Behind Even The Shadows

Verity Pursuit

Molly Moles

Scriverdea Publishing

Lewisville, Indiana

Scriverdea Publishing
4886 East 1100 North, Lewisville, Indiana, 47352
Printed by Amazon's Kindle Direct Publishing with permission

For additional information, contact Molly Moles using the listed address or email behindeventheshadows@gmail.com. Be sure to join @BEtheShadows on Facebook (with links to other social media platforms) for author updates and fan forums.

Verity Pursuit first edition, 2025
Fifth in the *Behind Even The Shadows* Series of six novels.

Cover artwork by Jane Christian
Photomanipulation, logos, and accents by Jacob Moles
Concept editing by Janet Hughes
Map created using Inkarnate.com with proper licensure

ISBN: 978-1-951499-18-1 (paperback)
978-1-951499-19-8 (hardcover)
978-1-951499-20-4 (eBook)
978-1-951499-21-1 (Audiobook)

LCCN: 2025906184

~ Dedication ~

To The One Who gave me the ability to produce the work I do ~ my Lord and Creator, God Almighty. May He be glorified in all I do, and may this book — and series — be a reflection of young Christian adults striving, growing, renewing, maturing, and perfecting day-by-day to follow Him and be in the world but not of it. Standing up to the sinful nature of those who do not submit to God's commands, while at the same time, showing them they do not have to continue in hopelessness and sin.

~ Acknowledgements ~

Sometimes "thank you" doesn't do justice; and yet what else can I say except, "Thank you!" for helping me make the publication of this novel a reality:
Janet Hughes   Jane Christian   Jacob Moles

~ Table of Contents ~

~ Pronuciation Guide ~

NOTES: Underlining: "hard" vowel. Capitals: stressed syllable.

Last Names:

Kevereux: KE-vr<u>oo</u>

Places:

Caudree: CAW-dr<u>ay</u>

Crullar: CREW-yar

Medd: m<u>e</u>d

Trofglen: TROUGH-glen

Yergo: YE<u>A</u>R-g<u>o</u>

Zervonith: zer-von-ITH

Miscellaneous:

Abaddon (plain): ab-<u>A</u>-don

Artemisia bed (fake medical machine): ar-tuh-M<u>E</u>-zuh

Bailiwick (code name): B<u>AI</u>L-<u>e</u>-wick

Cardiomyopathy (real medical term for heart condition): car-d<u>e</u>-<u>o</u>-MY-o-pathy

Chathum (cathedral): CHA-thum

Coadjutor (code name): k<u>o</u>-ah-J<u>U</u>T-r

Corpus Cathartarga (fake medical term for "body cleansing of pain"): C<u>O</u>R-pus · KATH-art-argah

Elysium (black diamond "metal"): uh-LI-sh<u>e</u>-um

Flezlick (river): fl<u>e</u>z-LICK

Machinate (ability name): MA-kuh-n<u>a</u>te

Monitorial (bay): mon-it-<u>OR</u>-<u>e</u>al

Nerfilgon (fake chemical): ner-FILL-gon

Santisk (park): san-TISK

Tantalum (metal): tan-TUH-lum

Trispinalfil (fake chemical): TRY-sp<u>i</u>nal-fill

~ 1 ~

Beside the dampened ticks, beeps, and dings that kept a steady cadence; the only notable noise was soft rubbing and occasional cracking of paper. Such large hands worked away at crafting such a delicate piece of art; the orange piece of paper beginning to take the shape of a rose with each successive fold, the eyes which oversaw each fold so critical. And yet, just as he was about to start another flower, his eyes widened as they darted to his left toward the bed. They then looked as if they sighed in despair as they went back to focus on their work.

With the sizable pile of flowers on the bedside stand, it was easy to tell Destan had been sitting by Callimay bedside for hours. He sat and watched her at first, but he got to the point he just couldn't bear to look directly at her. She looked so uncomfortable: the brace she had on to stabilize her neck didn't allow any movement and the tube jetting out of her mouth made him gag at times. Add to that the tubes on each side hooked up to reservoirs and her lying completely flat all the time; let alone she never moved? It's no wonder he was occupying himself.

Elder's gone so there's no need to worry about people I know doing things I never thought they would. ~ You're just too impatient about learning medical terminology. ~ Well maybe there's something I 'don't' want to be good at. Don't want to be 'greedy', you know. ~ I still say you refuse to learn because you can't pick it up easily. Kinda like how Calli complains about Chameleon not working as fast as she would like it to. Huh?

This bickering was cut short when her breathing became extremely shallow; him jumping up and bolting out the door to find someone.

"What is it, Doyen?" Torpid ran over, hearing the commotion.

1

"Calli. She's can't breathe."

Torpid ran into the room, but let a frustrated sigh linger when he saw the situation wasn't quite as dire as Destan had painted. Yes, she was having "trouble", but she was — in fact — breathing. She starting to hiccup, but it sounded more like wheezing. Torpid double-checked a few things and then called Doctor Gerould in, "You know more about her brain activity than I do."

They kept an eye on a certain monitor for a few minutes, not doing anything and allowing her to work through whatever it was on her own; much to the displeasure of Destan. But, she settled down and was resting peacefully within a few minutes.

"What was it?" Destan interrupted Torpid and Doctor Gerould's conversation. "Is she okay?"

"Just calm down," Doctor Gerould came over and put a firm hand on the distraught young man's shoulder. "As best as I can tell, aside from her fighting the airway — which, by the way is a very good sign — Callimay's 'mentally' having flashbacks just like she did when you threw her off White Cove."

"Huh?"

"Now I'm not going to testify to that being the exact reason, but what I saw then and what I'm seeing now? There's an unmistakable similarity in her brain activity."

"Will she get over this like she did then?"

"I don't see why not."

Destan slumped back in his chair, "Are you at least going to take the tube out since she's fighting it?"

"I'm going to leave that to Torpid."

His desperate eyes turned to the other man in the room, so Torpid answered, "I would like her to regain consciousness before I remove it so I know for sure the tissue is healed enough to withstand 'normal' stress and she's stable breathing on her own. I know it's not what you want — and she may fight it harder at moments — but maintaining her airway is vital for the time being."

Yes, it wasn't at all what he wanted to hear, but at the same time it was exactly what he needed to know. And really? In the grand scheme of things, none of this was a step back. She "was" getting better.

Once a few things were checked they left; Trever knocking on the door mere moments later. There was an extended period of silence as he waited, so Torpid asked, "Doyen? Emissary is here. Do you want him to stay outside?"

"Oh. I didn't hear him, sorry. No, he can come in."

Torpid consoled as he came back and put his hand on Destan's shoulder, "The second she responds to my questions that tube is out."

Trever went to Callimay's left side and sat across from Destan, not saying a word. He'd had time to wade through many memories, but was still working on deciphering exactly what happened — what Elder did; let alone why. There were all of these memories but he didn't remember any of the people. In a way he felt he was remembering someone else's life.

Well, he didn't remember anyone except Callimay.

The night they were separated smacked him square between the eyes — once it sank in — when she said "Everlyn". The look on her face was the exact same one she had when he hid her in the culvert they always played in at Santisk Park.

"Wear's Papa? Ez he otay? Wha happen, Twevuh?" She kept asking as he started pulling fallen branches over her.

"Just stay here. I'm going to go find someone to help." He hushed as he kept working, his eyes wide with fear as he labored to breathe. "We've gotta find Mama."

"But Twevuh, I too scare to be by mysewlf. And my head huwts." Her brown eyes cried; arms reaching out for comfort as she tugged on his sleeve. "Pweeze don't weave. Wha if du demon ghost finds me!"

"Just hold onto Mr. Ruff. Mama said he'd always keep you safe. — Here. Let me clean him off some. ... Alright. All fixed. There you go!"

She clung to the toy but he could tell this distraction wasn't helping.

"Remember what Papa said? If you go to sleep how your head stops hurting?" Trever paused as he kneeled down and smiled. "Crying is only gonna make it worse, you know that."

"I twy," Callimay tried, but failed, to stiffen her lip.

"It'll be alright. You're safe here. I won't be long and I won't ever let anyone hurt you. You know that. You're 'my' Everlyn. Remember?"

"But why tant I go which you? Woodn't it be safers for mes to be which you?"

Trever looked around and then scooted closer to her, sighing, "The way Papa talked? I— if something goes wrong you'll be safe. I might have to run, and since your head's hurting you won't be able to."

"You mean you die if you go! I tant woose you, Twevuh!"

"No," he put his hands out, trying to keep her wild imagination from flaring. "No I didn't say that! I said I 'might' have to 'run'."

"O-h. Awl white, den. I no good at wunning. Wemembu how Uncle Aweck 'awlways' catched me no madder what?"

"That's right. — Now if I don't come back by the time it gets light out… you remember what the big man with the shiny plate on his shirt looked like when we were here last week?"

"De man which de wealwee deep voice and de wong stick on his bewlt?" She sniffled as she pulled her stuffed animal close.

"Yes. If the sun comes up and I'm not back, go look for him. But 'don't' leave until then, alright?"

"Otay."

"Promise?"

"I pwomise. … Twevuh!"

"Yes, Everlyn."

"I wuv you."

"I love you too," he gave her one last, long hug.

"Pweeze come back," she whispered in his ear.

"I'll always be with you, Everlyn." He whispered back. "And I'll always watch over you. I promise. Nothing or no one will change that."

"Is stawting to snow," Callimay jumped in thought as she looked out in front of them. "Wiwl we have enough four a fowt?"

"I…"

"Big bwuduhs hewp since I showt. It get heavy and tawl wealwy fast. And den we awl pway togeder 'a-wl' day!" Callimay smiled as she started planning everything out; hugging Mr. Ruff and swinging him back and forth. "Den Mama cawl us four coco when we fwozen."

Trever didn't say anything for a while, but finally surrendered, "Sure, Everlyn. I'll tell Richie and he'll make sure it's a 'huge' fort."

"Oh goodie! Which du widdle holes for me to wooks out of?"

"Even the holes. Now just watch the snow and think about our fort so you can sleep. And remember: stay here. Alright?"

"I wiwl," she nodded, curling up against the embankment.

Gathering his courage, he nodded and then took off into the night.

He roamed around for what felt like hours, trying to find even one, single, living person. The area was bulldozed by the rebels who swept through with a wrath that didn't show any inkling of distinguishing innocent citizen from military. All Trever and Callimay's neighbors; even their friends? All those who stayed suffered the same fate as their family; but by this time the rebels had moved on.

The sight of such carnage was overwhelming to such a young boy; but knowing he didn't want what he saw happen to his brothers and father happen to his baby sister gave him what drive he needed to continue on.

There was a bright light that lingered for almost a minute on the northern horizon, followed by rumblings and quakes of a bomb's aftershock; Trever pausing as he watched in fearful awe. The sky was already hazy — a deep crimson color from all of the fires around the area of Quaverly they lived in — but that set the northern sky aglow for a while in the strangest way. For a second he felt like rushing back to his baby sister to keep her safe; but then he came to his senses.

After calling out as he ran down one more block — cold, scared, and almost to the point of utter exhaustion and severe shock — Trever turned back. He didn't want to go too far away seeing as how he didn't know how soon the sun would be rising; and then he was getting into parts of town he wasn't as familiar with.

As he rounded the last corner, he saw a car coming toward him. He ran up and waved his arms, crying out, "Help! Please! Please stop!"

The car came to an immediate stop and a middle-aged man who was extremely tall got out of the car; a look of concern on his face as he jogged up, "What is wrong, young lad?"

"Oh! You're with the military. Oh good!" Trever said relieved when he saw the uniform the gentleman was wearing; collapsing as he finished, "My sister and I need help. Someone killed our family. We're all who survived. I need to get my Everlyn to a safe place and we need to look for our mother."

"Oh?" He asked as he kneeled down. "Where is your sister? Is she close by?"

"She's—" Trever paused when he saw the other man in the vehicle. "That's the man who killed my family!"

"Are you sure?" The man asked confused as he looked back.

"I'm positive! My Papa cut him on his right cheek while he tried to fight him off! Did you arrest him?"

"Don't worry about him. Where is your sister? Take me to her so we can help." The gentleman said very calm as he looked back at Trever.

Trever was only nine-years-old, but he knew his question not being answered meant this man was hiding something. The man he knew killed his family wasn't in cuffs! And there wasn't anyone else around.

"I don't want my sister near him. Could you send someone else?"

"She'll be fine," the gentleman assured as he shut the door so this little boy couldn't see the other person and then kneeled to his level; his voice so smooth and calming. "Where is your sister? Take me to her so I can help you."

"No, I don't want him to know where she is."

"Tell me where your sister is, 'boy'." The gentleman's voice became stern as he got back to his feet.

"No!" Trever yelled as he turned to run.

"And where do you think you're going?" He grabbed Trever's arm as the other man got out of the car. "Baleck! Get back in t—"

"He knows. Me staying in won't help anything, Uncle."

Still furious but knowing he had to prioritize things, he turned his attention back to Trever as he grabbed his shirt, "Where is your sister? Where is Callimay?"

Terrified they knew her name, he screamed as he tried to pull away, "No! I won't tell! I don't want her to die!"

"Yes. Yes you will." Baleck sneered as he sauntered over. "You're going to lead us to that little Chameleon. Your father couldn't protect her… and neither can you."

"No!" Trever cried out in fear. "Please! Don't! She's never done anything wrong! She's my little sister. She hasn't hurt anyone!"

Not too much later, Trever had his head down as he stumbled and staggered in front of Elder and Baleck through the park. Anyone who would have been around would've known this poor little boy had been beaten and tortured. These two men — if you even want to call them that — preyed on this young child in every way that was inhumane.

They were willing to stop at nothing to find this little girl.

As they walked down into the culvert, Trever gasped: *Everlyn! Where are you! But I told you— just keep running. Please don't stop. Papa made me promise to keep you safe. Maybe this is—*

"Well… where is she?" Elder snapped.

"I told her to stay here until the sun came up." Trever cowered as he put his hands up. "I promise! I told her to stay here. See?"

"Tell me where she is, 'boy'!" Elder slapped him.

"I promise I'm telling the truth! I made her promise to stay here until it got light out. … M… maybe that bomb explosion looked like the sunrise to her? I don't know where Everlyn is! Please! Please don't kill me. I'm telling you the truth!"

"He's telling the truth, Uncle." Baleck huffed as he kneeled a few feet away. "See? Fresh tracks. I have a feeling with the snow being so patchy we won't be able to find her."

"Just go look." Elder growled as he jerked Trever toward him. "I'll take care of this little snake."

"Fine," Baleck rolled his eyes as he stood.

"Trever?" Destan asked when he noticed the tears streaming down his face. "Don't blame yourself. Elder did this. Not you."

He jerked back when he heard Destan's voice, taking a few deep breaths before answering, "When Everl— 'Callimay'. When she begged me to come back to her? When she said her name to me? It… It all came flooding back in such a painful and horrifying way. With all that happened after I pushed it aside, but… I've started letting—"

"I… I know what you're going through, in a way." Destan sighed as he leaned forward and clasped his hands together. "I'm just glad you're reacting like you are."

"Was Elder able— was he 'that' powerful to make me forget who I am… who Everlyn is to me?" Trever's face grew pale.

"There were drugs he gave you in addition to his mind control ability. One was the exact same one I had when I was processed and given my abilities. Mender told me it deadens your memories; wipes them out."

"Wha… I…"

"Elder told you that you had a silver deficiency, right?"

Still stunned, Trever just sat there in a daze.

"Those 'supplements' you've been taking every day? They were long-term aids to keep those memories dead. … Even early on Elder knew his powers weren't that strong even though he flaunted it like he was more powerful than God Almighty. He couldn't keep his hold on you like he envisioned he could and it was the truth he had to hide himself from. Drugs were his only option with you to keep his façade in his own mind; while he opted to use fear with everyone else."

"How do you know that?"

Destan took a deep breath as he rubbed his neck, "Calli and I have known for a while what happened to you. Elder's journal—"

"She's known this whole time about me!" Trever's voice cracked with anguish as he raked his uninjured hand through his hair. "She's known all along what—"

"It wasn't until we took that first trip to the Nest. When we met with Canary. That's when she found out." Destan clarified; doing everything to help Trever stay calm. "Don't beat yourself up. It was hard on her, yes. But she never gave up. … What happened between you two that day should show you that. She loved you and fought for you even though she couldn't remember you; nor you, her. She knew you were in there even though everyone and everything pointed to you being too far gone. Your mother even warned her not to try; but that didn't stop her even when her life was on the line."

Trever fought so hard but couldn't hold it in, "I… what have I done! I was actually strangling—"

"Look at me. As much as you could you kept her safe. Alright? You looked after her like no one else could during a time when she wasn't accepting help from anyone. Do you realize that?" Destan said firm, him almost stomping his foot as he stared him down; his tone softening as he continued, "She told me you moved in practically right after her adopted mother died; telling me how she found it so strange that a complete stranger would be so willing help like you did. She treasured your helping her. … And then you being so concerned about her after she was poisoned; telling me you always felt like she was a little sister to you? I don't think any of that was an 'accident'. Elder was powerful but he wasn't God. He could bend your view of reality and drug you to a certain extent, but he couldn't break your love for her."

"Why did Elder want her dead, anyway? What was so 'dangerous' about Everlyn as far as he was concerned? I mean she didn't have abilities then to threaten him. She was just a little girl. Why would he have our family killed?"

"Do you remember anything about Calli's fifth birthday?"

"Umm… not really. At least not right now."

"When your mother found out Calli was left-handed she got in contact with my father. They were friends from college and she knew he could help save Calli. My father constructed a serum — ability — which would allow her to quickly adapt to her surroundings: she'd be able to learn by watching others and mimic them. But without going into 'all' the details, Elder knew about it since your mother and my father both had contact with the Shadows; and he didn't like what was going on and tried to stop it."

"Wait! You're saying Everlyn had a special power back then!"

Destan sighed as he looked back at his sleeping wife, "It was nothing more than an aid to help her learn to be right-handed without losing her capability of functioning as a lefty. But logically speaking, it would allow her to learn anything that fast."

"But what's so wrong about that?"

"When does evil ever need a logical reason to do what it does?" Destan sighed as he stretched out a bit and then continued. "Elder wanted control; it's the whole reason he worked with my father in the first place… why he had an ability. For his plan to work he needed total chaos. If people could adapt, work silently as we have to get this evil overturned, he'd lose the fuel he needed."

"But why our whole family?"

"Elder was furious with your mother and wanted to 'pay her back' in a way that would hurt her more than anything — make her think twice before crossing him. And to be disgustingly blunt: he 'loved' mentally torturing people. It was his addiction that couldn't be satiated.

He thrived off the emotional turmoil he caused in others' lives." Destan sighed as he sat down on the bed and took Callimay's hand in his.

"Then why didn't he kill me!" Trever started pacing the floor. "That doesn't make sense if that was his thought process in this all."

"Elder said in his journal it would be more torture to your mother if he kept you alive and under his thumb. All the while her knowing you were hunting Calli down. … I…" *Excuse my interruption, but aren't things sliding in a 'bad' direction? ~ Oh. That's right. I hadn't noticed. Umm…* "You know what? I'll let Traceur know to give you the journal and video feed from the belvedere so you can see everything. And I'll get Canary's Shadow Box so you can see what things she was able to salvage from your home. Just go through it when you can and what you can handle at the time. Maybe it'll help you."

"I'm fine, keep going," he flopped into the chair.

"No, you're not."

"How can y—"

The armrest Trever was gripping crumpled in his fist like an empty chip canister. He jumped out of the seat, eyes wide while trying to keep his breathing semi steady.

"Like I said, just take this all in at the pace you can handle."

"What is this!"

He doesn't remember? ~ Well, I mean quite a bit has happened since then, so it's not 'that's surprising he's forgotten. "You have an ability, remember? And it's triggered when you're irritated."

"What!"

Trying to do what he could to be a guide and calming influence, Destan got up and came over; though made sure he was in between Trever and Callimay… just in case, "Remember when we were in the holding cell? How you popped your cuffs off? I mentioned—"

"Oh," Trever took a huge breath of relief. "Oh I'd forgotten that."

"I don't blame you, but let me warn you now: you need to make sure to keep a constant eye on your emotions. It might not be an armrest you're holding next time."

"Oh gosh!"

"Now don't spaz out on me." Destan fought to keep his eyes from rolling. *What is up with him! ~ Oh come now. Having abilities isn't*

something everyone has, usually. Him spazzing out isn't 'shocking'.
"Just keep that in mind and remember that armrest. Okay?"

"I will, for sure. — He 'is' dead, right?" Trever whipped his head around. "Elder, I mean."

"Fidus said he gave up right before they were going to take him off life support; which shocks me just as much as you, believe me. I didn't think he'd 'ever' give up. The way he'd been fighting up to that point? Always finding a way to slither out?" Destan sighed as he sat back; shaking his head. "But, then again, he was a coward. He'd probably call it 'dying on his own terms' but we both know better."

While he knew that helped, Destan could tell Trever was still struggling; he tried to open up some and see if it would help, "I… I know what you're going through. Having all these heavy memories come back and then seeing what Elder did to you? Granted it wasn't at the exact same time, but man? I get it. I almost strangled the love of my life when we were in Rayleen that last t—"

"What!"

I already told him this. ~ Give the guy a break, Boon. You're the one who mentioned it anyway and he's in a frenzy of sorts with emotions.
"Elder apparently thought it would be the most beneficial way to get rid of both me and her: have me to kill her and then let the guilt of what I did drive me to commit suicide. He told me so himself — in a rather covert way — at the celebration dinner." Destan offered as he brushed Callimay's hair back a bit. "When we went to Rayleen we'd gone through a rough spell, emotionally. I snapped. She did the only thing she knew to save me… and it almost cost her, her life. … After it was all over I kept blaming myself; and her violent reaction to it all made me feel even worse. It took me a while to realize what Calli knew from the start: Elder was twisting my frustration into deadly hatred. He takes thoughts, ideas — whatever you want to call them — and amplifies them. I know it seems like I'm blurring that fine line between saying folks can be 'possessed' to do things when we all know everyone has the choice to do what they do or don't do; but there are 'influences' we can succumb to if we're not watching ourselves. I was upset Calli was overthinking things when, in fact, if I would've cared to think about it for just five seconds: 'she' was the one thinking logically. But

he took that knee-jerk — stress on jerk — reaction I had and blew it up like a pineapple… and it burst everything else sky-high. He did the same with you. I know he did. You didn't want to kill her. That wasn't your original thought. I can't imagine it being so. He twisted whatever you were thinking so that's what it became."

A shadow was seen at the door, followed by a knock. Not thrilled he was interrupted but knowing it was probably best to give Trever a little while to come to terms with what all just happened, Destan went over and opened the door, "Oh. It's good to see you up and about, Auditor."

"How is she?" She tried to look around him.

"Mender would be able to tell you more," Destan stepped aside.

"I'm so sorry. I—"

"Doyen?" A man's voice from the hall asked.

He stopped and turned back, stunned to see, "Chicane? Coalesce?"

"Coalesce and I know what we did — to Auditor 'and' Liaison — was unforgiveable. Let alone my personal conduct up top." Chicane bowed his head in defeat as he kneeled; trying to be nonchalant as he hinted for Coalesce to do the same. "We put ourselves at your mercy and willingly accept the punishment you deem fit."

Destan sighed as he walked out and motioned for them to get up, not really ready to deal with this, "I know y—"

"Doyen?" Auditor interjected as she came back.

The worry in his eyes instantly flared as he whipped his head around, "What?"

She calmed as she put her hand out, "I apologize for making you think something was wrong. I just… thought I might be able to help."

Confused as to this offer, Destan stared at her.

"Let me handle them," she whispered as she patted his hand. "At least for the time being."

The comfort and relief he felt he couldn't express like he wanted to; him nodding as he bowed his head.

She patted his hand and then stepped forward to address the two young men in a loving and motherly tone, "I know you live in what you see as the overwhelming shadow of your sister, Chicane. And I know how much you've worked to prove you're capable of being strong without her; but don't push her wisdom and love aside. The only reason she does what she does is to protect you. She doesn't do it to put you down. Maybe she does come off as being far too authoritative for what you prefer in a woman, but it's because she knows if she doesn't she can lose you; and she doesn't want that to happen."

At first Chicane was put off by the mention of his sister, but it appeared what Auditor was saying began to make a small dent in that wall of resentment everyone knew he had concerning her.

"Find that balance of honor and respect with independence and responsibility. I believe you owe your sister just as much of an apology as me or Liaison." She finished as she eyed him a bit; turning her attention to the other young man. "And you, Coalesce? I think it best you remember something: just because someone — even someone you trust or who has some amount of authority over you — 'suggests' something doesn't automatically mean it's the right thing to do and you are not accountable if you agree to it. Even orders can be given in error. While the individual who suggests or gives orders for something to be done — or not — does take the brunt of blame, you are never immune or able to distance yourself if you participate. You follow like a blind sheep far too often; whining that you were just following orders or that someone who was higher ranked suggested it if something happens which puts you in a disciplinary circumstance."

The half smug smile on Coalesce's face morphed into a twisted pout; it not being lost to Auditor, "To truly apologize to someone you have to take responsibility for your mistakes. And I can tell you don't have that humble and honest attitude right now, which makes your apology to Doyen, me, and Liaison a lie. And I — for one — won't accept it. You always whine, throwing around excuses, and pass the blame on others. You have no capacity to take responsibility and be a mature adult… let alone a man."

That hit a raw nerve, but Coalesce didn't dare say a word with Destan standing right there.

"Maybe this isn't my place, but I believe that is why you haven't been added to the Veil." Auditor refused to give him an inch of leeway. "You two are polar opposites but equally as dangerous as I see it. We need 'men' to step up and do the right thing. — Chicane, you know that better than Coalesce. — You both need to become men. I know you can, but I'm telling you right now you're not. You're both hotheads who think this is a fun job where you get to roleplay as the good guy with cool weapons and special skills which make you the object of worship — albeit in your own mind. That is not — 'not' — what this is at all. You need to get your act together. And if you can't? I demand you leave. I'm 'this' close to demanding you both be expelled from here altogether. In your lack of maturity you could cause someone to die. In fact you almost did. … Let that sink in."

There was a prolonged time of shocking silence. Both Coalesce and Chicane looked like little puppy dogs who had their favorite toy taken away from them; scolded for playing with it too hard and ripping it.

Destan was even a bit shocked though thankful she said what he'd tried on several occasions. Each time was fruitless, so he eventually gave up. But hearing what she was saying to herself showed him how this "outburst" was something she'd harbored for so long.

"Doyen? If you will excuse me, I need to find Mender." She said rushed as she fought to hold in a sniffle. "I'm glad Liaison is doing well and I thank you for your concern for me and allowing me to do this."

"By all means," Destan ushered on; then turned to the two young men, "Well. What she said brings to mind what needs to be addressed with you two before something else happens. If you both are willing to reflect on the past, you know good and well I've said the same things on multiple occasions. While I'm frustrated beyond belief it took this much happening to get you two to be at least say something — even if you don't mean it, which is a totally different issue altogether — I'm willing to give you one last chance. One week. Go take very serious and personal inventory, then report to Traceur by five for your details."

"Yes, Doyen." They both nodded, giving him the Shadow signal.

"I hope you two realize this is happening to help you just as much as everyone else. If you're unsure or lost… 'ask'! Yes, there are some who are not as willing to help as other, but there are those who do and would jump at the chance to help you. But remember 'you' have to do the work yourselves and have the will to make the changes needed. Be 'men' like Auditor said."

They nodded again and then left, another individual coming up at that very moment, "Doyen?"

"You too?" Destan asked exhausted. "What is it, Fidus?"

"The Veil wants to know—"

"I… I can't right now." Destan's shoulders slumped and he fell back against the wall; him rubbing his face. "I can't do it, Fidus. Alright? I admit it. I can't keep going like nothing's happened. Calli kept me going before, but without her and all that's happened I need more time. I have emotions too, you know. I know in the past I—"

"I apologize if it sounds like I'm pushing you for an ETA. I… I didn't mean that. I was only going to say the Veil wants to know how you and Liaison are faring."

Destan stared at his second-in-command for a while, stunned: *Did I just hear that come from Fidus' mouth? ~ Keep it together now, Boon. You're beginning to crack. You know Fidus would never say that.*

"I… I understand it is out of character for me — even the Veil as a whole — but Elder's departure ushered in a much needed level of… 'humanity' I guess you could call it, in us." Fidus tried to find a good word to clarify; totally oblivious to what Destan was thinking. "I have seen to all your duties, but is there anything else I can do? Has Liaison regained consciousness yet?"

And with no time to catch a breath of air, in came tsunami wave number two. Destan had the split second thought Elder was doing this all to get him to lower his guard, so as the terror gripped him he took off without saying a word.

ℬ

He threw the doors to the cold, damp, musty room open and ran over: *If you dared fake your death…*

As he unzipped the black bag on the table in the center of the room, a slight stench that held the same natural musk Elder wore wafted out; it emanating from the lifeless, stiff, dusky grayed body of Elder.

Something inside Destan wasn't satisfied. With what happened for so long, seeing was "not" believing. He braced himself on the icy, metal table and closed his eyes. While he'd used Callimay's ability in this manner with her help a couple times — and more-or-less understood what to look for — he knew how good Elder was at hiding; and so he was exerting more effort to ensure he could find Elder if he was alive.

Though doing this while emotionally drained was causing him pain. But in this state he felt things he hadn't before. The harder he tried the more he recognized what he "felt"… "who" he felt. And the dear price he was paying was becoming too much — his knees giving out and his heart beginning to race. He tried to catch himself but couldn't.

Adding to this already worrisome situation he was in, Trever burst into the room, scaring him more than he thought possible at the time, "Doy— Destan! Something's wrong with Everlyn!"

"Calli!" He gasped under his breath, him jumping there before he could even get to his feet.

She was choking as she tried to reach up to her face where the tube was; him stumbling over as he reached for her hands: *Calli? Calli, listen to me. — Don't fight me. It's okay. Just calm down. That tube's there to help you breathe. Easy. … Calli? Calli you've got to shut your tie to me off. … Shh. I'm fine. You don't have to come look for me. Just turn off your ability. Let Liaison rest. Let yourself rest. Lance said you need to so you can heal faster. … Please. I'm alright. Don't worry about me. Please rest. I'm sorry I scared you. It's okay now. I need you to rest so I can see your shining eyes again real soon. Please, Calli.*

A few tears slid out from her still closed eyes as Destan rubbed her arms and kept talking to her mind.

Trever just then got back with Torpid on his heels. While Torpid was in shock to see him there ahead of them, seeing Callimay calming from what appeared Destan only touching her struck Trever more.

Before too much longer she was still. He kissed her forehead and whispered, "I'm alright, Calli. You're not abandoning me. I'm not going to let myself lose control. I promise. Just rest. I love you too."

Ѧ

Though that tiny slice of precious time with Callimay was helpful in every way imaginable, time decided to pass at a painfully slower rate than before; every tiny twitch of a finger making him jump in hopeful expectation. The pile of origami roses now accompanied by a plethora of other creatures grew and grew, some showing signs of being in a battle even though he did his best to fix them; Destan's battle against sleep proved it was going to leave scars on these little paper figurines.

Rocher immediately saw what Destan was doing the first day, so he made sure an ample supply of the specific paper needed for the tedious art was available; replenishing his pile in secret each time he stepped out. And there were a couple times he would leave a new design atop the stack so Destan would have a new challenge.

For as much as the origami kept him occupied, Destan found solace in something else after a while: it dawned on him what he did when she was in a coma… he read to her. And the way time passed after that was much more manageable.

She hadn't gained full consciousness, but she did enough one time; Torpid keeping his word and removing the breathing tube. Destan was out getting some air and working out at the time, and was completely deflated when he heard she was asking for him. And so he parked himself beside her and refused to leave.

Trever came and went, mainly to get the two of them food, but would spend much of his time trying to piece together the memories Elder tried to ensure he'd never remember. Every picture, trinket… everything he had that held memories were part of nothing but a big, fat lie. And while they were just things and the memories themselves weren't lies; the people who were there ruined what could've still been things to remember and cherish.

He trashed his place the first night in a fit of rage and hadn't bothered to do a thing about the chaotic mess since. The pills he was so religious about taking were spew everywhere; some crushed to the point there were piles of powder here and there.

Seeing this scene each night poked at him more and more until it culminated with him leaving without notice for Faberton to visit the graves of his family; him continuing on to Brigon afterward.

When he got back there was a bit of an uproar he caused and had to help control, but he knew the longer it was kept from Destan the better it would be.

Trever shuffled down the hall as fast and quiet as he could while looking to see if anyone was around.

When he got to the room, the blinds were pulled and he could hear different voices inside. Hearing what was said he knocked and paced back and forth while he waited.

It was a few minutes, but finally the door opened.

Needless to say Destan was shocked, "What in t— Majesty Presley!"

"I new good n' well my presence be unexpected, but when Trever told me oov thu situation I want-ne aboot tu hesitate in comin' tu be with hur. Is new a gud time? Has she come tu?"

Still trying to understand everything, he looked to Trever who just shrugged his shoulders; Destan twisting his lips a bit.

"Well, they just removed the drains." Destan looked back to Auditor who nodded, and then finished with a slight smile in his voice, "But she should be fine. I'm afraid she's still asleep right now."

Trever helped his grandfather to the bed and then Destan put Callimay's hand in his, "Trever told me thu one who did this tu hur be gone fer gud?"

"Yes."

"Blimey gud." He squeezed her hand as he nodded. "At least that danger be gone. … And how ya be, laddie?"

"Each day gets a bit easier," Destan sighed.

"Don't-ne lose heart," he encouraged as he felt for a chair and sat.

"How are things on your front? I know th—"

"Don't-ne concern yerself with such nonsense right new." Majesty Presley brushed off as he waved his hand in Destan's direction.

Ignoring the suggestion, he started thinking out loud, "I know I've got to decide what to do with the timeline right now in light of what Elder did. But I'm torn. Both are just as detrimental, yet beneficial as far as I can see. — Do we go ahead like nothing happened? But based on what we know, we'd be risking walking into a trap. Or do we wait and make them second guess everything so we keep control; all while risking losing political support?"

"Eye. It be a conundrum." Majesty Presley kept his answer vague to try his best to pry Destan away from such matters.

"What day is it?" He asked out of the blue.

"The tenth?" Trever replied, confused with the whole conversation.

"Then I still have a little time." Destan leaned is head back.

Doctor Gerould walked in a few seconds later, asking, "Did you ask Doyen what he's going to do, Emissary?"

"Oh. No."

"Ask me what?"

"There's the small, 'insignificant' matter of an alpha belvedere standing at one of the entrances to Bulwark which needs to be resolved immediately." Doctor Gerould eyed Trever in the most condescending way. "At least that is what I know to be best practice."

Destan looked over totally confused, "Huh?"

"Well… when I came back I went by the Minka. He flew out to meet me and followed me back." Trever fumbled as he tried to explain. "I said something so he'd stay outside, but I don't know what to do with him, it, whatever. And it's obviously got everyone else in a frenzy fit. I mean it's not like I meant to do it on purpose. And he's not all that bad, really. I mean at least to me he's super friendly."

Without a moment's hesitation, Destan shrugged as he replied, "You can let him in. And I—"

"Excuse me! Let a 'belvedere' in here? Have you lost your mind!" Doctor Gerould gritted his teeth; practically hissing at Destan.

His expression didn't waiver as he looked him square in the eye, "Canary severed his tie before she sent him to us. I checked everything inside and out and he's clean. — You can have Abacus double-check if you'd like. — And I'd prefer to have him here so Calli's got another layer of protection for the time being. Go get him, Trever."

"A… alright." He stuttered and then squeezed by Doctor Gerould as if trying to avoid being hit for doing what he was going to do.

"And what's going to keep him from picking everyone off, one at a time?" Doctor Gerould argued, not realizing who was there at the time.

The defensive edge still fresh from what he'd had to deal with up until now, Destan got in his face, "Elder was a million times more dangerous and you know it. The belvedere's saved my life 'and' Calli's, so I trust him more than most people. If no one hurts Trever or Calli everyone's fine. It's that simple. And if someone hurts either of them, then they deserve to be in fear of being bitten. — That's final, Mender."

"I'm holding you personally responsible if anything happens." Doctor Gerould emphatically pointed at him and then left.

"I apologize, Majesty Presley." Destan groaned.

"Eh, tis nothin' compared tu soom oov thu squabbles I be in on durin' my lifetime, laddie. Sit yerself doon. Ya sound weary."

A few minutes later Destan could hear barking and what sounded like a heard of horses thundering down the hall. He chuckled as he got up and opened the door.

The belvedere ran in and jumped on him, barking and wagging his tail more than ever, "It's good to see you too, Big Fella. Glad your face is healed over."

With his greeting now finished, the belvedere's ears twitched and he looked over toward Callimay. Destan let him go and he crept over and whined as he looked back.

"She'll be alright; just be gentle."

He cocked his head to the side as he stared at Majesty Presley, and then yelped back at Destan before nuzzling his nose under Callimay's hand; flopping his backside down and drooping his ears.

Feeling the lush, thick fur on the back of his hand, Majesty Presley reached out and petted the sad creature, causing the belvedere to whine and whimper.

Destan sat on the bed and bowed his head as he took Callimay's hand. The belvedere put his one paw on top of his and leaned his head against the bed: *You didn't forget after this long, did you, Big Fella?*

ℬ

After even more heated debate with Doctor Gerould, Destan's logic and reasoning won out; the belvedere happy to stay with Callimay while he and Trever saw Majesty Presley off.

"Ya be sure tu take time tu ponder it over, but inform me when ya make yer decision oon hoo 'n when ya wantin' to be proceedin'."

"I promise I will," Destan sighed as they continued on. "I'm leaning toward waiting — mainly because of Calli — but I need to sit down and think it through so I've got an exact timeline to give everyone so there's that assurance."

"As much as I no my opinion doesn't-ne coont in thu end, I be advisin' ya tu act on that instinct oov yers 'n wait. Ya be needin' her by yer side, laddie. I be welcomin' un audience tu speak with ya n' help with thu leaders I've done spoken with afir. But in thu end I respect thu position yer in and thoose oov thu people under ya."

"Thank you, Majesty Presley. I may very well do that."

"Now ya be sure tu tell Callimay I luv thu wee lassie 'n have all thu confidence that she be recovered soon. And tell hur I'll be seein' hur before loong."

Destan hesitated as he stopped near the awaiting jet, it appearing he was trying to find the courage to say something.

"Your… your offer to take her in still goes, correct?"

"Eye," he nodded as he turned; then reached out, looking for his arm to grab. "But don't-ne make me have tu fulfill that offer, ya hear?"

The air hushed with a serious yet somehow calm tension as Destan sighed, "I don't want to leave her behind any more than I want to find out the Monarch's son is still alive."

"Eh?"

"My point being: I'm not resigning and saying I 'am' going to die or even 'wanting' it to happen. I just want to make sure things are in place 'if' it does… because it's a reality I have to live with. I need that comfort knowing she'd be taken care of if the worst happened. And I would like to talk with you about specifics at some point so everything is ready."

"I understand. Thu Lord strike me if-in I don't-ne keep my word." Majesty Presley vowed as he patted Destan's hand. "And I be havin' Haggis makin' sure tu get all thoose details taken care oov."

"Save travels back. I hope to be in contact with you by the end of next week."

"I be lookin' forward tu it." Majesty Presley nodded as Aleck took his arm and helped him up the steps; nodding to Destan.

℈

Destan talked with Trever for a while before coming back in; mainly just to catch up and see how he was doing and where he had been. Seeing how he was handling things gave Destan hope he was going to be able to manage his emotions, and thus his ability, much easier than he himself did at first.

The belvedere, as always, was thrilled he was back with his humans and sat right beside Destan so he could be petted. — And having his "pal" beside him did make Destan feel some better, he had to admit.

"Doyen?"

"Come on in, Auditor. What is it?"

"Torpid's coming over to take her dural pain line out. I didn't know if you wanted to stay or not."

"I thought she was going to be sedated for a couple more days?" He asked confused as he got up.

"She is. That line has nothing to do with her sedation." Auditor smiled as she explained. "It's serving to help lower her sensation of pain that's associated with her broken ribs. It kept her from breathing extremely shallow so she wouldn't contract pneumonia."

"Oh. … Where is the line? I didn't see any others earlier?"

"Those were just all the drains to keep her lungs inflated. — I know, there's so much that the poor dear has connected to her it's hard to keep track of it all. — It's in her back, next to her spinal cord. Do you remember when Mender gave her the anti-venom injection? Well, it's in the same place just about."

"Alright. How can I help?" Destan asked as she walked over to the other side of the bed.

"Usually we roll the patient on their side to get to the line, but with her ribs in such a fragile state, if you want to sit her up and basically hug her it'd do the job just as well." She explained as she opened the box she had. "I'm going to put this soft collar around her neck so it's not strained while she's moved. Could you lift her head just a bit?"

He lowered the railing on his side and sat beside her; cradling her neck as Auditor slipped a foam strip under Callimay's neck and secured it in front, "She won't be in pain, will she?"

"If she feels anything it shouldn't be enough to cause her to wake up." She comforted as Torpid came in.

~ 2 ~

It was now just a day shy of four weeks since everything exploded at Bulwark. As he opened the door, Destan heard the usual excited tapping of the belvedere's paws. He kneeled to give him a few rough pets: *What's the big idea? Trying to keep me out, huh? I don't think so.*

He chucked as he got up, the belvedere bounding over to the bed and then turning and barking at him.

"Calli! You're awake!"

"I was wondering when you'd get back," she said rather hoarse as she tried to laugh.

"Oh, Calli." Destan sighed as he ran over, giving her as much of a hug as he dared while lavishing her with kiss after kiss. *I've missed you so much. It's so good to see your eyes and smile.*

"Cou—"

"No, no! Don't talk. Let me get Aud—" he stopped dead in his tracks and turned; his eyes glassy as he smiled. "Calli? I love you so much."

This display was wonderful, but to see her husband in this sort of tizzy worried her. But she wasn't able to say anything before he ran out. When he came back and sat beside her she calmed.

Callimay lifted her hand to his face, them both now crying. With all the strength she had left, she pulled Destan to her and leaned her cheek against his.

"You're gonna be alright. I promise you are. I know it's gonna be a long and hard road, but I'm not willing to give up. The hardest part is over. Whatever is left, I'll fight for you no matter what it is that comes along; or 'who'. You've fought all the battles you need to. Let me take over now. … I know I can't take the pain away — as much as I want to

— but I can at least make things as easy as possible for you." Destan vowed as he sat up. "Now, I do need to at least get you some water, alright? I'll be right back."

Her voice was as coarse as eighty-grit sandpaper and felt like it, but her questions couldn't wait; her grabbing his arm, "What about Elder? How is Trever? Did someone look at his hand? I remember Traceur mumbling about it before someone argued with Auditor—"

"He's gone, Calli. I checked myself; why I asked you to turn Liaison off. He showed himself as the true coward he was and gave up. — Your brother's doing well, his hand's healing just fine. —Just rest your voice until you get something to drink. Alright?"

She nodded and waited for him to come back; the belvedere much more composed as he followed Destan around.

Cool, fresh water felt so good on her throat. It was very similar to the feeling of getting that quenching drink on an oppressive, humid, summer day. And she did sound better, but it wasn't enough to make Destan happy. He left to find the first person available since Auditor hadn't come yet.

But of course just "this" much more patience was going to pay off since he met her just down the hall. While she had the right to be a bit perturbed about this; seeing this display of love and care touched her. And so she gladly "put up" with his jumpy nature.

Auditor came in, a warm smile on her face, "It's so good to see you awake! Doyen said your voice sounded really hoarse? … Well I have just the thing to help."

Doctor Gerould came in not too much later and after a quick check told Destan he could take her back to the suite by the end of the week. He explained in a very vague way what therapy she was going to need; Destan following him out and asking how he could help and if there was anything else he should do.

Trever passed by the two of them and then stopped; not but a couple seconds later backing up, "Huh? What are you— Everlyn!"

During the flurry of him rushing in and making over his baby sister, Callimay noticed something, "I— what's this for?"

"It seems your husband thinks I'm Veil material." Trever smiled as she took the thick, black leather lapel in her hand.

The reality of just how long she must've been out started to sink in as she looked at Destan shocked; him smiling and nodding as he replied, "He said he promised his father he'd keep you safe. Who am I to tell him he can't stay by your side to keep that promise?"

"The sleeves…" Callimay started as she recalled. "Oh Destan! Y—"

"Trever was a big help," he calmed as he took her hand.

"I'm so sorry. … And then if they let me in you'll have to—"

"There's no 'if' about it. You're a Veil." Trever piped in proud.

"Huh?"

"Fidus put you up right after Trever was added. Everyone agreed you'd proven yourself worthy aside from what was stipulated, so now all you have to do is have your veiling ceremony. And that can wait until you're good and ready. … But we'll talk about it later because I'm starving." Destan switched the subject as he sat down and took her hand in his, pausing and looking back up at her. "It's been a while since I've been able to say a prayer with you."

❦

To both their surprise, Callimay was allowed to leave two days early. Full of excitement, Destan vanished for a bit; all smiles when he got back and pulled the wheelchair to the side of the bed. And yet Callimay sighed, "Pain sucks."

"Well now, woman! Where'd this attitude come from?" Destan took a step back; his eyes ready to pop out.

"You didn't let me finish," she frowned as she twisted her lips. "I was 'going' to say pain sucks all the energy out of me."

"But it does suck, too, doesn't it?" He chuckled as he locked the wheelchair in place.

Setting the tone to a joyful banter did help both of them when the sharp and unavoidable pain came. Thankfully the second Callimay was sitting it released.

They moseyed their way back, the belvedere sprinting down the one hall as he barked; Trever trying to catch up. This sight made Callimay want to laugh, but her ribs demanded otherwise. So she sat there in agony because it just was too funny and she wasn't about to close her eyes and miss it.

After chatting a bit, Trever was glad to leave the fluffy sprinter with them so he could go get some work done in peace and quiet.

"Oh, you just aren't used to him yet." Callimay rolled her eyes. "It's just how he works."

"Eh, I'm cool without the touchy-feely from people, so it naturally applies to animals. — See ya a bit later."

The second the door opened, the belvedere squeezed into the suite ahead of them and hopped around. Callimay sighed as she thought about what was said between Destan and Trever earlier, "I hope this doesn't take as long as Doctor Gerould said it would. You said Total Eclipse starts… I guess it would be tomorrow, right? How in the world am I g—"

"Total Eclipse has been set on dusk status for the time being."

"Destan you can't do th—"

"Now just listen to me," he knelled in front of her; putting a finger to her lips and then brushing her hair out of her face. "There's no way Elder didn't tell the Syndicate what we're planning. Maybe he didn't tell where each, individual Veil is or exact dates; but I wouldn't put it past him to have done so. … So after talking it over with everyone and doing some praying, I've decided we're going to count our losses for the moment to hunker down so we can do our best to keep from losing anyone else. Yes, we run the risk of losing political support, but I'd rather lose that than someone's life when I had the ability to stop it."

It didn't sit well with her at first, but what he said made sense: they had to change everything or they were all at greater risk. And she was in no shape to do anything; she'd only be a burden right now. So this was going to be a win-win situation in the long run.

"Don't worry about anything but getting better, Calli; and at the pace that your body allows. Alright?" He smiled as he tilted his head.

"Okay."

"Good! Now," Destan continued as he turned and threw back the blankets on the bed.

"C… could we eat first?" She looked down and away, rubbing her arm. "I just… it'd be one less time I'd have to move. And—"

"That sounds like a great idea. What would you like to eat? I know Lance said it needed to be softer for the first week or so."

"Umm… well. How about— does soft lasagna count?"

"I really don't know. But I can ask. Just give me a minute, alright?"

"Okay," Callimay smiled as she laid her hands on her lap.

As Destan opened the door, there was a surprise waiting for him, "Oh good. We didn't miss you again."

"What in the…"

"Tabby finally couldn't stand not seeing Callimay after what we heard." Redje tried to explain. "We waited until Mender told us she was fully awake and doing well; so we're not here rouge. — I 'did' get clearance to come so all the technical areas are covered. — We tried a couple hours ago but I guess you guys were still in the Wing."

"But… I…"

"I promise we won't stay long, Destan." Tabitha put her prayer-like hands up to her pouting lips. "I just wanted to be here for you two for a little bit. Can I help with anything?"

"Where's Rose and Benjamin?" He asked as he looked around.

"The Utrees have them right now. You know I said I'd never let my children know about this place." Tabitha's eyes almost flashed.

"Destan? Who is it?" Callimay called out.

Tabitha stared at him.

"What?" He asked confused.

"May I come in?"

"Oh… I 'guess' since you came 'all' this way you can say hi." Destan rolled his eyes and huffed as he stepped back. "It's Rej and Tabitha."

All the joy and carefreeness in Tabitha disappeared; her standing there as stiff as a board clinging to Redje.

The belvedere barked and nudged Destan, reminding him, "Oh dear. I… He's not—Big Fella? Go in the other room."

Defiant as ever, the creature ignored what was said and sat just as pretty as ever and wagged his tail; perking his ears as he tilted his head while staring at the new people he could beg for attention from. He was not about to let this opportunity go to waste.

He wasn't stupid.

Or was he?

"I said go!"

Like a sad pup, he whined with tail tucked as he trotted into kitchen.

Tabitha had a death-grip her necklace as Redje held her; her trying to force herself to breathe. — Of course she felt somewhat embarrassed but her terror didn't allow that to truly register.

Redje encouraged her on; walking her over to Callimay and then standing guard in the kitchen doorway.

"Look, I…"

Not wanting the situation to get any more stressful than he knew it was, Redje put his hand out to quiet Destan, "It's okay. I'll just stay here 'til we leave. No biggie. — Even I had to take a second to figure it out. It's been a while since we've had a run-in with any dog in general."

"I can send him—"

"He's out of sight and she's 'okay' for the time being, so let's just keep it that way. The last thing she needs is to see him again." Redje put a firm hand on Destan's shoulder. "You had no idea we were here so there's no reason for you have him away. We both know he's different, but you know good and well how memories can tarnish things. So don't be sorry but don't overreact to try to accommodate. Got it?"

A lingering sigh of frustration hung in his breath, but Destan looked at his best friend and nodded.

"Hanging in there alright?"

"Better now that she's awake and back here." He took a deep breath as he leaned against the wall. "As far as everything else goes? Don't get me wrong, Fidus is good, but he's not 'Fidus'. I could really use you right now, Rej. Things would have been so much eas—"

Destan caught himself and looked over. Redje looked like he was sorry but at the same time not. Fidus was doing his job, he just wasn't "in tune" with Destan like Redje was.

"Look. I didn't— I'm not trying to guilt trip you. I'm not saying— I know that's what I said, but—"

"You're under a different type of stress and you don't have someone who 'understands' to turn to, physically speaking. Right?"

"You told me to pick a Christian when you left… now I'm seeing why you said that."

"Well, this gives you just another opportunity. Hmm?" Redje tapped him on the shoulder as he raised his eyebrow; then turned his focus to white fur in his peripheral, "So… you've got an alpha, huh? Male?"

"Yeah," Destan groaned as he pushed off the wall, the belvedere coming to his side; him trying to stay quiet, "I told you to stay in there! She's fine!"

"If we need to go…"

"No. No, Rej. You're fine. Calli must be in a bit of pain so he's just worried." Destan pushed on the whining creature to get him out of sight. "Stop it. She's fine. Okay? … No don't— Rej?"

"Huh?"

"Keep Tabitha distracted. I'm going to get him out of here for the time being. He's not going to stay put this close to her."

The way Redje went about it was so smooth with how he even worked his way into the conversation, but Tabitha knew what was going on. She kept her eyes glued to her husband, all the while knowing deep down she wasn't in any danger.

It was a challenge to keep the belvedere from whining as Destan dragged him out of the suite, but the second the door shut and the silence came, Tabitha relaxed.

Destan came back a couple minutes later, his lack of conversation triggering Redje to start, "Leave work at work and I told you don't feel bad. Focus on Callimay right now. … Where were you going when we first got here?"

"Oh! I was headed to ask Lance something."

"Mind if I tag along?"

"Not at all. — Calli?"

"Yes, Destan?"

"I'm gonna go ask Lance about the lasagna. Rej is gonna tag along."

Redje sounded worried as he looked over, "Tabby?"

She glanced around her for a few seconds and then gulped, "I… I should be alright."

He almost tip-toed over, kneeling in front of his distraught wife; taking the time to see to her regardless of others being around, "Tabby Bae? What do you need me to do?"

For a moment she just sat there, eyes closed, hand still clutching her necklace as a tear raced down her face; then took a deep breath, "I'm alright… now. I know it's not the same one, and it's not here. Go on. I'm sure you two want to chat, anyway."

"Sure?"

The lack of immediate response made Redje reach inside his jacket and hand her his two shadow knives, "This help an—"

Without a moment's hesitation, she snatched them out of his hands; but then stopped as her eyes got wide, "But what about—"

"Rej," Destan called out, him tossing a Katana to him.

After pulling the blade out of its sheath a bit, he looked up and half smiled, "It's been a while since I've used one, but I think I can still wield it if need be. Okay?"

Though it was a bit shaky, she sighed as her shoulders relaxed.

"Okay then. We'll be back in a bit." He kissed her forehead and then gave her a hug.

Ⅻ

"Well, he said as long as the pasta is 'floppy' it'd be alright." Destan announced with air quotes as he poked his head in the room. And of course Callimay shook her head as she rolled her eyes, a bit of laughter jumping from Tabitha.

"That was one of the 'worst' paraphrases I've ever heard." Redje all but punched Destan in the side. "That's 'not' what he said at all."

"It means the same thing," he shoved him back.

"Thank you for letting us barge in for a bit," Tabitha smiled as she patted Callimay's shoulders. "We won't keep you—"

"Oh, please stay." Callimay fought the urge to reach up to Tabitha. "Who knows when we'll get to see you again."

Tabitha looked at Redje, who looked at Destan, who looked at Callimay, who looked back at him. The look on her face disarmed him in every way. Yes, he wanted some time alone with her, but they hadn't had a meal with their best friends in so long; and they both enjoyed it so much, "Have you got a couple hours to spare, Rej?"

"We don't want to impose," he replied as Tabitha came to his side; him returning the Katana. "I'm sure you two would enjoy your first meal together better if you were alone."

"But—"

"We're not offended, Destan." Tabitha smiled as she handed Redje his knives. "We didn't come expecting to have a meal with you."

Destan thought for a little while: *Isn't this gonna wear you out?*

I know it will, but please? I'm not sure about you, but 'I' need this time with them before everything starts up again. I want to spend at least one more evening with them.

Alright. He smiled in agreeance, and then clapped his hands as he said, "Like Calli said: who knows when we'll see each other again. It'd be nice to have this time to chat and be together. Give us a boost of sorts before the last push."

"Well then, what can I help with?" Tabitha immediately replied.

"Well, I guess if you want to get some water boiling for pasta you could do that since it'll take forever." Destan suggested as he looked toward the ceiling. "I've gotta go grab what we don't have — which is almost everything — so there's not too much you can do yet."

"Mind if I tag along with you while you go shopping?"

"Let me ask if Calli wants to go, first." Destan shook his head as he walked over. "Would you like to stay here or go with me?"

After a bit of thinking, she replied; sounding a bit sad, "As much as I want to go, I'd probably last longer if I stay here."

"Calli they said they'd be willing to go." His whisper was pained.

"I know… but I also know you want to talk with Redje. Go on. Just don't take too long." Callimay brushed his hair to try and make it look as presentable as she could. "You need a haircut, 'so' bad. Land sake."

The pout on his face matched his hurt tone so well, "But Rocher told me it's officially long enough to put it in a traditional topknot. Sounded kinda fun to me. How do you think I'd look with—"

"Oh hush."

He winked as he let his hair go and patted her cheek, "I'll be back."

"I love you."

"Love you too."

❦

They all enjoyed a wonderful meal before Tabitha and Redje headed home; regardless of the previous objections given. And yet when the door closed after the final goodbyes were given, Destan and Callimay were glad to be able to rest. Neither of them dared dwell on it or say a word about it; because what Callimay said was true: they did need that time with their best friends. And while it left them exhausted, it was the kind of exhaustion they were happy to have.

"How about let's get you to bed?" Destan suggested as he put the last dish away.

She winced and hissed, "I can't even yawn! Ugh!"

Alerted but easily calmed, the belvedere — who was now allowed to return — bounded around as Destan pulled the wheelchair to the bedside, "I… I know this is gonna hurt— how a—"

"I should be alright." She tried to smile as she lifted her arms and waved him to help; her hiding a grimace. "Just take it slow."

Everything was going according to plan until she tried to take the one and only step she needed to; her legs giving out. Destan caught her, but at the expense of causing her to scream and gasp for air as she pushed away from him.

The belvedere snarled and growled as he ran to her.

Still disoriented from the pain, but trying her best to calm the creature, she put her hand out and in between gasps said, "No, Buddy!"

"Calli no!" Destan pulled her hand away as the belvedere bared his teeth and lunged at them.

In that instant of panic and confusion she started to fall, landing on the bed before rolling off and clipping the edge of the wheelchair.

Destan yelled as he threatened the belvedere; trying everything to keep his cool, "Let go! She's fine! I'm not hurting her on purpose!"

The belvedere released his arm and ran to the window, cowering while yelping and whining at Callimay. Never was the creature more confused with what to do.

Running to his desk, Destan heaved and hissed through his teeth as he started opening and slamming drawers.

Unaware of what happened, she asked as she rolled over and reached for the armrest of the wheelchair; the pain somewhat muffled because of the chaos, "What's wrong? What happened?"

"Not now!" He snapped at her as he ripped opened another drawer.

Callimay looked at the belvedere because of the commotion he was causing; seeing the streaks on his face and chest, "Oh no! Destan!"

"I said now not!" He argued as he shook his head; glass shattering as he threw a bottle against the wall before he rushed to the closet.

"Des—" she cried out as she grabbed her head, falling to the floor.

A few minutes passed before Destan came back out. He was knotting the wrap on his right forearm using his other hand and teeth. His brow still showed he was in pain as did his uneven breathing, but his posture and eyes showed he was much better; his slow gate proving he wasn't in danger any longer.

Seeing his wife unconscious on the floor, the belvedere lying beside her with his ears drooped, Destan ran over, "Calli? Calli can you hear me? Calli! I'm so sorry. I—"

As he turned her over she moaned a bit, barely opening her eyes to look at him. He knew by the look on her face she had a migraine, so he whispered, "Let's get you comfortable; then I'll get you something. … It's about time for you to take your pain medicine anyway."

In too much pain to lift her arms, she just nodded; Destan having to pick her up… which of course didn't sit well with the guard dog in the room. The creature started to growl, so he laid her down and stormed over to his computer, "I'd prefer to only have one arm semi disabled. … Now be quiet you unhinged, pessimistic, overzealous watchdog. Geez!"

With that safeguard on the belvedere, he went back to help his wife for what he hoped would be just a couple more painful seconds. But the poor thing was so racked with pain even after he spent so much time trying to help her get comfortable; she could barely swallow the medicine and had trouble catching her breath.

Once she settled back to rest, he went to clean the mess he made, rather upset with himself at how he reacted. Yes, he needed to take care of it right then, but he most certainly could've handled the situation in a much calmer way.

During this reflection time he double-checked his wound and sat in the dark; the belvedere poking his head around the corner of the door at one point, whimpering.

"Come here," he sighed as he turned and kneeled down, offering his hand to the creature. "I know, I know. You were just trying to keep Calli safe. You can't know exactly what's going on because you're still a dog. — And as much as I don't want to say this… at least I know you'll protect her from the monster that'll always be inside me. Thanks, Big Fella. … Just… just listen to us in circumstances like this. Huh?"

The belvedere bowed his head against Destan's chest, staying there until he got up to leave.

He sighed as he came out and saw the wheelchair: *Why does she have to go through all this? She's already been through—oh what's the use? It's not going to change anything. … Well, at least she's asleep. Thank goodness for that. I wish there were some way I could make this easier for her.*

A bit of helplessness crept in, him letting out a quiet growl as he shook his head. He took the bag off the back of the wheelchair, taking the small machine and leg wraps out: *Pretty self-explanatory, right? ~ Let's not get ahead of ourselves there, Boon. ~ It's a leg wrap. How hard can it be? … It's easier than putting that bandage on my arm, see? Nothing to it. Now all we have to do is… huh? Tube? What tube? H~ 'sure'. It's 'easy'. Ri-ght. You put it on upside down, buffoon. ~ A mistake anyone could make. Easy fix. Now all I have to do is turn this on and set it like the note says. … Done.*

Now satisfied with everything, he laid down; but instead of getting rest which he needed as well, he watched over the woman he so dearly loved. She was breathing shallow but nothing he wasn't used to. He pushed her hair out of her face, running his fingers through it: *If there were only some way I could take your migraine pain away, Calli. To give you some relief so you can get through the other pain. … Wait! Elder's journal. I remember he said Ginger had them when she was younger and he cured her! What*—"Big Fella? Watch over her. I'll be right back."

⅏

For hours on end he poured over the book, trying so hard to find where Elder mentioned Ginger. It was such a vivid memory, him still seeing it on the right-hand page one-fourth the way down, but at one point he thought he was tricked into thinking it was there.

Then the next page turned calmed those fears.

Now came the problem of figuring out exactly what was done. Yes, he wrote so much about what he did — Elder's record-keeping was the most detailed he'd ever seen — but it told Destan absolutely nothing. But surely that was because he didn't know much medical terminology.

But, even Torpid, Auditor, Doctor Gerould, and a half dozen other medical staff couldn't make hands or feet of it regardless of how awake they were. — How could someone be so detailed and yet so ambiguous at the same time!

Still bound and determined to find something right then, he started going through everything they found in Elder's quarters and station in Deep Dark. There were times he really had to watch himself: reading what despicable things Elder was doing wasn't something he was able to accept in a perfectly calm manner. Add to that the fact it was right under his nose for how many years: *If I would've only looked down when I was at his station. Those drawers were open! And you can't tell me~ He would've just made it so you couldn't see it. You know that, Boon. He'd done it all along in one way or another.*

But that wasn't his biggest battle he was fighting. Heavy eyelids were proving to be the most powerful "enemy" at the time. Taking the hint, he pushed the stack of papers to the side and got up.

What he pushed aside revealed a bright-colored note with a name hand-written. He paused, "Aldred Hilston? Huh? … I knew you were in Faberton working at that time, but—"

Glancing at the clock he knew Redje would be with Tabitha and Rose for lunch: *I'll leave him a message and then let things be 'till later.*

To his surprise, Redje answered the phone, "Well my goodness. We just got back to the house and you're calling. What's up?"

Oh that's right. I forgot. "You said back in October you ran into Aldred Hilston, right?"

"More like the opposite, but yeah, why?"

"See if Baron would be willing to meet with him."

"No need to bother him. I can do it."

"No. He had ties — what looks to be deep ones — to Elder, so I have no doubt he's got inroads with the Monarch to 'some' degree aside from those we already know about."

"I work with those types of people on a daily basis, Destan. He said he wanted to have coffee and gave me his number, so I'll just ask him. If someone else asked to meet, I'm sure he'd put two and two together. It's best to keep things as up-front as possible with him. Nothing's changed in that area that I noticed."

"Alright. I won't make you." Destan sighed as he picked up the page with the information he needed. "Ask him in whatever roundabout way you can what he knows about a treatment called Corpus Cathartarga or a machine called a Artemisia bed."

"Hold on there," Redje busted out laughing as he rushed to get a pen and paper. "Now what did you say? … I'm so glad you didn't go into the medical field like you told me you would."

"Huh?"

"I don't know much about medical terminology and such so maybe you 'did' say it right, but it sure sounded you uttered the Yeronich—"

"Rej you 'know' that's not what I said! I'll spell it and 'you' tell me how you'd pronounce it. Ready?"

Redje repeated the letters he wrote down, still laughing, prompting Tabitha to come see what was going on; Benjamin cooing and fixating on him when he saw him.

"Who are you talking to?"

"Just a sec, Tabby. — What was that, Destan? … Oh. T A R 'G' A. Okay. You redeemed yourself. It does look— anyway! I'll see what I can find. … Yes, I'll be discrete about it. What's this all about, anyway? Anything… oh. Alright. I'll get with him as soon as I can. … Yep, bye."

Destan sat back in his chair, staring at the far wall, glad he made some progress.

The next thing he knew, he was being shaken awake.

"Oh! What time is it?"

"Time for you to get back to Everlyn, that's what time it is." Trever said rather light-hearted as he slapped his shoulder and leaned on the desk. "By the way, what's with all this? And why are you wearing— w… why's your arm bandaged?"

"I may've found a way to ease — if not cure — Calli's migraines. She had a pretty bad one when she went to bed." Destan sighed as he stretched and stood up; then rolled his eyes as he held his bandaged forearm up, "And 'this' was courtesy of the belvedere."

"What!"

"Don't you 'dare' tell Mender. Well, just don't say anything unless he asks." He shushed as he waved his hands to calm Trever. "If nothing else he'd ~never let me live it down. It was an accident."

Now in a hushed tone, Trever kept asking, "What happened?"

"I'd forgotten to put the block on him as far as knowing Calli's emotions and pain level. I went to help her out of the wheelchair—"

"Let me guess…"

"I'm just glad I got it and not her. She wasn't paying attention; only heard him growl and bark. So of course she threw her hand out to calm him down." Destan explained as he yawned.

"How's she doing now?"

He took a few seconds and then replied, "She's asleep."

"Stop, doing, that!"

"What?"

"That mind thing you do. Creeps me out."

"Huh? … Oh. Sorry. I'll see you in—"

"Just come back when you're rested. Alright?" Trever shooed on, not wanting to think about what he saw as grotesque any longer.

ℬ

When Destan got back, he realized he didn't have his veil on… or his ensemble for that matter: *No 'wonder' everyone was so shocked. Makes much more sense now. And that must be what Trever was asking about. … Oh man! I'm beat.*

The belvedere was all but frantic, running to him and yelping as he opened the door.

In a panic he ran over, but when Destan found Callimay peacefully sleeping, he turned to the pitiful creature, "W… what's wrong, Big Fella? She's fine. Right?"

He kept pacing back and forth at the foot of the bed, stopping near her feet each time and stretching his neck out to try and reach her. Destan was still too tired to figure out what was going on; and once he checked her breathing and what else he could to make sure she was okay, told him to lie down so she wouldn't wake up.

~ 3 ~

When he woke up, the sight he was greeted with scared him for half a second. Callimay was wheezing; rolled onto her side. As he moved her, she moaned and started to squirm. Destan rubbed the side of her face as he had his head bowed so their foreheads touched, then once she was settled down got up to get her medicine ready.

By the time he got back the belvedere was acting the same way, "I know this bed is bigger than the one at the Nest or the Wing, and yes, she's laying in the middle; but geez Big Fella! Calm down!"

She was still asleep but he wasn't about to force her to wake up, so to keep himself occupied Destan got some breakfast ready. And while he worked he glossed over the papers Doctor Gerould gave him about what therapy she was going to be doing daily. They seemed easy enough because he'd done some of them himself, but he knew. He knew the pain she'd be in. He knew the constant struggle of fighting your body begging you to quit so the pain will stop. But for this therapy to help her, being in pain was expected and meant progress was being made. — Well pain up to a certain point, that is.

Sometimes knowing what was going to come wasn't helpful, so he felt it best to go into it all as support for her and not say much. His pessimism and helplessness wasn't going to help even though he would be wording it as empathy and concern — saying he knew what she felt — but he did his best to accept what things were and resolve to do everything he could to make it as easy as possible.

And to help test this mindset, she woke up and complained her head still hurt… and her left arm ached; moaning as he helped her sit up, "Ugh. I don't get it. By now it's usually gone."

38

"Shh. It's alright. Me tossing you like I did didn't help any."

"I know you didn't mean to. … Are you doing alright?"

"I'm fine," Destan nodded as he glanced at his arm, the belvedere yelping yet again.

"Why is he so noisy?"

"Only thing I can think of is he doesn't like that he can't reach you."

"Why don't you just let him on the bed?"

"Absolutely not!" His lips twisted as he huffed. "I'm not letting a half dog push me out of 'my' own bed in the middle of the night."

"Just while you're gone? He wasn't that bad when you were here."

"Oh Calli, you mean he—"

"It was only a couple times. He calmed down when I would talk to him." She said rather hoarse as she tried to calm her breathing.

"What's wrong, Calli?"

"I… I'm having trouble… breath-ing!" She wheezed as Destan took her hand and put his forehead against hers.

"Remember what Lance said: it's like hiccups. Listen to me and try to mimic it." He soothed as he exaggerated how he was breathing; making sure to do it slow and steady as he held her hands against his chest.

Before long she calmed herself so he helped her settle back, "Like your pillow fort?"

"It 'is' comfortable. I don't know why I never slept like this before." She made light of everything, her eyes looking worried as she finished, "C… could I… I mean would it hurt if we just—"

"Put the physical therapy off for a bit?" Destan smiled as he sat back down and took her hand.

"I know it's got to be done, but I'm… I'm just not ready for it. I…" *Not that I'll ever be 'ready', but I—*

"One day. I know Lance said to start right away, but I'm sure he didn't think what happened last night would. And if he wants to have a beef with anyone about it, well he can pin it on me. I am all for you getting a day's rest. Take care of the migraine first."

A sigh of infinite relief came from her, followed by, "I know it's important I get that all started as soon as possible. Just today."

"Just rest and if you 'need' something, let me know. I'll be back in a couple hours."

The belvedere followed him to the door, whining and nudging him, *You are just such a*— "Fine. Come on. … Don't let him push you around, alright Calli?"

"I won't," she smiled as he leaped with joy on the bed, snuggling close to her left side. "Ouch!"

"What did he—"

"My arm still hurts," Callimay calmed as she carefully set it on top of the belvedere's back and sighed. "He didn't mean to do anything."

Destan let out more of a growl than sigh as he sat down and pushed her bangs behind her ear.

"I love you."

"You're too good at this whole pulling me back." He replied, unable to keep from smiling. "But don't ever stop, got it?"

ℬ

Just as Destan got back to the suite, his phone went off, "Don't tell me you already met with him!"

"Well hello to you too," Redje scoffed, but couldn't hold back the boisterous laugh he was trying so hard to contain. "He was free and so was I. No need to put something off… especially with him."

"So what did he say?"

"Well," Redje sighed as he shut the back door and walked out toward the small campfire that was, by now, nothing but a pile of glowing embers. "I'm not exactly sure how to say this, Destan."

He let go of the door handle, eyes wide, "You guys are alright a—"

"We're all fine. It has nothing to do with that. I… well… are… are you sitting down?"

"No."

"Do it." Redje voice bottomed out.

He rushed to his desk and sat down, "Okay. What's going on?"

"When he first told me I thought I recalled the name but wasn't sure. Tabby confirmed my fear a bit ago— Destan? I… ugh! I really don't want to be the one to tell you this. And I most certainly don't want to do it over the phone."

"Just say it! Please, Rej."

"Baleck Willgun isn't dead."

40

"What!" Destan yelled as he jumped up, shoving his chair back.

The belvedere was startled awake and jumped off the bed as he barked. This sudden movement waking Callimay, "Wha… what's going on? … Calm down, Buddy. Whatever it is… just lay down."

Destan's eyes were so wide-opened that if they weren't already attached to his body they would have fallen out. He dropped the phone and stared through Callimay, frozen with fear: *Wha— but how? I don't— how did he get away? But I know I saw him— why would Elder want him alive?*

"Destan? Destan are you there? Destan? Hello?" He could hear Redje calling out.

He fumbled to pick the phone up after another minute, somehow able to get out, "Are you sure?"

"I'm positive."

Stumbling back, he caught himself as he flopped onto the chair, "W— what's he got to do with anything?"

"Aldred said the Die-a-door— well whatever you called it, he said your father designed it but Baleck was the one who finished it. That name was the one your father gave it, so his inquiring about you was rather blunt. … There's only one in the world and of course Baleck has it. … Destan? You there? Is— can I do anything to help?"

"I… wh— who—"

"Aldred wouldn't give me any more information… without you know what."

"Figures," Destan got out while still in a daze but his eyes managing to roll.

Redje poked the glowing coals, embers wafting into the air on the breeze. What could he say to help?

Doing what he could, the belvedere was beside Destan now, his head resting on his knee. This all felt impossible, but then again, Elder was capable of that at times, "Is he going to be staying in the area?"

"With what we discussed and your name getting thrown into the mix? I saw those itchy fingers growing in his eyes. He knows money's lurking somewhere in this for him. He won't be leaving anytime soon."

"L… let me think things through. I… I'll try to get with you… I'll get with you later."

"Take as much time as you need." Redje tried to encourage as he hung up the phone.

"What did he say?" A timid voice asked as the back door slid open.

"Just as scared and dumbfounded as I thought he'd be." Redje sighed as he felt a soft hand on his neck. "Just when we thought things were turning a corner, too."

"One man being alive isn't the end of the world. I thought Baleck wasn't even one who had abilities. Right?"

"Tabby it's worse than that and you know it." He looked up with determined eyes that were glassy. "If Elder faked his death, he could've faked countless others for decades. Hanger, Tri-claw, Puncture… they could all still be alive. And for all we know they could be inside; just waiting for the word."

"Y… you don't think—"

He jumped to his feet and took his trembling wife in his arms, "I pray he and his demon are dead, Tabby."

"H… he could be— no. No it's not possible. I 'saw' you—"

"Destan's said that already, Tabby. And I've experienced Elder's mirage myself."

"He can't be!" She screamed as she beat her fists on his chest. "He's dead! He and his belvedere are dead! I saw you kill them both!"

"Tabby-bae, I," Redje tried his best to stay calm and not let his emotions break open; him pulling his wife close. "I know I opened that door… I… I didn't mean to. I don't want you relapsing. Please."

She sobbed as she grabbed his shirt, "He just can't be alive. God please don't let that be so. How can I keep our babies safe if he is alive and comes here while you're gone! Even thinking about it causes me— look at what happened when we were with Destan and C—"

"Tabby," he cringed as he rocked her. "Tabby-bae you've got to stop thinking about it. It's just making things worse."

"What am I going to do! How… how can I…" her sobs became so severe she couldn't talk any longer.

℥

What else has Elder covered up? It's just as likely Nightmare's still alive! Maybe even— if Webb's alive I'm gonna—

Destan was cut off by Callimay wheezing. He flew over to her, the belvedere right on his heels, "Calli? Calli, relax."

She grabbed his arms, him gritting his teeth since she just so happened to latch on where the belvedere bit him; her panicking from another "hiccup attack". He put his forehead against hers like last time and went through the exact same steps so she could breathe easy again.

"What caused that?" She asked scared as Destan helped her settle back down.

"The muscles in your throat are reliving what happened; kinda like what happened at the mansion when I… well you get the idea. Lance said you'd have these spasms — hiccups — for probably a few more weeks. But in the meantime let's get your little fort built back. Huh?"

"My head hurts. And so does my left arm." She said rather slurred.

While her saying that wasn't something unexpected, and even the way she said it; what hit him as odd was she was just fine before. But he brushed it off and took a deep breath as he stroked her hair: *I'm sure since she had that spasm she pushed that pain aside.* "Just rest and don't worry. I'll be back in a few minutes with Lance." *Hopefully he's not in bed yet.* "Stay with her, Big Fella. But be careful."

And as it turned out, the person he was going after was on his way to check on Callimay. The belvedere wasn't pleased he had to leave her side; plodding over to the window and flopping down, him huffing as his ears drooped and his eyes glared at Destan.

It only took Doctor Gerould a moment before he sighed and shook his head, "She's running a low-grade fever. Hopefully it's an episode similar to when you two first moved to Rayleen… but I'm wondering."

"What?" Destan asked as Doctor Gerould checked her incisions.

"She 'could' have an infection. She was in ocean water and what we did was in a fight against time. The inherent likelihood of her getting an infection is high because of that, but I'd think by this time…" he trailed off as his face began to show more confusion than worry. "Well, they all look fine. And she's not reacting to them being touched."

While he drew some blood, he called for Auditor and asked her to bring a few things.

Trever happened to stop by during this all and stayed to keep Destan company. While seeing his superior in such an informal manner —

showing emotion — was still something he struggled with, at the same time it reminded him of the fact his baby sister was with someone who loved her deeply… and worried constantly.

Strangely enough, there wasn't anything Doctor Gerould could find to explain why she had a low-grade fever. It didn't concern him that much, him chalking it up to some type of episode like she had while in Rayleen even though he couldn't identify any type of toxins in her blood like he could then. He did say it was possible she could be having one due to her migraine, and since everything she went through was causing her body to do a type of reset it was reacting different this time.

Destan wasn't happy there was no concrete answer, but was reminded sometimes there wasn't an "answer-answer" when it came to medical abnormalities. Doctor Gerould assured him it wasn't anything he could see that would be worrisome and gave her a Halo treatment to help with what he knew was an issue.

Since he had the two of them there, Destan told them about the update concerning what could rid Callimay of these retched migraines forever; though since Trever hadn't heard any of it he had to explain everything afterward to give him the whole picture. He was irate to learn Baleck was still alive; ready to storm out for his pound of flesh.

"Trever, that's not going to do any good."

"It'll make me feel a whole lot better knowing that demon is dead." He fumed as he reached for the door.

"Stop!" Destan demanded as he grabbed his arm, calming when he saw the belvedere jump to his feet. "Let's talk outside. … If what Aldred said is true, then Baleck is going to be the only one in this world who knows how to use that machine. Can you remember when she was young and she'd have migraines, Trever? Do you?"

"Some, yes."

"How did you feel when you saw her like that?"

"It made me feel horrible since I didn't want her in that pain, and angry I couldn't fight what was causing it." Trever replied a bit calmer.

"They've gotten worse since we gained our abilities." Destan sighed as he let him go; pausing for a good long while. "But now I've found a shred of hope she won't ever have one again. I can't let it go. No matter if it is Baleck who is the one holding it."

"He murdered our family! I remember w—"

"He murdered my mother and only sibling, too, you idiot!" Destan shoved him against the wall, raising his clenched fist and then closing his eyes to calm as he bowed his head. "I… I know what you're going through. I k… I know the pain you feel. The anger burning you up? I get it. Okay? I… it's hard for me to deal with the fact he's alive; you're not the only one."

"What makes you think he'd help Everlyn? Are you dumb enough to think he'd be a person to keep his word?"

"I know he doesn't." Destan threw his head back and rolled his eyes; trying everything to keep calm but needing some amount of release at the same time. "But I also know he's a man who has a price. He'll play any side of the dice as long as he gets what he wants."

"Are you willing to pay his price?"

"Money doesn't mean a thing to me. I'd liquidate all of my assets—"

"What if it isn't money?"

"You mean what if he wants me to turn myself over?" Destan asked as Trever nodded. "That's what he asked for last time."

"How did it end?" Trever asked critical as he folded his arms across his chest, Destan not answering him. "He wouldn't take it, would he? It wasn't enough, was it?"

"Look, it's Calli's health we're talking about. When she wakes up I'll let her decide. Is it going to kill you to wait 'til then?" Destan negotiated as Trever frowned. "Killing — let alone murder — isn't the code of the Shadows… 'or' Veil. We're not the Radicals or Fringe. I didn't give you that veil and the title Liberator for you to malign and twist it into your own warped way of getting revenge. You do this and I won't hesitate to put a sanction on you, even with you being Calli's brother. — There's more than just Baleck out there who's a threat to Calli and you 'know' that. You want to risk being able to protect her just for the sake of ending one person's life? Will him being dead bring back your family? Will it? … Can you at least wait for her to speak her peace? She's just as much worthy of being his judge, jury, and executioner as you are."

The belvedere waited in the doorway this whole time; his happy expression helping the tense air soften. Trever's lips were firm and angry as he stood there in silence, absolutely fuming; he couldn't bring himself to admit Destan was right about Callimay being the one who could decide since this all was for her. He backed off and managed a nod as he left, but nothing more.

Callimay had rolled onto her side again, so Destan moved her back, rearranging the pillows and checking the machine hooked to the wraps on her legs.

She moaned as he tried to move her left hand to bring it to his chest, so he left it alone: *I'm sorry, Calli. Hopefully you'll feel better in the morning.* *Please, God. Please help me to lean on You. Help me be the support Calli needs. Help me lead her like I'm supposed to. Please strengthen her body so it can heal. Help both of us to be patient through this process of recovery. … And please help… help me. Help me be an example of You to Trever. Help me to show him how to cope with this type of frustration and anger. Help me to do better. I pray he's willing to listen and see what benefit there is to following You. In your Son's Name I pray, amen.*

~ 4 ~

Unlike what either of them expected or wanted, when she woke up, Callimay wasn't the least bit better. In fact she was worse. Far worse than Destan thought possible after what Doctor Gerould told him, "Oh my gosh, you're shivering!"

He bundled her up with every blanket he could find, then jumped to the medical wing.

Neurosan was the first one he saw and the first one into the room with him. When she saw Callimay, she gasped, "She's not shivering, Doyen. She's having a seizure!"

In one fluid motion, she ripped the blankets off — dumping them on the belvedere — and pulled Callimay over to her side.

"Why are you doing that? Her ribs—"

"She can asphyxiate since she's— she could choke herself very easily on her own saliva in this state." She paused, seeing the confused, fearful look on Destan's face. "And she's burning up— Nexus? … Nexus? … Why isn't th—"

"Who do you need?"

"Mender, Bracer, Coalesce… whoever is closest."

Before she had a chance to repeat her original question, Destan jumped back to the medical wing. Doctor Gerould just arrived and took off the second he was told what was happening.

Trever was moseying down the hall when he saw the two of them running into the suite. He took off like a sprinter out of the blocks, coming in to a room filled with the chill of fear; Destan and Doctor Gerould huddled around Callimay.

"What's wrong?"

"Shh," Neurosan calmed as she reached out and put her hand on his arm. "She's doing alright now."

"What happened?"

"She had a seizure but is resting now. Mender's trying some other tests to figure out what's causing this fever since it was probably what triggered it."

"She's alright?"

"As long as Doyen says you can, you can see her." Neurosan smiled as she nodded toward Destan.

He looked worried, but waved for Trever to come.

The belvedere was at the foot of the bed, still covered with the blankets, his nose poking out and resting on the bed.

Destan was rubbing her arm, trying to wake her, but wanting to do it gently because Doctor Gerould said she was still in pain. And it didn't take anything to see her breathing was labored; plus she was beginning to moan and toss back and forth.

Nothing helped for the longest time, but she finally opened her eyes. She blinked a few times, staring at Destan in confusion. As she tried to get up, she cried out in pain.

"Easy. Just relax, Calli. Everything's alright."

"W— who are you!" She gasped as her eyes darted between Destan and Trever. "Where am I? What's g— ah! … Ah. Wh-at happened?"

"It's me, Calli. It's Destan." He replied slowly, looking at Trever with fearful shock.

"Get away from me!" She screamed as she tried to move, crying out from the pain yet again. "How do you know my name!"

"Everlyn it's alright." Trever tried to calm.

"No. Please don't touch me." Callimay cried and yelped in pain as she shied away from his outstretched hand. "Who… who are you? Where am I! Wh… what happened to me? Why does everything hurt so much? What… what did you do to me!"

"Lance, what's going on!" Destan begged as he looked back.

Auditor just came in the room, her running over to Doctor Gerould as he remained calm and started filling a syringe, "Let me get her sedated. She's going to do nothing but fight us and cause herself more pain in the state she is right now; possibly injuring herself more."

"Why can't she remember me!"

"I don't know, alright!" He snapped as he looked Destan straight in the eye. "Be gentle, but hold her arms down so I can give this to her."

A few seconds slipped by, Trever doing what Destan couldn't bring himself to.

She wailed and cried, trying everything she could to pull away from the needle Doctor Gerould was sticking her with.

This terrified young woman couldn't fight the sedative, but tried to up until the last moment; her saying lethargic as she lost consciousness, "Don't! Please don't! What are you doing? What did I do wrong? Let me go. Don't touch me. Please don't… Please, God. Don't let me…"

Destan sat there, unable to move. It looked like someone pulled his heart out and stabbed it; letting him watch in horror as it beat its last few, useless beats before dying.

Once she was out he reached his trembling hand to her face, drying the tears which were still streaming from her closed eyes; his voice nearly stolen by the terror he felt, "Wha… what's happening to her. Why would she ever think I'd 'ever'—"

Confused himself as to why she would have such a drastic freefall of this kind out of seemingly nowhere, Doctor Gerould ran a few tests and didn't know how to tell Destan the news.

Able to hear every word Doctor Gerould said to himself, Destan ran to the phone, "Pick up, Rej. Come on. Please! Pick u—"

"Hewoah? Hoo dis?"

"Where's Rej?"

"Desan! Oh goodie! Iza can tewl you—"

"Get. Redje. I don't have time to talk."

"Otay. I get him. — Papa!" He heard her cheerful voice call out in no rush whatsoever; her chatting as she hopped along, "When awe you coming home, Desan? I hasn seen you en so wong! — Papa? … Mama, wears Papa? … Oh I no it knot time to go on our date. … Is Desan!"

"Destan? Redje's in the shower." Tabitha said as she took the phone. "What is it?"

"All I need is Hilston's number."

"What's wrong?" Tabitha asked as her eyes got wide and she froze.

"Just get me his number. Please!" He begged.

"A… alright. — Redje? Redje where'd you write Aldred Hilston's number? Destan needs it last night." She asked as she knocked on the door; doing everything possible to keep calm so Rose wouldn't notice.

There was a painfully long period of muffled voices on the line, then Destan heard Redje, "It's Venrow 7-8-2-1-0-3. What's going on?"

"No time to explain." Destan refused as he hung up, mumbling the number to himself as his hands shook while dialing the number.

"What are you doing?" Trever scolded in a hushed tone.

"There's only one person left in this world who knows what's going on." Destan growled, though his eyes were still fear-stricken. "I've got no choice but to find Baleck."

"Are you mad!" Trever grabbed his arm, completely irate.

The second he heard the phone line open, Destan blurted out as he shook off Trever's hand, "Aldred?"

"Who is this?"

"It's Destan Nevrille. I—"

"I wondered if this would come around to you contacting me." He said rather arrogant. "What do you want, 'Doyen'?"

"Tell me where Baleck is." Destan ignored the fact Aldred knew something he shouldn't.

"Baleck? Oh you mean Baleck Willgun?"

"I've got no time for this charade, Hilston. Where is he?"

"Oh come now. Nothing is ever 'that' urgent that you have to use my last name."

"I know he's alive." Destan began to spike. "Tell me!"

"I don't think you can afford to argue with me; you never could." He snickered as he sat down and stretched out. "Because you know if this keeps up I can't do anything for you. Why don't we meet and chat for a bit?"

"I'm good on my word, you know that." Destan started pacing the floor, raking his hand through his hair. "And this 'is' that urgent. Just tell me where he is. I'll make sure you get your money."

There were whispers and then the voice Destan never thought he'd hear again said, "Grave's Bycole, midnight. 'Don't' be late."

Baleck didn't wait for a response and the number was turned off by the time Destan called it back.

"Well…" Trever asked as Destan put the phone down and braced himself against the desk. "What did he say?"

"I've got to get to Trofglen to meet with Baleck by midnight." Destan said as he took a deep breath.

"Where at?"

"Somewhere called Grave's Bycole. I think it's on the Northeast side of the bay. — S… stay with her. Please? I'll be back as fast as I can."

Destan gave Callimay a hug and kiss, then gave Trever his computer, doing everything he could to keep him from seeing he was crying, "The damper on the belvedere's link to Calli is on here. … I… if I don't make— take it off when she gets better so he can protect her."

"I… uh… alright?" Trever replied as he took it, his hand and voice a bit jerky.

℔

Destan shut the door and leaned his back against it, still holding onto the handle. He muttered something while he had his eyes closed and then left. The walk was lonely and quiet, but it also gave him time to gather himself and get his emotions in order.

But, when he got up top, he heard the door open. Without turning he said, "Keep her safe. I hope I'll be back by caller's warning."

"Let me go."

"Trever, I'm not going let you get your pound of f—"

He caught Destan as he collapsed and laid him on the ground: no need to add insult to injury.

Trever took the money from Destan and returned the computer. He stood up and said determined: *If Everlyn loses one of us, 'I' get that honor. At least I get it first. She would grieve my loss, but I don't think she'd survive losing you… even if she can't remember you right now. — You have my word I won't lay a finger on him. At least not this time. I admit he's holding a trump card of sorts right now and I'm not the only one who's in line to get at him. But I 'will' get him.*

The second Destan said "Grave's Bycole" Trever knew exactly where in this park Baleck be. In fact Trever had been there before with Elder several times when he was younger for recreation and "family time". He even recalled that being where he would see Baleck routinely.

Knowing the deadline of midnight was going to be tight, Trever took his bike. He knew the one border security guard who would be on duty at the time, but wasn't sure if they would be willing to let him through.

"Kevereux, it's been ages," a young woman greeted from the darkness as she slid down a line which came from her perch.

This extremely slender, black-laden, mysterious, young woman had an aura of death following her like a trained dog. She sauntered over; her addressing Trever and his attitude toward her being quite mutual and familiar. Her purple eyes gleamed with a bloodlust that kept itself controlled in the moment; but it was clear it wouldn't take anything to unleash it.

How could he be so comfortable around someone this joyfully lethal? Where did he meet her, and why?

"It's been a bit, I know." Trever replied as he took his helmet off and stood up, smiling.

"Miss me?" She came up and he took her in his arms.

"Does that answer your question?" He replied after he kissed her.

"Who is she?" She whispered as Trever felt the blade of her knife on his throat.

"What do you mean, Kayla?"

"I know your cologne," she pressed it harder against his skin, her eyes burning. "And it doesn't smell like roses."

"Where's your swain? I saw him standing here as I was coming up." Trever whispered in almost a hiss as he motioned with his eyes to his blade against her side.

"He's my brother."

"You don't have a brother."

"What about the perfume?" Kayla shoved him back.

"It's from my sister."

"Cheater!" She tried to slap his face as he ducked to the side.

"Slut." Trever rubbed his neck, seeing blood on his hand.

They stood there, an arm's length apart, staring into each other's eyes; both of them with a look of betrayal that could only be satiated with violence.

"Come here, you." Trever sighed as he yanked her to him.

"I love you."

Such a horrible liar, really. "I know you do. I love you too." Trever gave her one more kiss. "So does this mean I get through?"

"What if I say no?"

"I don't have time right now." Trever pushed her away. *And I'm sure your swain didn't leave so you want me gone, too.*

"Let me guess: Elder sent you on a training exercise. … Am I right?"

Perfect out. Oh how you always seem to shoot yourself with these back doors you always hand me. "Yeah."

"Alright." Kayla backed off as an owl flew to her shoulder.

"Thanks." Trever smiled as he kissed her again; petting the owl. "I'll see you on my way back through if things go well. No guarantees I can stay, though. Sound good?"

She nodded and smiled, "Hope it's soon. Love you."

ᛒ

The keep at Grave's Bycole hadn't changed in the last nine years, and yet it felt completely different. All the memories he held dear associated with this place were heinous lies. Instead of a peaceful and picturesque place by the bay, it was a deafening ledge over a bottomless pit of deceit and inhumane cruelty.

He strolled along the waterfront, looking over at the thunderous waters of Arc Weir. Not a soul in sight… for very long, "Right on time."

But as the moon came out again, the person Trever saw was not whom he was expecting. The middle-aged man with long, true blue hair looked less than pleased as his baritone voice overpowered the low roar already in the air, "Did Doyen have second thoughts? Or is he hedging his bets?"

"He's… 'incapacitated', right now." Trever paused as he placed his knives on the post beside him.

"Incapacitated? … Interesting. I take it 'you' are the reason for it?"

"I know in time he'll forgive me." Trever didn't take his eye off the man for one second as he shoved his hands in his pockets. "I was under the assumption Baleck would be my contact."

"At the moment he prefers a bit of… 'ambiguity', as well as security given his current situation." The man hinted as he strolled up to Trever. "Allow me to introduce myself: Aldred H—"

53

"I know who you are." He folded his arms across his chest. "So, am I meeting Baleck or not?"

"Let us not get ahead of ourselves. All things in their good time." Aldred shook his head as he chuckled a bit. "I was promised payment for my services. Surely you are aware of how my services are rendered. And I still abide by best practice by ensuring it is secured… up, front."

Trever waited for a few moments, fiddling with the cube in his pocket, and then tossed it at him, "Here."

"Untraceable I take it."

"I've played the spy game long enough to know that's child's play. … Now since you've got your payoff, are you going to keep your end of the deal? Am I speaking with Baleck or not?"

"You are," Baleck answered from behind.

Out of the corner of his eye as he caught a glimpse of him; slowly turning, "It's been a while since we've seen each other… 'brother'."

"I'm sorry to see Elder's work on you didn't hold after his passing. You were a great asset as it was, but it and would have been greater now that you are Sinew."

"It didn't even make it that far. I saw before that just how vulgar you and Elder were… and apparently 'you' still are."

"He became complacent with you; flaunted you like you were some trophy that was indestructible and impenetrable. It was his one and probably only weakness. … I 'did' try to warn him." Baleck sighed as he came up to the railing. "You're looking well, all things considered."

"You look like you were dragged from Hummingbird Bay after Hurricane Fillmore hit."

"You remember that? Not one of my brightest moments. Oh it was quite a chuckle, wasn't it? — Things have been rough, I'll concede that. But by the tone of Doyen's voice it sounds like Callimay's circumstances are far from favorable."

"I'm not one to be diplomatic and such in these situations, so I'll put it all on the line: Everlyn's sick. Real sick. It started out as a migraine, but then she had a seizure—"

"Has she complained about pain in any of her extremities?" Aldred butted in, sounding inquisitive but looking worried as he walked over.

"I think her left arm was bothering her. Why?"

"What about a fever?" He continued to question.

"She's had a low-grade one, but I don't know for how long."

"Then it—"

"But that's nothing compared to the fact she doesn't know where she is or who any of us are. She even thought—" Trever cringed, seeing in his mind's eye the entire thing happening again. "She had to be sedated so she wouldn't hurt herself."

"I guess this 'was' worthy of that urgency. — She's end stage three." Aldred muttered to Baleck who tried to but couldn't suppress his groan.

Baleck's face changed as well. His eyes shifted back and forth as if watching a metronome keep a slower, yet steady tempo. He took a deep breath and surrendered, "I'll do it on one condition. And if it's agreed to I'll give the location."

"Alright," Trever nodded without hesitation.

"I know what powerful serum runs through Callimay's veins. It was given to her as an aid to make her blend into society when she was a child, but I know it's capable of more. Much more. Destry destroyed his work as I soon found out, but Callimay made a comment while I was fighting her about her knowing what both of our abilities were. Her momentary boast gave me a piece of information I feared was forever gone. Somewhere, Destan has information about the serum Chameleon. Give it to me and I'll do everything I know to save her life."

"So she 'is' dying."

"At a faster rate than I think you care to realize." Baleck warned as he started walking past Trever, Aldred following him. "I take it Destan contacted us just after he discovered she was experiencing amnesia?"

"Yes."

"Good."

"And with her being sedated it will slow the spindles' growth." Aldred added as the two of them continued on.

Baleck paused and looked over his shoulder, "If she's not treated within the next forty-eight hours I guarantee you: she 'will' die. The number Destan has will be available when he's ready to talk. ... And if you love your sister like you claim, and I saw when you were young, I would advise you to get back as soon as possible and persuade Destan to do as I say. — In other words: don't stop to see Kayla."

"I'm not a child."

"Aren't you… 'little brother'?" Baleck snickered as he sauntered off.

"Didn't you forget something?" Trever clinched his fists.

"Oh, those little nail files?" Baleck scoffed as he stopped at the post and looked over, picking one up and dangling it in the air. "You wouldn't dare even though you know what I've done. You can't afford to lose the only member of your family you have left. … And I'm the only one who can save her."

Baleck threw it right at Trever, its deep thud in the tree making the air beside his ear quiver.

"Elder was right, I have missed that adrenaline rush." Baleck smiled as he stood up from his follow through and glanced as his hands. "But that is for another time. — Hurry along little one. We'll have plenty of time to play later."

Trever snatched up the rest of his knives and jumped on his bike, tearing out as fast as he could.

B

Once out of the city he looked at his watch, guessing Destan would have gained consciousness by now. And he was fairly certain he'd be heading this way as fast as possible to stop him from doing what he'd sworn to do to Baleck. So, to make sure he wouldn't miss him, Trever headed back the way he knew Destan would be coming.

And sure enough, just over the border they met. Though the manner in which that meeting took place wasn't pleasant; Trever squirming as he ripped his helmet off, "Seriously! Can you stop doing that!"

"How else was I supposed to get you to stop? You couldn't see me." Destan breathed hard. "What happened? I swear, if you—"

"Let me first say I apologize for hitting you like I did. I just— if someone was going to die I knew it had to be me. Everlyn needs you more than she needs me." Trever was quick to explain. "And you'll be pleased to know I didn't kill Baleck. I know what I said earlier, but I got to thinking about what you said… and you were right. He's the only hope Everlyn has."

Destan calmed and smiled, then handed him his veil, "You're gonna need this."

"W… why are you giving it back to me? I dis—"

"You proved me wrong. Now take it. … And what happened to you?" Destan asked when he saw the blood on his neck.

"Nothing. Just a misunderstanding with— it's my personal affairs."

Now's not the time to be sidetracked like this, Trever. 'Please' grow up. "So what happened?"

"Let's talk on the ride back. There's no time to waste."

"I'll follow you back."

"Are you sure? You look pretty winded."

"I'm f— no, you're right. The last thing I need to do is spiral out of control." Destan corrected himself. "I know you can't stand it, but I'd prefer using Calli's ability than yelling back and forth."

Trever rolled his eyes as he started off: *So how does this work again?*

Just do what you're doing right now. Destan almost laughed.

Good grief! … Alright. Trever worked past what he viewed as the grotesqueness of what was happening. *So Baleck said he'd help. He said Everlyn 'is' dying. And if she doesn't get treated within the next forty-eight hours she's beyond help.*

Just forty-eight hours? What could it— *I… alright.*

Aldred basically said to keep her sedated. It'd help something, I forget what, from getting worse. … He wouldn't tell me where to take her until you call him back with your answer — he said the number you have will work this time. But… there's a catch to this all.

How much?

He wants Chameleon. — Not Everlyn, just the serum. He figured out you have the information and he wants it all. … You 'do' have it, right? Trever asked worried. *I mean what Everlyn told him—*

Yeah. Destan tried his best not to growl in frustration. *Yeah, I've got it. But what in the world does he want it for? He already has Challenger. I don't und—* *Oh no. He's going to fuse it with Challenger. If he~ Calm down, Boon! Adding itself to itself may do nothing. Stop jumping to conclusions. It's the worst thing to do right now.*

So, what are you going to do?

What other choice do I have that'll save Calli?

You're not going to give it to him, are you? I mean from what you've told me and even what I've experienced myself… do you realize he could wreak havoc on humanity itself if he had that? Are you just going to—*

If I do anything other than give him what he wants he could kill Calli without me knowing it. I have no idea what he'd do, and no one else has any clue what in the world this treatment or machine does let alone how our abilities work.

Well… then hold off on giving it to him. Make him take care of Everlyn first. Then once she's out and safe give it to him. You could get out of there before he even noticed he was crossed.

Trever, I don't lie.

So you're just going to hand him something he can turn into a weapon and use against Everlyn and everyone else?

He's stated his demands and I can't think of another way out.

I just gave you the other way!

I'm not going with your alternative, I can tell you that right now. Calli's life is in the balance. This is the choice I have to make so she lives. Baleck's not going to be 'gracious' in that area; he'll demand it up front and you know that.

I'd cheat, lie, steal… I'd be willing to murder someone to keep her alive. Why won't you? Don't you love her?

If someone were innocent and you ended their life… how were they a threat to Calli in the first place? *I love her so much I 'won't' do it. God hates every single thing you just listed you'd do for her. And as much as I love her I fear and love Him more. I know the same goes for her. I'm not going to warp my priorities just for the sake of physical and momentary rewards.*

This is a human life we're talking about! Not some prize from the carnival. … You know what? Just shut up. You're making me sick. We're almost back, anyway.

You, sick? If you listened to yourself with a rational approach you'd think the exact thing I am. What's gotten into you!

Destan could hear everything Trever was saying to himself but kept silent. Trever's trigger was irritation and the last thing both of them needed was for him to wreck the bike due to some involuntary reaction he might have. — This triggering his memory of what he almost did back in Rayleen the one time.

One thing out of that entire mess was true that Trever said: Destan had a choice. He did get to decide how it would work… yes, maybe it was only to an extent, but he did have "some" level of control over the situation. And even what he said to Trever started to sink in for himself: having Auditor or Doctor Gerould there while Callimay was being treated wouldn't help. They didn't know what in the world would be going on. In fact, every member of the medical staff had no clue what was even causing these "symptoms". He was running into this situation completely blind.

But if what Baleck said was true and Callimay only had two days left, then as much as he hated to he had to trust the man who wanted his wife dead not but a year prior.

Was that even possible, though? Did Baleck have the capacity for compassion at any point in his life that he could fall back on? Aldred did — well, as long as the price was right — but was that enough?

℔

The second Trever pulled in the lot he jumped off his bike, ripped off his helmet, and stormed off; not saying a word.

"You know what?" Destan said in a clear and determined voice. "Maybe you were right in surrendering your veil to me. Maybe you're not ready for this. You can't put the past where it needs to be so you can see the future clearly through the lens of reality in the present. I'd say I'm surprised to see you acting like this but with the influx of emotional experiences you've gone through in the last month I can see where this is coming from. … But that doesn't mean I like who you're becoming. It seems to be more and more evident that you — the real you — doesn't have a moral compass. You may say you love Calli but it sounds more like you're making her your god, an idol… an object. And I know for 'certain' she'd beg you to stop thinking that way. She'd tell you she's not that important. She'd plead and cry, saying she never wanted you to worship her. She just wants the love of her brother. She doesn't want someone to 'obsess' over her like you are. You take away her value when you do that. Lust isn't love. It never has been nor will it ever be. You're turning her into an object! Don't you see that?"

"Who died and made you god?"

"I never claimed to be, and God forbid I ever try to make myself out to be Him. I'm only stating the truth for what it is; telling you the blatant disregard for truth you have from your statements and actions."

"Just because my truth doesn't match yours doesn't make yours right. Okay, mister high and mighty?"

"Truth isn't subjective, but for the sake of things let's assume it were. If truth were subjective then there'd be no right and wrong: I believe you to be wrong based on truth and yet you say your truth supports your decisions. So are we both right since we can both have our own truth? Taking it a step further: that would mean what Baleck did to your family wasn't wrong because according to 'his truth' it was the right thing to do."

"Don't you dare… you can't—"

"Let's take this to what might be an ultimate end for us right now: if people have their own truths and they can't be questioned, then we have no right to push back against the Syndicate at all. We shouldn't be saving people from death because they believe what they're doing is right. … Do you see how stupid it is to believe that?"

No response.

"I can only push Baleck so far in this entire deal. He's got the trump card in his filthy, blood-stained hand. If he refuses to do anything for Calli until he checks what I give him then I'm left with nothing and the woman I love 'will' die. If I fudge with any of that I might as well be killing her myself. … Do you understand me? … Trever?"

He stormed up to Destan and got in his face, "Now that you've had your say you better let me speak my peace: yes, I worship Everlyn. And no, I don't see how I treat her as her being an object. — I'd do anything for her. I made a promise to her and our dying father that I would. And I will 'never' break that promise. I don't care if you are her husband. If you're going to put her in danger I promise you I 'will' remove you from her life… in whatever form necessary to keep her safe."

And yet you almost killed her yourself. "I feel sorry for you, Trever. So sorry." Destan cringed as he closed his eyes.

"Why?"

"Because I see myself in you right now. Not but a year and a half ago I was exactly like you in some ways. … I know what you're going through and so it hurts me. It does. Regardless of whether or not you want to acknowledge it, I get it. It's torture knowing that kind of evil is allowed to live and be free. — Why do you think I went there to the Society in the first place? — But she changed that. Calli reminded me of what I knew all along, what I thought I was practicing but wasn't. … I'm not going to force you to, but I'm going to make it clear: you've got to sit down and think this all through. The way you're acting and how you're justifying what you 'think' is best? It's a breeding ground for disaster. That's exactly what Elder fed on for his whole life! Don't you remember that? Sure, he's dead, but that doesn't mean you can go back to that kind of thinking without any consequence. Don't let it get that far. Stop it now. Go talk with Overseer when he stops by next week. Please. Just talk things over with him. I'm not making you, but I'm pleading with you as your brother-in-law: don't lose who you were before your life… well, before it blew up in your face. And I don't think it blew up when you found out who Calli was. I noticed it once you were added to the Veil… 'after' everything. I don't know what's going on in your mind, and I don't dare pry, but please! For Calli. For the love that kept you going all these years and brought you back to your senses and saved her life from your own hands. For yourself. For your sanity and because of your ability. Stop and think things through. Please."

Trever's face was chiseled with contempt and total refusal. He stormed off, leaving Destan defeated on all fronts. What was needed to be said was said, but negative responses were always the hard part. But what else was he supposed to do? Just let him alone, leave him unchecked, refuse to challenge him? Avoiding this wasn't going to keep the peace. In fact there was no peace. It needed to be restored.

And aside from his warped sense of values, he didn't understand the extra physical power he now had. Destan felt it was his obligation to help because without Callimay's help there was no way he would be alive at that very moment. Trever needed that same help.

He sighed and bowed his head, him seeing his watch bringing him back. Destan jumped to the suite only to find Callimay was worse, "If her fever gets any higher—"

"Is she having another seizure? What do we do?" Destan asked in fear as he dove onto the bed.

"No, Destan. She's just shivering a bit." Doctor Gerould calmed as he put a strong hand on his shoulder; then backed off a bit. "I wish she'd start sweating. It's the only thing—"

"Shivering? Then why didn't you put a blanket— where are they?"

"Destan, she has a fever. Bundling her up will only fuel it. You cut its 'food supply' — within reason — and it dies."

"But…" he stammered, mortified with the condition she was in and trying to stop this helpless feeling from growing.

"I'm… I know it's hard. And I know there seems no end in sight to what's happening. We're trying everything we— oh." He snapped his fingers. "Do you have any thicker sheets or a super thin blanket?"

"Huh?"

"I finally remembered what I was thinking about before you got here. While she does need this to help break her fever, I don't want her to instantly get chilled at the same time." He paused when Destan's brow furrowed. "A sheet would keep her from being directly exposed to the air so she can retain enough body heat so she's not violently shaking while her body has the ability to release the heat it needs to."

"Oh. Okay. Umm… let me go look."

A few minutes later Destan came out with a small stack of different sheets, "Will any of these work?"

It didn't take him long to find one, but he stopped when he looked over, "What are you doing?"

"I'm just looking for this," Destan sighed as he took a briefcase from under the bed. "Baleck's conditions are for me to surrender my father's information on Chameleon. Why? I'm not exactly sure. I have an idea, but with as far out as he can be with his ideas…"

"You're not going to do that are you? While it is a supplementary aid, even so… it's extremely powerful, Destan! In the wrong hands—"

"Lance, please." He begged as he flopped onto a chair. "I already went through this all with Trever on the way back. I 'have' to give—"

"Just hear me out. I'm not actually telling you to not give it to him. But why not put a failsafe in? You're good with computers. Talk with Abacus. There must be a way of it 'appearing' to be there and good, but once it is accessed it… well, corrupt the file or whatever."

"Even if I did that, if he checks things out first—"

"Have it on a delay. I mean with technology today that is possible, right? — Don't worry about hypotheticals. You could spend a lifetime indulging them. … When does he have to know?"

"Forty-eight hours. I've got no time to do what you're suggesting."

"There's just got to be a way out of this without risking him having that information."

Is there? Destan groaned as Doctor Gerould went back to Callimay. *Is there really a way? Am I just so out of it that I can't see it?*

He was in a trance of sorts as he looked through the files to find what he needed, not noticing Rocher, "I beg your forgiveness, Sir. I did not mean to startle you."

"It's… it's alright. What is it?"

"I had a discussion with Liberator and ascertained what transpired. What is your plan of action? I doubt I need ask if you plan on handing over such sensitive information of which your father fought and died to keep secret from this evil human… is it?"

Destan slumped back in his chair, throwing his head against the headrest, "Will no one in this place give me any encouragement that doing the right thing will work!" … *Calli, where are you when I need you? — Please, God… help me stay strong.*

"Do not see this as some form of rebellion against a greater force. How could one as you describe, loving what it made, see your devotion and desire to save her life as something worthy of punishment? This is done with only the intent to save Milady's life and protect others! Never was there a more noble cause to put love above all else."

"Have Python ready to move in the next fifteen." Destan leaned over the desk, unwilling to even entertain this flawed thinking. "And Raven. I don't know how far we'll have to go. And depending— Calli may not even be able to fly. I just don't know. So… have them both ready to go. And get Fidus. I need to speak with him."

"As you wish, Sir."

As he looked the paperwork over, the idea of "doctoring" it on this front alone was stupid and ill-conceived: *Yeah, I have every other serum father made to reference as far as quantities and compound names. And I'm sure there 'is' a pattern, but~ Boon, let it go. Don't do this. ~ Letting Baleck have this 'is' dangerous no matter what he does with it. They are not wrong when they mention that. ~ But you know this isn't the 'right' way to do it. Hell is much more dangerous and will last much longer than anything he could do. ~ I seem to be the only one left who believes that. ~ Sounds more like you're giving up. ~ Then you tell me what other option I have that not only protects Calli, but keeps Baleck from getting his hands on this. I'm all ears, seriously. I don't want to, but I can't think of anything else!*

Fidus showed up just as it looked like Destan was finishing up, "You wanted me, Doyen?"

He nodded toward the door and then followed Fidus out, pausing and looking back to where Callimay was as he closed the door, "I'm not sure how this is all going to go. The last timeline we discussed… go with it. Fi— I'm praying nothing happens, but I've got to face the facts that if something does go wrong things can't fall apart because I didn't make sure everything was ready to go on without me."

With his reasoning, how could Fidus object? It was nothing more than what steps they took during any other circumstance such as this. And so he nodded as he took a deep breath, "Understood."

"And…" Destan quieted to almost a whisper as he looked around before continuing. "Keep an eye on Liberator. He didn't say it outright, but I know he saw 'her' again."

Fidus groaned as he rolled his eyes, "I'll be sure to keep an eye on things. Where is he, anyway?"

"I haven't any idea." Destan sighed in frustration as he rubbed his forehead. "When we g—"

"No need to worry. I'll be sure he reports."

"Just lay low about that all right now… but keep him on a double shadow. He's getting 'trigger happy' if you know what I mean, and with this all going on and him having an ability that's uncontrolled?"

"I won't say a word to him and will make sure he's watched." Fidus assured as Destan turned back to go in the room. "I trust you've taken the necessary precautions to ensure this transaction — if you will — won't cause problems?"

Not again. Destan cringed as he sighed.

"Did you consider running a Trojan with the download? Condenser was speaking with me just a few minutes ago and said we have them built into all standard drives now. Machinate even told me she doesn't see why she couldn't render it invisible altogether."

"What good would that do?"

"As she told me, it would allow her to infiltrate their computer from within, through the guise of what would for all intents and purposes look like a viable copy of the information he is demanding. And during this all we could pull information they may have from the Syndicate at the same time."

Exhausted from this constant battering, Destan said, "Just do whatever, Fidus. Alright?"

He dragged himself back into the room, and at the first sound of the belvedere whining, rushed over to Callimay. She was starting to wake up, Doctor Gerould busy filling a syringe, "Destan? Try and keep her still. Can you do that for me?"

He gulped as he sat down and hugged her as tight as he dared; not willing to hold her down like Trever had.

As Doctor Gerould turned, he could tell Destan was crying, his head buried in the pillow beside her as she tried to push and pull away from him. His deep voice was crumbling as he begged her to be still, trying to tell her he was there and she would be alright.

It was cruel to him to see how Destan had come so far and was on the brink of losing the only person in this life he cared about; the one who had helped him more than anyone else become the man he was so proud of. And not only that, but "she" was the one pushing him away; unknowingly begging him to let her die alone.

He'd seen how Destan put up with rejection his whole life from so many people, but Doctor Gerould only remembered him being anywhere near this distraught once… and he lost that person in the end: *God? Please let him keep her. He needs her.*

She was crying as she drifted off, her hands quivering as Destan held them in his against his lips. — Though it wouldn't have been any stretch to say some were Destan's tears rolling down her face.

His body was shivering just as much as hers was. He wanted this all to end. He wanted the turmoil and pain gone. He wanted to rest… and he wanted to give it to his love who was put through more than he ever was. The fleeting thought of finding one of the last operating ships left on Quidoria and leaving for the Homeworld passed his mind a time or two… but then he thought about all of those left and how that guilt would never let them leave: *I don't know what to do, God. I… I feel lost in a way without my Calli. What am I supposed to do? How can I trust the man who was more than willing to murder her less than a year ago? — Why, God? Why! Please tell me! I'm begging you! I don't know if I can do this anymore. I just… I don't want to lose her. Please. … What am I supposed to be learning! I— I can't do this by myself!*

By this time the belvedere was on the bed and howling in the same sad and mournful tone as when they were back at the Nest.

This cry from the creature was a mirror of the fact Destan started giving up. No avenue he had left seemed to show any glimmer of hope. For some reason he couldn't find one where his love would make it. Whether it was through Baleck's deception, him not getting her to the meeting place in time, or her just not surviving the treatment: *Boon, keep yourself together. ~ How can I! Look at her! Ca… My Calli is dying. Dying! Don't you understand that? And I have no guarantee Baleck will do what he said. His word is worth just as much as a million federation cyberbits. Nothing! — I know he has me between the sunrise and a cliff… but what if he takes Chameleon and runs? What if he's been leading me on, saying he has the equipment to do what treatment is necessary for Calli when he doesn't? If he's paid enough, I wouldn't put it past Aldred to be in on it; as cruel as this is even for him. … Maybe everyone is right. They're all saying I need some kind of safeguard. ~ Stop and think about this. Deep breath. ~ It doesn't need to be something deep or misleading. If I can just hold out until he treats her. … But even then I'd be running the risk of losing and leaving everyone on Quidoria in danger. I'd be betraying the trust of countless people who are relying on me to keep them safe if I gave that to him. ~ You? Alone? ~ I'm the head of this all so everything that happens falls on me if it fails. … I mean how much can he know about it, really? Father did it all in secret. If he thinks it's so special then maybe it would work to alter it. If something is strange about it he'd just see it as its unique properties. Maybe it's just a matter of taking a bit of everything and combining it~ You mean make your own truth? ~ N… no. I~ Don't you dare think for a minute that a little wrong here mixed with good intentions there will justify what happens in the end. If you're going to stand in the truth, then you better make sure you stick it out to the very end. What would Trever say if he saw you doing what you accused him of not but a half hour ago? ~ This is different. ~ Now you just shut up and listen to me. Elder twisted you before, but this? You're doing it all on your own. You've been through life and death with Calli multiple times and yet this one is somehow different? You've got two 'days', not seconds like when she was dangling off the cliff during training. She trusts you to know how to get through this without compromising what is most important. Don't betray that trust, no matter if she can't remember it right now: a promise you make is a promise you keep until it's fulfilled... in this case, the possibility of physical death. Don't betray the trust God has in you. You need Him more than her; 'especially' right now. 'He' is The One Who will get you through this. And He is The only One Who can actually heal her.*

Just like the times he was able to free himself from Elder's hold, Destan's eyes widened as he jerked back. He was allowing the pressure from everyone else to make giving up the "easiest" option.

In fact he was letting his priorities freefall at a dangerous rate.

I can't be like that. I 'can' get this together. I 'can' find a way. I've... I've just got to stop and think. Pray. ... And get Baleck called so he doesn't back out.

"I guess you suppose my facility is in this hemisphere and where the weather is favorable. Rather a dangerous assumption to make, wouldn't you say?" Baleck scoffed as he answered the phone.

"Just tell me when and where." Destan said, trying to stay calm and composed as he motioned for Enforcer, Fidus, and Rocher to come over. "I have everything you want."

"Do you happen to know of the Port of Monitorial?"

"On the east coast of Agroos Union?" Destan clarified, writing down things as fast as possible for the other three to read.

"Aldred will be at the private pier on the north edge. Come alone."

"Wait!" Destan said in desperation.

"Really, Doyen. I believe you underestimate the time constraints." Baleck scolded, his tone hinting he was rolling his eyes. "The weath—"

"Let me bring one person. Please. Just her doctor. ... Please. I..."

"Begging? — I'm dealing with children everywhere." Baleck voice sounded like he took the phone away from his ear for a bit. "I took you for better than this, Doyen. How utterly degrading that Elder could fall to such immature individuals. … Very well. I understand your lack of trust and understanding; and I admit I admire your true concern. But where Aldred says he has to wait—"

"Alright. We're leaving right now. — Lance?" Destan called out as he ended the call.

"Yes Destan?"

"Can Calli fly?"

"I honestly don't know. Baleck would be the one to ask."

"I— ugh! Alright. … Come on, Baleck. Don't d—"

"What now, Doyen?" Baleck argued.

"Can Calli fly in the condition she's in?"

The edge in his voice softened a bit, "Is she still fully sedated?"

"Is she still sedated?" Destan asked as he jogged over.

"Fully." Baleck corrected.

"Fully?" Destan repeated.

"Yes. But for how long I can't guarantee." Doctor Gerould replied.

"I heard him," Baleck cut Destan off. "As long as the initial takeoff and ascent is in that timeframe of her being fully sedated she should be fine. Same for final descent and landing. When should I tell Aldred to expect you?"

"Five hours. Six tops."

"Very well." Baleck replied as he hung up the phone.

"Rocher?"

"I'll fly," he replied without hesitation as he turned to leave. "And I'll call ahead to have Martimus ready."

Destan grabbed what Baleck wanted before rushing over; during which time Doctor Gerould double-checked some calculations to see if he could determine if and possibly when she would need another dose.

"Her left arm is causing her so much pain that I thought it easier all around for it to be protected as much as possible." Doctor Gerould explained when Destan saw the sling she had on.

"Doesn't she need something more to wear? It's the middle of winter and we're headed for even colder climates."

Doctor Gerould refused as he gathered what he needed, "I'm sorry, but not right now. I know it's hard to see her like this, but trust me when I say this is helping. The fever's levelled off which is a 'very' good sign; so hopefully it'll break soon. 'Then' you can bundle her up to your heart's content. … Keep the sheet on her and bring a robe or another sheet to cover her with when we're outside. But they need to come off the second she gets in if the fever hasn't broken. Got it?"

A minute later he had her floor-length coat in his hand as he bolted out of the closet.

The belvedere knew something was wrong and did what he could to comfort Destan. He sat down and bowed his head as he took Callimay's free hand in his, the belvedere jumping on the bed and putting his paw on top and bowing his head.

Fear of not knowing what was going to happen was reaching a mini climax for this young man. For one of the few times in his life he had no "control" over what was happening. He'd become used to having the upper hand — or at least a cover to divert his opponent's focus. Being laid bare and helpless like this reminded him too much of the times he lost people he loved.

And to make matters worse, he had to trust someone who wanted him "and" his wife dead: *It has to be different this time. Please, God. Please let it be different.*

His hands shook as he slumped over more and more. And by the time he opened his wearied eyes his forehead was resting on Callimay's forearm. Her skin felt like a heated stone: radiating endless heat, not cooling when something as cold as ice was placed on it. He leaned over and gave her a kiss, whispering something to her, then sniffled as he — with the gentlest of a touch — gathered his beloved wife into his arms.

Still wanting to help, the belvedere stuck to Destan's side and kept perfect pace with him. Destan shook his head right before jumping to Raven, "I'm sorry, Big Fella. You've got to stay here. … Alright? Watch over Trever."

He laid down and hid his face from Destan, whimpering and whining; then after Destan jumped, lifted his head and howled.

✣

Tension paralyzed the air as the two men accompanying Destan and Callimay rushed to get ready to go. The weather was less than desirable and Destan knew Rocher was going to need help, "I'll co-pilot."

"No. Stay with Milady. I am capable of manag—"

"If we crash what good is doing all this?" Destan refused, trying to push away the fear that was trying so hard to overtake him.

"But can you focus at the level I would be required to give you trust in? Forgive my boldness, but you would be more endangerment than help, Sir."

"I have to. Most of our pilots are down sick and the others are out on details. Ace and Arial have yet to finish their solos, and then the class of—"

"I'll co-pilot," someone interrupted as they stormed in.

"Huh?" Destan asked confused as he turned to see who rushed in.

"Just trust I know what I'm doing, alright? There's no time to waste. Ground check finished, Sentinel?"

"Yes," Rocher nodded rather stunned as the half-crazed, half fear-stricken person passed him and went into the cockpit. "Sir, did you—"

"It was Elder, alright? Let's go." Trever said annoyed.

The only response Destan could give was a shoulder shrug and nod to Rocher. He went back to Callimay, having Doctor Gerould sit with him to keep an eye on her.

Rocher and Trever did an amazing job keeping the aircraft as steady as they did through the blizzard near the border of Ferdinan and Agroos Union. They were okayed for landing, the strip cleared just enough for them to touch down; but were grounded until the storm passed… for good reason.

❦

Wind peppered the all-terrain with ice and snow as Doctor Gerould drove along at a snail's pace. Destan began to wonder how in the world they were going to be able to travel by boat: *If the wind is this bad here, it's got to be at least ten times worse on the open water. It was one of the many reasons that whole place was abandoned.*

Their inching along paid off. They arrived when there was enough of a break in the storm for them to see part of the pier. Doctor Gerould pulled them in as close as possible and then helped Destan bundle Callimay up. They braved the horrendous wind to shelter her, making their way down to the lone naval vessel; sloshing waves of icy water slapped the waterfront in a way which made you feel terrified and chilled to the bone.

Usually he would keep watch for any persons nearby, but Destan couldn't think of anything but making sure Callimay was safe. Doctor Gerould knew this and did what he could to keep watch; though, with the amount of snow and the speed at which the wind was carrying it along? It was nearly impossible.

Aldred came out just before they got there and hurried them in. Destan sat down on the first seat he saw and clung to Callimay, Doctor Gerould having to remind him in a whisper, "You need to take her coat off. … Destan."

"Huh? … Oh. Right."

"We were both beginning to wonder if you would make it through." Aldred mentioned in a calm tone as he looked at a few gauges and then turned around. "But I guess I should never underestimate the lengths you'll go to and resources you are willing to use. — By the way, do you have my payment?"

"Yes," Destan nodded as he handed him another cube.

"You know I've always enjoyed working with you. You're always so very cooperative, Doyen. Or would you prefer me to call you Destan?"

Nothing.

He rolled his eyes, sickened by the emotion that wasn't in the form of a reaction to what he knew; asking more direct, "How is she doing?"

"Fully sedated per your instructions." Doctor Gerould answered as he looked around the highly advanced interior of what turned out to be submarine. "How do you have access to these types of technologies?"

"Now I do believe you are delving into areas of questions better suited for a different time." Aldred smiled as he held the cube up to his eye, then walked over to what looked like an incubator. "The more preliminary work we get done prior to making it there the faster this all will go… and the better her chances of making it."

"What do you mean?" Doctor Gerould questioned, storming to his feet so he was between Destan and Aldred.

"To know the map of the spindles, a full scan of her nervous system needs to be made." Aldred explained as he tapped a screen and the incubator opened; not bothering to look back. "And then of course all baseline vitals need to be recorded so accurate adjustments in treatment incriminates can be made during the entire process."

"What are spindles?" Doctor Gerould continued, leery of every word coming out of Aldred's mouth. "How are they mapped?"

He frowned as he turned around, crossing his arms across his chest, "Spindles are caused by an accumulation of the amplifier found within any serum. If you've looked through both Destan and his wife's files, and I'm sure you have, you'll probably recall mention of things such as 'Nerfilgon' or 'Trispinalfil'. Those are two types of amplifiers; each with an affinity for a specific type of tissue found in the body. — Though cemented to its contact points, it remains in its fluid state to a certain extent to allow normal bodily functions to occur without hindrance. — Very much how waters undisturbed look like smooth glass, while choppy waters looks like rugged rocks; under prime conditions these amplifiers form a pearl-like, smooth finish over whatever tissue and cells they are targeted to interact with. When something is askew during cementation, rough points begin to harden with jagged edges forming, these points being easily flaked off; them adhering to other portions of the serum within the body: though at the point they're free-range — to our knowledge — they do not affect the surrounding tissue. Each time the ability is used when these are present, the possibility of these malformations growing/flaking increases. It can happen with any serum, but ones being in one-hundred percent interaction with the nervous system are one-thousand times more likely to form if even one calculation is the slightest bit off or cementation is interrupted in any form. — If these areas where the flaked off amplifier accumulates continue to grow and shed, they become what are known as spindles: sharp, long projectiles which harden to the density of cortical bone and damage tissue around them… in this case, her brain. The scans we perform are able to identify not only spindles, but even those initial rugged spots no MRI or CT-scan could ever imagine showing."

"What would have caused this sudden onset, though? If it takes time, why are symptoms just now showing and it so life-threatening?"

"The flaking from steady buildup due to constant usage of a serum from a botched processing can go completely asymptomatic for years. The speed of her deterioration, in particular, is undoubtedly due to a single event where her ability was activated and then immediately 'aggravated' like never before. I would imagine her migraines have been caused by the flaking and spindle growth, mainly, so it was probably the last massive one she had which brought this all on."

The belvedere! Destan's eyes bugged out. *When he bit me and I—*

"How many times have you done this?" Doctor Gerould continued.

"Are you going to risk us not having ample time to save your wife or are you going to do as I say?"

Destan said shaky as he put his hand on Doctor Gerould's arm, "I understand, Aldred."

"Just lay her with her head at this end."

It was almost as if the machine was made for her by how perfect the size of it was. But that was lost in the shuffle from Destan constantly fiddling; taking the extra time to fix her hair so it wasn't pulling on anything, making sure her clothing wasn't binding her, and so on.

Perturbed by this fuss, Aldred was about to make a snide remark when he paused, "While you're at it, you can take the sling off as well."

"Oh. Alright," Destan replied in a daze.

Aldred asked a few questions, imputing the answers in the computer on what Destan now realized was the machine his father invented.

A few minutes later the lid began to close.

"Please don't!" Destan begged as he grabbed Aldred's arm. "Please."

"Even if I could leave it open you couldn't hold her hand." Aldred huffed. "It can't gather the information it needs if two individuals are within its scan radius and the scan can't function unless it is closed."

"Well…" Destan scrambled to think. "I…"

Doctor Gerould came to Destan's side, trying to put his suspicious nature aside to support him, "The faster this is done the quicker she can get out."

🕭

Not too much longer they surfaced inside the infamous "city inside a mountain" — a massive mountain with formed with a major part of the southern base missing. It was a stunning place, but its location left this architectural marvel dilapidating for over sixty years. Illuminated by some orb in the roof of the cave — a feat in and of itself — the look of all the building faces carved out of the stone walls was similar to what was known as Gothic architecture on the Homeworld.

Aldred got the submarine up to the dock and opened the door, turning back as he addressed Doctor Gerould, "You'll remain here."

"Very well," he sighed as he stepped back.

Suspicious of the compliance he was given, Aldred went back to the machine, warning Destan, "We have a long walk ahead of us. I 'hope' you understand it won't be one to easily to relay information about."

Confused, Destan stared at him.

He 'is' that desperate. Who would have ever guessed? "It will be much more comfortable for her to make the rest of the trek in here."

"I…" he stammered as he rubbed Callimay's hand.

"The encasing is a sheet of glass I'm sure your Kunai are more than capable of penetrating if something were to go wrong in your eyes, or you felt she was being threatened." Aldred offered as he unlocked the machine from its base so he could move it. "Follow me."

🕉

The powerful storm was nothing but faint, whips of echoes; those even fading as they entered one of the cathedrals. Destan's hold on the bed Callimay was in was a death grip, and still, there was something he felt he couldn't stop thinking of, his mind wandering off to thoughts of his father: once again. His talents were saving her. And yet it was such a depressing thought to know this loving heart and bright mind was gone. The only other two capable of such things being obsessed with greed and power.

Aldred was at ease this whole time, him strolling along. Even the feeling of their footsteps cracking the eerie secrecy that captivated the air; triggering the sky-high cathedral ceilings to weigh down on them? None of it phased him in the slightest.

What Aldred said earlier now made sense: this was just like walking through a maze house with all the staircases and narrow passage ways which would periodically open into yet larger cathedral-vaulted areas.

There was something familiar about this place but Destan wasn't about to entertain why; and yet this maze-feel he knew was the source. But what was it? Everything looked the same and felt as if it was impossible to turn so many times to the left without ending up where they had just been. It truly was a mind-melting experience. — On that front alone it's no wonder this place was abandoned!

And yet — much to Destan's surprise — they now found themselves at what appeared to be a dead end. There were windows along the far wall showing what little could be seen of the outside world; the sun giving every effort to break through the thick storm clouds.

Making a left-hand turn, Aldred opened a door, guiding the bed in and allowing Destan to go ahead of him.

This spacious, damp, and rather drafty room was dark except for the far left portion where several advanced machines were; one person whom Destan could hardly bear to know was still alive, standing there.

"Welcome to my home," Baleck smiled as he turned and greeted.

Destan couldn't get any words out. He wanted so bad to speak his mind, but if he irritated Baleck too much he could refuse to help. And part of him was just furious this man was living practically right under his nose. — Hiding in plain sight was the safest thing for evil, too.

Once Aldred shut the door he guided the bed to its station, Destan rushing over and taking Callimay's hand as soon as there was enough room for him to get his hand in the cover's opening.

Baleck and Aldred talked some, but Destan could only get himself to focus on one thing at a time; and right now Callimay had it. The only reason he heard the one thing they mentioned was because her name was spoken; and to be exact, it was her hand they were talking about. He looked over only to find her left hand was contracted, swollen and blistered. The shock took a second process before he reached over, daring to remove her wedding bands before something irreversible happened to her finger — her hot skin at least helping with that.

Not a moment later he fell to his knees and wept, unable to keep himself together anymore. And of course this "act" of such care and devotion appalled Aldred, "Enough of this. Where are the files?"

"Couldn't it wait until you're done?" Destan tried to get himself together as he stood. "I have them with me."

"Now. Hand it over."

"Why won't you believe me? I've never given you reason to doubt my word, Aldred."

"I'm an impatient man, Doyen." He reached out as he stormed over. "You have no room to negotiate. Quit getting this high and mighty thought that you somehow having any say about what will happen. There's no way for you to have any higher card on us."

"Give him the drive, Destan." He heard Baleck say in his calm, authoritative, evil tone. "Don't make things any more stressful than they already are."

"But— a… alright." He sighed as he reached for it.

Aldred ripped it out of his hand and stormed over, plugging it in and going through everything; muttering to himself as he worked.

A minute later, Baleck walked over, "Is everything there?"

"Yes?" Aldred answered a bit confused.

"What?"

"Look at these numbers and you tell me."

Baleck looked at the screen and then back to Destan with an overbearing look of suspicion. Destan's eyes were wide as he asked, "What's wrong? That's all the information I have. If something's missing I don't know where to f—"

"It's only that these numbers closely correlate with both what Callimay and you have already." Baleck's eyes narrowed. "It's just very… uncanny."

"I don't know anything about those things." Destan defended as he took Callimay's hand in his. "I gave you what you wanted. Don't do what you did last time. You've played with her emotions, but I beg you: don't play with her life."

"I won't," Baleck sighed as he walked over to an ornate wooden box and appeared to do some puzzle atop it which opened it. "I give you my word… as worthless as that may be to you."

He came up with what looked like an iridescent blanket and started to put it over Callimay. Destan grabbed his arm and asked frightened, "What are you doing? The doctor said she couldn't—"

"The bed only acts as half of the device, Destan." Baleck explained as he pulled away and kept laying it over her; his expression looking like it was attentive — almost caring like a doctor would be. "This is the other half. In fact this is the part your father entirely completed. … And as far as her fever goes, it should be the easiest portion to treat."

It struck Destan all at once… was Baleck truly understanding about everything? Buy why? Why this sudden shift? His tone and how he acted wasn't like who Destan remembered from any situation before; let alone a single minute ago, "Wh… why did you agree, Baleck?"

"I'm a man who's loved a woman as well." He sighed as his hand lingered on the edge of the bed; him looking into the darkness at the other end of the room. "As I came to that last time in Kerogen I heard a shot and saw Ginger fall to the ground. I didn't see a soul around, but regardless, I knew 'he' had it done. I stumbled and clawed my way to her side. — Elder may have spared my life, but he sentenced me to a far worse punishment. He made sure we both suffered while she slowly bled out. … I couldn't save her as it was, but finding I had no abilities whatsoever to get her to where she needed to be? … She cried as she gasped for each breath, telling me what Elder made her swear to never tell me, grieved she couldn't continue to let me live the life I'd always wanted. It was then I realized the abilities I thought I had weren't what I wanted. I wanted her. She'd become my life. And I lost her. So I lost my will to live. — Aldred's kept me alive these miserable months for some reason. Maybe fate knew you needed me so it had Aldred find me. I don't know. — Elder reached out and told me when he was dying, and at that moment I laughed and smiled for the first time in ages. I couldn't have been more pleased to know he'd been outsmarted."

He paused when he heard what sounded like a gasp; him turning to face Destan, "I'm not expecting you to understand everything, and I'm not in any way changing my view, but I couldn't allow even my worst enemy to go through the pain I endured. This isn't the kind of death any spouse should endure. … While I plan to meet you later in a difference capacity, know that bridge isn't being crossed here and I 'do' intend on doing everything possible to save her."

Destan looked more frightened than ever. How could anyone be this detached and yet caring?

Noting this, Baleck cleared his throat as he stood tall, pushing aside the inkling of emotion as he glanced at the box beside him, "Consider this my one last acknowledgement of your father's abilities as a medical genius. Perhaps it was fate that gave him this idea in the first place: to be his daughter-in-law's savior."

Nothing felt real to Destan except the terror inside of him. Part of him regretted bringing his love to this calloused husk of a conceited and twisted man. Everything that happened in that field flooded back and he couldn't stop thinking this was a trap.

But how would he know? Who else could help Callimay?

"Just as a precautionary measure, though… say your goodbyes to her now." Baleck hesitated as he turned back. "As much as I know how to combat this, if she isn't willing to fight though the pain, or if the process takes too long — she won't make it."

Destan's frozen body jerked out a nod and turned to Callimay, taking her in his arms as he wept: *Dear Lord? Please give my Calli the strength to fight through this pain. She's done it so many times before; please continue to give her the strength she needs. Help her remember I'm here. Help h— God, please. I don't want Calli to die. Please. Don't let what I've hidden from her kill her. Please don't let Elder have this victory. Don't let satan have any enjoyment in this. God please. I know this treatment is designed to help, but I know it's because You allow it to. You are the reason this all came to being. Nothing such as 'fate' can take Your place. Please let it be in Your will that Calli makes it. Please. It's in Your Son's Name I pray, amen.*

"We need to get started," Baleck put his hand on his shoulder.

Destan put her hand back under the blanket and stepped back, trying to accept the fact there was no stopping this. He had to accept the responsibility for what happened; for the choices he made and the risks he was taking. This decision was made without Callimay's input whatsoever… and yet it was her life on the line. Guilt started to inch its way into his heart because of his doubt; but at this point who could blame him and what could he do to stop it?

For this first part — which felt like a year and a half — there wasn't a single word said. Aldred and Baleck were busy watching different monitors; imputing various commands to them at certain times.

After an hour passed, the only thing Destan noticed that was any different was Callimay pouring sweat.

This was a good thing, right? He wanted to ask, but with as focused as the other two in the room were, Destan tried the only other person he knew: *Lance?*

What is it, Destan? Doctor Gerould replied concerned as he jumped to his feet. *What's going on? Are they done?*

Calli's pouring sweat. … That's a good thing, right?

Even with my limited knowledge, yes. That's a wonderful thing. He sighed as he reached back and sat down. *Are they done?*

No. Both Baleck and Aldred aren't anywhere near Calli. They're not even looking at her. There's nothing in the bed moving, either.

Well, it's a form of treatment none of us have any clue about. — It's incredible to think your father was the one who started the work that brought this about. And Baleck seems to be a medical genius in his own right; albeit his dedication to the Oath being very… 'selective'. But it is what it is and those 'god complex' doctors and medical professional sadly exist even to this day. — How is everything else? … Destan?

Huh?

Has he looked at what he asked for?

Yeah.

And?

He was suspicious… I think Aldred still is.

What did you end up doing, anyway?

"What is going on?" Aldred fumed as he furiously started working.

Destan froze when he saw Baleck tensing up as well. They grumbled with each other for a bit and then sat back down and looked at a few things. He looked at Callimay and saw she was starting to move, her expression looking like she was in pain.

"What's going on?" He asked worried.

"Shut up, Doyen." Aldred ordered as he came over and did some work on the computer that was on the bed itself.

"What's happening to Calli?"

"Let us work, Destan." Baleck quieted as he pushed him aside to work on the computer opposite Aldred. "I'm showing fifteen-hundred."

"Seventy-two thirteen." Aldred shook his head.

"Run it again. Better yet, reverse it." Baleck growled; still as level-headed as ever.

After a couple minutes, Callimay progressing to the point she was starting to convulse, Destan ran to calm her but Aldred held him back.

"But she's in pain!"

"Of course she is! That's what's supposed to happen: the spindles are being pried off her nervous tissue so they can be flushed out. You touch her and we have to start this all over again. ... If it's even possible." Aldred demanded as he shoved him back.

"I told you she was going to have to fight through this." Baleck eyed him. "This is the most critical time. So pray or call out to your higher power or god or whatever you call that you worship. She's going to need it since she's not responding."

"Calli!" Destan gasped in horror as he dropped to his knees.

Aldred replied once the test was complete, "It's lower, but still nowhere near your number."

"What is it? Mine's come up."

"Forty-seven."

"Better. Mine is at thirty-two." Baleck said a bit more relieved. "I just don't know what's causing this imbalance. ... Destan? Destan!"

"What!"

"I know about her arm and head, but are there any other injuries she has?"

"I... I don't know all the names of everything."

"Well do your best," Baleck huffed.

"She has nine broken ribs, at one point they said something about air and blood around her lungs, and her neck... I... it was something about her not being able to breathe." Destan tried his best to recall but sounded like an absolute bumbling idiot; him being too out of sorts to remember what on a normal basis he would know. "She had a brace on for a while and there was—"

I should've let the doctor come. Aldred moaned as he rolled his eyes.

Latching onto one comment, Baleck whipped his head around, "Which side does she have more broken ribs on?"

"I... I don't know." *Lance?*

Yes?

What side does Calli have more broken ribs on?

Her right side, six of them. What's going on?

"Six on her right side." Destan blurted out.

"And you didn't ask him, Aldred? Seriously? I 'told' you what Elder had done." Baleck scolded as he continued to work.

Then you babysit them next time and tell me if you can get any work done. Aldred whined as he kept working.

"Well that made a world of difference… recheck yours now."

There was another period of time where there was nothing said, then Aldred replied, "I'm down to fifteen-hundred."

Baleck sighed and leaned his head back, "Good. Now we can continue. Set it back to backflush first, then start with the pairing. — Destan? Tell me what you did to the Chameleon serum. You changed something in it, didn't you."

"No. I swear I didn't." He shook his head furiously as he stumbled to his feet. "How is Calli? Is she going to be okay? Did that help any?"

"Don't try to change the subject. The numbers in that paperwork are almost 'exact' matches to Liaison done with the components of Challenger. You really should have been a bit more creative even though you don't understand all this."

"I did 'not' change anything. What I gave you is exactly what was on my father's drive. If something's wrong 'he' changed it. — What's wrong with Calli!"

"You're a horrible liar, Destan. Tell me what you changed."

"I didn't! I'm telling the truth, Baleck."

"I touch this button and Callimay's gone forever." He threatened as he put his hand over the computer. "You have no choice but to assume I'm serious."

Destan bowed his head, trying to keep himself under control, "God as my witness: I'm telling you the truth! My father took Challenger and formed Chameleon from it; his other notes explain that. And my doctor told me when he compared Liaison to Chameleon they were extremely similar and didn't know how father missed it. … Baleck please! You've got to believe me! Why would I risk Calli's life for this! How could I think of tricking you using something I have no knowledge about? It'd be outright murder if I did!"

Baleck withdrew his hand and stood there for a few moments, then walked back to where he was working, "How are things now, Aldred?"

"Stable. The backflush is almost complete."

With this distrust firmly established, Destan would flinch each time Baleck would take his eyes off of what he was working on, his heart racing and eyes darting back and forth between them and Calli: *If he thought I'd mess with it, why even ask me to give it to him?*

Time dragged on and on, Destan not knowing what time it was and terrified because the distrust felt like it was going to explode at any second. Add to the terror the fact he was called a liar eating at him so much he almost couldn't stand it? He was a glowing bed of coals ripe for sparking into an open flame.

Callimay's left hand which had found its way from under the blanket while she was thrashing about wasn't contracted anymore — if that was any consolation.

But things weren't over yet. Baleck could still do something.

At one point Aldred got up and spoke with Baleck in a hushed tone, eyeing Destan the entire time. Baleck sat there for a while and didn't say anything, but eventually nodded to him.

Aldred came over and worked for a bit on the computer on the bed, then took a chip from the bed back to Baleck. They both poured over the information and then Baleck got up and came over while Aldred left toward another part of the room, "Well, I've done all I can. And as far as what this machine can tell me, Callimay's spindles are gone. She should never have any of these side effects from using her ability again. And not only that, but she shouldn't have debilitating pain from her broken ribs. There will still be discomfort once she wakes up — and it is only a temporary relief — but it will last long enough for her to regain the strength she needs to be able to endure what pain she will have in the future. I'm sure what she feels will be nothing like what she's endured in the past. … She should regain consciousness on her own in a few hours."

"I… I don't know— thank you, Baleck." Destan fell to his knees again; a tiny bit of him repulsed to say such a thing but unable to not say it. *The very same man who murdered my family now saved the woman I love. Is there any way possible that he—*

"I will caution that there is one area which was beyond my control; and that is her mental capacity. How much she retains from recent events is only something you will know when she wakes. She may — in some aspects — be… 'different' than she was before. While this isn't necessarily something you want to hear, it is a small price in the grand scheme of things that may need to be paid in order to have her alive. … In other words: the spindles 'did' do damage to her brain. But until she is conscious, the extent of that damage won't be known. … Do you understand what I just said?"

The lights in the other part of the room turned on, revealing a completely different setup of machines and such.

Baleck sighed as he continued, "And so to finish your end of the bargain you'll stay and see the true potential of Chameleon."

Still trying to process the bombshell news he was given, Destan had to do a hard one-eighty when he realized what was just said and what the meaning behind it was, "Now you wait just a minute. Trever told me you said I just had to give you the information. He said nothing about me staying."

"Little brother has been known to lie," Baleck thought out loud as he looked up and tapped his chin; then continued, "I do hope you understand I'm not letting you off the hook 'that' easily."

Knowing Callimay was so fragile, Destan tried to keep things from escalating, "Let the doctor take Calli back. I'll stay for as long as you want me to. There's no need for her to. You said she wouldn't wake up for a few hours and you gave me your word that you wouldn't let her meet her end here if you had anything to say about it. Isn't that right? Or were 'you' lying to me?"

Baleck stood there, his lips firmly pursed.

"How many Falconers are waiting? … Tell me you liar!" Destan charged at Baleck and grabbed him by the collar. "Why would you say you know the love a man can hold for a woman if you would save my wife only to let the Monarch butcher her the second you save her? Just what kind of liar are you! … Tell me!"

The two men glared at each other for an unbearable amount of time, Aldred stepping in, "There's no Falconers here, Doyen. You're more than welcome to take her back to the dock and see for yourself."

While he was met with a glaring rebuke from Baleck, he assured him, "I'll accompany them to the dock and then bring him back. — I trust the good doctor knows how to operate a rather simple auto pilot system, correct?"

"I'm sure he can manage," Destan nodded.

"Very well. — Baleck?"

"Go ahead." He stormed off. "But don't take long. I don't have time for all this."

"You'll need to carry her back. The Artemisia, as you know it, needs a couple hours to recharge." Aldred explained in a grumble as he left to open the door. "Put her coat on and come on."

Destan then realized he forgot to bring it with him, so he took his veil off and wrapped her in it. The blanket slipped off and fell on the floor as he scooped Callimay into his arms; burying his face against her neck as he gave her a kiss.

℥

When they made it to the dock, Doctor Gerould immediately started checking her; smiling and taking a much-needed deep breath as he patted Destan's shoulder, "She'll make it. She's fine."

"You can operate this type of auto pilot I was told?" Aldred asked rather arrogant as he nodded toward the controls.

"Yes?" Doctor Gerould replied confused. "But why?"

Take care of my Jewel, Lance. Destan sounded choked up as he knelled and gave Callimay a kiss. *Tell her I always loved her and I was just trying to keep her safe.*

"Where are you going?"

"To keep my end of the bargain, apparently." Destan sighed as he stood and followed Aldred back. "May the new moon continue to rise on you."

"M… may the stars— you come back. You hear me?" Doctor Gerould refused to acknowledge as he fought back tears. "Don't you dare leave me to tell you wife this."

"Don't keep her here any longer. Get her back safe." Destan nodded as he turned and left. *Thank you for everything you've done over the years, Lance. It didn't go unnoticed. Unappreciated? … Well we both know that's different. I'm sorry for those times.*

I'll get a team sent as fast—

Don't you dare try anything until you're one-hundred percent sure you're safe! Just get out and then get everything settled before worrying about me. If chaos breaks out, too many lives will be at risk.

I…

That's my final order.

As they walked along, Destan reached out: *Please just listen to me, Trever. Alright?*

What's going on? How's Everlyn? He replied worried as he threw his magazine to the wall and ran to the window. *Is it all done? Where are you? I'll come—*

She's fine. They're on their way back. Meet them at the pier if you can. — Trever? I… I don't think I'm coming back. At least that's the way it's looking. Destan sighed as he looked back and saw Callimay through the window. *G… get Calli to Brigon. Your grandfather said if anything went wrong he'd keep her safe. … There's always a chance I'll survive this, but don't wait for me. Leave the second you're able to. … If I can I'll meet you there. If not? Be the man she needs you to be and the one I know your father trained you to be, Trever. Don't worry about everything else. Fidus has everything—*

You idiot. You better come back.

If that were Redje saying it, Destan would've laughed, but he could only cringe: *Trever, please! I'm not 'wanting' to die, but I have a bad feeling about this all. I'm just glad Baleck agreed to let Calli go.*

Just leave. Baleck's a liar anyway. What he dishes out he gets.

I'm not just gonna lay down and die. Destan sounded so frustrated as he followed along. *I'm just trying to make su—*

You are the biggest coward I've ever k—

Destan cut his connection. It was hard enough for him to realize he might never get to see Callimay again; his eyes on a swivel looking for something to help him get out of there. But to have his choice mocked and torn to shreds like Trever was doing without thinking this was to stall for time so she got to safety?

The fleeting thought that the submarine was rigged crossed his mind, but his heart refused to entertain that dreadful though realistic thought. Without that surety of knowing she was safe, he "would" die there… and it wouldn't necessarily be at the hands of Baleck.

"You're back much quicker than I thought," Baleck stood up and said shocked as the door opened.

"It's easier when things are kept short." Destan took a deep breath, things finally beginning to fall into place so he was able to focus on his surroundings. "Especially when the situation is like it is right now. … Don't you think?"

"I hope you understand this is done as a precaution." Baleck said as he showed Destan what was in his hand, Aldred having a gun drawn and pointed at him.

"Just get it over with." Destan rolled his eyes as he put his hands behind him. "Though you think you would've learned these really don't work 'that' much in extreme cases."

Once the feelers were locked and turned on, Aldred went back to the computers and talked with Baleck for a short time. He then walked over and took a cloth and put some liquid on it.

"Anything you care to say before we begin?" Baleck asked as he pushed Aldred's hand down; addressing Destan.

"You don't have to do… 'this'; whatever you've concocted. Power isn't everything folks chalk it up to being. You admitted there was such a thing as love. It is a powerful thing in-and-of itself."

"The only one I loved is gone; taking it with her. Power is all I have now." Baleck's eyes narrowed as he yanked the cloth to his face. "A man's own power is all he can trust and rely on when alone."

Baleck stumbled and staggered, still grumbling but now slurred and inaudible; Aldred trying to help him. The second after he got on what looked like an operating table he was out cold.

Aldred began hooking him to the various monitors and equipment in a flurry. He looked at Destan with an expression of utter contempt, glaring at him every free moment he had.

While part of him was curious to see what happened to himself to gain his abilities; if what he was seeing was any indication of what was to come… it was extremely boring. So as Destan sat there, he closed his eyes: *Rej?*

Nothing.

Destan waited a few minutes and then tried again.

Still nothing.

It was worth a try. … She's still asleep. It's best if it does end up the way I'm starting to think it will. Feelers were a pretty smart idea, really.

He opened his eyes and jerked just slightly — wincing a bit — when he saw Aldred standing not but five feet off, staring through him. As if glad he was in pain, Aldred rolled his eyes as he scoffed and stormed back to where he'd been.

This prompted a thought, "If you don't mind, I have a question to ask you, Aldred."

"What is it, Doyen." He snarled as he kept at his work.

"So is Baleck only injecting himself with Chameleon? Or is he doing one of his infamous 'mixtures' I read so much about?"

"And what is it to you?"

"Just trying to help the time pass and understand what's going on." Destan tried to be as non-confrontational as possible, him fighting the urge to shift how he was sitting.

"Time will pass at the rate it always does. And understanding is a thing of perception. You know what you need to." Aldred's arrogant tone was just as strong as ever, him finishing to himself: *We're almost there. Once this is over I'll get the payoff I've been promised and you get what you've wanted for quite some time.*

Destan didn't catch the last part of what Aldred said, because what appeared to be strange little things started happening: Aldred started moving the monitors he placed and then switched out the liquids which were being injected, then monitor after monitor would flash red before everything — one by one — came to an abrupt stop.

I'm no expert here, but this sure doesn't remind me of anything I ever remember reading about. ~ You're telling me. What in the world is he doing? ~ Maybe part of what has to be done if you mix serums?

Not too much later everything popped back on and did some sort of reboot cycling; Baleck seeming to have a seizure for a moment.

Aldred let things "run their course" and then turned most of the machines off. After watching the others for a while, he removed all but five monitor patches. He sat and waited, writing things down every once in a while, then when Baleck began to stir he was more attentive.

The saying that how you come out of anesthesia is how you would be as a drunk… if that's true than what kind of guy is Baleck, actually?

Destan began to tense up when he saw Baleck was instantly coherent when he came to; which didn't take nearly as long as he expected.

Aldred helped Baleck sit up and asked a few generic questions before being questioned himself, "Well… how did it go?"

"Just as you predicted with the amplifier mod," Aldred helped steady him. "Each overloaded for a moment, then returned to normal for the remainder of the cementing."

"So you didn't lie, Destan. I applaud your integrity and must admit my error for believing you capable of deception in such a situation. — I know the effect as a whole will take some time, but I can already feel a difference in my body." Baleck's attention was diverted as he looked at his hands which were trembling. "This excitement and power rushing through my veins. What a feeling of absolute power you must feel each time you tap yours!"

Destan's eyes widened with fear as he watched what was unfolding. Baleck began to pace the floor, staring at his hands and snickering every once in a while. Aldred tried to get him to calm and sit down, but he wouldn't hear of it and became more and more agitated with each attempt made.

Flashbacks started compiling as Destan started to piece together what was happening, "Baleck. You need to listen to Aldred. You need to calm yourself."

"But these emotions fuel this power! Why would I stop them?"

"That's the whole point! These emotions will fuel a monster who's just begging to be released and incapable of restraint! It only hungers for destruction and death. I know! You know it too and you know what the end will be if you don't—"

"You don't embrace it like it is intended to be, you weak fool! The monster isn't one at all."

"Baleck, you've got to get a grip." Destan's voice almost sounded scared; him understanding how Callimay would feel when he would start to spiral out of control. "You'll drive yourself insane and kill yourself if you keep this up!"

"I'm already insane! You took away what I had left in this life!" Baleck lashed out as he turned on a dime to face Destan; him breathing heavily, his hands still trembling as he pointed at him.

"I'm sorry about Ginger d—"

"This burning is nothing compared to the anger and pain of losing her. So it's not her, you idiot. Killing Elder. Him dying at my hand was the only duty I had left. It was the only way for me to have peace and comfort. I was thrilled to know he was dead, but furious to know it was not at my hands. I have all this revenge but no one for it to rest upon. … So it now rests on you."

"Aldred don't!" Destan gasped as he jumped up, instantly doubling over from the feelers shocking him.

Only trying to keep at bay the danger he knew was lurking as well, Aldred had what appeared to be something to sedate Baleck with, but was unaware Baleck was in possession of a dagger. As he reached out to take hold of Baleck, Baleck turned and stabbed Aldred, laughing the entire time, "Oh how I missed this feeling."

Stunned was the only way to describe the look Aldred had as he clung to Baleck's arm before crumbling to the floor and staring into nothing; choking as he tried to say something.

This high he'd felt before began to build in Baleck, him turning to who was his only other source of prey at the time: Destan who was still on the floor, hissing to fend off the pain so he could keep aware of his surroundings as much as possible.

In a moment of panic, Destan reached out to Callimay, worried she woke up and reconnected with him. — Thankfully she hadn't.

Rej? Destan asked himself again, sounding more desperate this time. *Rej are you there?*

A few moments later he heard: *Destan?*

Oh thank goodness.

What's going on? Where are you? Why did you hang up s—

You'll help Calli, right?

Of course we will, but we won't leave you out. He started to joke, but could tell something was wrong. *What's going on? You sound like you're in pain.*

Unless Baleck trips or turns the dagger on himself, I'm not making it out of here. The walls in this room are lead-lined. There's nowhere for me to jump that'll do any good. I'm in feelers and just lost the pick I had. I'll probably only be able to jump a couple times before I'm spent.

Baleck? *W… what can I do?* Redje asked, sounding choked up. *Can I call someone? Is anyone—*

Just tell Calli I loved her so much. Tell her I'll see her in a bit and I'm sorry we couldn't go home to Rayleen to start a family. … I think that's the thing I regret most. Destan closed his eyes, Baleck standing right over him practically foaming at the mouth. *I— there's so much I want to tell her, but there's just no time.*

I'll tell her.

Thanks for not giving up on me, Rej. You and Tabitha both. No one could've asked for a better pair of friends or comrades. Take care. Stay safe; physically and spiritually. Tell Rose—

Destan? Redje opened his eyes as he shot up. *Hello? Destan? Are you there?* "Destan!"

"What's wrong?" Tabitha shrieked as she tried to get her bearings.

Redje was staring at the wall, a look of shock plastered on his face; his eyes overflowing with helplessness and confusion.

"Redje what's wrong?" Tabitha asked again as she gripped his arm.

"Destan's… he's… I… it can't be." He mumbled under his breath.

"What can't be? Redje you're scaring me."

"He was doing that mind-speak thing like you said Callimay could do just now. He said Baleck had him pinned down and he wasn't going to make it out. … He was talking and then… and then nothing."

"Are you sure you weren't dreaming?" Tabitha began breathing hard. "Redje it could have been a dream, right? I mean, how'd he find Baleck so quickly? And why would he confront him with everything else going on? That doesn't make sense."

"If it was a dream, it's the first dream of its kind I've ever had: I was awake. — What are you doing?"

"Calling someone to find out exactly what in the world is going on." Tabitha sounded determined as she put her hand up for him to be quiet. "Nexus? Where's Doyen? … Well, get Mender. And hurry. — Can you still hear him?"

"No. He just cut off like when a call drops. I tried to—"

"Tell me Destan's with you." Tabitha asked when Doctor Gerould answered the phone. "Redje said he was talking with Destan and he was with Baleck and not able to get out of where he was… alive?"

"He's not. And as much as I don't want to believe… by his last comment he made to me and what you just said, I… don't know if he made it out. How—"

"No!" Tabitha screamed as she dropped the phone.

ℬ

The storm let up enough for Rocher and Trever to get clearance to leave. And after talking with Redje and Tabitha, Doctor Gerould was in just as much emotional shambles as they were. He gathered as much strength as he could muster and told Rocher and Trever — Rocher taking it better than Trever, but not by much.

That discussion was a hard one, but when he came back and saw Callimay he didn't know what to do. He didn't want to be the one to tell her what happened. Yes, Redje and Tabitha said they were leaving right then for Brigon and would meet them there to help as much as they could, but he still held the responsibility of being the last one to see him alive. He was the last person who could've done something to get them all out of there together. And what did he do?

Fear, sorrow, anguish… guilt. Guilt was truly what was haunting Doctor Gerould. He knew all along something wasn't right and Destan was exhausted from all he'd been through in such a short time. How could he just sit back and accept what he was told? Yes, he wasn't as proficient as most Shadows, even, but he knew how to fight: *I had time to do something. My reactions are fast enough I could've— it was just Aldred; and we all know he's no fighter. I… why didn't I at least try! Callimay will hate me when she finds out, and I couldn't even think of blaming her. This 'is' my fault.*

Meanwhile in the cockpit, Trever kept stewing in his anger while Rocher channeled all his grieving anger to ensuring nothing more happened; snapping at Trever to get a grip and do his job.

It worked better than any effort Destan made.

Rocher contacted Fidus, telling him to send someone who could keep this under wraps until they knew for sure — he wasn't about to accept Destan "was" dead until he physically saw his body.

Of course Fidus agreed they couldn't jump to conclusions and needed proof either way, "I'll take care of it."

Even after landing and explaining the situation to Majesty Presley, Callimay was still unconscious. Trever took off in frustration, leaving Doctor Gerould and Rocher to wait on her to wake up; though they were hoping Redje and Tabitha would get there first.

ℬ

The one trusted with this vital and delicate detail was Traceur. When given the news it took her every ounce of courage she had to keep her emotions hidden. And as she powered through and prepared to leave, she started remembering what Destan had said and done at pivotal — or just memorable — points in their work relationship. Remembering what made her smile or laugh was the hardest; the tears becoming so heavy in her eyes at times.

Compared to others details which were of this caliber importance, the trip to her drop off point was short, and yet it felt far too long and agonizing. There was far too much time to remember things which filled the pit of sorrow* in her heart at the time.

And then as she surfaced at the far dock of the cove, an altogether different level of dedication and focus washed over and drowned out her emotions. What she'd done for so long and was so good at flipped its "on" switch and she went to work.

She looked for the "invisible" trail Destan would have left, but soon found herself being guided by voices. At one point she had to hide in one of the larger vestibules while a group of Falconers filed by with some kind of machine: *What in the world? What kind of incubation chamber is that? What are they doing… or growing in that thing? I've never seen anything like it!*

After snapping a couple pictures, she heard them mentioning a name she recognized… and hoped was there.

When she made it to a dead end, the trail now gone, she started looking in every offshoot and working her way back. As she entered one, the hair on her neck stood up. Traceur heard what sounded like someone moaning, and then, "At what point did— do. At what point 'do' the Shadows rise?"

Her heart started racing and her eyes got wide as she replied in a quiet voice as her right hand slid behind her, "With the afterglow."

A younger man with icy white, flowing locks stepped into the light; his outfit screaming Falconer just as plain as day. He looked concerned yet relieved, "Is it appropriate to ask whom am I speaking with?"

Not the least bit suspicious or defensive, she replied, "Traceur."

"I'm sure you're well aware who I am."

"Linton Swinchpuck. I know of you, yes." She nodded as she stepped out, still sensing someone else was in the room.

"I will contact you later to explain what I know about this all, but for the time being you need to get him to safety." He turned and pointed to a shaded corner behind him. "He's alright, but had more than his fair share of hits from feelers."

"Doyen!" Traceur gasped when she got close enough to see who it was. "How c— Linton?"

She ran to the door, stopping short when she heard him speaking with others outside. Realizing what they were talking about, she ran back to Destan and calmed him, shielding him with her body so those who came in wouldn't see them.

They left not too much later, but Traceur waited a while longer in case that wasn't everyone or some came back "just in case".

During that time she did what she could to bandage Destan's wrists and find out what happened. He kept apologizing for the uproar he caused, though she said had he not she wouldn't be there and no one would've known where he was or if he were alive, "You picked the perfect people to let know so it was contained and yet handled as fast as it was."

While meeting Linton was something beyond her wildest dreams — as far as her personally-held mission within the Shadows — seeing her commanding officer alive and in a far better state than she hoped… it was near impossible to keep her joy from overflowing in her eyes. And yet she felt so awkward because she wasn't the type to be like this.

Traceur had to support him, but about halfway he was able to move on his own; and before long they were all out sprinting to get clear.

Right before they got to the docks — which had no cover — she had him rest while she ran to get things ready and then did recon to see where everyone was. Then once she was satisfied, she went back for Destan and they ran for it.

During her last sweep, Traceur still felt like someone was watching. As she looked up to one staircase she caught a glimpse of Linton. He waved to her and looked pleased as he turned and left.

✤

Seeing the water encase him when they first got under shook him a bit, but he closed his eyes and tried to get his mind off what he narrowly escaped. Yes, he lived through it; but at the same time everything was such a painful blur he really didn't know what happened. All he knew for sure was what he saw right then and there… and he was beyond grateful to be alive.

The water currents were more disruptive for them than Aldred because they weren't as deep. And then when they got back and he got to the vehicle the cold began to bite at him; this reminding him how much he wanted to see Calli and hold her close.

Destan first called Doctor Gerould, him not being able to say anything before hearing the desperate plea of his father figure, "What did you find, Traceur?"

"Me, thankfully." Destan replied.

"What on— why did you—"

"I'm just about as surprised as you are, Lance. Is Calli awake?"

"No. Confrere and Helpmate are on their way here right now after the conversation you had with him."

"I'll… I'll call them. Calli 'is' alright, right?"

"She's doing just fine. Still asleep, but doing just fine."

"Good." Destan said relieved as he sat back. "I'm on my way to you right now. Just hang tight."

"Should I let everyone else know that's here?"

"Yes, please."

"Alright."

As the phone clicked Traceur looked over, "Why 'did' you—"

"Let's just say I had a gut feeling that wouldn't go away no matter how hard I tried to find a way out of there: each plan I had kept falling apart." Destan sighed as he rubbed his face, then winced as he shook his wrists. "Call Helpmate."

Tabitha answered as she sniffled, "Please tell me Redje was wrong."

"I'm sorry I scared you guys." Destan replied. "I really didn't kn—"

"Oh thank you God." Tabitha started crying. "Thank you so much."

"Is Rej there, Tab—"

"I'm here. … Please don't scare me like that 'ever' again. If I wasn't so torn up I'd probably punch you. Even so I still might."

I'd not only deserve it, but welcome it. "I'm sorry."

"I'm… I'm just glad you're alright and we don't have to do what we were preparing ourselves for." Redje took a labored, deep breath; this wild string of events wearing on him. "So what happened, anyway?"

"I'll tell you a bit later after I can gather all those details for myself. Everything's jumbled up right now. Plus I've got to get Fidus called so we can get things calmed down."

"Alright."

"Are you okay?" Tabitha's strained voice pleaded.

"As far as I'm concerned? I'm alive and nothing that happened will be permanent. You two get home."

"Understood." Redje sounded relieved. "It's… it's good to hear your voice again. And in a better tone at that. — By the way: what did you want me to tell Rose?"

"Oh. Right. Tell her 'Desan' misses her and will try his best to call her soon to talk. She picked up the phone earlier and I was pretty short with her."

"I'll do that, though I doubt she'll remember you being upset." Redje laughed as he reached over to grip Tabitha's hand. "Tell Callimay we're praying for her to heal quickly."

"I will. Safe travels back."

Once all the phone calls were finished, Destan leaned his head back and tried to rest a bit. And yet he could tell something was on Traceur's mind, "What's wrong?"

"Why was Linton there?"

"Huh?" Destan asked confused as he sat up.

"Linton, the Queen's nephew. What was he doing there?"

He took a split second to think, then shook his head, "He wasn't there. At least 'I' never saw him. Are you sure it was him?"

"I didn't just see him, I 'talked' with him; I know it's him because he knew the code I'd sent him long ago. He was the one who kept you hidden from the Falconers. Though there was something strange about them. They had very different uniforms and such. I can't quite figure it out, but there was something — I don't know — 'off', about them? Anyway. Linton only told me he'd get in contact with me to explain what he knew about this all, later on." Traceur tried to push aside what was truly bugging her. "You think he's final come around?"

"You know as good as I do it's hard to tell with him. It may be just another one of his diplomatic 'services' to keep balance and order in the family."

"Maybe," Traceur thought as she tapped the steering wheel. "But somehow… the look on his face and the sound of his voice? It was like he wanted to come with us but couldn't."

"When did he say he'd contact you?"

"He just said later."

Destan's mind wandered off in thought as he looked outside: *We hopefully can get going before this picks up again.*

"Well, we're here." Traceur announced as she pulled up to the chopper. "I'll get in contact with Fidus about the other info on my way back. Let me know when you are on your way back."

"I will. And let me know if you hear from Linton in the meantime." Destan nodded as he opened the door, wincing as he shook his hand. *How I hate those feelers. Geez!* "I… I'm alright. Don't worry about me. Just get back to Bulwark. And be safe."

"I will. You too."

For the first time in what felt like a lifetime, Destan was able to relax and rest; sleeping the entire flight to Brigon even though the sounds in the chopper were well out of the range of what would be considered "ambiance" to most people.

ℬ

Rocher was the one who met him and rushed him inside, it striking Destan how much emotion he was showing. But the second someone else was around, he clammed up; making Destan chuckle oh so slightly: *'There's' the Rocher I know.*

When he got up to where Callimay was, Doctor Gerould greeted him, "It's a load off my mind to see you. … How are your wrists?"

"Well, my hands are still attached. Other than that there's not much of a positive."

"Let me—"

"No. No, I'm seeing Calli first. Is she awake?"

"Not yet, so just settle down. It won't take me but a minute to—"

"I kinda feel like I've come back from the grave. I 'need' to see her. Traceur cleaned them so they'll be fine a while longer. Please, Lance."

Unable to fight that desperate plea, he stepped aside and nodded him on.

This bedroom was even more elaborate and ornate than theirs at the mansion… and rightfully so for the princess his wife was. It was dark outside, yet the snow reflected what moonlight there was, giving a soft glow to the outside world and the room. Not nearly what the belvedere was capable of, but still enough light for him to see.

Destan pushed the fine lace and sheer fabric of the bed canopy aside so he could see the woman he came so close to losing — yet again — and then leaving her alone… again. He smiled as tears ran down his face; so relieved to be able to see her. She looked so peaceful; her softly breathing as she slept.

With that reassurance of "seeing" her, he all but collapsed next to her; though doing it so he wouldn't disturb her. He reached over and took her left hand, trying to endure the pain; taking his wedding band off her thumb and putting it back on and putting her rings back on.

As he lay there, now content with things, thoughts started spiraling; him still trying to wrap his mind around the fact he did make it out of that all. And then out of the blue, something Baleck said jumped out: Callimay's brain "had" been damaged. To what extent was she going to be "different"? Would it truly be permanent? Surely it wouldn't be so bad that she couldn't remember him… right? Of course she did that one time, but that was just due to the pain she was in.

Right?

His battered body fought his mind on how much energy could be expended on such a wild thought as he sat up and looked around the room: *Of course it's all the way on the other side.*

Not having your hands to help get yourself out of bed when you were exhausted was looking to be a rather impossible task for Destan, but determined to prepare himself for what could be the worst case scenario when Callimay woke up, he couldn't give up.

Just as he got up he heard a knock at the door. He rushed over as fast as he could and whispered, "Who is it?"

"It's me, Destan," he heard Doctor Gerould.

"Come in."

After glancing at Callimay, Doctor Gerould asked, "Will you let me look at you now?"

A nod toward the sofa Destan was originally headed for was all Doctor Gerould needed to know.

While prepared to be chewed out for being reckless, what was said by Doctor Gerould was the total opposite, "If your father had the chance to make the choice for your mother as you did for Callimay, he would've in a heartbeat. Don't beat yourself up about what 'might' have happened. The feathers you ruffled will tame in time."

"I..."

"Everything in hindsight is always clearer: what you could've or should've done different. But the fact is we can't make decisions after the situation is over. A true leader is made from those who are willing to sacrifice themselves in situations where emotions are high, time is short, and in your case: the outcome is life-or-death." Doctor Gerould kept on in a calm tone as he tended to Destan's wrists; stopping for a moment and looking him in the eye. "I know I'm not your father, but I know beyond the shadow of a doubt he'd tell you he was proud of the decision you made."

The stunned look on Destan's face brought a sliver of a smile to Doctor Gerould's; him letting out a bit of a sigh as he finished, "He kept hoping you'd grow out of your teenage rage before he died. But I can see now that you've used it to help you — you've learned to control it and make a very important decision that was going to hurt you either way. Emotionally 'and' physically, that is."

His last comment hit Destan a bit odd, making him suspicious, "How bad are my wrists, Lance? Just tell me."

"I could never keep you in the dark very long, could I?" He half chuckled as he nodded; his voice borderline depressed. "I don't know why I try to soft-pedal things with you when I know it doesn't work, but I guess it's just hard for me to tell the son of my best friend things like this. … I don't know if you remember the one lab bust we made about… oh, six years back? The one in northern Yergo? Well I followed up on those who had this degree of damage and they, in the sense of hand usage, were invalids. The nerve damage was beyond repair and the muscle and tendon burns caused irreversible damage so they had contractures to various degrees. — But! The fact that you're still able to move your fingers and you feel pain is hopeful. All your combat training has helped you in a unique way: it strengthened your hands and wrists. So, you can take more than the average person. … I won't give a concrete prognosis right now, but I believe there is hope. And quite a bit of it. You just have to be willing to suffer through being served and helped for a while."

That last bit frustrated Destan, and Doctor Gerould knew it, "If you don't, I can guarantee you that you'll lose the usage of your hands for the rest of your life. And what would Callimay say, knowing you had a chance to save it?"

"How long?"

"Twenty-four hours of absolutely nothing. And I mean 'no-thing'. Which also means you 'have' to ask for help for 'every'thing. Got it?"

Destan nodded as he sighed, staring at his hands.

"In that time I can make arrangements for the tests that will need to be done before surgery."

Surgery? Right now? Are you serous! Destan groaned as he hung his head. *That's gonna take months to recover from.*

"You and Callimay are alive. You've got to remember that during all of this no matter what comes from the tests. That's why I said what I did." Doctor Gerould tried his best to be positive. "Now that's about all I can do for now, but is there anything I can help with?"

"No," Destan stared at the floor.

"I can help you back over to Callimay. No one's here."

"I'll just stay here, Lance. It's fine."

"Why?"

"Something Baleck said came back to me that's had me worried in another way: he said he wasn't sure how damaged Calli's brain was by this all. He said it 'was' and that she might be 'different'." He glanced over to her; his heart aching a bit. "Who knows what state she'll be in when she wakes up. And if— I can't scare her if the worst happens. I just can't do that to her. I don't wanna see that wild fear in her eyes thinking I did— I can't do it. I just couldn't stand seeing her like that and hearing what she thought I would do to her, again."

While it was something he should have considered, it was rather shocking for Doctor Gerould to hear this: *Well this all just— it's either nothing or everything.* "Let me get my halo and do some scans on her right now while she's still asleep. I can't say I'll find tiny issues, but I'll be able to help prepare you."

Unable to fight sleep long enough for Doctor Gerould to finish the scans, Destan passed out for a few hours. When he woke he had to take a few minutes to figure out where he was.

No one else was in the room, but on the end table was a note.

> *There was indeed some damage, but not what I was fearing I'd find. Just be gentle and patient with her when she wakes up. Aside from the damage, remember she is somewhere she may see as "strange". And with her mental state when I put her under, she may have lingering memories of that.*
>
> *I trust you'll know what's best, but I just wanted to give you this small reminder: if you need anyone or anything, just call. I let Aleck know your hands were injured, so he has someone trustworthy outside the room waiting at all times who can help you if needed.*
>
> *I'll be back around three or so.*

While knowing this was helpful, it hurt at the same time. They'd come so far but still had one major push to go… and this all happens. In a way he wondered if this was what the Syndicate wanted to happen: him to do this to himself so he'd be incapacitated and unable to utilize his ability to protect and defend those he needed to.

But, those thoughts were for another time. Now is what he needed to concern himself with. And so he did his best to prepare himself for what may come; trying to figure out what would help Callimay the most as well as keep her safe if she couldn't remember him.

And then if she had some motor issues? That was controlled by the brain as well. Doctor Gerould didn't say anything about where the damage was or what it affected.

Lord? Please… please heal my Calli. Everything that can be done physically for her has been done; and so I ask that You fix what is left damaged: please let her remember me so I can help her. Please let it be in Your will that she doesn't lose who I know she is. … And help me. Help me heal physically so I can take care of her. Help me mentally to have the confidence to make the choices I need to within the coming days. Help me emotionally to take things in stride and continue to win the fight against my anger and rage. Just help me, God. Please. Help me learn, grow, and mature as I'm supposed to. Please push this despair and worry away from me. Give me Your strength so I can keep going as I need to. … It's in Your Son's name I pray, amen.

When he opened his eyes, he noticed motion where Callimay was. He got to his feet and now realized more than his wrists were injured, him hobbling over as he hissed and grunted; fighting the urge to grab his right leg.

She was crying and mumbling something as she tossed, worrying Destan the worst was coming. He kneeled beside the bed and prayed again, hearing her cry out as he finished.

"No, please!"

Everything now second nature to him was having to be suppressed on more than one front. He had to sit there and wait to see what would happen; let her work through what it was she dreamed about. And then he could only talk to her. In his mind, even though he could still use his arms, it didn't matter if he could "half-hug" her; anything short of holding her, his strong hands reminding her she was safe with him? It wasn't going to cut it. But if he was going to have any chance at having the usage of his hands in the future… he couldn't do anything.

Callimay looked as wild as he'd seen her a couple times as her eyes darted around the room; her breathing unable to slow and settle.

In that moment Destan prayed no one would come in. The last thing she needed was someone else in there.

"No, no, no." She cried in a whisper as she clutched the bedspread close to her. "God please don't…"

As she turned toward Destan, she yelped and jerked back.

But she stopped. Her eyes widened and softened as tears began pouring out of them.

Leary and scared, the bedspread still in her death-like grip, she inched toward Destan who sat there on the floor like a statue that was capable of nothing but crying; his head bowed enough so he wasn't making direct eye-contact with her but still able to see her.

Hearing voices outside, Destan suddenly remembered: *Lance don't come in. Please! Not yet. Don't let anyone come in. Calli can't handle that right now. Please!*

The voices vanished, making Callimay question things.

Curious enough to look around, she scooted toward the foot of the bed, her flashing her fiery gaze at Destan from time to time to make sure he hadn't moved. — Each time she saw he hadn't moved helped her calm that much more.

This last time she looked at him, though, looked almost sympathetic. Her head tilted a bit as she stared at him; it appearing something about him interested her. Not willing to get closer, she stretched her neck out a bit so she could see everything below chest-level. It was then a real change started to occur. Whether it was the bandages or traces of blood still on him, she gasped a bit as her eyes became glassy.

And then out of nowhere she looked at her left hand and stared with thoughtful and curious eyes at the rings she had on; her other hand now beginning to let go of the bedspread.

Not but a few moments later she took them off and examined them closer; her starting to mumble something too quiet for Destan to hear.

Amidst all this emotional carnage, a small sprig of hope began to sprout in Destan: Callimay was moving around without pain. This was proof what Baleck did worked.

Then the memory of one of the teenage boys he fostered a few years ago jumped into his thoughts out of nowhere. He remembered a letter he got three summers ago: the girl this young man married had a stroke she thankfully recovered from, but from then on she would wake up every morning not knowing who he was... that they were married. Destan recalled how the words the young man used showed how hard it was for him, but that his love for her grew because he was reminded he had to wake up every morning regardless of anything and "choose" to love her. She was still in there, he knew that, and he wasn't about to go back on the promise he made… the very thing Destan had to work with him so hard on.

Now he understood. And now his one sprig of hope was joined by another, then another… that single sprig now in an entire field of young plants just waiting to bask in the bright sunshine that was on the horizon. The light still had to get over the rugged mountains in the distance, but the sprigs didn't fear the wait. They knew they would survive until then and that the sun "would" come.

His hope knew it was worth the wait and both him and Callimay would come through this for the better. They just had to wait and be patient for the time being.

She turned to him and looked at her rings and then back to him; continuing to do this for a while.

My ring? He lifted his left hand to show his band. *Well at least that was the first thing she remembered of me… not—*

Her eyes widened as she scurried to the edge of the bed, freezing for a moment before reaching out and taking hold of his hand so she could see the band better.

Of course the last thing he wanted to do was scare her, but what she did was causing him more pain than he could hide. Him grimacing made her jump back, but she stopped short of panicking when she saw the bandages again, "I… I didn't mean to. I'm sorry."

Trying to be calm and quiet, he took a deep breath before replying, "I'll be okay." *Come on Calli, just stop and think. I know it's still in there. I know 'you're' still in there. Take your time. Just don't push me away. Please.*

Again, her eyes widened even more from hearing his voice. She clutched her chest as she took a few labored breaths, trying to find something that made sense to her on the bedspread. Unable to find what she needed, she looked up to him again and asked in almost a whisper, "A… are we… umm… married?"

Destan bit his lip and nodded.

"D… do you… do you know why I can't remember anything? I assume… you know my name, right?"

The tears in his eyes couldn't hold on any longer; him nodding yet again as he replied in a soft voice, "Callimay. Your name is Callimay."

That hit a rough spot, her wincing as she covered her eyes.

"I'm sorry." Destan begged, fighting the urge to move closer.

A few seconds later she asked, "Y… you call me Calli, don't you?"

His heart sighed in relief as more tears streamed down his face, "I always have and I always will."

"Some…" she tried to catch her breath as she looked around him, it still looking like she was in some pain. "Something happened. … It… it hurt. I remember pain. … But I… I don't—"

"Just take your time," he dared to interrupt. "Don't force—"

She put her hand out for him to be quiet as she shifted how she sat, "I remember a dog whining and it was so hot but cold at the same time. … And I was in so much pain. It hurt so bad I couldn't stand to move. But I couldn't keep myself from moving. B… but I don't know why."

The air in the room was even anxious to hear what she would say next; after a few minutes her finding more fragments of memories, "Then there were raised voices; but they weren't angry. I… I remember your voice. … Yes. That's right. It was your voice. You… you sounded scared. Like you were crying? You said someone's name… I think. I…"

Callimay rubbed her face as she worked to remember, Destan fighting the urge to fill in the blanks for her.

A couple more minutes passed before she said more; her tone and breathing almost perfectly calm, "Lance. You said Lance. Didn't you?"

He nodded in an encouraging way.

"There was someone else there, wasn't there? Another man?" Her eyes started begging for help.

"Trever?"

She mouthed the named a few times, her blurting out, "He's my brother, right? He… he was trying to keep me from moving so I wouldn't hurt myself. Right?"

"Yes."

"I… the only other thing I can really remember is you crying. After that it's blank. — What happened? What made me forget everything? Forget you?" Fear started clawing away at her voice. "Does it have to do with you being hurt?"

"After that 'should' be blank, Calli." Destan worked so hard to be calm and stay where he was. "You were injured. It caused you to get sick and forget. Lance is the one who put you to sleep so you wouldn't hurt yourself and the sickness wouldn't worsen. You stayed like that until you were treated."

"Did the doctors say I would remember everything eventually?"

"They… well they're not sure, Calli. Your mind has been hurt really bad. It's going to take time."

Her lips quivered as she tried to mouth a word to say something, but nothing would come.

A couple minutes passed, him unable to wait any longer, "Calli?"

"Destan?" She looked at him terrified. "That's your name, right?"

I'm not even mad I was the last name she remembered. "It is."

"What if I never remember?"

"Don't ever worry about not remembering the past," his smile made every effort to look sympathetic without somehow causing the dam that held back his tears to burst. "I'm here. I'll help you fill in those empty spaces with new memories."

Callimay scurried to the side of the bed where he was and then stopped as she begged, "Promise?"

"I promise."

The next second Destan felt her shivering body against his; her crying as she clung to him.

"Calli?" He did his best to not raise his voice; though she jumped back anyway. "I just… I need to move my hands. Th—"

"I forgot again! I'm so sorry!" She gasped as she bit her lip, trying not to cry. "Did I do that?"

"No! No Calli you didn't—" he tried to calm; but grimaced when he realized he couldn't even wave his hands. "You didn't do this, Calli. This happened after you were treated."

Her eyes swelled with fear, "W… why? Who would do that?"

Destan took a deep breath and sighed before looking her square in the eye, "There are some very evil people who do not want either of us to be alive. Just know that for right now, okay? As you start to recover and remember, I'll help explain more. We're safe now; those people are gone. They'll never hurt you."

"Are you going to be okay? Is that why I'm not in a hospital to recover?" She looked around, terrified now. "Is it safe here?"

"We're safe here. Don't worry." His eyes followed her as she started running around the room. "It's okay. In fact, Lance is right outside helping keep us safe. Okay? — And as far as I go, I 'may' need to leave for a bit to get surgery. But know I will always do everything I can to keep you safe no matter where we are, and I will only leave you with those I know we can trust. Ones I know will never hurt you."

Callimay gasped when she looked back and saw Destan struggling to get to his feet; her running and reaching out to support his forearms.

He looked up, their faces just inches apart, and froze… just like she did. Even though having her so close was a comfort to him, he didn't want her to feel uncomfortable; and so he made himself uncomfortable which made her start to feel the same way.

The flash of a thought ran through her mind of what she cried out before she lost consciousness and what nightmare she woke up from in the first place: *Why am I trusting him so fast? These may not even be my real memories. Right? … Right? I…*

Time paused for a few moments; Callimay beginning to remember something so vivid she couldn't deny it being real, "Y… you're wearing the cologne I like. I remember… I got hurt once and you had to carry me. I remember smelling it then. And… and you bought me another bottle of the rose perfume I wore when we met. I… I somehow lost the original bottle I had. … Right?"

"Ca—" Destan was cut off by her kissing him.

$$\sim 5 \sim$$

They stayed in Brigon while the extent of Callimay's injuries were checked, rechecked, and checked again. — The process was almost a month of emotional torture for them. — Starting every, single day from scratch wasn't something either of them wanted to do: Callimay crying herself to sleep as she fought to stay awake because she didn't want to forget. And even though Destan needed surgery, leaving her alone wasn't something he was willing to do. It was understandable; but if he didn't get this surgery before the end of the month? His helpless state was assuredly going to become permanent.

If I could just find something to help her so she would wake up calm. That in-and-of itself would be amazing. Destan thought as he sat and waited for her to wake up. *But what? What can I figure out before I have to leave tomorrow?*

His attention was diverted when he saw the door open and someone poke their head in and gesture as if to ask if they could come in; him nodding them on.

"I may have something." Doctor Gerould whispered as he sat beside Destan, showing him a small recorder. "I'm obviously not sure, but it can't hurt anything to give it a try. Eavesdrop told me about this type of therapy and it sounds just like something Callimay would be responsive to since she enjoys listening to music."

"Music?"

"Certain styles of songs as far as tempo, note range, and melody have a profound impact on one's mind. — I remember vaguely some of that information being pounded into me during school, but it was in holistic therapy classes which, at the time, I wasn't interested in. — But she told me this 'may' help. She's dealt with a couple of our own who have suffered what you could call chronic amnesia, but obviously their circumstances were much different. And so it's the main reason she's not sure if it will work. But she did say it can't do any damage so there's no reason 'not' to try."

"What do I need to do?" Destan's voice sounded so encouraged.

"Turn it on when she's getting ready to go to sleep and keep it on throughout the night until she wakes up. It's as simple as that." Doctor Gerould replied as he hit a button on the side of the recorder and adjusted the volume a bit before setting it on the nightstand beside Callimay. "She did warn that this first time wouldn't be a true tell-all because she wasn't hearing it when she went to sleep. So keep that in mind. … I know you love a perfectly quite room to rest in, but for the time being you'll need to—"

"That's not a problem." He cut off as he focused on his sleeping wife. "If it helps even a little I can handle it."

"Aleck said the chopper would be here around eight tomorrow."

"Who did you get to take your place while we're gone?"

"Enforcer is coming with Auditor."

Destan let his shoulders drop as he sighed and nodded.

After a bit of back and forth discussion, Doctor Gerould sat with Destan for the next hour to see if what was suggested would prove to be helpful. The music was very calming and relaxing… Destan smiling a bit because it reminded him of Callimay.

How could this not help her? Even if all it did was help her not wake up in a terrified screaming rage that was worth it to him. He'd learn to adjust to the noise.

Signs of her stirring started showing, the two of them bracing for whatever would come… but hoping so much for a positive outcome.

An amazing answer to prayer unfolded in front of Destan when for the first time in almost a month he saw his wife wake up like she usually did. He couldn't help but jump on the bandwagon immediately: she was going to be emotionally stable while he had to be gone. Sure it was only three days, but even a day with her having to work through being terrified when waking up was enough burden on him. Now? Now he felt he could breathe a bit and focus on himself.

While she didn't remember him, Destan was content with what progress had been made. And by the time she "came to" — which was quicker than usual — even she was more relaxed about being apart, "So I didn't scream or anything?"

"Not once," he smiled as she put her arms around him.

"Do… do you think the music can really fix this? I mean… do you think I'll quit forgetting everything every, single, day like this?"

"Seeing what it did with just a good, solid hour of use? I have faith this is going to work, Calli." He leaned his cheek against hers. "We just have to keep praying and not give up. Maybe we'll have to spend time finding the right kind of music, but I won't stop until every song that has this capability has been tested. Okay?"

She tried not to cry, "I'm sorry."

"Sorry for what?" He pulled back a bit so he could see her face.

"I know you're hurt and there's so much going on right now—"

"You didn't 'do' anything to bring this on, Calli." He wanted so much to wipe the tears from her face. "It's not like you wanted this to all happen. Right? … Then there's nothing to be sorry for. God's using this as an opportunity to help us grow and keep our priorities straight. If we weren't dealing with the Syndicate it would be something else I have no doubt. Please don't feel bad, Calli."

"I just… I just remembered how hard it is for you with— I just don't want you to go through this all alone. And I know you are."

He sighed a bit as he barely shook his head, "But Calli I'm not. You know that. Even if I'm alone in the middle of nowhere I'm not alone. — But I also understand what you are trying to say. — Remembering moments like this helps me. I 'know' you are in there. You just need more time to 'wake up' right now."

‽

As he stood in the hall later that night, Majesty Presley came over and started chatting with him about his surgery. Somehow Trever came up; the fact he was still nowhere to be found, "I don't understand why he's acting so contentious lately."

"Destan, he be workin' thru more than I think ya realize." Majesty Presley calmed as he stood across from him and clicked his tongue a bit. "Even when he be here last time, he be on edge and constantly annoyed by things he'd be seein' and rememberin'. He not be quite sure how tu process 'em all. He still be — in a way — a young laddie. Give 'em time. He'll be coomin' 'round, I be sure oov it."

Destan sighed, "Did he tell you where he was going?"

"I'm afraid he didn't-ne." Majesty Presley shook his head. "In fact, I didn't-ne even know he left 'til ya said somethin'."

"Trever," he growled under his breath. "Don't do this."

"When ya be headin' back? … Of course I be assumin' ya are."

"If all goes well tomorrow and Calli is stable, we should be headed back in a couple weeks." He commented as he continued to stare out the window. "Should I… do you think I should just leave her here with you? I mean, it would be safer given the circumstances right now."

"Ya know good 'n well she wouldn't-ne take tu it, bein' apart from ya durin' such a time as this. I know she be dreadin' just ya bein' gone fer a few days right new."

"I know. But at the same time, how many more 'pot shots' can she take in this state?" Destan grimaced as he leaned his shoulder against the icy glass. "Yeah, Elder's gone, but I've got to face facts: what we have left to do is extremely dangerous. I know she gets to the point she remembers what is, generally speaking, going on… but that takes a good part of the day. I'm not sure—"

"While her involvement in things may need-be adjusted a bit, let me be remindin' ya that separatin' ya will oonly cause ya booth stress 'n worry that'll bring ya nothin' boot ill-timed decisions, dangerous mistakes, and quite possibly bring aboot fatal outcoomes. I'm not aboot tu order ya one way er thu other — I couldn't-ne even if I wanted tu — but I offer ya this advice as Callimay's grandfather: let her be with thu man she dearly loves. Let her make her oon decisions. Let her be by yer side." Majesty Presley encouraged.

Out of the blue, Destan sneezed a few times, then replied; sounding a bit congested, "I am the leader, but a 'good' leader listens to those under him to make the best decision."

"Are ya alright, laddie?"

"With everything… I might be catching a cold." Destan shrugged off as he sighed. "It wouldn't be anything I can't bounce back from."

"This be riskin' yer surgery?"

"I doubt it." He continued to be casual about it all; then sighed when he saw the look on Majesty Presley's face, "I'll ask Lance when I see him in a bit."

Now satisfied, Majesty Presley leaned on his cane as he nodded, "Eye. … I best be off tu take care oov soome matters. If~in ya don't see me, make sure ya let Haggis know when ya be leavin' so I knew tu be with Callimay. Eye?"

"I'll make sure he knows."

♅

Destan stayed there at the window for a while, hoping Trever would show. — What would make him leave after what his baby sister went through? Why wasn't he there for her like he said he would be? — It frustrated him to have this "family" problem on top of everything else.

Then again, how much "damage" did Elder do that he had to cope with and work through? Was this place a major trigger for him? He had been there when he as old enough to recall it.

He sniffled a bit as he stood there, watching what little he could see of the snow swirling and blowing around. While all these thoughts of Trever, his surgery, Callimay, and everything else whirled around in his mind like the snow; he had to admit that compared to times before he was quite relaxed. It were as if the peace he knew he had all along was something he didn't fear taking hold of during such a time as this. And the benefits he was reaping for doing so made him regret not doing it sooner.

~ 6 ~

Wide-eyed and running as fast as he naturally could, Destan flew down the halls to Callimay's room when he got back… only to realize when he got to the door and looked at his hands which were both in casts — he had to wait for Aleck or one of the others to catch up to him. A stark reminder of his dependence he was going to have for a while yet; he knew it wasn't going to be forever. The inconvenience now was just that: now. So he found the closest chair and sat; only to hear voices in the room followed by footsteps headed to the door.

"Majesty Presley."

"What perfect timin' ya have, laddie." He smiled as he stepped back.

"Who is it?" Destan heard Callimay ask.

"It be yer husband, wee lassie." He chuckled as he turned in her direction; then finished as he turned back to Destan and walked past, "Don't-ne bother with me, we kinna talk later. I be sure ya have some things tu talk oover toogether."

As the door closed, Destan looked over in almost shock.

Callimay smiled as she came over to him; taking his hand in hers, "How did it go? I know Doctor Gerould told me some, but I want to—"

"Is it true?" He lifted his hand to her cheek; his voice full of uncertainty. "Is it really working?"

She nodded as she wrapped her arms around him, "Better each day, I think. I may see about trying some other songs if this kinda plateaus, but for right now? It's enough."

His shoulders slumped as he leaned his face on top of her head, letting a massive sigh sprawl out and relax.

"Did Trever ever come back?"

Callimay sounded sad as she stepped back a bit, "No. I don't have any idea where he is. I even tried to reach out and find him, but it's too exhausting for me to do that right now. — How did it go?"

"We'll know in about a month." He glanced at his hands.

"Are… are you okay?"

"This?" He cleared his throat as he half-grinned. "It's just some cold or bug. Nothing major they said."

"I… I meant… Destan what happened to cause this? Will you tell me what happened to me that put you in that position where you were in feelers?" She tired her best to be calm and collected.

He rubbed his face with his forearm as he sighed, then gestured toward the sofa, "Are you sure you can handle it?"

"As sure as I can be without knowing."

They sat down, Destan looking like he wasn't completely satisfied with having this conversation; him stating his conditions, "I'll tell you what happened, but I won't use anyone's names. Okay?"

Callimay's face was splashed with confusion as she tilted her head, but after blinking a couple times she nodded, "O… okay?"

"I just need a bit more time before I tell—"

"If it's—"

"Now just calm down," he huffed, her biting her lip. "I didn't mean it that way. I need Fidus and some others to gather some intel so I know for sure before I say anything using peoples' names."

Well that sure was a whole lot of reassurance for nothing. ~ Be quiet. Whatever — 'who'ever — it was, they're very dangerous so Destan has to make sure they are where they can't hurt us. ~ You're right. With what I'm dealing with right now I can understand him waiting. "I really don't know why I'm so bent on knowing right now. I'm sorry. It's all in the past anyway. And if you say things are alright then I trust you."

ℬ

Before it was time to go, those two weeks speeding by so quickly because of all the progress Callimay was making — as well as Destan — he stood and waited at the opened door of Raven. The weather was so uncertain. It even felt anxious for him.

Not a single, solitary moving object or person could be seen: *Where are you, Trever? Why don't you ask for help? I know sometimes it's hard; you feel like you're not being a man when you ask for help, but it's really not that bad. … In fact it makes all the difference. Things turn out a whole lot better when you do.*

Though, when they got back to Bulwark, there he was: all smiles when they stepped foot on the apron. He asked how he could help and chatted with them both as they started for the suite; a total reverse from what Destan saw from him the last few times.

"How long has he been here?"

"He arrived not too much later after I found out you were alright." Fidus whispered out of the side of his mouth as they both watched him. "And as far as I can tell, he hasn't been to see her since."

"I guess I should have asked you if you'd seen him when we talked." *Keep it together, Boon.* "Good." Destan sighed. "Where's Traceur?"

"She's actually meeting with Linton right now. Western edge of Faberton near—"

"Shotput?"

"Yeah. — By the way, you sound terrible? What's wrong?"

Ignoring the question since his focus had been diverted, Destan's eyes widened as Callimay winced a bit, "Are you doing alright?"

"It's good to see you up and about, Liaison." Fidus smiled as Trever helped steady her.

"Thank you," she replied as she took Destan's elbow. "I just stepped funny, Destan. Don't— wait. He has another name here, doesn't he?"

Aware of the situation, Fidus brushed it off as he waved on, "Don't concern yourself with those minor things right now. It'll come back in due time."

"I… I remember it started with… uh," She shook her finger at him as she worked to think. "It started with…"

Not aware of the situation, Trever began to panic, "Everlyn? Are—"

I'll explain later. Destan was stern as he glared at him and shook his head. *Just let her think it through. She's okay.*

She looked up to Fidus and smiled as she blurted out, "Doyen! His name is Doyen, right?"

Destan and Fidus both smiled and nodded.

For as happy as she was to remember that, she pouted a bit as she looked at the three men, "There's something else, isn't there? Your leather coats remind me of something. … I mean there 'is' something special about them, right?"

Feeling as if he were almost going insane because Fidus and Destan weren't worried about her forgetfulness, Trever stood there in shock.

She looked back and forth several times and then snapped her fingers, "Oh! I get one too! There was a test I had to take. And someone else… what was his name… he had to come with me."

Fidus broke a sliver of a smile as he nodded again; his forbearing side shining so bright during this all.

"I… I guess you don't know yet." She sounded so apologetic when she looked at Trever's face. "I've had some sickness that made me forget everything, and so while I do remember quite a bit, there are some things which are still really fuzzy. Could you remind me who you are?"

Still not satisfied, but unable to withstand the smile on her face, he surrendered and said light-hearted, "Trever. Or either of my other two names that I go by here: Emissary or Liberator."

"Trever…" she tapped her lips with her fingers. "Seems like I knew a Trever a few years ago. I think he was a— it was you! Y… you're my brother, aren't you? — He's the Trever we were talking about who was missing, right, Destan?"

While a reassuring nod came from her husband, a sigh of relief caused Trever's bugged eyes to finally close as he answered her, "That's me. Though what's this about me missing?"

"You didn't know, did you?"

Taking the major hint from both men's glances, Trever replied rather vague, "Well, I knew you were sick and forgot who we were, but I didn't know you were still having issues with it."

"I'm sorry."

"Don't be, Everlyn. It's alright."

Trying her best to fight off a yawn while keeping her balance was Destan's cue, "Let me get you back to the suite. — I'll be back in a bit. Let me know if Traceur shows or drops contact in the meantime. — And Trever? Let Majesty Presley know we made is back safely… and where 'you' are."

"I will, don't worry. — Would you mind telling me if you're going to be down for a few days?"

"Huh?"

"You sound like a gargling whale." Trever almost scoffed.

"Oh," Destan smiled when he realized his voice still sounded rough. "I'm fighting something off, but I feel fine. It's just some cold. I'll be sure to keep in mind this is what a 'gargling whale' sounds like."

"I'll make sure he takes it easy." Callimay assured Fidus who was standing a bit off and stopped when Trever asked. "I'd say it's more like allergies, but it's the middle of the winter."

"It's just from the overload of stress and cold." Destan brushed off. "The doctors said it wasn't anything to be worried about."

"Very well," Fidus nodded and then left.

All things with Trever aside, I wish I knew what was up with Fidus. He's almost clingy and it hits wrong. ~ Eh. I'm sure he's just emerging more and more out of that frustrated and bitter state. Whatever he's got hidden inside was what Elder used, but now he's able to process it and hopefully put it behind him. ~ I... sure. We'll go with that for right now. ... And as long as Trever keep heading in the direction he is, I can keep things even-keel easier so Calli can rest and not use her ability. I know she said she tried to use it the one day, but I really don't think she understands how to do it. Which is okay. ... At least for a little while longer. Even if— I can wait a bit longer. I have no doubt once she's rested and able to use it, it'll all come back... just like everything else.

❦

When they got back, the giant fluff ball of happiness was waiting right at the door. While a lapse of thought and preparation on Destan's part — he wasn't sure how Callimay would handle this — she was thrilled to see the four-footed creature... even though she didn't recognize him one bit.

"Aren't you a 'beautiful' dog!" She gasped as she reached out; the creature snuggling close to her. "Oh my goodness... do you know me? — Is he yours?"

"No," Destan hop-kicked the door the rest of the way and then sat beside her. "No, he's actually yours."

116

"When did I get him?"

"Not that long ago," he reached over and rubbed the belvedere with his arm since he pawed at him.

"Who gave him to me? Did you?"

A horrifying wave of shock slammed into Destan at that moment. Her forgetting what happened to her mother was something he'd dealt with once before, but having to explain it again?

How do I word this so we don't have to talk about that all right now! ~ Well there is one way that is quite technical but vague at the same time. ~ It is the truth, and that's all that matters. "You inherited him from your mother."

She looked at him for a second and then sighed, "Oh."

Nothing but painful silence was left in the room, and the belvedere knew it; him curling closer to Callimay as he whimpered a bit.

But she didn't let this hold her that long, "Well, I'm sure there's a long story behind that all that I just don't remember; but maybe it's best — at least right now — that I don't know?"

Relieved she was content with her lack of memory and respected the likelihood of his full knowledge made Destan smile as he did his best to brush her hair behind her ear, "For right now let's just keep working on you healing. Then we'll sort everything like that out."

~ 7 ~

It amazed Destan how something as simple as music could hold so much power. But then again, was it so surprising? He remembered several times when his father was annoyed or frustrated in the evening; how his mother's playing relaxed him in what seemed to be an instant: *I know if mother were here she'd be calling everyone she knew so she could make recordings. It even might've been enough of a pull to get her and grandmother to reconcile. ~ Where did that come from? ~ I was just thinking. I really wish I had some recordings of her playing. It would be so~ Now just hold on. ~ You didn't let me finish. I'm not about to risk Calli relapsing just for some sentimental idea. This has been working since… it's been almost two months now. No need to change it. — But I really do wonder if there's a recording somewhere. She did play a stent for that one popular violinist. … I wonder…*

As he rolled over, he frowned and flung his hand toward the far corner of the room: *And what do you think you're doing! Get off the bed! Go on! … No. Get. Off. … I don't care. She's fine right now.*

Only seeing facial and hand gestures, the poor creature still knew he was being banished; whining and yapping as he pleaded his case.

When I'm gone you can come back, but not until then. He huffed as he eyed the pitiful creature that flopped down in the corner; staring at him with his big puppy eyes. *And I'm immune to that so just stop it. You're not dying. Hush.*

ᔆ

The morning passed by quicker than he expected, and so when he got back toward lunchtime he found Callimay walking around the room, holding her hands in such a way he now knew her to do when she was trying to remember something; him smiling, "What is it?"

"I found these drawings in my nightstand." She led him over; picking up the sketches. "Do you know what they're for?"

He took a bit to look them over — he'd never seen them before — and then replied soft and calm, "They're for your veil, looks like."

"Oh!" She dragged out and nodded as she took them back to look over again; moving her thumb when she noticed something. "Did… did I draw these?"

"Sure looks like it."

She twisted her lips as she looked at the page, Destan's first guess at what she was trying to figure out not at all what she asked, "But I don't need one, right? My mother had one, didn't she?"

Destan had been hoping so much he wouldn't have to tell her what happened, but here it was: her memory picking out that singular fact without knowing any context, knowing it to be the truth.

Of course deep down he knew it was inevitable, but this timing just wasn't good. It wasn't good at all.

"Calli? I…"

"What's wrong? Did I not remember—"

"You are right about that. I didn't mean… your mother's veil isn't wearable anymore. I… w… when she was— it was cut in two then shredded before we got it." Destan tried his best to get out while trying to keep as many of the details as possible from her.

While she didn't understand what he said, something made her shiver in fear as she crumpled the page in her hand; blurting out, "Why couldn't I save her, Destan? Why did she have to—"

"I'm sorry, Calli, " was the only thing he could think to say as he held her.

Not accepting his embrace she pushed back, eyes wide, "Wh… why did I say that? H… how could I have saved her? I don't even know my real mother. My adopted mother didn't even know about this place let alone— what am I remembering, Destan? It's scaring me."

The moment she crumbled to the floor the belvedere ran over and sat beside her. Destan kneeled down and tried to wipe her tears away; her knocking his wrist to make him leave her alone. He tried not to hiss through his teeth so loud, but she heard it and was scared for an entirely different reason, "Oh no! I... I didn't..."

"Easy," he took a deep breath and put his other hand out to calm her; the one which had been smacked now safely against his chest so it could rest. "It's okay. I know you didn't mean it."

Callimay buried her face against the belvedere and wept for a bit; apologizing while trying to understand what she was remembering... even though she couldn't remember it.

During this time Destan tried to find a soft way to help her work through these memories; him saying when she looked at him, "I know it's hard right now with your mind so fuzzy, yet it still has those bright, clear instant memories that jump out of nowhere like this. And I know the past has ways of ripping us apart inside no matter how much we try to move on. But I know you understand what I keep back I only do so to help you. I knew you'd remember this sometime or another... I just didn't figure it would be this soon."

"I... I found my real mother? And she died?"

He nodded as he bit his lip and bowed his head.

"It was at night, wasn't it?"

Knowing there was no stopping her from finding out, Destan sighed as he nodded again.

"The belvedere was there. And there were people chasing us." She kept on as she looked around the room, her eyes latching on to the fruit bowl on the table; her pausing for a while before finishing with tears running down her face, "Trisan. She said—"

Nothing was capable of keeping the floodgates closed. She bawled and wailed in Destan's arms for quite a while, not able to get anything out that made sense; and he didn't dare say anything.

For as much as he hated seeing her like this, he knew all too well she needed this. She needed to cry her heart out and grieve because, to her, this was the first she knew of it. How could he bear to stop her and tell her she needed to get herself together?

Sobs stabbed at the silence in the room, Callimay's eyes showing just how devastating everything was to her, "I... I have the capability to protect others somehow; not just talk to them. I did it earlier that night when we first met the belvedere."

Now he stepped in, "Under the stress and the circumstances we were in, you did all 'you' could. That ability isn't one you mastered yet. — And your mother stayed so we could get away. Had she come with us we might not've made it."

"But what good is me having abilities if I can't use them when I need to? I was under stress when I thought that belvedere was gonna hurt us. Why didn't— I'm nothing but a useless—"

"Callimay Rose Everlyn Nevrille." Destan said a bit more firm as he planted his forearms on her shoulders. "If you don't know how to do or use something on a consistent basis, then not being able to do or use it under pressure does 'not' make you a failure or useless. It's not like you did it — or in this case didn't — on purpose. You 'wanted' to save her. You 'tried' to save her: you fought me and the closing door to get back down to her. But your mother wanted you safe, and she knew you were safer away from her. All she ever wanted was to see you again and make sure you were safe and happy. She got that, Calli. And she wasn't expecting to. I'm not sure why, but she knew things were bad even before we met. She chose that night on purpose. Even before she knew about you she knew that was going to be her last night of freedom."

"What?"

He let his arms fall to his sides as he hung his head, "The blood moon. It's a day of mourning for Shadows and Veils since the Syndicate started using those rare lunar occurrences as their 'judgment days'. We've lost quite a few Veils and Shadows… and people we loved and worked to protect on those days. I'd forgotten it was one of the days I gave her, but when she said that one specifically; how it was the only one she had left… I started putting two and two together. Then when she kept evading my questions when I first talked with her I pretty much knew things weren't going to end like I'd hoped they would."

"She knew she was going to die that whole time?"

"I'm fairly certain, Calli." Destan soothed as he wiped her face. "But she got to see her little girl she'd been searching so desperately for, for so long. She had you in her arms and got to talk to you for what little time she could. It may not have gone like she hoped and dreamed it would, but the look on her face when she saw you? Do you remember it? … God gave her what she'd been asking for all along: to see you.

She had a peace about everything at that point. — I think the reason she couldn't find her Shadow Box for the longest time was because she had it out to look at everything one last time."

He gave her time to calm down, then reached over and gathered the drawings which were crumpled and spewed around: *You've been away from your job for how long, been under this much pressure, and 'still' do a great job like this? You truly do have a talent for this, Calli.*

The belvedere sniffed the one and then sat up and tilted his head as he looked at Callimay. She managed a half-smile as she petted him, sighing, "Do you think the design will be alright?"

Of course the creature barked happily and then hopped around; her laughing a bit as she wiped her face, "I meant Destan, silly."

"Oh! Me?" He played along as he peered over.

Even crumpled and creased — some parts smudged at this point — the detailed yet somehow simple sketches made Destan beam, "I don't see why not. It looks like you. And there doesn't seem to be anything 'wrong' with regards to code. At least none I can see."

"Would you be willing to take me to wherever I need to go to get it made? … I mean, do you have time right now? Or is it something that has to be given to someone else for approval?"

Destan glanced at his watch and nodded in a confident and up-beat way as he stood; helping her up as well, "I've got a little time, yep. But are you sure?"

Her legs felt like leaded gelatin; her starting to fall back. Destan caught her, but the belvedere was startled and jumped up; knocking into her accidentally.

"Easy, Buddy."

The belvedere yelped and threw himself away from her, then laid down and looked at Destan with drooped ears, "I'm not mad. — Are you sure you feel like going? There's no rush. We can go later."

"No. No, I'm fine. And I've been resting for how long up to this point? I think I need to move around a bit more."

𝕯

As they walked along, Destan had a thought; him hoping it would be a good distraction from what he knew Callimay was still thinking about,

"So… if you had to design my ensemble and veil, what would you have done different?"

"What?" She started to laugh as she looked up to him, stumbling since she wasn't focusing on what she was doing.

"Careful! … I was just curious is all."

"Oh," she kept hold of his arm as they started off again. "Umm—oh! Your arm's doing alright… right?"

"You're fine. It's my wrists that need special care." Destan brushed the side of her face.

"Well… I'm not sure. I… well I can't really remember much about my job. I don't even know if I could draw like this." She took the pages in her hands and stared at them; but then snapped to, "Not that I won't ever be able to, but right now— why did you want to know?"

"I was just curious what your thoughts were on the 'look' of my ensemble; if your professional eye had something against it at all."

She rolled her eyes a bit as she looked up, but smiled, "For as much as I know about things right now I wouldn't change a thing."

"And why do you say that?"

"Yours looks like you. Sure I say that mostly because it's the only one I've ever seen you in, but it really does look like you. I know you're not a showoff. You're determined and straight to the point. You do what needs to be done and don't let things get in your way. So I think it shows that. … I do remember how your veil wasn't your choice, but all that shows is that you and your father are so similar."

"I wasn't a fan of the split side seams, but, father had Seaxes — like you — so he had to have it like that so he could get to them."

A longer moment of silence was followed with a slow nod and a drawn out, "O-oh."

"What?"

"That made me remember something: I did it to look like yours, not so I could use my knives."

Why am I surprised? "Miss matchy-matchy." Destan exaggerated as he bent over and kissed her on the cheek, snuggling the side of her face. "What's wrong with my wife? Doesn't she have a style of her own that she wants to use?"

"Oh…" she fussed.

"Oh…" he mimicked as he stopped. "You're beautiful when you get mad. You know that?"

"Destan," she gasped in a whisper as he kissed her again.

"What? I haven't had any onions. My breath shouldn't be bad." He put a hand up to his mouth and breathed.

"That's not what I meant," she said hushed and wide-eyed.

"Well, what was it then?"

"I just— there were others walking by."

"A-and?" Destan dragged out as he raised his eyebrow.

"Well I just… I don't know. I guess… well it kinda feels strange as far as this place goes. I remember us being serious and formal here. So this all just doesn't feel right to me." She replied flustered.

Makes sense, Boon. ~ I know, I know. This is going to be a process.

"Destan?"

He smiled as he put his arm around her, "You are right it 'was' like that — and still is to an extent, I guess — but things have changed. Now I don't want you to feel awkward, so let me know like you have."

ℬ

The belvedere sat down rather pitiful and huffed, but waited in the hall and watched the two of them through the glass windows.

Little bits of memories — what felt more like déjà vu — started stringing together as she wandered around.

Destan looked around a bit and then called out, "Outfitter?"

"Doyen! Good to see you're back." He popped out of the back room, and paused. "Let me guess: I've got another veil to make?"

"You would be correct." Destan chuckled as he guided Callimay over to the counter so she could support herself on it.

Outfitter sounded rather concerned as he came up, "Are you sure you should be up and about right now, Liaison? — And what happened to your wrists, Doyen?"

"This is all because I've been resting 'too' much." Callimay brushed off. "And that is because he was trying to keep me safe."

"I'm fine, Outfitter. Don't worry." Destan almost rolled his eyes. "The whole reason these are like this is to keep them protected."

"Feelers?"

"What else?"

She smiled as she handed Outfitter the papers, picking up on Destan not wanting to continue this line of conversation, "Doyen said this would work for the design. What do you think?"

"The first thing I'm going to say is that: you know they come with sleeves, right?"

"Well…" she took a bit to think. "I guess since I won't have any that's probably why I designed it without them. — Destan? Right?"

Outfitter looked at Destan confused; Destan mouthing "Canary" and then gesturing with his eyes toward Callimay. He mouthed "Emissary" with his eyes wide-opened to which Destan nodded.

This guy really 'does' live in his own world, now. ~ Well in order to make sure he keeps his sanity I'm sure it's forced to a certain extent. ~ It's not an easy adjustment for him, I know. ~ Just wait for it to be our turn to do that. ~ If Outfitter can do it, then I can, too.

"Oh. Well then. I… umm… I understand why you didn't put much effort into that part. I'll add a simple straight sleeve and…" he fumbled, trying to sound sensitive and respectful while keeping his mind focused on the discussion. "I'll be sure they're easy to remove. … I… I'm so very sorry for your loss, Liaison."

"It's alright, Outfitter." Callimay managed a smile. "I know many don't know about it. I didn't even know for a while myself."

He looked over the sketch some more, finishing as he smiled, "I think it looks like a perfect fit for functionality and your personality; something that comes out in everyone's design whether they admit it or not. I'll get started on it right away so it'll be ready by week's end. I have the measurements you gave me last time…"

"They should work just fine." Callimay's smile brightened. "Thank you, Outfitter."

ℬ

When they walked out, Mr. Utree stood up from petting the belvedere; smiling as he explained himself, "I know you said to wait until you got back and settled in… I hope this wasn't too soon. Cill was bent on me getting here as soon as possible to see how you were. In fact everyone was getting antsy about finding out how you were."

As was her usual when she met people she didn't recognize and yet remembered, she stared at him for as she rambled about what she could associate with him, "Y… you. You're… you're someone I met on a Sunday. We ate at your home. Is that right?"

Understanding of the situation, Mr. Utree nodded.

"Pricilla! That's your wife's name, isn't it?"

"I'm glad you remembered my better half first." His smile grew.

"I'm not supposed to say her name, am I?" Callimay gasped when she realized what he was wearing.

"It's okay. She doesn't have a title so there is no other way to refer to her." Mr. Utree calmed as the belvedere rushed to Callimay's side.

"You're one of the overseers from the congregation in… in that town Destan and I were in. Right?"

"I am."

That connection was all she needed for her mind to be at ease and fill in the rest of the gaps; her giving him a hug out of the blue, "It's so good to see you, Mr. Utree!"

"I'm glad you were able to make it." Destan smiled as he reached out to shake hands but stopped. "How are things in Rayleen?"

"Continuing along as usual. Little things here and there that are shifting, but life is like that. — Other than the obvious with you two, how are things progressing? You sound a bit worse for wear, Destan."

"I'll be alright before you know it." He turned his one hand over and tried to move his fingertips a bit. "Should know more next week."

"He sounded much worse while we were in Brigon, but I agree he's still not that great." Callimay commented as she shook her head.

"Would you like to join us for lunch?" Destan changed the subject when he noticed his watch.

"If you wouldn't mind, I'd enjoy the chance to be with you both."

"Want to get something out, Calli? Give us both a bit of a break?"

"Alright. Come on, Buddy."

As they started off, Destan turned when someone waving caught his eye; returning the gesture to Outfitter. It was then he realized, "Calli?"

"Yeah?"

"Why didn't you do the whole, not remember but recognizing thing with Outfitter?"

"Huh?"

"Like what you just did with Overseer. Why didn't you do it with Outfitter? Did you actually remember him?"

This struck her too, "Oh. I guess I didn't, did I?"

A bit more time than he thought should pass did, so Destan repeated, "So…"

"I don't know, really. I mean I did feel like I knew him, but I didn't have that 'need' to remember why." She sounded stumped as she twisted her lip. "That is odd, isn't it?"

"Well don't get all worked up; I was just curious."

ℬ

While they were at lunch, Fidus rushed in and pulled Destan aside, "Traceur said you need to see her right now."

"What is it? I'll be done in—"

"She wouldn't tell me what it was, but she did say it couldn't wait."

"A… alright." Destan replied a bit worried. "Calli? I… I've gotta take care of something really quick. Okay?"

"Alright."

"Would you excuse me, Overseer?"

"Of course," he smiled as he waved on. "I'm sure Callimay and myself can pass the time."

"No, stay here with her, Big Fella." Destan pushed the belvedere away as the creature ran to his side, ready to go help with whatever he was going to do.

ℬ

Traceur looked wild-eyed with terror when Destan got to her station, her pacing back and forth at an alarming rate.

"What's wrong? What did Linton say?"

"I saw his body, Doyen. I swear I did! He was dead! I was part of the detail that brought him back." She began rambling, her clenching fists making the leather of the back of her chair pop as her nails skipped across it.

"Easy," Destan calmed as he pulled another chair out for her. "Just start from the beginning."

127

Taking the hint, she took a deep breath and perched on the edge of the armrest, still looking nervous and worried, "You said Aldred was where you went, right?"

"Yeah. So?"

"Well… Linton told me what he saw when he got there. He wasn't anywhere around. He saw a trail of blood which led into the inner portions of the city, but didn't have time to investigate; and those with him didn't care."

"I'm not too surprised they don't care, but the fact he made it out of there does." Destan shook his head a bit, but then sighed, "Not that I'm unhappy he got out of there — in fact it's the total opposite. I just don't know if that effort was in vain or not."

"He… he also said he found Baleck on the floor beside you: foaming at the mouth, hands contracted, back hunched over like some old man, bleeding out from what looked like a self-inflected wound. 'He' stabbed himself in the head, right? I mean…"

Destan sighed as he slumped back in his chair, "Yeah, he did."

"Why!"

"When he got done with administering himself Chameleon — or whatever cocktail he made with it — he started laughing maniacally and rambling on with himself; getting irritated with Aldred and myself more and more with each passing moment. I'd seen this behavior once before, but it was over a much longer period of time the decay took place." Destan thought back as he trailed off; then snapped to, "Regardless, I knew what was happening: he was falling into what is called frenzy mode — he was a cliffhanger. I didn't know why, but then Baleck told me he was furious I'd killed Elder. That he wanted to do it himself. … Sure he said he did it all on purpose because he knew how to control that 'power' he said I was too weak to, but I just can't understand after all he saw how he could believe that."

"You mean he did that on purpose?" Her eyes got wide.

"It's what I understood. He still harbored all the anger against Elder for killing Ginger while letting him live; letting him watch her die that day in Kerogen when we thought they both died. For whatever reason, he chose that kind of death as his only way out of the torment he was in." *Which means Aldred wasn't trying to kill him, he was trying to counteract it. But then what was he looking to get out of it all? What payoff was Baleck going to give him?*

"Wait. Isn't that what you suffer from?" She asked as she sat back in her chair and tilted her head.

Destan sighed as pushed his hair back with his forearm and leaned forward in his chair, "The exact same thing. It was a true out-of-body experience. One I'm glad I've had but pray I never witness again."

"But ho—"

"Calli." Destan calmed as he sat up and took a deep breath, glancing to where his wedding band would be as he smiled softly. "She's able to calm me from the inside. Her ability allows her to get through to me when no one else can. Kinda like what people call that 'still, small voice'? Well it's similar to that. …. Kinda."

Traceur sat there and stared at him. Destan knew what she was thinking so he replied, "It's alright. I'm not going to snap like he did. Getting to 'that' point of rabidness requires time and enough fuel on the fire. — And yet… there was something 'way' different between Baleck and myself. — Anyway."

"But…"

"I could, yes." Destan explained in a calm tone as he tapped the table top a few times with his brace. "That's why I'm always trying everything possible to keep myself from getting angry. That's my fuel. The glowing coals are always there because of the conditions surrounding my processing — when I got my abilities. But Calli's able to keep enough water on them so they don't spark so easily."

"I just… never realized." Traceur replied shocked as she relaxed in her chair. "I mean, you 'are' alright, right?"

"I'm fine. … Believe me, you'd 'know' if something were wrong."

"Why do you sound so hoarse?"

I must 'really' sound horrible for everyone to be mentioning it. "I think it's from everything emotionally and physically. It's nothing 'that' bad, believe me. I sound a million times worse than I feel. Okay? — So Aldred was gone and Baleck killed himself. Then what? Was that it that's got you so worked up?"

"Oh." Traceur shook her head. "Linton saw you had feelers on so he took them off and moved you to a different room."

"Did he say why he was there?"

"He said Baleck contacted the Monarch saying he would have you there. Apparently he contacted them several hours prior to say he had a high-standing Veil in his sights."

He must have done it when I took Calli back. Destan grumbled in frustration. *It's a good thing I pushed like I did to get her out of there.*

"I supposedly 'caught' Linton as he was leaving after moving you." Traceur continued. "He said the machine in the room was something the Syndicate's been trying to get Baleck to turn over to them for years, and worth just as much to them as you; so they were okay abandoning the search for you just for it." *Rather absurd that a machine is worth that much, but...* "He said what it was, but I wouldn't dare repeat such a word. It looked like some advanced incubator or space tube."

"It's a machine my father dreamed up and Baleck made a reality. — Confrere thought the same thing, but believe me: it's not pronounced how you think it is. — It somehow recognizes certain types of pain and doesn't just deaden it like pain meds, but treats and I guess cures it. At least that's how I remember Baleck describing it."

"Why was he there, though? And getting you out of there?"

"I was going to ask you that."

"I was afraid of that. He didn't say anything and I didn't ask. I was trying to keep things on track, but there were so many questions that would come up from each thing he'd say it felt like."

"Maybe it was his sign of repentance."

"Huh?"

"I guess you didn't get the report yet: last we heard his movements hinted to him joining the Syndicate. Yes, he's seen as the leader of the major part of the Swinchpucks who refused to put their lot in with Vashti and further blacken the name they'd worked for generations to build... even excluding her from breeding rights of the dire wolves and eskimos; doing everything to cut her access to them. — Obviously that didn't last long. — But what we've caught wind of as of late is that he's been having talks with Vashti; something he's never done. If he joins them outright or tries to play both sides in keeping with his known public 'neutral' stance; either does more harm than good for us in the end. But if him helping me and meeting with you means what I think it does — his meetings with Vashti an effort to gain some kind of intel we can use — we may just have gained another ace in our hand."

"Well, if what he says holds any weight and means anything: 'I' think he's siding with us." Traceur said slowly and quiet as she took an iridescent blanket out of her satchel. "He said take this as his oath."

"What!"

"He also said without this that the machine they took can't function for its intended purpose. That machine's gotta be more important than we realize. Why would the Monarch be looking so hard for it? Why would they turn down finding 'you' of all people for it? … Why would they want it in the first place? It's just some medical device, right? I mean what you said is rather astounding as far as what it can do, but it's not like it raises the dead or anything. … Doyen?"

But how did he know that? Destan took the cloth in his hands and set it on the table, running his rough fingers over it; a hint of Callimay's perfume still on it. "I'm baffled too, Traceur. It doesn't make sense that they'd let me go for it."

"He said it would be in safe hands with us and he would work to get us all the specs on the other part so we can replicate it."

"What else did he say?" Destan whipped his head up.

"He was doing a great job of keeping his cool, but between my endless questions and the time restraint he was under I could tell he was paranoid; like he was scared someone was watching him. At one point he just cut off and said he would try to get in contact with you directly within the next week to discuss things."

"If we can get the Swinchpucks on our side then we can cripple the Syndicate financially. And it'd be instant because they're the source of the Syndicate's ties to the Homeworld. If we can get that money away from them, Total Eclipse will be able to be set in place and we'll get this done and over with much sooner… and with what I am hoping is less loss of life and more hope of it sticking, politically."

"There was one thing he told me right before he left. He knew it'd be of interest to you, specifically." Traceur said rather worried.

"What?"

"It's… it's what I was all worked up over to begin with; and still am. He… he said… he said the Prince is alive." She barely was able to say.

"What!" Destan slapped the desk; instantly leaning over in pain and hissing for a bit before finishing. "The Prince, he… Tor— I don't u—" *How can Elder still wreak havoc on us like this after he's dead! ~ Because he did it before he died and you're just now finding out. ~ I know but— oh no.* "Did he say anything about a man named Webb? Maybe called him Dodge?"

"No. Not that I remember." She squeaked as she pushed herself against the back of her seat.

"If he's alive— did he say where they were?" He flashed his eyes at a now cowering Traceur. "I… I'm sorry. Give me a minute."

Destan walked away and to an empty room; walking around in the darkness. He muttered a few things again and again; stopping and leaning against the wall as he rubbed his one wrist at one point.

He began to wonder if he needed Callimay, but knew asking her to start right now would cause her more pain than she could endure at the time… plus she didn't remember how to use it, so really, how could she could help him right then?

But would it cause her pain? Didn't the treatment deal with that? Or was that something that would stay with her forever because it started with her other ability?

Even if she could remember I can't risk having her try right now. I can do this. I know what's going on. I've just got to stay focused and calm down. Elder's gone so I don't have that added temptation to keep going. I'll talk with her later about trying to figure out how to do it again. ~ Come on, Boon. You can do this.

Once he was calmed, Destan came out and found Traceur hadn't moved; him sitting down with a sigh, "Thanks for the 'subtle' reminder. I appreciate it. — Did Linton say where the Prince was?"

"He said he would be attending the Moonlit Mingle in Zervonith next month. Something about it being a memorial for his Duchess?"

"Figures he would come out for her. … Alright." Destan nodded as he started to think. "Get in touch with Ivan. Tell him to expect to hear from me in the next couple days so he needs to have things ready to go. And then get with Outfitter. Calli's going to need a new wardrobe and mine's going to have to change."

"Is it safe to take her?"

"She's the safest she'll ever be with me. And I highly doubt she'll let me go by myself, even if she doesn't know the Prince is there. — Is it 'in' Shipsherow?"

"Yes. … What are you planning on doing with him?"

"Hopeful— I don't know…" he trailed off as he tapped the desk for a bit. "You know good and well I tried to get information out of him and what good that did. I… I just don't know. I mean I 'do', but—"

"Understood," she sighed as she gave him the Shadow signal and stood. "I'll get with Ivan."

How in the world am I going to tell her all this? With the way she reacted with figuring out about her mother? Destan cringed as he started walking back. *And what if Webb didn't get disposed of, either? If she had to relive what he— God, please no. Elder's MO seems to be 'let one live and the other die' so 'please' let it be this way with those two. — God? Please let Webb be gone. I don't want Calli to be in fear of him again. Please. I'm scared of what he's capable of. I don't want him to hurt her like that ever again. And I don't want her to go through remembering what happened. I'm so glad she's forgotten. I don't want her to remember. I can bear that memory alone. Please. Let her forget. Let her forget this for the rest of her life.*

When he looked inside the restaurant he hated to know what he knew and how that changed what he thought would be the rest of this fight. He wasn't going to lie to her, but couldn't he wait? *Boon, the last time you tried to 'protect' her it did worse damage. ~ I know. I just… I don't want her to—*

"Destan? What's wrong?" He heard her sweet, worried voice. "You look upset? What happened with your meeting? Is everything okay?"

"I… we… let's finish lunch and our visit, then we'll talk. Alright?" Destan tried to smile. "Everyone's okay. It's nothing like that."

ℬ

Putting aside what he knew wasn't easy; but, since Callimay wasn't listening to him he didn't have to worry as much. Even so, he knew she would notice him being distracted. So on their way back he smiled and put his arm out for her, "So. Calli. Random question."

"Okay."

"If you were going to dye your hair any color — any color at all —
what would you choose?"

At first she played along, joking, but ended up sounding somewhat
hurt when he wasn't laughing with her, "What… I mean what kind of
question is that? … Don't you like my hair the way it is?"

Smooth, Boon. 'Real' smooth. "No! I mean yes! Yes, I love your hair
the way it is. I… I was just… a wig, then. What color would you want
a wig to be if you wore one?"

Comforted that this truly appeared to be a joke, she put it back on
him, "Well my own, of course."

"Oh, come on. Think really hard." Destan prodded as he smiled and
fake-pouted. "Play along with me. I wanna know."

While it seemed so stupid, she was a good sport and thought really
hard for a little while.

And a little while longer.

Finally, she replied, "Well, I guess if I 'had' to choose— oh that'd
just be stupid. — What is this all about?"

"What color? The stupider is looks the better."

"Why are you asking?" Callimay stopped and glared at him.

"You tell me what color and I'll tell you why. Deal?"

"Orange."

"Perfect. — Because we're going to Zervonith for a real quick trip."
Destan nodded as he started walking again.

"Why? What's there?"

I don't want to do this. Why can't I just wait until—

"What is it?"

*She knows something's going on so you have to spit it out. And
maybe she won't even remember him.* "I…" *You're right. Maybe she
won't.* "Does the name Toreon strike a chord with you?"

"Should it?"

Oh what a blessing. ~ Just keep it calm and keep it quick. "Eh, I was
just curious." Destan shrugged as he put his arm around her and
started off again. "He's extremely difficult to get in contact with and I
need to see him before we get much else done right now. He's going to
be in Zervonith next month, so that's pretty much the only time I have
to do so."

"Oh." She sounded upbeat about everything. "But why do I have to have a wig to go?"

Having to explain what was rather simple panged Destan every time, but they faded quickly when he considered the fact she was alive, "Zervonith is one of the three 'eccentric' countries on Sinpur."

She looked up for a couple seconds and then snapped her fingers, "Oh! You mean the place— do I 'have' to wear a wig and everything?"

"Oh come on. It'll be fun." He bumped into her a bit as he winked. "It'd be a nice little break, don't you think?"

"Going all the way there and through all this trouble just to meet 'one' man?" She grumbled under her breath. "Who is this 'Toreon' guy anyway? You're think he was some… Toreon?"

They were right outside the suite by this point and Callimay refused to go in. That name was starting to sink in, "Why do I feel that he was someone 'really' important? I mean why else would you go to all this effort just to meet him?"

I don't know about you, but I'm not liking her being so logical. ~ Please stop Calli. Please. "Well it's not like folks coming here is very easy. Especially right now. Let's go—"

"What aren't you telling me?" She shut the door and faced him. "Who is Toreon?"

Destan looked everywhere but in his wife's eyes as he tried to scramble and think of something.

"Is he someone I know?"

Somehow he forced himself to reply, "Yes."

"Toreon…" she kept repeating as she tapped her lips, then asked, "Is he someone you wanted me to forget?"

While he wanted to be jovial and play off of when the two were vying for her; he knew better. There was no stopping her now from figuring this out. All he could do was find a way to limit the "damage". A defeated nod was all he could manage.

"Then he's someone who is 'not' good." She paced back and forth.

"Calli, please."

"If he's someone who's tried to hurt us and you're going to meet him, then I've got to remember 'why' so I'm prepared." She stood her ground. "Why are you meeting him?"

"Well... he doesn't know we're meeting." Destan muttered as he scratched his neck. "And I'd like to keep it that way."

"Then..." *This guy must be 'evil'. What did he do? Where... why does his name sound so familiar? ... Toreon?*

In his last-ditch effort to get her to stop, he reached out and put his arm in front of her so she'd stop walking. And hopefully, thinking.

But, all that did was trigger her memory, "Tore— he... you mean the one who... t... tell me you're kidding. ... Destan? Destan, please!"

Part of him wanted to start kicking himself — he knew exactly what memory he triggered with what he did — but the terror on her face kept him focused on helping her work through what he'd hoped and prayed she would never remember, "I wish for the life of me I were, Calli. I... when I met with Traceur, the contact told her he was alive."

"But how!" She pushed him away as she started breathing hard. "Y... I remember... you told me he was dead! — Destan, what's going on! The... the contact must be lying. He can't come back. He's dead!"

"He could've, but it checked out. Elder saved him somehow." Destan tried to calm; Callimay losing her balance and falling to the floor.

The belvedere barked from in the suite and pawed at the door.

Destan ran over and fumbled to open it, Callimay clinging to the creature's lush fur as soon as he got to her, "What's going on! H... wait... wait just a second. There was another one who hung around him. He was even worse than Toreon. I remember. He..."

Now Destan was terrified.

Her eyes kept widening as memories came into focus, her screaming as she scurried away from the belvedere and pinned herself against the wall, "He can't be. Tell me Webb's dead! I... he can't... why would he b... Destan? Destan please tell me that disgusting—"

"I don't know anything about him one way or another." He knelled down and wrapped her in his arms tightly so she wouldn't flail around; every fist she pounded into his chest hurting more than his stressed wrists. "I looked and looked and couldn't find anything about him. I'm hoping and praying he's gone."

"He can't... not again, Destan. I can't... I just can't..." she sobbed and screamed as she continued to fight. "He's got to be dead!"

He started crying as he buried his face in her hair, "I'm sorry."

$$\sim 8 \sim$$

While they were out for their daily walk a couple days later after Destan's therapy, Outfitter stopped them, "I finished your veil, Liaison; but I wanted to make sure you knew Liberator stopped by and took it. — And I made sure to make it so the sleeves will give this time, Doyen. I apologize for the slipup with Liberator's."

Destan looked down to Callimay and grinned, "Ready?"

"You mean we can go right now?"

"Well you'd need to change so you look 'official', but yeah." He chuckled. "We've got down time right now. — And I mean the Veil when I say 'we'. — This really is nothing more than a fancy ceremony. Everything 'important' has already been done."

"Alright," she shrugged as she waved to Outfitter who was leaving.

As they continued along, Destan began walking slower and slower; worrying her. She looked up and stared for a bit, a memory hitting her out of left field, "If you need some time—"

"I'll be alright." He tried to smile as he put his arm around her. "I just hope this is the last time."

"Since Trever got a new title does that mean I will?" She tried to get him to think of something else… even though it was still connected.

"Yes. Yes it does." Destan replied a bit thoughtful. "Hum…"

"Who picks it?"

His face looked like he caught a whiff of something sour and rancid as he frowned, "Usually the one who put you up for a vote."

"What's wrong with that?"

"That'd mean Fidus would get to choose it."

"Well… it is a rule?" Callimay tried to encourage.

"No." Destan shook his head as he took a deep breath, trying to not be so serious. "No, it's not. And I think we've 'broken' enough 'rules' at this point that it wouldn't really matter. At least that's what Fidus was talking about yesterday."

"Then ask him if you can."

"It's alright, Calli." He smiled as he stopped at the door. "You get to say whether or not you want the name, so even if I did pick something you could tell me no."

"I get to tell you no if I want?" She acted so shocked.

"You already have, you rebellious woman." Destan all but belly-laughed as he threw his head back.

"Oh shush. — I'll get ready as fast as I can."

☨

As they stood outside Deep Dark, Destan paused and took a deep breath to gather himself, "Stay here while I get everyone ready, okay?"

"Alright."

"You. Stay. Right here. Don't move." He exaggerated.

"O… kay?"

She doesn't remember. "Just wait here."

Why is he so concerned about this? I mean it's not like I'd get killed for going in there. "As long as I don't hear you yelling or no one starts chasing me, I promise you: I will not move one inch." Callimay raised her hand.

"Good." Destan smiled and gave her a kiss. "I'll be back in a bit."

Callimay stood there and rocked back and forth on her heels, discovering there were knives in her sleeves: *Well that's kinda dangerous to have there. … Oh! They snap in. That's really handy!*

Seeing the tiny blade made her pause. She turned her ankle out and compared the rings on her boot to the handle of the knife in her hand and then bent over and tugged on it: *Oh! I have more? Land sakes that's quite a bit! Why in the world would I need so many? … And yet I remember using these. And I used them quite a bit. But when? Why?*

Several Shadows passed her as she worked to remember; nodding or smiling as they greeted her and kept going. And while some things were obviously still lost to her, this wasn't and hit her as being not just strange but extremely awkward. Every other time she remembered meeting someone they always looked preoccupied and detached. She remembered how Elder had everyone to some extent under his thumb, but those who were here were of a professional and serious demeanor anyway. Why were they all of the sudden "coming out of their shells": *This just doesn't make any sense at all. Why would th—*

"Hey." Destan repeated as he kissed her. "What's my beautiful wife doing? Talking to herself? … You've got a worried look on your face. What's wrong?"

"Why is everyone so… how do I put it… happy? And why do I have all these knives everywhere in my outfit?"

Destan chuckled a little bit as he brushed the side of her face, "Well to answer your first question: I thought the same thing at first, but I've come to find what — for the most part — is to 'blame'… and it's you."

"What did I do!"

"It's not bad, Calli. — I shouldn't have said blame at all. — When Elder died, everyone to some extent had a shock of reality hit them. As if their mind that was held captive without them knowing was all of a sudden released and they could fully understand and see what had happened. … You come in because they finally saw 'why' I acted the way I did. It reminded them why they're fighting: for those they love. Fidus said they had an 'awakening' if you will. They gained their lost humanity — concern and care for others."

She looked at him stunned and never said a word.

"Your eyes are so clear." Destan sighed as he leaned his forehead against hers. "You have no idea how much I've wanted to see your eyes like that again, Calli."

"So what about these?" She brushed off and showed him her hand.

"Those are your hummingbirds." He tilted his head. "Remember?"

"Hummingbirds?"

"Yep. Tiny little feather-like knives that'll slice through pretty much anything… if you have the right force behind it."

"Hummingbirds…" she trailed off as she flipped the small knife over. "Oh! Oh I used them— Justice Wan. … Your eyes! How are they! Did anything ever—"

"I'm fine." He framed her face. "That was 'months' ago."

Callimay pouted a bit in frustration as she looked away, muttering, "I wish I could just remember everything."

"At least you don't have to start over from square one every single morning." Destan reminded in a soft and loving way.

Her shoulders dropped as she sighed, "You're right."

"It'll come, Calli. Just give it time, and ask me if you need help. I… I know I'm keeping some things back, but maybe I've been going at this wrong. I don't know. … Maybe this all is a way God is using for us to grow stronger together."

It was something to shutter about when she thought of two people in particular she just remembered, but she had to admit, "At least when you do tell me things or let me know details I'm finding them out in a 'controlled' environment where I can work through— well, you 'put up' with me working through it all."

"I'm happy to, Calli." He raised her chin. "'More' than happy to. Okay? … Okay."

ℬ

When they came in, all eyes turned to them; the hundred or so people she could see snapping to and giving what she now remembered was the shadow signal. And with each step forward, little bits of memories started stringing together to fill the missing pieces of what happened in this very room and why Destan was so firm about her staying put.

Destan wanted so much to say something, but he didn't want to add that jolt to the list right now. She was working through it — taking it in stride — so there wasn't any reason to mess it all up. So, he put his arm around her and smiled when she looked up to him.

Fidus was standing with Trever in the middle of the circular room, him holding what Callimay knew was her veil.

When they got to the bottom of the stairs, Destan at first thought she was nervous, but the next second he realized she was scared. He leaned over and whispered in her ear, making her smile for a tiny second as she shied away; and then gave her a kiss and nodded to the two men.

She took a deep breath and let go of Destan's hand, almost forcing herself to walk to Fidus and Trever while Destan took his place.

Trever gave her a hug and then stepped back.

"You all know why we are gathered right now," Destan's booming voice filled the hush, startling her. "Cal— 'Liaison'," *Now I'm doing it.* "Was granted the right to join us given she surmounted the weighty task of passing the regimen to become a Shadow. And beyond anyone's expectations she proved herself more than worthy to bear the honor and duty of a Veil. — Yes, Fidus already set forth the official vote, but I would like to request a flash vote if everyone would indulge me and grant Liaison's request before we continue."

Callimay looked around to all of the approving voices and then back to Destan himself.

He took a deep breath and continued, "Fidus? You were the one who tabled the grant and was the original deciding vote. I see no need to deviate from such a precedent."

"As you see fit," Fidus nodded to Trever and they walked to their respective places.

Trever got Elder's spot? Callimay asked shocked.

It only seemed fitting. Destan smiled. *He was his 'disciple' if you will, and what Elder taught him — for the most part — was beneficial.*

Everyone in the room jerked a bit when she turned on a dime and screeched, "What did you just do!"

Oh geez. I didn't. ~ Ugh. "Calli, I…" he tried to calm as he ran over to her. "I'm sorry that—"

"What did—"

"It's okay." He pulled her aside and sat her down. "Calli remember how you used to be able to talk to me without anyone hearing you? That you could even listen to what I was saying to myself?"

"You're… you're talking mad, Destan!" She managed to keep to a hushed growl as she gritted her teeth. "That's impossible—"

She's forgotten something she remembered? ~ Minor setback. It's fine. Probably just nerves making it flare a bit. Keep calm. ~ I hope this won't be something that happens every time she gets like this. "You remember when we were at the Society, don't you?" He rested his forearms on her shoulders, looking her square in the eye. "Do you remember when you came to look at your grade; how you heard me say something and yet I told you I never said it out loud? And then you heard me a second time but noticed my lips didn't move? … Calli?"

Her eyes were bugged out, as if she were too scared to look away from him, but in reality she was working to remember what he said. She remembered going there, being with him, and even something about her checking her grade for some specific reason; so obviously the rest must be true as well. But she couldn't remember it. And what a thing to forget!

She took a hard swallow after a minute or so and nodded, Destan finishing, "I'm able to do similar things, too— it's nothing mystical or anything like that, Calli. Our bodies were injected with chemicals which have enhanced our senses to a rather outlandish extent. That's why you got so sick and lost your memory: the chemicals you were given weren't given correctly and they started hurting your mind."

"Those… those were real conversations we had?" She tried to catch her breath as she stumbled to a seat. "They weren't conversations I dreamed up?"

"No, Calli." He kneeled in front of her. "No, those all happened."

For a split second he was scared she fainted, but she was just letting out a major sigh of relief, "I thought I was going crazy."

"Are you sure you're okay?"

"Can I still do it after what happened?"

"Yes. Baleck said t—" Destan clapped his hand over his mouth.

"Baleck? Wasn't he…"

Not now. Oh 'please' not now. ~ You sure put your foot in your mouth that time.

Catching a glimpse of Trever and Fidus, Callimay blushed as she wrung her hands, "I guess… I guess I made a scene, didn't I?"

She forgot. Oh thank goodness. Destan glanced back to everyone to hide his emotions; and then turned and smiled to her, "It's fine. They all know you've had a hard time. Don't worry about it."

He stood up and turned to the rest and put his hand out as he nodded, "Thank you for giving us that moment."

A few hushed comments were made, but Callimay didn't feel like anyone was upset or making fun of her.

Destan took her back to her spot and then resumed his.

"For votes, Liaison, the one the vote is being cast for or against must use their beacon to receive the verdict. I am aware you do not know everyone's signal, so at the conclusion I ask for a verbal confirmation to aid you." Fidus explained as he draped her veil over his viewing box and looked around the room for agreement. "The vote will take two minutes as you've witnessed before — and I hope you recall to some extent. Your beacon should be set to receive only. And as I understand, the style you have would thus be two demarcations."

Callimay nodded in acknowledgement as she took a shaky deep breath, trying to smile; but then stopped and raised her hand, "Umm. Excuse me. I'm sorry. What's my beacon? — Did I forget to get it from the suite, Destan? I didn't know I—"

Destan looked to Fidus, part of him still not convinced he was calm and cool about the "informality" of what was going on, but was met with an encouraging nod and pan of the hand.

He took a breath of relief and motioned for her to come to him; taking her hand and reaching behind her ear. "Calli? You already have your beacon with you. It's right here. Remember?"

After jerking from hearing the sound when hers went off for a split second, a few more seconds of confusion passed before the lightbulb finally came on, "Oh! I had it put in not too long ago, right? Doctor Gerould was the one who put it in."

"That's right." He smiled and nodded. "Just leave it set like it is right now, okay?"

She nodded and so he sent her back to where she needed to be.

"This vote does not change the prior vote. This request I see it as yet another representation of her utmost respect for the due process in the Veil — not referencing her temporary lack of recollection as any sign of disrespect — and her desire to know first-hand rather than base her knowledge off hearsay. Even in her moments of fuzziness she asks for clarification. … A yes vote — turning your beacon on — will affirm your vote in support of Liaison. A no vote — silence — will let your change in decision be known, but will not change the outcome. … Are there any questions from Liaison herself or anyone else? I know that some of this may not sound familiar to you."

"I'm fine," Callimay put her hands behind her and smiled.

"Then let us begin. Set the timer." Fidus said as the lights went out and the clock face lit up.

Calli?

"Huh?" She whipped around.

Just think to yourself. He put his hands out. *I can hear you.*

It still sounds stupid. How in the world could he hear me.

I asked you the exact same thing the first time you heard me. Destan smiled as he winked.

She fought of the urge to yelp, and just shivered in place.

Remember to look down, he gestured as he turned his back.

Oh yeah. That's right. She replied rather nervous. *This was that scary part last time.*

This is nothing like before, Calli. If it were, there would be no way I would leave you there by yourself. It's alright.

Everything happened as every time before, the only difference being Callimay hearing what Fidus and Destan heard and her not scared of the silence and unsure what was going on.

When they were done, Destan looked perturbed as he turned.

What is it?

Ask your brother.

She looked over and tilted her head: *Huh?*

Hey, she's the only one who's supposed to listen! Trever rebutted as he pouted.

It's good to see she's comfortable with this so quickly. I wonder if she realizes it or not? *Just blame my suspicious nature, Trever. She's my wife, and if someone's changed their mind I needed to know exactly who it was.* Destan's eyes narrowed as his lips twisted even more.

I was only joking. I turned it back on at the very end. Trever rolled his eyes. *You knew I was kidding the whole time.*

Callimay looked back to Destan, still confused, while he shook his head and grumbled: *It's nothing… 'big'. We'll talk about it later.*

O… kay?

"You heard the resounding responses I assume, Liaison?" Fidus asked; trying to keep everyone's attention.

"Yes," she nodded as she snapped to.

"Could I hear a quick roll call of everyone who voted no?" Fidus asked as he looked around.

Silence.

"Then with that lack of response the only other alternative is that everyone voted yes." Fidus nodded to Destan as he picked up her veil and they both walked toward her.

Callimay tensed up, prompting Fidus to stop.

"I… I'm alright." She stammered as she pushed against Destan's chest so he'd stay at arm's length. "I… I was just having flashbacks. I… I'll be alright. Just give me a minute."

"Elder's gone, Calli. I promise you he is. Fidus isn't going to hurt you." Destan sighed as he kneeled down. "And if he ever dares to I won't hesitate to step in. Just take a deep breath me for me, okay?"

Fidus offered the veil to her; Destan nodding her on as he stood there, smiling. Though Callimay could see the pain in his eyes because of what he was going to have to do once she put it on.

"Outfitter said he only basted the sleeves on… whatever that means." Fidus whispered as she turned to put her arms in the sleeves. "He said you would understand."

"I do. Thank you for telling me." Callimay tried to smile as she leaned away and slipped her hands into the black leather.

The thick leather weighed so much; it was almost overwhelming. How in the world was she supposed to move with this on!

But the more she thought about it, she knew part of it was her being so nervous: *Destan's was never 'that' heavy and it's obviously heavier than mine. I remember that.*

Startling her a bit, the magnetic snaps — which truly didn't make much of any sound — felt like they shattered the silence in the room as they snapped the front part of her veil shut.

She was glad it was so dark because of what Destan told her — her face feeling like it was on fire: *I never thought I'd say this, but I've finally seen someone who makes that thick, bulky, heavy leather look beautiful. But you make everything you wear look beautiful. … Ready?*

Trying everything she could to keep herself together, she looked up to his glassy eyes and whimpered, "I'm sorry you have to do this."

"Well," he managed that sliver of a smile as he raised his hands. "I can't. Fidus has to."

"Oh. Okay." She bit her lip; trying to keep her hands from shaking and her breathing steady.

What's wrong?

"I… I just need a minute — like I said."

Destan motioned for Fidus to step back as he cleared his throat, "Before we begin — though I think it rather obvious and I thank you all for the help you have been through this all — I am not able to fill the role that is supposed to be mine in this moment."

Everyone nodded; a few hushed comments heard.

Trying to buy Callimay even more time without drawing attention to her so she could work through what he knew she was remembering, he continued, "It has been the standing code of the Veil that any member who is added and had a previous family member in our ranks — who died while fulfilling their role — should undergo this Right of Respect. … It is known by you all that Cal— 'Liaison', and Liberator are brother and sister. And it is also known their mother was one of us whom we lost recently: Canary. One who gave her life to protect the child she'd worked to find and keep hidden from our true Nark; and out of the hands of the Syndicate."

He glanced over to her, sighing as he finished, "It is also known that I, for one, do not understand all of the logic and reasoning behind such a right; but I will fulfill my role in respect for the valuable life that was sacrificed and my love for the precious life left to forever more bear the burden of that death's memory. — I ask my fellow Veils, as I did last time, to look at the raw seams and remember the raw emotions still felt at times by the person wearing that veil. Time helps us grow around our grief and heal what can be healed, but surpassing that, I believe the understanding and encouragement of others is what helps those in this circumstance. Remember the sacrifice, devotion, and loss, but most importantly: remember the life left behind. And also remember we each carry the burden of loss differently."

The lights went off again as a red light shone down on them, scaring Callimay as she sniffled.

I don't know how in the world you knew this, but your dream was accurate in that way. Destan sighed to himself as he came up to her and wrapped his arms around her; closing his eyes as he took a deep breath. *Lord? Help Calli and myself right now. Keep us strong. Help us remember the blessing of those willing to sacrifice themselves for* others; like we remember how Your Son did so long ago. Help us to use those memories to push us toward a future where we continue to bring glory and honor to Your Name. It's in Your Son's Name I pray, amen.*

"A… amen," she quivered as he kissed her on the forehead.

I'm going to stay right here while he does it. Okay? He took a deep breath as he took a step back and nodded to Fidus.

There was a painful silence as everyone looked on… it wasn't just Destan and Callimay who were emotionally worn by this. Everyone in the room was doing their best to show a good front, but so many of them closed their eyes or looked away as Fidus reached out.

His grip got tighter and tighter on the leather, bracing himself for the force he was going to need to break the thread used to keep this grade of leather sewn together.

Destan muttered something to himself as he took a deep breath, and then a series of pops and shredding noises burst through the silence.

Callimay let out what almost sounded like a yelp as she felt the sudden jerk and heard the noises; fighting everything inside of her that wanted to scream.

Fidus quickly dropped the sleeve and did the other one, not wanting to drag the Right out any longer than necessary because of her already fragile state and the immediate barking heard.

Part of him wondered why they did it so soon, but he had to admit that waiting wasn't going to necessarily help any: *Who is to say she would remember anything about this place without being here? Or that coming back at another time wouldn't trigger some other memory. … Or what I almost did to her.*

As the second sleeve hit the floor, Destan wrapped her in his arms as he whispered, "I'm sorry she's gone, Calli. I wish that part of all this were a horrible nightmare."

She replied in a what was nothing short of a mind-blowing, calm tone as she rubbed his back while the room went dark, "Mama was right. She said you'd protect me and keep me safe. … You are, Destan. You are."

When they looked up, Trever had braced himself on the railing in front of him. Even Fidus looked like he was fighting to hold back a certain amount of emotion.

Now composed as much as possible, Destan walked Callimay to the empty place in the ring of viewing boxes, confusing her: *Wait. Aren't these places for the most senior Veils?*

He smiled as he ushered her on: *We're husband and wife: a team. Different sides of the same coin. I'm the most senior Veil here, so— even if anyone objected 'I' would've made this your place. It was your mother's and rightfully yours. You've more than proven your worth to this group within the Veil, Calli. And even though I know your mother didn't want you to be here, I'm sure she would've wanted you to be right where you are if it came to that. This was what I talked about with everyone before I came for you. Everyone is okay with it.*

Destan gave her a kiss and then took his place — which just so happened to be right beside her: *Kinda nice how that all worked out, huh? Almost like it was planned.*

She smiled as she sniffled.

"It has been the long-standing practice that the Veil who put the individual up for consideration to join us should have the honor of giving our newest Veil their new title." Destan addressed everyone, and then switched directly to his second-in-command. "Fidus? You were the one who first spoke up. In your interaction with Liaison, watching her perform through various stages, what title do you propose for her which would show her worth and status within this body?"

"If I would be allowed to," Fidus began what almost sounded like a vain effort of procrastination. "With the rare circumstance this is, I believe you yourself could offer a better title which would show her importance and role to us since you trained Liaison. That and the obvious connection of you being married to her, I believe, warrant your position to do such." *And I was not able to find a title which gave her the justice due her. What one word could describe the immeasurable value she has been to us all?*

Bewildered at the comment verbally given… and nonverbally, Destan saw how yet again his second-in-command changed so much from the rough, methodical, logical, and one-track-mind man he was even two months ago; let alone four years. While there were times he would delay to find an answer in the past, the fact is he always "did" find an answer. He almost didn't know what to say, "I… I appreciate your willingness to gift me this honor. I admit even I am at a loss and not prepared to give Liaison her new title."

He paused for a while, scrambling to think of a title worthy of the love of his life. While this wasn't a permanent name she would have, this was a perfect opportunity to remind those around him of the Godly woman Callimay was and how that impacted them all. She was the one who supported him all along… in fact she supported everyone in that room during a very precarious time. She was the one who encouraged him to stay when she found out about this side of his life. — That is, when she understood what was going on. — She did so even though he felt he wasn't going to be able to "juggle" being a husband and the type of military leader he was.

Of course he wanted to just call her Calli, but he knew that wasn't fulfilling the purpose of such a title. It was also to protect her identity.

Destan started thinking about his father and mother, something running through his mind as he stared as Callimay's smiling, flushed, and somewhat wearied face. It slipped out when he talked with Doctor Gerould the one time and it was a perfect fit; though not something "original" by his standards.

It's just: would everyone else see the title as something acceptable for their situation and purposes?

There was only one way to find out.

"This name has held a special place in my heart for a long time, and is one of the words I used to describe her when I vowed to her on our wedding day my oath of love and commitment. It was also the name my father always referred to my mother by: his Jewel. I never understood why, and pet names seemed trivial to me — at best; but I now know it wasn't a pet name he had for her. It was the embodiment of what he thought of her: a precious and rare part of creation who would only be found once in this life and was given to him for the specific purpose of keeping safe and protected while having the freedom to be who she wanted to be. — You are my Jewel. And to whatever extent anyone else in this room assigns, you are theirs as well. The break of gleaming light you brought here is what revealed the thief we'd overlooked and been blind to for 'far' too long. It took such a precious treasure to lure him out; and we came 'this' close to losing that same, precious treasure."

There was a time where waves of whispers ran through the room; some not able to be contained to a true whisper. And with those couple audible remarks, it helped the nervous pit in Destan ease.

"Whereas this title may be a bit… 'nonconventional' to our usual style, the description and reasoning for its use is nothing more than what I see as the most fitting title any Veil could be given." Fidus voiced his approval after he worked to clear his throat; trying to find a diplomatic way to word it. "It is always left to the new Veil to have the final say whether or not they would accept the new title, so, Liaison? This new title is given to help add a layer of protection to both you and the Veil, in addition to giving a clear understanding of your role in the Veil. You have not been known by your other title for more than a handful of time, but being part of this group requires nothing less than complete secrecy and strict adherence to codes of conduct." *Though she already knows everything even though she may not remember it.*

And I don't ever regret telling her. Destan eyed him.

"I understand," Callimay nodded. "And I see nothing wrong with the title Doyen has proposed."

"Very well, then," Fidus took a deep breath. "Let it be known from here forward that the newest member of our ranks is known by the title of Jewel. All channels needing to be utilized to inform Veils in active details should be opened to convey this news as soon as it is safe."

There were a few Veils who left at that point, followed by a brief time of silence which Destan broke, "And if there is nothing else, let the Veil be lifted so the Shadows can be seen."

Any inkling of tension left in the air was snapped in an instant; it now feeling like it was more of formality than tension. Some came up and congratulated Callimay, while others waved or nodded to her before returning to their work.

As everyone went their own ways, Destan came over to his wife who hadn't moved and kneeled in front of her, "Calli? I know this may be a difficult thing for you to do, but please do it for me. It might seem a trivial thing as far as what good it might do, but it would make me feel a world of ease if you would. Every tiny thing counts right now as far as keeping you safe, and I don't want to risk my precious Jewel being taken away from me."

She tilted her head and smiled, trying to think of what in the world he was talking about as he took something off his belt, "As beautiful a reminder as yours and my wedding bands are… they catch and reflect even the moon's light in a brilliant way." *And they better with as much money as I spent on them.* "I… I got a new set for us until this is all over. I know they're nothing compared to our real ones, but—"

"I… I never even thought about that being a problem, but you're right! My goodness!" Callimay smiled as she started to take hers off, then offered her hand when she saw his eyes widen. "I… I know you're only doing it to help keep me safe."

Destan took them off and then slipped on the elysium set with black spinel which looked as much as her original set as possible. He then stood so she could put his on; though it was difficult with his brace.

"This is one memory that I've had for a while. In fact it's one of the first ones I remembered." She fought off some tears as she rubbed his hand. "It somehow feels strange doing this a second time. But I'm not sad. There's nothing wrong with this. If anything, it makes—"

"Everything match better," Destan made a face.

Callimay huffed, a bit flustered, but defended, "Well it's true."

"I'm just— hold on there. I'm not able to let our real rings just sit in this box." He shook his head as he reopened the box she had.

He had her lift the liner where two chains made of the same black metal rested. He took one out and slipped her bands on them, smiling as he handed her the box with the other chain and his band.

As he started to put the chain on, he stopped, "If you don't mind, Calli? Could I keep yours and you keep mine? Kinda keep a bit of each other close while we get through this last push?"

This little display of beautiful love and affection was almost too much for her; her trying her best to not cry as she looked up, "I… when did you…"

"When we were in Rayleen and I said I had to leave for a while… I know you probably don't remember, but it was when we went back for the Verde ball. I know it upset you, but I had to go get these and then make sure my 'real' band was engraved." Destan admitted when he saw that she noticed the inside of his band. "Well that was at least half the reason I had to go and didn't want you to come."

"W… what was the other half?"

"I… it was getting in contact with your mother." Destan sighed. *Though I guess that turned out to be a fraud. And quite possibly what cost her, her life. ~ Now let's not start that again.*

"Oh! Well, that explains why I couldn't go. — Yes, I remember that. When you got back I was talking with and 'for' my old stuffed dog and you thought I was talking about you." She smiled as she put his band on the chain and then put it on. "I think it's wonderful to have this little reminder of the man who loves me so close to my heart. Especially right now with everything going on."

~ 9 ~

Destan had more than the usual amount of stressful decisions to make in the days that followed; his voice regressing a bit. There was a day where he actually didn't feel too well, but he pushed through — against any and all of Callimay's wishes, "But you've got to rest."

"I'm fine," his frog-laden voice croaked as he continued with his workout. "It's not like I'm dying; I've been through much worse than this. You need help getting back into the swing of things so—"

"But has this ever happened before— and don't talk about when we were in Brigon." She refused to budge; her curling up on the floor and looking up at him rather pitiful. "Just because you're used to something doesn't make it right… or in this case: healthy."

She just won't make this easy, will she? ~ I for one agree with her. ~ You just never agree with me, regardless of what's going on. "Calli?" He sighed as he sat down beside her. "Calli I—"

"Your eyes are so bloodshot," she cringed as she reached over to him. "Why are you doing this to yourself? You don't need to."

Out of nowhere, he felt this spark of anger flare; quickly reminding him, "Calli? I… could you help me? I know I said— please help me!"

"Help? How?" She popped up and followed him as he started pacing the floor; her getting scared. "Destan, what do I do?"

She doesn't remember. … God? Please help me. "Just…" he put a hand out to her as he braced himself on the closest table; trying to keep his vocal tone stable at least, but still hissing, "Just help me!"

What am I forgetting! It's… I have to remember. I've got to! ~ But what are you supposed to be helping with? ~ I don't know, but I don't want to ask. He looks so ups… upset? Upset. … Angry. Anger. Rage. …

153

Oh no! How could I forget! "I'm sorry!" She yelped as her hands began to tremble while over her mouth. "I don't remember h—"

Seeing his eyes flare again made her stop talking. She did her best to not cry as she frantically tried to figure out how to talk to his mind, but after a minute or so she still couldn't figure it out.

"It's okay." Destan calmed as he took a deep breath, going to a knee. "I've been fine — as you can tell — but this flared out of nowhere really bad. … Do… do you remember? It doesn't hurt much, does it?"

"I don't know if I've turned it back on." Callimay sounded panicked as her eyes darted every which way. "I know what I can do, but 'how' I'm still fuzzy on. I'm trying! Believe me. I'll fig—"

"Don't get yourself that worked up. Just relax and try to remember. I've caught this one so I should be okay." Destan said even for himself, a growing part of him becoming worried he'd waited too long to bring this up. *Me getting mad at myself for slacking off about this isn't going to help a single, solitary thing.*

Noticing his shoulders drop, eyes soften, and breathing level off as he got to his feet helped her relax. She flew to his chest, trying not to cry, "I'm sorry you have to be the one to remember things I sho—"

"It's okay," he held her close as he leaned his head on hers, sighing. "I'm alright now."

Part of her wanted to keep on apologizing, but the other part knew that wouldn't change a thing. In fact, it might trigger another ember to spark. So she tightened her hold on him and silently scolded herself; still trying to remember how to use her ability.

Calli? Can you hear me? Destan asked after a bit, making sure he wasn't mimicking her ability.

Nothing.

Hum. I wonder how I can explain how I—

Destan?

There you go. He let out a large sigh as he let her go and lifted her chin so he could see her.

Can you hear me? Her voice sounded like she was lost and scared.

Yeah. This is what it sounds l—

"Something's wrong," she screeched as she pushed him away and looked at him horrified. "I should be able to— I can't 'feel' you! I know

I'm supposed to be able to. But it's like you don't exist to me anymore. How is that possible!"

"What do you mean?" He asked; fighting the fear that was trying to claim the top spot in his mind.

"I remembered I usually know what emotion you're feeling — even just your presence — but I can't. You're… it's like you're dead to my senses." Callimay's hands starting to quiver as she backed away from him even further. "Destan, what happened to me! I thought you said the person helped save me? Was me losing my ability the only way to save me? I have to lose you so I can live? I don't want that!"

Just stay calm. ~ Baleck 'could' have done~ Yes, but we don't know that for sure. Don't make this any worse than it is already. "Do you mean you can't feel the pain anymore?"

She reached out for the nearest chair and collapsed, trying to think, "I… I guess so? I hope so?"

"Just try again." He kneeled beside her and smiled, rubbing the side of her face as he encouraged. "It's okay if it takes a while. And if you can't get it right, I'll try to figure out how to help you remember. We learned how to use these in the first place without help, right?"

Callimay nodded and started trying again, but remembered more of what she was trying to say, "There's just some deeper attachment that's not there anymore. I don't know how to describe it other than I can feel you in my mind. The closer you are or the more emotions you feel, the more I feel you."

He took her hands in his and squeezed them as much as he could, "How about this: close your eyes. … Now tell me what I'm feeling."

"But I—"

"Yes you can. Just try. Tell me what emotion I'm feeling. We'll start all over again and learn this together. Come on. You can do it."

Destan could see her eyes darting back and forth even though they were closed, her hands almost twitching as he could tell she was fighting to figure out what he was feeling.

Flashbacks to what their time at the Society was like, it was a source of calm for him even though he couldn't let go of the fact Baleck could have lied to him all along about what he did.

A few moment later she blurted out, "Nervous!"

Thank you, God. He sighed as he bowed his head, his hands falling off hers. "You're so used to feeling the pain that it being gone makes you feel like you're not connected to me."

D… Destan?

Yes? He tilted his head so he could see her face out of the corner of his eye.

Is this how I did it before?

Yeah, he leaned back on his heels and smiled.

So… so this is how it's supposed to have been all along? I mean as far as how things were supposed to feel?

What's different now compared to what you remember?

"It…" she looked up and mouthed a couple things, her expression rather confused. "It's like it's 'cleaner', if that makes sense. Maybe it was my migraine fog that kept it that way. But now I can feel 'you'. … I know it's a horrible explanation after I just said I couldn't feel you."

He continued to smile as his eyes filled with tears, "I'm so glad that torture is over for you. So very glad."

She started to cry as she slipped her arms around his neck, "I would've gone through it for the rest of my life just to keep you safe."

"I know you would've," he gave up trying not to show emotion. "But I'm forever thankful you don't have to."

🕉

After a long but much more stable afternoon and evening, Callimay got around to calling Tabitha to get input on what to do for her wig; trying to come at it from a thought process that saw this trip as a unique adventure… and not a mission to take down the very same person who'd done so many horrid things to her.

At first she was doubtful there would be anything she would like, "I get it's supposed to be 'really' crazy and out-of-this-world, but what 'is' that? The color alone is enough for me to think it fits that."

Tabitha laughed as she looked back to see why Benjamin was crying, "Sweetheart, what happened?"

"Iza just gave him a hug, Mama. I pwamise!" Rose jumped back.

"Remember, you can't hug him like you hug your Papa." Tabitha gently reminded as she picked him up and rocked him back and forth.

"I sowy Benamin." Rose hushed as she reached up for him. "Pweeze wets me hold you."

"Come over to the computer and you can hold him there." Tabitha gestured as she started back. "I'm sorry about the interruption."

"Oh, don't think anything about it." Callimay smiled as she waved on. "You're busy. If I need to—"

"Oh no. You're fine." Tabitha said as Rose climbed onto her chair and she sat Benjamin on her lap. "Now be gentle."

"Awl white, Mama." Rose nodded as she whispered.

"Now!" Tabitha let out a sigh as she clapped her hands and sat down. "Where were we?"

"Trying to get past the fact orange isn't crazy enough for hair." Callimay made a bit of a face as she put her elbows on the desk to support her head.

"Oh yeah. Well, let's think. Now your hair doesn't have to look 'stupid', just flamboyant. … What about a flower?"

"Like a real flower?" Callimay asked confused.

"No. Take your hair — or in this case a wig — and fix it so it looks like a flower." Tabitha laughed as she looked in her book. "Let me see if I can find one. … Hum."

"Ooo!" Rose gasped. "Iza wike dat won, Mama!"

Tabitha stopped and leaned over to show it to her, "What does it look like?"

"It wook wike Mammy's tiddy tat." Rose said lovingly as she giggled; her legs swinging back and forth, banging the table leg.

"That's right. I— oh, I'm sorry Callimay. I got sidetracked."

"You're just fine." She sighed, sounding almost a bit sad. "What is the one she liked?"

Tabitha turned the book so she could see the hairstyle for long hair that look like the sides had been pinned in such a way to make them look like cat ears.

"Oh. Wow. That's kinda neat."

"Let's keep that one in mind, then." Tabitha reached over and got a pad of paper, putting a piece in that place. "Now I know that flower one was here somewhere. … Oh come now. I know it's in this book. … Where are you?"

"Why awe you tawking to du book, Mama?" Rose asked as she tilted her head, her hair following suit and flowing like a fountain across her right shoulder.

"I'm talking to myself, Sweetheart." Tabitha leaned over and nudged her nose against Rose's.

"I wove you, Mama." Rose nudged Tabitha's nose back.

"I love you too, Sweetheart. — Now! My goodness I'm getting so distracted today."

Callimay tried to smile, a tear not able to hang on; it falling down the side of her cheek.

"I… I'm sorry. I'll have Rose—"

"No! No, please don't. I haven't been able to see her in a while." Callimay said it a raised voice and then trailed off.

"Wear Desan, Cowimay?" Rose asked as she waved her hand.

"Both hands!" Tabitha gasped as she reached out.

"Oh! Iza forgot." Rose grinned as she snuggled Benjamin closer to her. "We don't wanna dwap Benamin."

"No, we don't." Tabitha breathed a bit easier. "I promise I'll find that hairstyle here before long, Callimay. I'm sorry."

"No rush. Destan will be a while yet."

Tabitha went and got a couple other books, unable to find the elusive hairstyle she had been looking for this entire time; but finding some others which were interesting.

At one point Callimay could see the cover of what was the first book, and as she focused more on it she realized, "Is the one you're looking for on the front, Tabitha?"

"Oh for the love of," Tabitha threw her hands in the air; her, Rose, and Callimay now laughing; sending Benjamin into a fussing frenzy.

"Mama?"

"He just doesn't like loud noises, Sweetheart." Tabitha calmed as she took him in her arms and snuggled him close to her face. "You're just new to this all, aren't you? Yes. I know. Just calm down. Shh. … There you go."

"When you and Desan have a baby, Cowimay?" Rose asked as she leaned on the table so she could get as close as possible to the camera.

"I…" Callimay said stunned.

"Roselyn!" Tabitha scolded.

"What, Mama? Don't Desan and Cowimay wants a baby?" Rose asked confused as she flopped back on her chair.

"Shh. They do, they just can't right now."

"Why not?" Rose continued to question. "What's so hawd about it?"

Tabitha looked up and saw Callimay was gone.

Meanwhile, as Destan finished drying his hair he heard howling. He looked over and threw the towel down, bolting over when he saw Callimay curled up on the floor, hugging the belvedere, "Calli! Calli what's wrong?"

"I… I don't… I can't…" she just couldn't get her words together.

"Destan?" He heard Tabitha call out.

"What is it?" He asked wide-eyed as he sat down at the computer.

"I'm sorry. Rose… well Rose asked when you were going to have a baby and why you hadn't already." Tabitha groaned as she rubbed her face. "I didn't know she— I'm sorry, Destan."

"I…" he stuttered, understanding why Callimay felt that way; and starting to feel that same pain he knew she was. "S… she didn't know and doesn't understand. It… it's alright, Tabitha."

"Tell Callimay I'm so incredibly sorry." She sighed as she looked over her shoulder. "Redje's getting ready to— Rose, stay here. — Oh, Benjamin. I'm sorry. Mama didn't mean to. Shh. — Destan I—"

"Tell Rej we said hi." He said rather somber as he nodded and waved her on. "We'll talk to you later. It'll be okay."

Destan dragged himself over to Callimay and collapsed next to her, letting her crawl into his arms as he whispered, "I love you."

"I love you too," she sobbed as she gripped his hair and buried her face in his chest.

~ 10 ~

The belvedere sniffed each, individual article of clothing stacked in two different piles on the bed. Callimay was all but yanking each article out of the box, huffing each time she chucked it behind her and reached for another one.

Rustling could be heard in the direction of the closet; the belvedere jumping back and barking when he heard boxes crashing to the floor.

"I'm fine," Destan laughed as the sound of the belvedere thundering toward him shook the floor; the air shaking as the belvedere barked. "Geez, Big Fella! There's no way these boxes could 'do' anything to me. 'Believe' me."

A minute later, he walked out with a box which was about the size of a briefcase. He looked over to Callimay due to the odd sight of green fabric flying through the air in what seemed to be a steady flow, "What are you doing, woman?"

"Why are all my clothes green and yours orange?" She sighed in frustration and desperation as she slapped her hands on the edge of the now empty box. "Did I— I 'know' I made sure to… ugh!"

"Huh?"

"You told me I needed to pick my color and it needed to be the same for everything. Well look… Outfitter made all of your clothes or—"

"Hey, hey, hey. Calm down," Destan came up behind her and wrapped her in a bear hug. "Mmm. Your hair smells really good."

"It took him almost five weeks to get this done after I finally got the designs made! He even pulled a couple Shadows to help because it took me so long. We've got to leave day after tomorrow if we're going to get there when you wanted; which means there's not enough time t—"

"Calli." Destan rocked her back and forth as he groaned. "Listen to me. Yes, orange is your color and green is mine, but by the traditions in Zervonith, the husband and wife switch clothing colors when they're married to show their devotion to each other. — And I think it's so you can tell who belongs to whom. — Anyway! They're the way they're supposed to be. I didn't bother telling you because knowing you, if you did you would've been asking me nonstop what my clothes looked like… which would ruin the entire purpose of you designing your own clothing in the first place. Outfitter already knew ahead of time, so there isn't a thing to worry about."

She sighed as she relaxed and leaned her head back against his chest, then complained when she saw the box he set down on the bed, "I left my wig in the bathroom on purpose."

"That's not yours." He chuckled as he reached over and picked it up; tapping her nose with it. "This is mine."

"Can I see it?" Her eyes sparkled as she reached out.

"No." He snatched it away.

"Destan!"

"I don't even know what you finally concocted with Tabitha. Plus, you're always the one saying, 'no, you have to wait,' so I'm putting my foot down: I get that same privilege." He tossed his head a bit as he put the box up higher so she couldn't reach it when jumping. "Besides, I've had my wig much longer. I'm not going to be the one who has to reveal their secret first."

"Oh…" she fussed as she flopped on the bed.

Destan was going to mimic her, but he couldn't help but laugh for a bit before finishing as he tucked it under his arm and started picking up his clothes, "I've gotta admit, I'm surprised Tabitha didn't tell you what mine looks like. She's the one who redesigned it. My first stab at it wasn't 'good enough' apparently."

"She said she couldn't remember what it exactly looked like since, and I quote, 'that was a wedding and two babies ago'. But she did say if she had remembered she would've told me."

"That little nark."

"Destan Quinton! Take that back." Callimay stomped her foot, the belvedere whimpering as he backed away.

"It's fine, Big Fella." He smiled as he leaned over and gave her a kiss. "We're just joking with each other."

"More like joking at the expense of Tabitha."

"Alright. Alright," Destan rolled his eyes as he took the box and bopped her nose again. "I'll make you a deal. We'll put ours on together so we can watch each other struggle; and be shocked at what the other looks like. And then thank Tabitha for making us look like stunning idiots."

Callimay laughed as she took his hand, "Deal."

ℬ

After dinner that night, as was their usual, Destan gave her another language lesson. The Yeronich language was one of the most — if not the most — intricate one in existence, but he knew she would be able to pick up on it enough for what they needed. And in a way, he enjoyed this hard task Callimay had to get through. One: he knew it wasn't a pass/fail thing since she would be a complete outsider; so there was no possible way for her to know everything from the start nor would she be expected to. — In fact, if she did that'd be an automatic red flag. — And two: he enjoyed teaching her extremely challenging things. It was what they first did together and what he had treasured for so long.

The only part he didn't like was when she would beat herself up for not getting it the first time. And it seemed to be worse now that she remembered she was supposed to have a little "helper".

She tossed the papers onto the seat next to her and curled up in his lap, "If I said it once, I've said it a million times: it looks like someone beat their hands on a keyboard and fumbled through saying it out loud, settling on the very first pronunciation. … Ugh! Chameleon isn't— I don't remember how to make her work."

"I think 'you' are just burned out. You're trying to learn too much, too fast, because you know you have Chameleon. 'You' are capable of learning without 'her'." Destan stroked her hair. "You don't have to be fluent before we get there. People would be more than understanding if you struggled with it, let alone the fact I'd miss out on getting to play the role of interpreter."

"But after all this, all I can say is: hello, my name is, and goodbye."

162

"That's where I started." Destan reached over and picked up the papers. "Let's take a break, huh?"

"Do you know how to speak Yeronich fluently?"

"Yeah. Pretty much."

Callimay let a sigh of frustration drag out of her mouth.

"But I took a year's worth of classes, Calli. A 'ye~ar'. A real, whole, full year." Destan reminded as he slapped the pages against her leg; finishing in a chuckle. "And even though I might know the language, my accent can get me in trouble."

"Really?"

"It's hard to believe but I admit I have an accent. And there are a couple words on the last page even I can't help you pronounce. Which is why I put them at the back." Destan smiled as he shifted in his seat. "And you know, as a total side track? I think I could get used to your makeup and hair like this. Not that I'd want us to move to Zervonith after everything's done, b—"

"Well there's no way I could get used to yours."

Destan let out a boisterous laugh, and then replied, "You should have seen the look on your face when I took it out of the box."

"I couldn't believe you were serious about moving to Zervonith when you were a teenager… and actually 'wanted' an emerald green rattail that you would need to brush and style every, single, day." Callimay messed with the locks of green hair that came down to almost his waist.

"And I couldn't be happier that never happened." Destan wrapped her in his arms and pulled her close. "Now! Back to the topic of my accent, Ivan said he'd be more than happy to help out when he arrives. It'll even help me."

"You said the one day he was your 'mirror'. What did you mean by that? Or is that something I just forgot?"

"I don't think I have told you. Basically 'mirror' is the code for those who physically fill the spot for the several identities — if you will — I have around the world. I obviously can't be in each and every place at the same time, so there are a select group of Veils who are very similar to me in build that don't mind having colored contacts and living in what can be called the lap of luxury." Destan explained as he did something with his phone, then stopped and set it down. "Well, maybe that isn't the best way to describe it. They have jobs and responsibilities as would any 'regular' well-off person in the country each of them are in. And they are fulfilling a Veil's detail by being there: it's not all fun and games. With their high standing, politically and financially, they've got major details to fulfill that can get sketchy at times. But there are nice perks that keep things evened out. Zervonith is probably the one with the most perks."

"How many are there? Mirrors that is."

"Seven including Fidus." Destan replied as someone knocked at the door. "Right on time. — Good to see you, Ivan. Let me introduce you to my wife. You know her as Jewel."

The young man who walked in, for all intents and purposes, looked like Destan's twin brother. But, his ensemble and veil showed he was quite opposite of Destan in his personality. And yet his voice was so much like Destan's: strong and deep with the unmistakable Kerogen accent undertone.

"Guess I need to be on the lookout for a Jewel of my own, now," he smiled and bowed as Callimay walked over.

"We're looking into it," Destan nodded; the slightest hint of a chuckle in his breath. "Timelines aren't cemented until after we get—"

"Wait. You mean 'I'll' have my own mirrors?"

"Wherever we need to go where I already have an established identity and mirror, yes." Destan replied as he took her hand.

"I know there's much to debrief on, but I know there's another pressing matter right now." Ivan panned his hand for them to go ahead of him.

"It's like you know Jewel already," Destan chuckled as they walked to the sitting area. "But, let's just keep this simple since she's a bit burned out. — What would help you the most right now, Calli?"

This was a good question; one that took her a little bit to find an answer to, "Why don't you just talk with each other and then stop to explain to me what you're talking about every once in a while. It should help prepare me for what it'll be like when we get there. And I tend to do better when I watch." *At least that's the way Chameleon is supposed to work.*

Woman? Quit using her as a crutch. 'You' are the one learning. She's really just there to help your right hand. Destan eyed her as he sat down; proceeding to have a debrief with Ivan.

He had a few slipups which Ivan and himself had a good laugh about, but for the most part he talked so fluent you would have assumed he just got off the plane from Zervonith — they both were lightning fast in how they talked, and half the time Callimay felt they were slurring words together. She found herself preferring Destan and Redje yelling at each other to this.

It took a while, but she was eventually able to pick up on certain words and phrases; being able to get the gist of what was being said. — Of course if Destan was talking about her it was easy to know because of the smile on his face and the sparkle in his eye.

They talked for a while; Ivan now giving information about the Mingle itself. And then he turned his attention, "Jewelra? Kreugne diada vengua ta ganka wick ne?"

She sat there like roadkill mere moments before impact; mouthing what words she heard. The words sounded so familiar but held no connection to anything. — Maybe if she opened her eyes more she'd be able to hear better?

Calli. You can ask him to repeat himself. Destan tried to help.

"Could you— I mean: breugne diada— no, diado quanpu uhh… wank diado side? Inpa?" (Could you-female— you-male repeat… what you-male said? Please?)

"Zinphanack!" (Of course.) Ivan smiled. "Kreugne diada vengua ta ganka wick ne?"

It was slow but she started chipping away at it: *Kreugne is would. And diada is the female version of you. But I can't remember the rest… ugh! ~ Come on, Rose Petal. You can do this like Destan said. ~ Can I? What is vengua, anyway?*

She tried for a bit longer then sighed, "I'm sorry, Ivan. I know you're asking me a question, but I don't know what it is. — You all talk so fast. But I know everyone will so I need to get used to it. Could you maybe give me a hint?"

"We 'do' slow down if the person is having trouble understanding, Jewel. I'm sorry I didn't. Let me try it again." Ivan encouraged as he thought about what he said so it was clear; him and Destan chuckling as he fought to speak slow and clear.

"Kreugne diada, vengua ta, ganka wick ne?"

"Did you ask me if I would talk with you?"

"Close enough, yep!"

Would you… vengua. What is it? She twisted her lip.

Calli. Destan smiled as he waved his hand so she'd look at him. "This isn't a test. You got the gist of what he said."

"I know," her shoulders dropped as she closed her eyes. "I just want to— want! Like! Vengua! I remember now! You asked if I would 'like' to talk with you."

"Very good."

"Goodness gracious. … Why on top of everything else did they have to make a new language? Wasn't it enough to just change the entire way they lived?"

"Because they could, that's truly the reason why." Ivan winked as he sat back. "So, would you?"

"Not really, but I won't know what I know until I try." Callimay sighed as she smiled at Destan. "I'll try it for a bit."

~ 11 ~

As the sun's rays stretched out over the sky the morning they left, Enforcer stopped by, making sure Destan knew their luggage had arrived. Fidus came by as well and told him there was a quick meeting that he and a few others needed to have; Callimay "officially" allowed to participate.

It was still as much of an adjustment for everyone else as it was for Callimay; her excited to be able to come in whenever she wanted. But as she followed Destan — stopping when she walked up to her box — the rest of the small group continued on to another area. He turned back and smiled, waving her on to keep following, "This isn't anything as formal as that all, Ca— Jewel."

The fear she'd had started creeping up as she rushed over and took his hand. Was there something she wasn't allowed to see, something she shouldn't say, still? What if she—

Just take it easy, Destan slipped his hand around her waist and pulled her closer. *You're not gonna do anything wrong or get in trouble. And believe me when I say no one's going to make fun of your hair or outfit. I mean look at me! They're not saying a word about it.*

She couldn't help but snicker a bit, but quickly let that fade when Enforcer said something.

Trever walked by at one point and backed up, taking a double-take of his sister. She tried to be subtle and get him to stop staring, and it seemed to work… that was until he came back by and made a funny face at her. And then he found an excuse to come back by so he could do the same thing; making it so very hard for her to keep focused on what was being said, let along her composure.

167

Destan almost got upset the one time, but seeing the look on both her and Trever's faces disarmed him. In some ways they were still little kids: they were treating each other the only way they knew. And Trever was the older brother who naturally knew his job was to get his little sister in trouble, knowing she wouldn't ever be in real trouble. — Who would dare get mad at his sister with him around?

ℬ

Right as they were about to head out, Destan was working on severing all the ties to the belvedere when his phone rang, "Could you get that?"

"O… okay." Callimay sighed as she picked it up, then paused. "It… it's a blocked number."

He jumped up and ran over, calming himself before he answered, "When do the Shadows rise?"

"With the afterglow."

He relaxed and sat down, taking Callimay's hand in his as he sighed, "I was wondering when you would be able to get with me. … It's good to speak with you too, Linton."

Callimay's eyes lit up as she sat on his knee.

"I'd enjoy meeting as soon as possible, but I'm heading to Zervonith to— Oh? … Y— you are?" His eyes got wide as he looked to his wife who was just as surprised. "I see. Certainly. … No. They'll be someone with me. … I'll send you information once we arrive, just let Traceur know how to get it to you. … Very well then. I'm looking forward to seeing you under more, shall we say, 'controlled' circumstances. … You as well. Goodbye."

There was a knock on the door followed by Trever poking his head in, "Are you two ready to go? Raven's fueled and cleared."

"Do we know where Toreon's staying?" Destan asked as he swiveled his chair around, part of him expecting to see Trever acting out again but pleasantly surprised he was calm and collected.

"At the Syndicate Lounge, why?"

Why would I have thought he would be anywhere else? Destan sighed as he tossed his phone onto the desk. "Nothing much. Let me finish severing the Big Fella's tie to all of us and we can go."

"Alright. I'll meet you there." He nodded and turned to leave.

168

"Hey Trever."

"Yeah Destan?"

"Thanks for letting Rocher go back for—"

"Don't think anything of it. I'm glad to use these skills, finally." Trever pat-slapped the door as he winked.

☙

A few minutes later they were walking down the halls toward the underground tunnel that would get them to the airstrip. This walk was going to have them pass much more "crowded" areas unlike when they went to Deep Dark, and just as Destan expected, everyone they passed had to take a double-take of the two of them.

In a way, this reaction made Callimay feel better: she wasn't the only one who thought she looked a sight. Her sky-high, vibrant orange hair was shaped and fixed into a bouquet of flowers with "adorable", oversized, cat ears — Rose wasn't about to let her not have them. She still had what resembled the style of her normal bangs, but they were almost as long as her normal-length hair. Everything else was up in super-tight braids while the lower part of the wig was buzz-cut on her neck. This massive, stark contract of orange hair to the deep, rich, emerald green color of her flamboyant traveling dress and matching coat made her look beyond disjointed; but it truly couldn't compare to the combination Destan had on. His spiked, emerald green hair with matching cat ears — a quaint similarity — and the long rattail which was tied only at the bottom, looked like the greenery top of a carrot. His velvet-embellished orange lounge coat and bell-bottom pants with a lacy, ruffled dress shirt screamed the vegetable comparison even more. He had his fur coat in his hand, refusing to put it on until he got cold… and conceding that he would at the latest when they got to Zervonith.

"I know. I know. 'I' was the one thinking of moving there in the first place, you don't have to remind me. All green wasn't as noticeable so it didn't stand out as that ridiculous."

"Just don't freeze to death before you decide you're 'cold', okay?"

"I promise," he chuckled.

It was still unfathomable to Callimay how people could think this was normal and wanted their children to grow up in such a culture.

Yes, they had the freedom to choose what they wanted, but they didn't get a choice to say no: it was basically illegal to wear "boring" clothing.

But then she remembered these people were all about the outward appearance. It was normal and what they saw every day; and from what she gathered, those people truly enjoyed that aspect of their lives.

This outward focus left some to be desired in the way of comfort… well at least for her. Callimay's six-inch heeled stilettos were a bit of a challenge for her to wear since her outfit was quite weighty and they were lace boots with only a ribbon sash to strap them to her feet, ankles, and lower legs. And then it didn't help her time away from everything was causing her stamina to suffer.

"Calli, I can carry you for right now."

"No." She smiled as she gripped his forearm. "I'll be alright. Let's just walk slower mister 'always on time'. Alright? Last time I checked flights are often delayed. And I thought we were 'supposed' to be late?"

"Gotta get that switched around in my brain, don't I?"

"We both do. But we will… try. Right?"

"Challenge accepted."

ȸ

While the jet ride was — for the most part — enjoyable; Trever wasn't as "understanding" as Rocher was with Callimay's fear. But let's face it: what big brother wouldn't take a stab at their sister's "insecurity" they saw being silly?

It was late-morning when they reached the eastern part of Yerlonga where they would stop to give Trever a rest and grab some lunch while the jet was refueled.

As they started the final descent, since there were only patches of clouds here and there, Callimay got a closer aerial look at much of the snow-covered world most of Indalla was. And yet there was this strict line showing where it was just too warm to stick. What an odd and yet amazing sight to see!

Once the jet stopped, Trever almost instantaneously popped out of the cockpit, "Who's hungry!"

Oh for the love of— "You, I guess." Callimay blinked slowly as she gave him a blank stare.

"You're 'so' right." He shook his finger in the air as he nodded. "I'll go find a good place and get us a table."

And before anyone could say another word he was gone.

Once back in the air, Callimay would talk about what things looked like and ask what other things were; reminding Destan of the times they would fly back in Rayleen before everything… changed. It hurt him a bit she wouldn't remember it, but then again, it might not have had the same value to her at that time even, as it did him.

He had the added benefit this time around of not having to keep an eye on the instruments. His attention rested on his wife to fully witness her amazement with the world around her. He knew she was scared to death inside, knowing why they were going, but was so glad she was trying everything she could to find a silver lining and keep hold of it.

This entire trip was going to be one shock after another for her. He'd done his best to explain as much as possible, but explaining wouldn't do "seeing" justice. Who knows what memories she still had yet to remember that would be triggered when she saw Toreon. Destan tried to figure out a way she wouldn't have to meet him; but there just didn't seem any way possible for that between how the event was structured to her stubbornness.

While the thought of her having this reaction did concern him at first, it hit him while talking with Ivan that anyone who was new always reacted with utter shock to pretty much everything around them. No one would be concerned if she did the same — they wouldn't know it was because of seeing a certain individual.

When they crossed the Bright, Zervonith came into view. It was coated in a thick, stark white blanket of snow which stretched from the Purity Mountain range where the country bordered Hagzell, to the western coastline where the mouth of the Flezlick River emptied.

As they got closer, Callimay could start to make out where the roads and such were; at one point her able to see individuals; these little dots of colors practically glowing against the white background.

ℬ

It was a bustling airport, but the area of customs they were going to be entering was smaller since they came by private jet. Trever sent them on since he had other checks and clearances to go through as the pilot and said he would meet them at the curb.

While a bone-chilling wind was the first to welcome them, it still was a beautiful day. It was nice they didn't have to walk so far for that reason, but for some odd reason her legs starting to complain.

Warm air rushed out to greet them at the doors opened, Callimay finding herself staring at everyone. Especially those who looked to be security. Oh what a test this was for her self-control! Of course they had their uniforms on, but their hair was… very individualistic.

Everyone seemed so friendly, so she was at ease from that: *I couldn't imagine coming here by myself. It was hard enough going by myself to the Society. Looking back, I understand why Mr. Ionba was shocked I was going. — If he knew I was here… he might have a heart attack!*

I'd never want you to go anywhere alone. Destan interrupted as he rubbed her hand. *And as long as I'm still breathing, you won't be. I promise you. If anything gets to be too much, just let me know. Hmm?*

She smiled back as she looked up and leaned her head on his shoulder, "I will."

Once they got through customs it was off to find their way through the airport to where Trever would be. Destan took his time because he knew the checks and such Trever was going to have to get finished aside from going through customs himself, but wasn't expecting what happened to fill the time they had.

A middle-aged woman popped out from behind a support column and gave Callimay a little wrapped box as she exclamed, "Ick sewn yariv ta jeek diada, Ruza!" (I'm so happy to meet you, Rose.)

After that, Callimay couldn't understand what she was saying: *Destan? I… I know she said something about being happy to see me, but what was that last part? Did she say she knew you were leaving to get married?*

Pretty much. Destan chuckled as he replied to the woman, "Ruza es gild teramooph Yer'nich." (Rose is still learning Yeronich.)

The lady looked so worried as she gasped and gave Callimay a big hug, seeming to talk faster now as she took her hands.

Callimay looked at Destan with a scared expression as the woman kissed her on the forehead: *I'm sorry, Calli. She's… how should I put it? 'Over exuberant' when it comes to newcomers? I was hoping she would be gone today. … Just be glad she kissed you on the forehead.*

I… just wasn't expecting it. She started to calm as the lady stepped back and talked with Destan some more, him translating so they could leave quicker.

❦

By the time they got out to the street, Trever was leaning against the cycle, "And here I thought 'I' was the slow one."

Destan huffed as he helped Callimay into the two-seater side car: *Just be glad you didn't have to meet with who we ran into. Though the more I think about it, the more amusing it sounds.*

"Seriously! Stop doing that." Trever jumped as he hissed.

If I start talking Lingual too much they're going to get offended and some might get suspicious, alright? Destan said rather direct as he glared at him. *If you would've taken the time to—*

"Fine. Just… just keep it short."

All but a pet peeve to Callimay when it all came down to it, but still something she couldn't help but notice, was what nothing short of the severely disjointed nature of every single person's styles in clothing. She couldn't wrap her mind around the logic of it: *I get fashion is a thing of 'preference', but goodness gracious. If I would have grabbed a dozen magazines from each major Homeworld culture and ripped out clothing pictures, put them together 'blindfolded', and done every color opposite of what was in each picture… I 'still' could've put a more complete outfit together than what most of these people have!*I know you're listening, so answer me this: what if people start staring at me for having what I am starting to think would be referred to as 'boring' or maybe 'strange' clothing?*

Yours is a bit 'bland' to use the correct term, but people would see you as someone in what's called 'transition' and not, Destan cleared his throat as he began to gesture in a grand way. *'Cultured' to the point that you feel free to let yourself go and not be bound to mankind's mold of expected appearance.*

Well at least using 'some' kind of mold would be nice. At least it'd be an improvement. My gracious!

Oh you just wait until we get to the Mingle. Your little designer self is going to be screaming her head off. Destan joked as he waved to someone on the street. *She might even walk out on you altogether, come to think of it.*

Oh dear. I hadn't even thought— she froze, trying to hide her facial expression as she waved as well. *They wear 'something' halfway decent, right?*

We're not in Medd, so yes. Destan nodded, sounding relieved.

Thank goodness for that!

♌

The house they stopped in front of looked more like a bunch of giant mismatched shipping crates someone cut holes in for windows and then smashed together. It wasn't a stretch to think even a five-year-old could've done a better job of making sure it was stacked "nicer"; but this was what this society thrived on at every level: brazen.

This three-story house was in the middle of town, right on what looked to be one of the main thoroughfares. It took up the entire block, barely leaving room for any yard and no room for any fence. Well at least no traditional fence — between the sidewalk and the laughable amount of a yard was a self-enclosed moat with the brightest orange Koi fish Callimay had ever seen, "They're huge! Are they all orange?"

"There are green ones…" Destan looked around her and then beside him. "But looks like the rare things have run off for the time being. Probably inside. Guess yours wanted to greet you first."

"Mine?"

"They're orange. Thus, they're yours."

"Oh. I guess I didn't realize how much you had to change for me." *This just gets more and more bizarre. ~ Whoever heard of someone buying fish that matched the color of the hair their spouse has!* "Wait. How do they survive out in this weather?"

"It's a special tempered glass enclosure that keeps the water the temperature they need." Destan explained as he walked up to the door. "Looking forward to unpacking everything?"

The door swung open to reveal their luggage neatly stacked right in front of the door.

"How did it get inside?"

"No one locks doors here." Destan steadied the door and then whipped around to pick her up. "Man, your outfit 'does' weigh a ton! I— surely there was a different fabric you could've used. I know you don't remember all of what you are capable of, but—"

"It's really not much heavier than my wedding dress, Destan. And I remember you picked me up very easily then. Are you okay?"

Her worried gaze wasn't about to win him over, "I'm just out of practice; it's been a while. I'm fine. But why didn't you—"

"It's warmer this way. Plus, this is as light as we could get it without it looking… well, looking—"

"Like is should?"

Callimay rolled her eyes, then asked, "What are you doing?"

"They don't frown upon carrying your bride across the threshold. And this is the first time you've come to my home here. So…"

While this all distracted her for a blissful moment, she felt more than a bit insecure knowing the doors weren't locked. When Destan set her down after giving her a kiss, she made a bee-line to the door and started looking at the knob and the doorframe.

"There's nothing there, Calli," he sighed as he came over, knowing what she was looking for. "But it's only the exterior doors. I can lock all the interior ones. — Most don't have locks on any of their interior doors even, but you'll see three locks on each 'important' door in this house as well as all the windows. And all for good reason aside from just plain privacy. Plus there's 'hidden' security I had installed because of— well I'm sure you get why. I'll make sure to double-check them every night. Okay?"

Knowing there was a level of security Destan set in place himself, she took a much needed breath as she closed the door. It was then she looked around the room and started to take in everything. It was vastly different inside than what the outside showed. Though she couldn't think of the architecture style's name, she knew it was a very popular one in a country called the United States of America during the very first space race during the twentieth century on the Homeworld.

She started trotting from room to room, leaving Destan behind. But when he heard a shriek he came running, "Calli!"

"I..." she calmed as she started laughing. "I just didn't know what you meant by the fish could get in the house. I wasn't expecting to be able to walk into their 'home', if you will."

He closed his eyes and took a deep breath, then tried to keep from laughing when he saw his wife standing in the mid-calf water with pretty much all of the green Koi fish surrounding her, "Looks like you've got a fan club. — Told you they'd be in here, didn't I?"

"Well duh, I'm the same color as them! They probably think I'm some over-grown queen Koi or something." Callimay bantered as she picked up her drenched skirt and started tip-toeing back. "Stop biting my skirt! Shoo! I don't want to step on you. Please move. I d— ah!"

Destan rushed over and reached out to catch her so she wouldn't face plant into the water, "You're too nice to them. 'Make' them get out of your way. They can handle it. Believe me."

"I... I'm sorry." She blushed as she gained her footing and hopped back. "I didn't... I..."

"It's alright. ... Calli?" He reached for her hand.

Still dodging his gaze, she pulled back, "I... I should go get changed. Could... could you bring, well, any of the luggage up? I can find something for the time being."

"A... alright." Destan replied a bit stunned. "Calli, really. I'm fine. It's alright. That didn't— Calli?"

❦

This distance between them did nothing but become wider, and it was beginning to annoy Destan. That night at dinner he moved his seat so he was right next to her, but she wouldn't pay much attention to him. He sighed as he turned in his seat, bending over so he could see her face, "What's wrong? You've been distracted like this since y—"

"I... I'm just trying to help." She fiddled with the orange peels on her plate, trying her best to hide she was crying. "I know it's h—"

"I'm alright." Destan blinked slowly as he groaned; putting his arm around her and leaning his head against hers. "Yes, it's hard at times; but I've had a couple hard reminders as of late to keep things in perspective: I have you with me. You're alive, you're alright, you're not in pain, and bless The Lord your memory came back. Seeing you smile and hearing you laugh is what matters most to me because that means you're here with me. … Remember what you told me? How, 'as long as you can keep going I can too'? Well I 'can' keep going, I promise you, Calli. But in that I need you to tell me if something is wrong. … 'Is' there something wrong?"

"I just know you have so much weighing on you in every other area." She sounded so depressed as she took his hand, still not looking at him. "And I— I just want to help like I'm supposed to; not make things harder. Especially not now."

"It wasn't your fault that happened earlier. Those green Koi can be more than the usual type of stubborn. I've tripped over them a time or two myself." He tried to pull her up from this emotional pit she let herself fall into. "And I didn't have anyone to catch me."

"You mean—"

"I've face planted a few times in that water; wig and all. — I should've said outright about them having free range of the floor in the drawing room, that's my bad. — Everything's in the past and there's nothing to worry about, alright? It's not like me catching you was sinful or anything. … Calli? Calli I'm okay. Please— Calli look at me. You're my wife and I'm your husband. I know the first part of our marriage was very… lacking. And by that I mean in 'all' areas, though that one's kinda at the forefront with all this. … And then when things finally started changing we made that promise; but it isn't one that'll last our entire lives. I know everything piled on top of each other makes moments like those really awkward, but don't think of them as being sinful and evil. Okay? I know you're doing everything you can to help. That wasn't your fault. I know it was an accident. And I'm okay. And the bottom line is: that wasn't wrong. Okay?"

"Okay."

"Good. Now let's get these dishes thrown in the washer and get ready for bed. Huh?"

~ 12 ~

Before she knew it, the big night arrived. Even though they'd spent so much time talking things over — what various backup plans would be in place if different things happened — Callimay felt she was still a knotted bundle of nerves with no clue what to expect. It got so bad she couldn't get anything with her outfit, makeup, jewelry, wig… nothing would cooperate.

And so she waited for Destan to get done on the phone so he could help her with even the tiniest of things.

"For as much as we'll ever know, he doesn't know we're here, Calli. And hopefully by the time he figures it out it'll be too late." Destan tried to comfort as he double-checked her wig. "How does it feel now?"

"Better." She took a shaky breath as she handed him her necklace.

"Now I'm not saying to 'get a grip' or 'don't be nervous'… that might strike everyone as a bit strange with you being so new to this. And I'd never ask you to do it especially under these circumstances." He twisted his lips as he fat-fingered his efforts to get the clasp to open. "Just… just try to think of this as a strange dinner party and dance; and do your best to forget about Toreon. … I know it'll be hard, but try, Calli. Alright? I know this is still a mission, but I'm gonna tell you right now I can see how you do better being caught off guard when you need to do something super important. And it's not bad to be like that, okay? In fact that's really helpful; you blend in better so you can stay hidden longer. Which also means you stay safe longer. Now deep breath. … And now look at me. … I love you."

"I love you too," she smiled.

"Now. Put your hands out." Destan lifted them and let them go, them steady as ever. "Good. Now you can do me a favor."

"What?"

"Make sure I look presentable… by the standard here."

"I… Destan." She groaned as she took the brush from his hand as he sat down.

"Calli?" He exaggerated as he looked up over his shoulder at her.

"Fine. Just promise me you'll never 'ever' wear makeup when we leave here. And I mean 'ever'!"

"You have my word."

After all the "pleasantries" were out of the way and she checked his outfit once more, she looked at the clock, "I'll admit, being an hour late to such a formal even seems… well, wrong. And then the dances they do? It still doesn't make much sense."

He smiled, "It's not 'that' different. You still have to follow my lead, and you're amazing at picking up on anything I do. Plus, once you see it being done I'm sure you'll get right into it."

"Let's hope Chameleon is wanting to work tonight."

"Oh come now. You were doing fine before you knew about her. — Now where's my ray of sunshine?" Destan lifted her chin.

"She's right here." Callimay sighed as she gave him a hug. "Why didn't you give me a name like Sunshine or Ray?"

"Why do you think?"

"Yeah. Neither sound the slightest bit 'spyish'. Jewel is borderline, but works." She started fiddling with her handkerchief, trying to not sound nervous as she laughed.

"Just stay close to me. Everything will be alright." Destan closed his eyes as he pulled her close. "I'm right here."

🕉

As they stood and looked up to the grand stairs that led to the hall, the pulsating sound of Classical Electronica-fused music making the air tingle; this all reminded Callimay to brace herself for an experience she never thought possible. It was at that moment the part of her that was a bundle of nerves felt more understandable: she felt like this because she was excited to see what this was like. Yes, she was terrified in a certain aspect, but getting to attend a Mingle wasn't something just anyone got to do… even if you did live in Zervonith. This was a once-in-a-lifetime chance she wasn't going to squander, part of her critical about fashion bracing to be driven insane included.

Destan's persona did a total flip and was in "undercover mission" Doyen mode — technically known as deep recluse — but it wasn't something anyone but Callimay could notice. He embraced every fiber of the culture he'd planned to be part of and with all the flare and fanfare; taking his wife's hand and starting to strut up the steps while photographers snapped endless shots of them. All the while each step keeping perfect time to the tempo of the music he could hear.

He was enjoying this "showing off".

This all served as encouragement to her: *It's go time, Rose Petal.*

They stopped outside the door and Destan took his cane off his belt and smacked it on the ground.

The doors slid apart inch by inch, the music and atmosphere of the building rushing out to greet and whisk them away for the evening.

Two men — one from each side — skated up to and around them before taking their coats and asking Destan's name. They then nodded and left.

Okay. That wasn't too bad. ~ Their outfits? ~ Like I said: it wasn't 'too' bad. I 'can' do this.

Yes you can. Destan squeezed her hand, him winking when she looked up to him.

As the music stopped, everyone turned their backs to Callimay and Destan as an announcement of their arrival was given.

Once the music came back on, everyone went back to what they were doing… ignoring them. — They had to go to people to get them to say hello.

Okay, fine. They 'have' to do something different just for the sake of being different. But really? I mean what is wrong with these people! It's not like there's anything so 'binding' in society about acknowledging someone and saying hello. I mean manners do exist here, right?

He couldn't help but chuckle to himself, but let her mind flesh out what she needed to. This "distraction" was going to work in her favor on more than the front of blending in with everyone… it was going to keep her from obsessing over Toreon: *Maybe we should've gone out more like this the past few days. Maybe that would've helped her sleep better. ~ At least she kept her memories under all this stress. ~ And I can't be more thankful for that, let me tell you. I was scared to death when she woke up screaming last night.*

While she knew it was to be expected, she still hated what many referred to — in the most brazen, endearing way — as her "pathetic" knowledge of the language. It made all of her interactions so long and tedious. Plus she was depending on Destan to focus on that instead of everything else.

Several of the women complemented Callimay's dress, but she could tell there was still some sort of distain in their tones. — That and the comments they made to themselves. — She didn't know everything they said, and for good reason, but was able to put together how they were less than thrilled with her choice. A couple even offered to take her to their couturier to give her a "proper" wardrobe: *Calli, don't worry about it.*

But I tried so hard! And this was my 'job'! I got 'paid' to do this! Callimay's sigh sounded more like a fume of anger as she fought her stinging eyes. *I know I'm still trying to remember that all, but even Outfitter said I was—*

Watch this. Destan winked as he interrupted the lady speaking with them, "Ruza tadend here boluse hereowenus." (Rose designed her dress herself)

"Usafa fesznku ne!" (Forgive stupid me) She said wide-eyed as she kneeled in front of Callimay. "Ki apukagize." (I apologize)

"Diada… kuden ko— toe. Toe." (You didn't see— know) Callimay stammered as she frantically reached out and helped her to her feet.

The word about her designing her own outfits spread quicker than Callimay had even seen a rumor at the Society move. And yet unlike the Society, a half-dozen women came up to her and apologized for their comments they made earlier.

I'd say for as much as they disregard so many 'normal' traditions and rules as well as basic courtesy, they at least admit when they go too far. If that's anything. She tried to find the bright side. *I mean they even came up themselves to do it.*

The end doesn't justify the means, though: it's because of their image being tarnished that they go overboard like this. … Guess that really didn't help you any, did it? I'm sorry, Calli.

I know you did it to try and help me. I mean they're not Christians, so I have to keep that in mind; but they still have the choice to say anything at all. And some are actually honest about the apology which I admire and am thankful for. — You're right. I shouldn't worry about this. It's not like we're gonna live here or my reputation of being a designer, which doesn't exist, hinges on whether or not I can design clothes to suit their styles. Callimay replied more confident as the music stopped.

Don't look back, Destan put his arm around her and turned her back to himself. *Remember? For formal introductions to groups the group turns their backs. *

"Unava Unavo, hunep finds toon dine booka: Toruon Philpod, Lyton Swinpook." (Ladies and Gentlemen, our special guests for this evening: Toreon Philpod, Linton Swinchpuck)

Callimay's confidence ran as far away as fast as possible. The instant thought of her disguise not enough to keep Toreon from recognizing her paralyzed her. She remembered how Dakoe said Toreon could see through his masks when he would shapeshift… so how would the one she was wearing be any different? And her voice? There was only so much she could do naturally to make it different even when fumbling to speak a new language.

But feeling the firm, strong hold of her husband's hand on hers made her pause: *You can do this Rose Petal. Destan needs you. Calm down. Be like Canary was: a true warrior under immense pressure. You're her daughter. You can do this. ~ Mama had done it much longer than me at that point in time, though. ~ He's more likely to figure things out if you avoid him or don't talk to him. ~ I know. I just wish I had more time. I'm not ready. Not that I ever would be but I didn't think he was supposed to be here yet. Destan said he wouldn't get here until we'd been here about two hours. ~ Just stay with Destan and things will be alright.*

The music started back up so they went about their business, but it appeared Toreon's attention immediately rested on them.

Linton escorted him to them, acting as an intermediary for their entire conversation.

During the introductions they had with another pair, it hit Callimay: *He's going to know I understand what he says.*

Yes, he will, but if he has regard for the culture here as I think he does, he won't dare directly speak to you using Lingual. — Directly, that is. — And he should also assume you've given it up and won't respond to it any longer. So just go with it for now.

A… alright.

"Diado arm newne." (You are early) Destan's higher tone squeaked out a greeting as he hugged Linton. *I got your oath.*

"Ki apukagize tweed krequed finaze. Tweed desirque hoove june evoone wick diade." (I apologize we broke custom. We wanted to spend more time with you all.) Linton translated as he nodded to both Destan and Callimay — his eyes resting on her. *Can you hear me?*

She smiled as did Destan as they looked at each other and nodded.

Tonight won't work. It will have to be at some other time.

"Ki funve." (I understand) Destan nodded as Toreon came over and gave him a hug.

Destan kept his cool so well during the entire conversation. His emotions kept stable and this helped Callimay calm and "go with it" like he told her to.

And then something clicked… as if her training fully came back to her. Even Destan could tell this and it helped him be at ease knowing she was ready to do her part and make sure this evening was as productive as possible in light of this setback with Linton.

"Could you tell them I heard about their recent marriage?" Toreon asked Linton. "And tell them I brought a gift for the bride."

Lindon nodded and translated; almost sounding nervous.

They both thanked him for the gift and soon sent him on his way to mingle with the others so they could settle into their place as members of this group of people who were there to enjoy the evening; biding their time for what was coming.

Callimay switched so she was listening to everyone while Destan would switch between Ingrid and Toreon's abilities to keep an eye on everything: *Everlyn? Destan?*

Yes Trever? Destan replied.

You've got Falconers swarming outside.

I know. Destan sighed as he looked in the direction of the main entrance. *Any sign of 'you-know-who'?*

Not that I can see. Maybe he 'is' dead.

I can only hope. … Calli had a nightmare last night that made me wonder. She kept crying and saying everything seemed so real, seeing Toreon in our bedroom.

I'll keep an eye out. Trever continued to scan the area. *They're heading in but through a side door.*

Probably to the private vestibules. I'm sure Toreon will be there part of the time. Destan continued to take surveillance. *And with Elder's protection now gone he's got to take extra precautions. How many would you say there are?*

I'd count at least two score. … Should I take Everlyn out yet?

Destan looked at her: *I'll let you make that call.*

I'm fine, Trever. She sounded determined and confident. *As long as he doesn't know who we are and Destan feels things are at least semi-controlled, I'll stay. I've got to for us to have the best chance at catching him.*

Alright.

After they talked with the various couples Destan said he wanted to make contact with, Callimay asked surprised: *They think glitter is an actual color here?*

Huh?

Look at that girl's dress and her hair. They're nothing but glitter — no single color.

Oh! Destan chuckled to himself. *Yeah, it's a 'color' in that sense.*

You mean I could've chosen that!

Absolutely not. Destan reprimanded, though there seemed to be a hint of sarcasm in his voice. *I can put up with wearing a wig that's long and some makeup, but you'll never catch me wearing anything with glitter on it.*

What about your wedding band?

I… Destan realized he'd been caught on a technicality, but didn't let it sidetrack him. *Okay. Okay. — But as much as I'm joking about everything there is a point about it which is true. You couldn't wear glitter even if you wanted to.*

Why not?

It's a color reserved for women who intend on staying single.

Oh. … You mean they make that decision in their teens?

Some, yes. Destan nodded as the music stopped and they turned their backs to the stage. *But most do it if they were 'left at the altar' so to say, or if they were cheated on and now divorced. Odd, but true: to remarry here is basically illegal —frowned upon to the point you'd be kicked out of the country, even in the sole situation God permits remarriage. Why they clung to that single moral ideology — even though they took it too far — out of everything I couldn't tell you.*

Toreon spoke to the group for a few minutes, Linton translating. To say they were both disgusted when he talked of his devotion and love for his "late love" Gallia — how the tragic loss of her would continue to leave him with a heavy heart and no hope to find another like her — was beyond understandable.

Still the same, stinkin' liar.

Well, at least he's consistent and we're not the only ones who know what he says isn't the truth.

Huh?

Linton. Can't you hear his tone?

Guess I didn't pay much attention since that's kinda normal.

Oh. Right. I forgot.

A few more comments made her realize he was starting to spiral out of control: *Destan! … Destan? Destan listen to me. … Destan!*

What! He snapped back; his fiery eyes burning.

You're upset, I know. She started rubbing his hand gripping her other, trying not to wince. *But… but don—*

Destan closed his eyes as he worked to calm his breathing.

It's difficult for me to pick up on your emotions, now. I haven't relearned that part yet. She explained as he turned to her and kissed her hand. *I'm sorry I let it go that far.*

Let's dance some. It'll help. He smiled as he put his cane in its holder on his hip while the next song started, others around them getting ready as well.

This is going to be so awkward. She sighed as she mimicked how he was standing. *What are we doing first?*

You know. This is one of the songs we practiced.

Oh. … Electronica. Contemporary-controlled ballroom.

Good job. Destan smiled as he laid his hands against hers. *Just like we practiced; I know you can do it. Have fun with this and keep your eyes on me. … Think of it as a small reward with all that we're doing on this trip. Huh?*

Most of the couples didn't pay any attention, but there were those who were keeping tabs on her to see how she would fare.

These hybrid dances were the first distinction Zervonith made for itself when it was established as a country. A prominent individual in the country — who was a classical musician — toyed with the idea of "breaking the mold" even further than previous artists in centuries past had done with creating what were called "epic" versions of some of the most well-known pieces. Needless to say that idea became reality. And it was the first of many which would follow in rapid succession.

To execute these dances correctly required a keen ear for musical progression as well as fluid movement to switch from one form of dance to the other; as well as knowledge of cadence to know which ballroom dance it would switch to. It took most people years to master it; but as usual, it appeared Callimay was well ahead of the game.

After their first dance was done these couples who were observing her came over to tell her how amazed they were. It hit her the wrong way at first, but then she realized they were glad she was "immersing herself so quickly" and commented that her musical background had an impact on her abilities.

Linton cut in at one point and requested to dance with her: *Jewel?*

Yes.

Doyen?

I'm listening, Destan replied as he nodded the two of them on.

Now is your chance. I'll entertain her so there's no suspicions as to why you'd leave. Linton urged as his facial expression became quite serious. *He's going to the only private vestibule without Falconers. Why, I'm not quite sure. But this will be the best opportunity you have by far.*

The music intensified in volume, this seeming to give Destan a bit more confidence… and yet he was leery: *Calli? What do you think?*

There's something Linton's hiding but I can't quite figure out what it is. It's like it's not directly tied to what he's telling us. She strained to use her ability. *I… I'm sorry. I ca— wait. Did you tell him about your plan? How does he know about why we're here?*

The vestibule is empty, but then again… there might be some other type of trap in it. Destan looked to where Toreon was going. *While I didn't tell him exactly why we were here; I know he's not stupid. I… well… I'll go. He is right about this being my best chance, but I don't want you t—*

Does Linton have a weapon on him?

No.

Then I'll be fine no matter what he might try. Go. Callimay encouraged. *I love you. Don't take too long.*

Destan sighed as he turned and started in that direction: *If 'any'thing starts to feel wrong, get to Trever. Don't worry about me. I'll find you.*

Won't everyone notice?

If you're in danger it doesn't matter. Destan said much more serious as he took hold of his cane.

He didn't flinch at all when Toreon came up and spoke with him before gesturing him on and opening the door.

Callimay could see Toreon's evil smile grow as Destan nodded and followed: *Lord, please keep him safe.*

❧

The vestibule was dim; Destan using Ingrid's ability to make sure things were safe. And while it was odd there wasn't anyone already in there at the bar, there wasn't anyone hiding. He switched to Callimay's ability and could tell Toreon was totally relaxed and going along with this event as a whole: *Just keep this up. Make everything easy and simple all the way around. No need to cause unnecessary problems.*

The up-tempo music muffled to a low, pulsating rave as the door closed; magenta neon lights giving the mist-filled room an aura that felt relaxed for where they were. Toreon sauntered to the other side of the room where he brightened the normal lights a bit and retrieved a couple glasses and a bottle which was half-full of some clear liquid.

"I don't mean to be disrespectful, but I take it you're familiar with Lingual?" Toreon asked as he motioned for Destan to sit down.

"Yes," his high tone was remarkably distant from his usual one; him leaning back in the lounge chair, propping his cane beside him. "I appreciate your decorum earlier. It was quite appreciated as a whole. And I know I speak for more than myself."

"Oh think nothing of it. Accommodating to different cultures and practices is something I very much enjoy; and Linton was more than willing to offer his services. I think he secretly enjoys it, actually. Being an arbitrator for languages is in his blood. His knowledge of so many different ones baffles me at times." Toreon chatted as he poured the drinks. "Ice?"

Destan replied as he shook his head, "I'll pass, thank you. — If you don't mind my asking: does Linton frequent here for field tourneys?"

His eyes became a bit curious from Destan's refusal of the drink, but finished fixing his and came over, "As a matter of fact that is exactly why he comes here. Apparently what we have in Crosswall can't match the style and quality here."

"There is a certain level of 'passion' in the players here that I will whole-heartedly agree 'lacks' in those I have seen in other countries. Said with respect, of course."

Toreon began after he took a drink and sat down, "I have to admit, during my stay here I haven't found someone as fluent as you are. Did you reassign here at some point?"

"I am a transplant of sorts, yes. But finding those with their original knowledge of Lingual is not as uncommon as you might imagine. I'm just not as bashful about using it in… 'controlled' environments, if you understand what I mean. Especially with my wife."

"Kerogen by chance?" He questioned as he peered over the glass at Destan. "I only ask because your accent sounds familiar."

"You would be correct." Destan fiddled with the lead goggles he had on his other hip, feeling a slight shift in his demeanor. "No matter how hard I may try, that baggage does linger. Though it's not nearly as much of an issue as it was early on."

𝕭

Callimay was still working to figure out what in the world Linton was hiding while not focusing so much she lost her level of awareness. He more-or-less appeared to be frustrated… almost like he didn't want to hide what he was hiding. But what was it? Why was he so worried? What was it that was causing this reaction in him?

At this point Destan had been gone much longer than anticipated, but he let her know when she asked: *So far so good. He sure seemed to be baiting me earlier with me refusing some of his offers. But now? … I am cautiously optimistic things are going well. I'm just hoping that me taking it slow like this doesn't backfire.*

Just stay safe.

You sound tired, Calli.

Linton agreed to stop after this dance. She sighed a bit. *I didn't expect I was going to be dancing this much nonstop; let alone the mix they've used has been nonstop rave. But I'll make it.*

Once the dance was over Callimay struggled, but finally got out a request for some punch. Linton smiled, being so patient with her and helping her correct a few errors. But just as he was about to answer, he looked behind her and his facial expression drained.

She laughed, a bit confused with it all as she turned and looked; and after a couple seconds of frozen terror she screamed when she realized who was standing not but five feet from her.

This individual's eyes looked at her with the most terrifying gleam — a gleam she had blissfully forgotten.

Everyone who could hear her looked to see her scrambling for the front door, the young man who just arrived jogging after her.

𝕭

Meanwhile, Destan and Toreon continued chatting, Destan seeing his perfect opportunity opening up to him, "You wouldn't happen to have any pecans, would you?"

"Of course," Toreon paused as he stared at the wall. "Oh crumbs. It looks like your bride — your precious 'Calli' — wasn't thrilled with the present I got her. So sad. I worked so hard on this surprise, too."

189

Destan jumped up and looked back, seeing Callimay running out; him instantly feeling dizzy.

He fought through it and looked back, but Toreon was gone… only his laughter lingering in the air. It was then he realized: *The mist. It should've cleared long ago. I can't believe I… I fell… I can't…*

Of course everyone was confused what was going on, Linton even looking shocked. He looked back to where Destan had gone; weaving his way there when he wouldn't answer and wasn't coming out.

He put his sleeve to his nose when he opened the door; the smell of this mist far too familiar to him. After a couple seconds he went in and got Destan out; helping him to another room.

The second Destan was able to understand what was going on, he jumped to his feet… having to grab his head as he staggered for the door. Linton did his best to help, but when he saw the look on his face he wasn't sure if there was any sense trying to explain.

In groggy anger, Destan threw a wild punch, glaring and grumbling as he stumbled to the door; completely ignoring what Linton was trying to do and say.

ℬ

Callimay was hysterical. Flashbacks of when she was at the Society and running through the labyrinth started to reform; though this time it was an unknown cobblestone street with endless alleys going in every direction that was the setting for this heinous series of events.

She didn't dare look back from the fear of if she did she'd see he was far closer than she thought.

Trying to help build some distance, she ducked into a side street that was rather dark and then the first alleyway she could find. And with the sound of his footsteps seeming less and less, it appeared to work.

He never said a word the whole time, but that wasn't his MO… that was Toreon who was the verbal tormenter. But if she had to weigh the two, this silence was more terrifying.

Just as she was about to take another sharp turn she took a misstep and went tumbling. A moaning gasp dared cross her lips as she looked up and saw him coming. She couldn't give up. Not now.

As Callimay got to her feet, she fell again: *What! What's wrong? I—*

"Grates and heels have never mixed. Ever." Webb finally spoke as he stopped about ten feet from her. "I'd think you'd know that."

Callimay wailed as she clamored to crawl away from him.

"Toreon's my superior, and yeah sure, up to this point I've obeyed his command about you… but enough's enough." Webb leaned over and ripped her mask and wig off. "He's taking too long and I don't care to wait any longer."

"No! Please no!" She cried as she flailed, scratching his face and screaming for help.

The next moment, Webb's smile changed to a pained, empty look and he let go of her. Callimay saw the bloodied blade of a knife sticking out of his chest, blood streaming down his shirt as well as out of his mouth; spraying on her face when he coughed.

Behind him, the person who dealt this blow had their hand around his neck and whispered in his ear; though still loud enough Callimay could hear, "I told you what would happen if you even tried. You really thought you could get away with this? 'No' one touches her except me. Not even Destan can. … Goodbye ole chum."

With one quick twist, Callimay heard a snap and then Toreon let Webb fall on her. She squirmed to get him off and then looked up at Toreon, mortified.

They both heard shouts, him turning to see it was Destan.

Toreon disappeared just as Destan appeared right beside Callimay.

"Calli! Calli what happened?" Destan asked out of breath as he knelled beside her.

"You know, you should keep a better eye on your wife, Destan. The most unsavory of characters come out in this part of Wen Square at this hour. But, no need to thank me." Toreon called out. "I'm sure I'll see you before long. Take good care of my glasses for me in the meantime."

Destan looked up and saw Toreon standing at the head of the street. Linton stopped at his side and then they both disappeared.

Linton played me for a total— "Calli, please tell me you're alright." Destan asked as he turned his focus to her, ignoring the fact he could hear someone running toward them.

"I… I ca…" she wheezed as she pinned herself against the building wall and stared at Webb's body.

Trying to calm her, he put his hand on hers, only to have her scream at him and claw at his face, "Calli. It's me."

She started crying when she saw the scratch marks she left on his cheek, reaching out to him with her quivering hands, "D… Destan?"

"It's alright, Calli." He consoled as he took her in his arms. "He— you're alright, aren't you?"

The person who had been running toward them this whole time stooped over Webb's body and then rushed over to them.

"We need to go," Trever whispered as he looked around. "That band of Falconers isn't far behind me."

"Looks like we can still get back to the bike." Destan looked back as he grabbed Callimay's wig and mask, then gripped Trever's arm.

The next moment they were at the bike; Trever having to fight off the urge to voice his disgust, shock, and fear.

Callimay was nothing but an empty, over-sensitized, and paranoid shell of herself; her screaming every time Trever had to hit the break or would accelerate, after which she would just stare off into nothing.

Destan looked at his watch at one point and sighed: *Head straight to the airport. Call ahead to ask for clearance. There's no time to stop at the house.*

What about your passports? Our detail won't get on their shift for another three hours.

He hissed as he slammed his fist on the side of his seat: *Why did I fall for this all!*

Feeling Callimay's grip on him tighten as she whimpered reminded him that one, losing his cool right then wasn't going to fix anything, and two, her clinging to him like she did when Webb was causing her to have the nightmares tore him up inside. What she must have gone through when she saw him… he should have been there for her!

But he was fulfilling their mission. He was doing what he went there to accomplish in the first place. They knew something was off, and yet neither of them ever suspected this was the reason why.

It's going to take more time for me to get them since she won't let me— *You know where the main bedroom is on the third floor?*

Yep. Trever grunted as he made another sharp turn.

The purse Calli had when we arrived?

It took him a few seconds since he was trying to navigate, but replied: *The green one with the feathers and super long fringe?*

Yeah. It should be on the large vanity.

⅓

Their stop at the house took longer than either of them wanted — they weren't in that purse — but they were able to get to the airport and avoid any of the authorities who would've been on their way from the Mingle. And with a dead Falconer… that would've spelled nothing but a death sentence to stay.

With the timing of everything, the airport wouldn't grant pre-clearance requests; so instead of fighting it and attracting attention, Destan did what he could to help everything go quicker.

A couple checks weren't clearing no matter how much Destan and Trever both tried. But while they knew it was a clearance they needed to pass for their own safety, both men knew something was changed in the data so they wouldn't get clearance. They weren't in the air "and" in international airspace, so they weren't safe. And they didn't have access to any other air field close enough to make a run for it.

"We can't keep going around in circles," Trever hissed as he threw down the clipboard.

"But neither of us are mechanics," Destan glanced to the terminal as he kept trying to adjust things. "And if we don't get this right we could all die." *We're out of time, though. ~ Come on, Raven. Tell me what they did to you, girl. What's wrong?*

Trever looked out and saw the security detail headed their way; bolting for the cabin.

"Trever don't!" Destan threw his headset on the one instrument panel as he tried to grab his arm.

The next second the lights all came on in the cockpit, the two of them standing there for a second, staring at each other.

"Get the cabin door closed and check on Everlyn, I'll get things started." Trever pushed past and grabbed his headset. "Go!"

Shots ricocheted off the fuselage as Destan fought to get the cabin door closed — it wasn't designed to be closed from the inside. Add to that he was still dealing with the after effects of whatever drug he's been given "and" Trever started taxiing? It make it much more of a dangerous situation than what it might have appeared to be.

There was the reality that the fuselage was severely damaged, but there was no stopping now. Trever called ahead to their one and only location in Medd.

"Why there?" Destan questioned as he sat down.

"When they find out where Raven's registered, of course they're going to expect us to make a break for it there. We've 'got' to have the fuselage looked at, and that's the closest and safest place to do it."

Destan let out a cry of frustration as he raked his hands through his hair; him realizing when he looked down at the radar, "We can't."

"There's no way we can jump the gap with that in question, I don't care how good of a pilot either of us are, with the altitudes we dare keep with this all in question, turbulence over the Bright right now is 'way' too high."

"Would you rather have a rocky trip or have an air fight?" He stared him down. "One of the highest ranked Falconers was murdered tonight. There's no way Toreon won't lie about 'how' he died. We 'have' to take that risk. It's our only shot. So we all need to be prepared to bail." *This is an absolute nightmare.*

Trever's face froze with this realization.

Knowing they were in a race against time to keep their trek back to Bulwark clear; Destan contacted their team in Vock to get things ready for an emergency landing and inspection as well as plotting the rest of their course back to avoid detection.

The second he got off the phone, Destan knew he had to address the elephant in the room. For them to focus, they needed to air out what happened before things got any worse, "I found out about the same time you did, I'm sorry."

"Why would you leave her with him?"

"Now hold up there. I didn't leave her with that sleezeball. I left her with Linton and 'only' because she said she was fine." *Me losing it is the last thing that needs to happen right now. — Lord? Give me strength. Please! Trever most certainly isn't going to be of any help in that area right now.*

"Why didn't you send her out to me?"

"I 'told' her if she felt she needed to she could. I didn't make her stay there. She even told you she was fine with staying. Remember? … And she might have originally intended to go to you when she ran out, but couldn't think straight." Destan took a deep breath as he forced his fingers to spread out on his knee.

Tension was beginning to build at a rapid pace between these two with the discussion that continued; Destan finally ripping his headset off, "What's happened? You were so supportive right after finding out about who Calli was, and then there was that spell where we were at odds because of our conflict in values, then everything was back to normal once we got back from Brigon… and now everything's off kilter again? What's going on, Trever? What have I done to lose your trust? — Calli!"

"What's wrong? I heard shouting." She looked around, her fearful gaze resting on a resentful Trever and then Destan who was wide-eyed.

Without a second thought, Destan jumped up and rushed back to her, "It's alright now, just go back and rest. I'll be there in a minute."

She pushed him back and looked over, whimpering, "Trever?"

"G… go get some rest, Everlyn. I… everything's okay." He said a bit more compliant as he glanced back at her feet, not wanting to see the remaining blood that was still smeared on her face. "I… it's okay."

"I'll be back in just a minute." Destan ushered her on. "I promise."

"O… okay." Callimay nodded as she folded her hands across her chest and turned to leave; stopping when she heard beeping.

The three of them turned their focus to the radar; Destan and Trever freezing when they saw the speed of the incoming aircraft.

Sensing something was so wrong it was dangerous, Callimay broke the silence, "What is that?"

Unable to get a word out for a few seconds, Destan stared at her, causing her to scream, "What is that!"

"Everlyn?" Trever calmed as he whipped his head around. "I know what just happened was terrifying and you need time to process it all, but you have got to listen to everything we tell you and do it exactly when we say. And I'm not going to sugar-coat this: that's a fighter coming after us, and they're not just going to ask us to 'pull over'."

"W… wha… I…"

Knowing what Trever said was what needed to be said, Destan still knew all too well Callimay wasn't going to be able to handle this alone. He looked back, Trever nodding him on, and rushed her out into the cabin. He opened a cabinet and grabbed what looked like backpacks, handing one to his bewildered wife as he started putting his on, "Just fasten it on like I am, okay?"

She fumbled around, still in shock, so he reached to help; only to have her scream and claw at him again. He fought the urge to yell — part of him thinking that was the only way to get her attention — and instead grabbed her by the wrists and looked her square in the eye, "I'm sorry, Calli. I am. But you have 'got' to listen to me. We don't have time for this. If you don't get that put on correctly you can die when we have to bail. So you need to either do what I just did or you have to let me help you. … Are you listening to me?"

Whimpers and sobs jumped out as she tried to free her wrists; but when he finished she calmed and let him help her.

He had her sit in the seat closest to the emergency door, making sure she was buckled before he snatched another pack and ran back in the cockpit.

The second he got his headset on, Trever jumped up and threw his parachute on, "I… I'm sorry about earlier. I just get thrown into this memory fear of sorts: not knowing what's going on and not having control of the situation when Everlyn is around just scares me. I just remember what happened last time and… I'm sorry."

Glad the tension was broken and the fear of what "might" happen gone, along with a reason as to where these flares were coming from, Destan sighed as he relaxed a bit, "I can understand that."

Trever popped his head out and smiled as he waved at his sister, then jogged back and took his seat again, "I got with our crew in Vock and they're sending a sub. It may take them a bit, though."

"Which way is the current drifting?" Destan looked at a map.

"Thankfully we'd be heading straight toward them. Water temps are the only issue… are there any extra clothes out back?" Trever asked concerned as he flipped a few switches.

"I don't know if there is enough time for that," Destan groaned as he checked the radar. "How much is the difference right now?"

"Half hour max, they said."

Without saying a word, he jumped up and ran out; only to find Callimay gone but her parachute still in the seat. He ran down the aisle terrified, scanning the seats as he worked back, then threw open the door to the lounge.

She screamed as she jumped back, Destan instantly consoling, "I'm sorry! I didn't know where— y… Calli taking off your parachute was dangerous. We may need to bail at any moment. You've got to keep it on. Okay? Let's get back."

As they started back, the jet veered to the right harder than even Destan would've anticipated necessary. He jammed his back against one of the armrests as Callimay fell on him, but gritted his teeth and threw his arms around her so he could protect her.

Light flashing outside following by a shockwave and the jet being peppered with shrapnel cemented what Trever said. While she didn't understand exactly "why" this was happening, she wasn't able to even ask because she was so terrified.

"Destan!" Trever yelled at the top of his lungs.

He got himself and his wife up; doing his best to stay upright and running as the jet bobbed and jerked, "What?"

"If those bullets weren't bad enough, left wing's damaged. I can't keep her steady." Trever grimaced as numerous lights flashed and warning alarms sounded. "I don't know if I'll be able to avoid another."

"Come on, Raven." Destan mumbled under his breath as he grabbed the controls. "Just a little more, girl. Hang in there."

A new and blaring alarm sounded, Callimay yelping when it went off; making Destan snap at her, "Buckle up now!"

Her hands shook like only a few times before, but she got it fastened a split second before the jet began to roll to the right. She screamed as she gripped the armrests, Destan and Trever letting out agonizing yells as they worked to control the battered jet.

The night sky lit up to their left like last time, the window on that side cracking when part of the shrapnel slammed into it.

"Go," Trever grabbed Destan's arm. "Get my sister out of here."

Destan nodded and flew back to Callimay, unbuckling her as she started thrashing and screaming for her brother.

Of course her parachute was nowhere to be found when they got out to the cabin, so Destan hugged his wife and yelled in her ear as he strapped something around her, "Do 'not' let go of me no matter how scared you are. Do you understand me?"

Unable to hear her reply, he took her cinching her arms around his neck as his answer. He took a deep breath as he made a fist and slammed the emergency button next to the door.

Her ears popped as she felt herself being sucked out the door; her blacking out.

When she came to, she didn't know what was going on other than she was freefalling. She heard an explosion above her; the light giving the water below them more definition. While the terror she felt kept her death-grip on her husband at full-strength, there was another type of terror that was starting to build momentum as they continued to plummet... Destan wasn't holding onto her.

Destan? Destan can you hear me? She screamed. "Destan!"

She couldn't see much of anything, but she could feel something wet on the side of her face that was warm, *Destan! Destan wake up!*

The next second she felt something slapping at her arm, the snap of billowing fabric heard right after as they jerked up.

Only now that their freefall had broken did she dare move her head, seeing Destan was out cold; a major gash on the side of his head. She tightened her hold as she started to cry, the sound of the water below them becoming audible.

While she wasn't a swimmer, she did know how to tread water... by herself. The sound of the water becoming more and more pronounced made her fear drowning: *How can I hold him up at the same time! I can't—* *Destan! Destan I need you to wake up. Please! I can't— I don't... Destan please! — God please wake him up!*

When they finally hit the frigid water she panicked; letting go of Destan so she could hold her nose.

The second she surfaced for air she realized what she did, but all she could do was watch in horror as the parachute disappear under the water in what felt like slow motion. She tried to reach with her hands to feel for him, but he wasn't there.

"God please!" She screamed.

But before she could start crying, something — someone — burst through the water right next to her. She looked over and saw Destan slumped over something; then saw her brother's face, "Trever!"

"You okay?" He grunted as he repositioned Destan.

"Let me help!" She worked her way to him.

"I got him." He feigned a smile as he went under for a second.

Part of the fuselage impacted not far from them, Trever yelling, "We need to swim, Everlyn. And turn your beacon on to send and receive. The sub should be here in five minutes or so."

All she could think to do was pray the sub would be there quicker than they thought. She knew Trever couldn't keep up much longer, but she also knew she wouldn't be any help. The roar of the jets was still heard, but farther away at the time. And an amazing answer to prayer, while the jets were completing their sweep pattern and coming back, the submarine surfaced so they could get in before they circled back.

ℬ

Feeling like she was "trapped" in this submarine was unnerving, and she was chilled to the bone, but seeing the state Destan was in pushed Callimay past it … for the time being. He was worse than she expected but much better than Trever feared; those who came to get them rushing to tend to him while getting information from Trever.

"Must've hit his head when he got ejected. I was still in the cockpit at the time." Trever hissed a bit as he stretched. "Naw, I'm not that bad. I can wait."

Trying to piece things together, Callimay asked, "Destan had a belt around me. Why wasn't it attached when we hit the water?"

"So you didn't hear me, did you?" Trever chuckled as one of those helping out gave him something to clean the cut on his side with.

"Huh?"

"After I cut you lose and released the parachute, I was yelling at you to let him go when you hit water and I'd take care of him. I knew good and well even if you could swim you wouldn't be able to support his weight 'and' the parachute."

She tried to think back, but couldn't remember him ever doing those things, let alone yelling to her.

199

"I'm just glad your instinct kicked in and I didn't drift too far from you guys." Trever brushed off the person as they tried to help him.

"Is he okay?" Callimay asked as the person checking Destan's head made a face.

"Well, it could've been worse, I can tell you that. He's gonna have a headache like none other when he wakes up, though. — Flipper? Radio ahead for an ambulance."

"What!" Callimay shrieked as she shot up in her seat.

"He needs an MRI done to be sure there's no bleeding on his brain or other damage, Jewel." The middle-aged man assured as he kept working. "From my experience he should be just fine, but there's always that risk. It won't take that long."

�

Being freezing cold and sitting with Trever in a hospital waiting room was oddly familiar and yet strange to her. She yawned as she fought to stay awake, him reminding, "Turn your music on, Everlyn. Just in case you do drift off you don't have to worry."

"Oh dear… I don't," she panicked.

"I… give me a minute." Trever scrambled to think, finally snapping his fingers and getting his computer out. "Oh thank goodness the water didn't ruin it."

A couple antagonizing minutes later Trever had the music playing; Callimay almost not able to rest because she was so worked up.

"Just rest, Everlyn. I'll wake you up." Trever put his arm around her; him taking the phone from the one Shadow who walked over. "Yeah?"

"How are things?" Fidus asked in a rushed manner.

"Well: Mirror in Zervonith is toast, Linton ratted on us so we lost the Prince 'and' Raven, and Doyen's in rough shape. … He should be just fine, but he's getting an MRI just in case." Trever didn't feed into the concern as his sister curled up next to him. "But other than that we're safe. Trying to work out a way to get back as quick as possible."

"So the Prince is still out there?"

"I don't know what all he can do, but we need to see about finding a way to track him if he just 'appears'."

"I agree. I'll get our people working on it."

This conversation somehow lulled Callimay to sleep, Trever not bothering to wake her up when Destan got out; instead carrying her to his room and leaving her there while he went to make arrangements for them to get back to Bulwark.

And when he got back, he sat with her and thought things through on a more rational level as he brushed his sister's hair out: *Was Linton, the Mingle— this whole thing a ploy to get them out in the open? It sounded rather fantastic and simple. I just don't understand how no one thought this might happen. And the drug mist? Doyen would be the first to notice it. How did he not think about it possibly being that? … But, then again, there was no way to know about him knowing. All the intel we got was clean. Even I couldn't find any info about Webb. Where in the world did they have him hidden this whole time? And then with how Linton acted? There is always that possibility of him baiting us — I mean Doyen even kept talking about that this whole time. And Everlyn 'did' say she could sense something was wrong, but… what can be done about it now? All we can do is salvage what we have and get back as fast as possible. I'll figure out a way. She can get me into places. He wouldn't be expecting me right under his nose.*

But the one thing Trever couldn't wrap his mind around was the fact Toreon killed Webb. It made no sense. From what he'd been told they were chums, comrades. What did Webb do to cause Toreon to snap like he did… and in such an instant and lethal way? Something was still missing. And as he looked down at his sleeping sister, he knew she was the only one with that answer.

ℬ

Destan was medically cleared within a few hours, and aside from the splitting headache along with a sore back and shoulder, he was doing fine. He knew Callimay was still terrified of what happened to him — let alone what she went through, so he powered through the pain to help her be at ease.

While far from favorable, but the best that could be put together with such short notice and trying to navigate the pronounced Syndicate security everywhere, they had safe transport that would get them back to Bulwark… in about two days.

Knowing the danger they narrowly escaped was still close, Callimay was skittish once they got off the ship at the dock in Werthington on the west coast of Prig, "Where... where are you going?"

"I'm just stretching," Destan calmed as he sat back down and sighed. "And I wanted to see if Trever was on his way or not."

"Oh," she nodded furiously as she grabbed a fistful of her skirt.

His voice cringed as he reached out and rubbed her hand, "You sure you're doing okay? It's okay to tell me no."

She tried to smile as tears began streaming down her face, "We need to get to safety first. I can hang on. It's okay."

He sighed as he leaned over and wrapped her in his arms. "I'm so sorry things... I lov—"

"I love you too." She cried in a whisper, pushing back so he'd let go.

"Bus will be here in about ten minutes." Trever announced as he jogged up, smiling as he raised a bag. "Got us some snacks since it was on my way."

❧

The second she stepped on the bus, she knew something was off, but she didn't dare say anything; all she did was make an excuse to get off. Of course Destan and Trever didn't think anything of it and excused themselves as well; the bus driver reminding them when he'd be pulling out.

When they were out of sight of the driver Callimay turned on a dime, Destan running into her.

"We can't get on that bus."

Trever almost said something, but Destan put his hand up and replied, "Didn't feel 'natural', did it?"

"You felt it too?" Her eyes got big as she gripped his hand.

"Yeah, and I was a bit put off. Those guys are better than that. — Could you go tell them, Trever?" Destan looked over his shoulder rather put off.

"I... but..." she tried to keep her brother from leaving.

"Calli, that bus is full of Shadows and a couple Veils." Destan chuckled as he patted her hand. "I guess since they were put on short notice and with all the Syndicate is 'over doing' they're on edge."

"Then…"

"Everyone in that bus would willingly give their life to protect you, not take it, Calli."

Ashamed, she turned away from Destan and started to shrivel up as she cried.

"Here now," he groaned as he walked around and kneeled in front of her. "It's okay. I'm glad you picked up on that awkwardness and acted on it. It means you're able to notice things even now. … Calli?"

She managed a nod as she wiped her nose; them turning to see who was jogging over.

"They got the message. We're ready to go." Trever panned his hand.

đ

About halfway through their trip, Destan got a phone call from Fidus. And while at first they were just talking about "normal" things, at one point Fidus paused and then flipped the conversation on its head when he told Destan there was a caller, "He said it's urgent that he speak with you."

Anger burned in him for a few seconds as he thought about things, but steeled himself as he glanced up to check on Callimay before replying, "Patch me through."

"Are you all safe?" The almost frantic voice begged.

"Linton, what in the world happened?" Destan didn't give an inch.

"I thought about— I'm sorry. I was hoping you could get everything finished before Webb showed up. I knew he was going to be there, but… but I didn't know until that night. I didn't know how to get info to you quick enough and hoped it wouldn't spell disaster if I just let it go. I messed things up, I know that…"

Destan closed his eyes and tapped his fist on the armrest, continuing after Linton finished his rambling apology, "How can I believe a word you say? You were pretty chummy with him when I last saw you two."

Silence was the only response for a few seconds, followed by Linton speaking in more of a whisper, "I can't afford to break with them in the open yet. There are those I love as well whom I want to protect. Vashti and I are already on pretty thin ice; doing that would've sent her on an instant rampage."

203

While he knew he could be walking into more lies, Destan decided to flesh this out and see what information he could get, "How did he know we were going to be there?"

"I don't know. I've tried to get him to say something about it without raising suspicion, but— it wasn't me who told him. I swear. I know—"

"Tell me where Toreon is right now."

"Still here in Shipsherow at the Lounge."

"Are you sure?"

"I can see him right now: he's carrying on with some of the Elites about your jet being taken down. The federal authorities have been in and out for the past h—" Linton paused, switching the conversation. "Well don't let them sleep in too late."

He's either a 'very' good liar, or he truly is scared to death of being found out. "Call that same number when you have more time."

"Alright, dear." He nodded to those walking by, checking his watch. "I'll try to call tomorrow morning before the kids head to school since I need to be a translator for some people who are leaving, and then get a couple other things done before I leave."

"Toreon's leaving tonight?"

"Yes. I'll make sure I call with enough time to talk to them all."

"I'll make sure I'm available. Bye."

ꟿ

Sure enough, by the time they were over halfway through their trip on the submarine to Ferdinan, Linton called.

"Do you know what happened to my wife?" Destan asked, sounding half infuriated and half desperate as he glanced back at Callimay.

"All he said was that Webb was going to overstep his bounds and touch someone he'd sworn to never touch. That there was no room for such a violation at any rank and he needed to be removed because of his disobedience." Linton recounted in a hushed tone as he stepped away from the window. "I'm not sure if that helps any."

"He 'was' going to? Those were Toreon's 'exact' words?"

"Yes."

Oh thank goodness. Destan slumped in the chair and let his hand drag down his face.

Linton sighed as he walked along, "I didn't know about the escort of Elites or Webb until we were on our way. Thinking back I know it was totally possible for me to say something without anyone knowing. ... I hope y—"

"I know you want to meet face-to-face — as do I — but I need to know this now: whose side are you taking?" Destan demanded as he stared out in front of him with the most serious expression possible. "I know this might be forcing your decision, but after what my wife went through and the situation I now find myself in, I 'have' to know... even if that means I'm risking your support by doing so."

"I understand your concern and the necessity for this. ... I know I've been known as the one to 'play both sides of the coin', but I've come to the realization I'm morally not capable of that any longer. There's a tie a person has that supersedes anything else." Linton began rambling, worrying Destan as Trever sat beside him and listened. "The saying is that the blood of the covenant is thicker than the water of the womb; and it's right. Toreon's actions, though at surface-level may seem just in his protecting your wife from Webb, I know were only done out of greed and selfishness. This 'discarding' people who he likes or claims are close to him when his authority or 'ethics' — if you dare to call them that — are brought into question? Or outright challenged? Well this type of reaction is him. Not many even within the highest Syndicate officials know this: Toreon had a twin brother. I say 'had' because when he was six he found out his brother was left-handed. He murdered him without a second thought... stabbing him to death using his own left hand."

"What?" Destan asked wide-eyed.

"It was buried as quickly as possible. And when I say that I mean those who knew were physically buried." Linton explained as he sat down and reached for his drink. "The only reason I know is because Toreon bragged about it all with the most vile of pride when he was visiting me over spring break; just two months after he committed the murder. — After that I could tell he was hounded with strenuous teaching... which resulted in him now being right-handed and tight-lipped about that 'accident'."

Both Destan and Trever were left speechless.

"In fact, the hidden truth is that both Vashti and Olderon are left-handed." Linton sounded much more bold as he scoffed a bit. "Why they turned on those who were like them and in the same breath were able to escape the Eradication I really don't know; but that's something else entirely. — I've had my squabbles with Vashti and Olderon for years, but since I became I father I came to see just how deadly what they're objective is by what they've instilled in their son. They're a far worse evil than the actual groups who caused the Homeworld to sever trade ties with us. This has to stop… now. No matter what. So I'm joining you. … But, I… I do have one request."

"What would it be?"

"Once this gets out, Vashti won't hesitate to come after the rest of the family. She has no love for the bond that is there since she is not 'blood' kin. In fact she's only ever wanted control over the family name and money; and so the moment she discovers this treachery she'll execute every individual she 'thinks' turned against her; all in the name of justice." Linton's voice strained a bit. "Is there any way for you to help me get whoever in the family agrees to hold out and stand against Vashti into hiding?"

Destan looked at Trever for a while, as if reading his options on his face, "Give me the names and locations of who the family members are and I promise you I will do all I can. There is still a risk with it, but I will do all I can."

"I completely understand, and thank you in advance for your help. Tell your wife I'm sorry about all that happened. I know it's really not much, but tell her I hope she's able to recover from the experience soon… and if there is anything I can do that may help — though I'm somewhat at a loss as to what that may be — please let me know. I want to make up for my mistake."

"I'll tell her, thank you."

"I'll be in contact soon."

~ 13 ~

After the initial shock of what happened settled — which took much longer than either of them wanted or expected — the following few weeks flew by. Linton's family members who wanted protection took Destan's offer gladly; staying in Kerogen at the mansion was more protection and they knew they had to take this risk to stop what was coming. Pickups were staggered and sometimes lengthy to coordinate with what would be normal vacation destinations and such to avoid as much unwanted attention as possible.

Things went smoother than even Destan was anticipating, but wasn't about to complain or contemplate the hypotheticals of a trap lying in wait for them. Elder had no inkling about this plan — getting the support of Linton was just a pipedream Destan and Traceur had — so logically speaking, there was absolutely nothing the Syndicate could have prepared ahead of time.

Linton sent his children with some cousins — his wife refusing to leave in case something did go wrong — though he eventually got her to go ahead of him. He made it clear he was going to stay with them for the first couple weeks at least to be sure everyone was settled and things were stable; giving his word he would relocate to wherever Destan instructed for as long as necessary.

A rather odd realization to have but one Destan just couldn't look past or forget; this last conversation with Linton ended so much different than he envisioned when he originally thought of Linton joining them. Looking at Callimay's face during their talk — knowing how her being with him was his biggest source of immediate help — he encouraged Linton to talk things over with his wife and bring her.

While he wasn't quite sure at first, Callimay spoke up with how she felt being away from Destan; tacking on his children coming even though Destan frowned and shook his head. His tone changed in an instant and said he would talk it over with her to make the best decision for them and thanked Destan for his consideration.

Her suggestion was considerate, but it truly wasn't something they could handle. And yet, at the same time, he had to admit she was right: if his wife came his children needed to as well. What parent in this type of situation would want their children where they couldn't see them so they would be able to protect them… and in this case that would be more than three countries away?

❦

Even though she was moving on from what happened, Callimay hadn't told Destan what exactly happened. That was until the night Linton was arriving — just about an hour prior — she gave him peace of mind knowing Webb didn't "do" anything before Toreon showed up.

Really, though, as she thought about what she was saying, that memory didn't feel real. Yes, she saw Webb die… but with her memory already so shaken and scattered? Let alone the fact she remembered going through the whole "he's dead" emotional roller coaster? Going through it a second time made her doubt it happened. And who could blame her? There were a few now whom they "knew" were dead who escaped by Elder's hand, so it was understandable for there to be this lingering fear even with Elder himself dead. — Of course Destan hadn't dared tell her about Baleck yet. For the most obvious reason of him now being dead and bringing that up not being of any benefit.

Trever stepped up in a big way when they got back, it becoming quite apparent the "someone" Destan was furious Trever was seeing… well this person was the gatekeeper to an amazing opportunity to get intel no one else could get now with Canary gone.

But even so, Destan wasn't sure how this would go. Dealing with this individual was still a longshot, "How do you even know she'll take you back with her?"

"Believe me. She will." Trever assured in a rather fond tone as he glanced at the old picture in his hand.

"Calli's 'not' gonna be happy at all when she finds out."

"I know she won't, but I've got the best chance of anyone."

"That's providing she can get you where you can find it."

"Kayla knows her way around. She'll get me in. — Look, I know you've been against this all from the beginning. Don't think I didn't recognize those I'd find close by on some occasions." Trever confessed as he glanced at Destan out of the corner of his eye. "But maybe by doing this I can get her to come around. She's a good girl deep down. We have our squabbles, but I know she does it just because that's how I like things."

"You're sure she doesn't have a sister?"

"Positive."

It just couldn't be her. Right? I mean Ingrid acts nothing like what Trever's saying. She's not clingy, wanting, jealous, and attached. That's the very thing she ran away from. Destan mulled over as Callimay walked up. "Have you gotten with her?"

"I never do. It'd be a red flag if I did."

"Unders—"

"What's this?" Callimay asked as she looked at the pictures on the desk. "Ooo! A snow owl. … Come to think of it, you know I've always wanted to see one and never thought I would; but I actually did! It was beautiful. And it has purple eyes just like this, too! It—"

"You what!" Destan all but jumped back. "Where'd you see it?"

"It was… uhh. Let me think. … Oh! It was when you went to get me the roses that day at the Society. Remember? What you actually asked me about when you came back? The thing I said I saw? It was this bird. He was just sitting up there in the tree, staring at me. I couldn't get over how pretty he was… or she. — But when you got back it was gone." Callimay pointed here and there as she explained. "What about it?"

Bone-chilling silence.

"What? Are you gonna tell me it's Ingrid's owl or something?" She half-laughed as she pointed to another one of the pictures on the desk; then widened her eyes, "Y… you're… I mean I know she's a Strigidae and they have those, but—"

"You're sure the bird looked like this? The eyes?" Destan worked to steady his voice; taking a hard swallow. "And you think this is Ingrid?"

"I may not remember a lot of things, but I do remember this." She almost rolled her eyes in frustration; now thinking this was a prank. "The purple stood out to me so much because they didn't look real. Of course I'm sure. And of course that's a picture of Ingrid. Look how she's holding her right hand. It's a common position Vock's High-Fashion Model Agency teaches. I only know because I worked with that agency on several occasions. It's their trademark, if you will."

Destan and Trever looked at each other, more and more concerned.

"Would someone please tell me what's going on?"

"Did Ingrid ever talk about a sister? Twin sister, maybe?" Destan sat her down and started asking in a soft tone.

She thought for a little while and then answered, "Well… I— no. No, I don't remember her talking about family at all. Why?"

Again, Destan and Trever looked at each other.

"Everlyn? … There… well there's this girl I know. I've known her for a very long time and I'm really close to her."

"Oh?" Callimay asked confused. "A girlfriend?"

"She fits the description of Ingrid almost to a T. It's just there are a few physical attributes that are different and her personality is just about the polar opposite." Trever tried to explain but just couldn't quite get a complete thought together while trying to be subtle. "The bird is hers, and this is a picture of her… not Ingrid."

"You're positive, Calli?" Destan handed her the picture and kneeled in front of her.

"I…" she stammered as she looked at the young woman. "Yes. Yes, I'm sure it's her. Even her piercings are the same in their location and what she would wear."

Trever took over at this point and finished explaining, "As far as I know from what Kayla told me, her bird is the only one left on this planet. — And you're right, those purple eyes aren't its natural color. The bird isn't even all natural. But it's not what the Sisterhood uses. It's what the Syndicate used before they got their hands back on the dire wolves and eskimos. But, snow owls are rare as is and easy to pick off by a steadied knife or spike, so they don't use them the way they intended for long-term. In fact, they ended up only using them as surveillance cameras. They couldn't do much else. — Anyway. Kayla has strong ties to the Syndicate, like Destan told me Ingrid does, and I'm going to go with her to see if I can find any more information on these 'Elites' Linton mentioned being at the Mingle. Doy— Destan told me he heard that name used before: Mama used it, but didn't give much details other than they were 'strange'. So, we talked with some of the others and it's sounding like there's something there we need to know about, and quick, before we start doing anything else. None of our contacts have any detailed or concrete information, so hopefully I'll find where they're keeping them hidden and who they are."

"What?" Callimay asked scared as she whipped her head around.

"You know all the new security measures placed around Bulwark?" Destan asked, waiting for her to nod before he continued. "Well, it's because I have a strong feeling these Elites aren't just high-standing Falconers. Your mother contacted us about a group of Falconers who were only connected by the Society a while back — she didn't use Elite then, that was later on — and then once again later on saying they were 'strange' like Trever said. I... I think they have abilities, Calli."

"Then that m— Trever, you can't go! If they have abilities y—"

"Everlyn, I have to. I'm the only one who would blend in quick enough." He calmed as his baby sister ran into him to hug him. "Time isn't something we have much of right now. Especially if they are who we think they are. The sooner we find out the sooner we can figure out what our next steps will be."

"But if they find you—"

"Look at me, Everlyn." Trever paused as he pushed her to arm's length. "We've all been in danger since we joined the Shadows. In fact you've been in danger since the day you were born. ... If you're going to lose one of us I 'know' it has to be me who makes that sacrifice. You need Destan more than you need me."

"I need you both!" She bawled as Destan came up behind her and wrapped her in his arms.

"I'll always be with you, Everlyn." Trever recalled telling her when they were both so young. "And I'll always watch over you. I promise. Nothing nor no one will change that. And don't think I'm that easy to take down. I'll put up a fight like they've never seen to get back to you."

"Please don't say that." She reached out as he took his veil off.

"I won't be needing this for a while. That and Destan said you'd want something to keep while I was gone. … And you know? Maybe when this is all said and done we can build that snow fort you asked me about the night we got separated." He smiled in a thoughtful way as he laid the leather coat in her hands. "The Nest has snow all year round and that's where we're headed once this all gets taken care of."

"Trever please."

"Everlyn," his voice hushed in the most tender of ways as he framed her flushed and tear stained face with his steady hands; trying so hard to hide the pain he felt from the memories that came to mind as he continued. "I didn't find Mama in time and I'm sorry for that. But you found the man I told you to find if I didn't get back in time. … I know you don't remember it and so what I'm saying makes no sense, but know it makes me feel like less of a failure back then by saying all this now. — Stay, you hear? Listen to Destan. Don't wander off again so I have to come looking for you."

The belvedere walked over and sat between Trever and Callimay, looking sad and confused.

"I now know what Mama meant by Mr. Ruff would keep you safe." Trever smiled as he knelled and petted the creature. "You take good care of Everlyn for me, alright?"

Hearing her name made the belvedere look at Callimay and perk his ears as he barked; his tail unable to stop thumping against the desk leg.

"Good. … Keep her safe like you have all along, Destan. I'm sorry things got so strained between us when you needed someone. Guess I'm still not used to sharing Everlyn. … You know where I'll leave contact I can get out." Trever finalized as he took a step back. "If things go as planned I should meet you at the Nest in two months."

"May the new moon continue to rise on you." Destan nodded, still trying to corral Callimay's flailing arms as she tried desperately to reach out for her brother.

"Please. Trever!"

"I love you, Everlyn. I always have… and I always will."

And with that, he jogged out of Deep Dark; never looking back.

Destan waited a few moments, then let Callimay go; knowing she needed to at least be given the chance to go after him.

She bolted, screaming as she raced up the steps, clinging to Trever's veil while the belvedere sat and looked at Destan who gestured to her. He took off as well; barely squeaking out the doors to keep up.

℔

When she got outside she could hear the sound of Trever's bike. She wailed and screamed as she fell to the ground: *I don't want to lose you, too! I just found you. Please! Why does it have to be you who goes? … Please, God. Keep him safe…*

The belvedere snuggled beside her and howled until Destan came over and picked her up; oversized snowflakes beginning to drift down. In a way it felt and looked as if the weather were sorry for her and was trying to comfort her; the soft sound of snow at night was always such a comfort to her in the past.

In the distance Destan could still hear the faint sound of Trever's bike and said a prayer himself. He was trying to think of something to help Callimay, and then remembered, "How would you like to head out to the waterfall?"

"Don't you still have that one big meeting to do? I thought Linton was coming in tonight?"

"Fidus can look after that until we get back. It's still a few hours off, anyway." Destan shrugged as he started walking toward the one side lot, glancing at his watch. "You need time to process what just happened and it's my job to give you space where you can do that. … Unless you need something else. — 'Do' you need something else?"

"I just want Trever," she sobbed and hiccupped as she swiped the tears from her face.

"Then we need to pray; and keep on praying." Destan encouraged as he stopped and set her down.

"Okay," she nodded as she got down on her knees and took his hands, the belvedere mimicking how the two of them looked.

℔

Later on after Callimay had time to come to terms with everything and then all of Destan's duties were taken care of for the day, he came back to the suite… but didn't see her anywhere.

213

"Calli? Calli, where are you?"

No answer.

He shrugged it off at first and moseyed around to look in every room; a moment of panic creeping in right before he caught a fleeting glance of her on the balcony behind the kitchen. Destan could hear what she was saying to herself and smiled as he waited.

When she turned to walk back in, he asked, "How's he doing?"

"Good so far," she wiped her face. "I don't know how much you heard, but he said I should be able to talk to him every day at this time. They all keep 'normal' hours, and all he has to do it think to himself, so it's easy and no one knows. ... And he said if he did find something he'd try to just tell me when I talked to him so he wouldn't have to risk being followed or exposing what he was doing; but told me to tell you not to abandon the drop off point altogether."

"That's great to hear!" Destan encouraged as he leaned his head on top of hers. "Now he'll have even more protection since he won't have to get out as much. And it's all because of you that he'll be safe."

"Yeah," Callimay tried to sound optimistic. "How's Linton doing?"

"Things are coming along great. Everything at the mansion is stable as humanly possible. So everything else is ready except..."

There was a pause she wasn't happy with, "Except what?"

"I... I can't justify moving right now; knowing there are these 'Elites' out there, no matter what they're capable of?" Destan slumped his shoulders. "Toreon by himself is dangerous enough. But if he has a squad or more of people with abilities who think just like he does? I'd be signing death sentences for practically everybody we know if I dared go now. ... I know we took him down once before, but Toreon's no idiot. And even with Trever— he's not anywhere near ready to use his ability in that kind of situation whatsoever. And even if we had time so I could work with him, we can't be everywhere at once and we don't know how to combat the other abilities. I just... I wish there were a way for me to know right now so I could get other things finalized. I know several are in limbo because of this. ... I mean 'do' they have abilities? If so, is there a list of what serums were used? How many are there? And then if they don't have abilities, well what in the world do they have a new title for? Why does Toreon have himself surrounded by them? What's their purpose? Are they stationary or field? If they are field then what on earth have they been doing that we don't know about? How c—"

"Now hold on," Callimay put a hand to his chest and stared him down. "Talk about me needing to calm down, well now it's your turn."

Destan half-laughed as he took a deep breath.

"What about the information we got from the drives at the Society? Or Elder's personal possessions?"

"There were groups of names I found but never any pictures to run recognition on or what abilities they had. — Sounds odd, but it could be because Mr. Freigh liked physical records more than digital… and those are all burned to a crisp, now. — And as it would happen, the names of those individuals are quite common, so cross-checking them with what Canary sent wasn't of much help because the ones that did match could very well be accidental since it was only a handful. … But if our hunch is right, and knowing how they operate, I wouldn't be a bit surprised if they are the same and they had most of them change their names as a precaution. — And like you thought, since there still seemed to be holes in what we found I 'did' look in Elder's stash. He wasn't a hoarder when it came to his computer; gutted the thing what looks like daily. Paper, though? I think Baleck would have been on him like he was on Mr. Freigh."

Hopeful with where he was going, Callimay egged him on, "So?"

"Even then, it wasn't anything tied to the Elites." Destan sighed as he shook his head. "Granted, I didn't think about looking at any of it until right after Trever left, but at least I'm not kicking myself for that lapse."

ℬ

With no solid information but a very strong inkling to the Elites being something much more dangerous, Trever abandoned his original idea and made sure his talks with his baby sister were much more surface-level to avoid any hysteria; using the drop-off point to get the more weighty information to Destan where she couldn't see it. — He was okay with his baby sister "prying" his mind, but not his brother-in-law.

Trever knew he got in at the perfect time at the perfect spot, on the cusp of figuring out what was going on. He almost let thing slip on a number of occasions, but the thought of his sister being "extra" if she knew about what was actually going on all the time wasn't something he wanted to deal with.

Of course Destan was against his withholding — knowing all too well how easily and devastating that could backfire — but during his last discussion, Trever promised he would tell her everything the next day; him very hopeful he would have all the info he needed so his "confession" to her would be taken better. … Or so he hoped.

And so with all this knowledge, Destan worked everything out so he could stay with Callimay when she planned to talk with him; trying to keep things casual.

While the clocks in the room were not mechanical in that they had that faint tick which would announce each passing second, something in the air gave that notation of time passing. Perhaps it was how anxious Callimay was, or maybe it was Destan's hoping what he feared would not be reality. And maybe it was a combination of both.

The clock flipped to midnight and she was nothing but smiles as she reached out: *Trever?*

Silence.

It's okay. Take a slow, deep breath. This has happened before. ~ I'm nervous. ~ Why? ~ Well, maybe it's because Destan's here. ~ Oh come now. That's ridiculous. … Try again. *Trever?* "He's not answering."

"Just because he's not ready exactly at the stroke of midnight doesn't mean something's wrong. Maybe he's had a busy day. — He's probably just a bit late. Going deep recluse like he did requires him to put that all first." Destan calmed as he ushered for her to sit back down. "You only tried twice and almost back-to-back. Just give him a bit. I'm sure he's been a few minutes late a couple times, right?"

Trever? Trever are you there?

Still nothing.

"Something's wrong."

She is the best little sister to have, I gotta say. Destan smiled as he took her hands. "It's alright. Give him longer… like a few minutes. It could be he's really tired and slept through his alarm."

Those few minutes passed with the same thing happening.

Callimay was about frantic, pacing the floor now.

"I… I can't even feel him, Destan." She froze mid-step and flashed her terrified eyes at him. "It's like when y… you were shot! I—"

"Calli, calm down," he did his best to remain the voice of reason and assurance; getting up and wrapping her in his arms. "Remember how things are a bit different now? How you can't feel the pain? This is probably part of it. He's there. He could just b—"

"But I'd be able to tell he was asleep. I… I don't know how to explain it Destan. I—"

"I know what you mean," he sighed as he let her go. "I know there's a difference. But remember: you couldn't 'feel' me once you got better. Maybe that has s—"

"But Trever's different. Our connection isn't the same." She started crying. "What happened to him, Destan?"

"Let's give it a bit. Try him at… quarter till one. Okay? Give him some time." He glanced at his watch and then reached out, rubbing her arms. "Something may have come up so he's having to be extra careful right now. Try not to think of the worse thing possible right out of the gate, huh? I mean, if — and I mean 'if' — something has happened, you need to be calm and steady so we can figure out how to get him back safe."

"O… okay. Y… you're right," she shuttered and shivered as she closed her eyes; Destan beginning to pray aloud.

So many of her emotions felt the same as in times pass, and yet they were all different. This was her brother, not her husband.

But one thing was most definitely the same: time decided to play its cruel game of dragging its feet so much you had to drag it behind you as it whined and clung to the doorframe as you tried to make progress.

The moment it was a quarter till, she reached out again… but there wasn't any reply. She tried every fifteen minutes, but nothing. They both stayed up well past sunrise with nothing but the same result.

Needless to say, at this point Destan was worried: *Even if he were sleeping he'd be up by now and would know Calli was talking with him. And I can't see him being that stupid to play this kind of 'joke' on her. Me? One-hundred percent yes. Her? I just can't see it. ~ And if he was needing to take extra precautions this should still be enough time. ~ Which means… there's gotta be another reason. ~ But what could make it impossible for Calli to reach him? ~ I don't even wanna think if that's possible.*

S

Sleep was something long forgotten at this point; the next couple hours spent in Deep Dark trying to get information from those close to Trever to see if they could figure out what was going on.

At one point Callimay got herself together and came up with something: she tried to reach out to those who were nearby location-wise to Trever to see if maybe she was exhausted in that aspect and didn't know it.

Sadly it worked as it was supposed to.

Bent on figuring this out at all costs, Callimay stayed up for the next two days straight trying every so often to reach out and find her brother. But it did nothing but reinforce the fear inside her. It built and built but something else won out; her body couldn't take it any longer. And much to the panic-filled shock — and relief — of Destan, she passed out mid-conversation.

When she woke up, Traceur was at the door talking with Destan. She heard Trever's name and rushed over, "Did you find him? Did he get news out? Is he alright?"

"Sh… she just went to the drop off point to see if he'd left any kind of communication." Destan calmed.

There was a moment of painful silence.

"And?" Callimay egged on.

"There wasn't anything, I'm sorry Jewel." Traceur bowed her head.

"Maybe he is in a pinch right now, Calli. We can't give up."

"Oh, Destan," she bawled as she ran out to the balcony.

"I'll have it checked as often as we dare to." Traceur nodded, pretty sure of what Destan was going to say. "Linton just arrived for his first official meeting. … And then Majesty Presley wants to speak with you."

Lord? I need Your help so bad right now. He dragged his hands down his face and sighed. "Alright. I'll be there as soon as I can."

~ 14 ~

Unlike what anyone expected, two weeks went by with no word: good "or" bad. It was the strangest thing. To Destan it didn't feel hopeless and yet the inability for Callimay to reach him gave no other logical conclusion but that something "did" happen. But there was no increase in security, no broadcasts, not one, single indication at all that they'd discovered him.

This whole time Callimay drifted into what could only be described as a long-term emotional breakdown; she couldn't function. She'd become so bad that she gave up on trying to contact Trever. — Destan tried a couple times, but he knew his range wasn't anywhere near hers.

While he hesitated to do anything at first, Destan had to remind himself everyone was understanding and willing to help. They knew his wife's background wasn't like theirs, but they also knew what she was capable of when needed. So he had her duties waved and asked if Traceur and Auditor would check on her when he would be gone.

She wandered around the room aimlessly and didn't want to go for walks or even drives out to the waterfall. She'd lost interest in just about everything and had stopped eating on a regular basis; the belvedere about at his wits end.

When he could get her to go for a walk there was this obvious distance. She would apologize and try harder each time, but she just couldn't get out of this hole she'd dug herself into. And part of it was she didn't "want" to. She wanted to be alone… and Destan knew why and could empathize with her. She was scared. Scared he was gone. Scared she lost the last member of her immediate family that she'd longed to have back for so long. But he knew her doing what she was doing — or in this case not — wasn't right. She couldn't go on not taking care of herself just because of this unknown. He made the choice himself; full-well knowing every single risk.

But Destan also knew it was hard for her to make that distinction at times. Even he had to admit he felt the same pressure. And so he tried his best to support and encourage her however he could.

❦

When they came back inside, Traceur ran up behind them, "Doyen? Could I have a word?"

"Of course," he gave Callimay a kiss and walked to the side a bit.

"You two need to go to the drop off." Traceur said quite serious.

"Is it that bad?"

"I'll let you be the judge of that. This is all I got." She handed him a note that just said where to go and what timeframe. "I'd leave within the next half hour."

"Alright," Destan sighed as he turned around and walked back to his wife; clapping his hands as he tried to sound upbeat, "How would you like to go on a top-secret mission?"

"Okay," she said rather monotone as she rubbed her arm.

Destan sighed as she passed him and headed back to the suite to put her ensemble on: *Even just a week ago she would've asked Traceur the same three questions she did every time someone asked to speak with me or she saw someone. — Calli please don't give up. This isn't you. … And you're not alone. I'm here. Don't… don't you see that?*

❦

As she was getting ready, Destan looked at his phone. The last text he got from Trever was to tell Callimay happy birthday. He sighed in more of a groan as he leaned against the wall.

The door opened not but a couple minutes later and he saw her all decked out. She was carrying Trever's veil as well as the soft suitcase that held the knives and spikes her ensemble held.

"Would you like some help with those?"

"Alright," she sniffled as she tossed the leather envelope on the bed. "Where are we going?"

220

"Somewhere we 'technically' shouldn't be."

She shrugged her shoulders as she took her Seaxes out.

His efforts to peak her interest were not hitting the mark. In fact he felt like he wasn't even aiming in the right direction at this point.

As he was finishing loading her boots, a memory shot to the front of his mind, catching the ire of his wife, "Why are you smiling?"

"Huh?" He whipped his head up.

"What's funny?"

"Nothing," he reached over and took the last few mini spikes in his hand. "I was just recalling something I remember Rocher telling me."

There were a couple moment of silence, followed by her asking, "What did he tell you?"

Well at least this randomness came in handy. "Rocher told me once that it was a long-standing tradition through my grandmother's culture that — and this was a 'long' long time ago this custom was in effect — the husband would do his wife's hair and makeup because they didn't have mirrors, or at least really good ones, at that point in time. It was kinda one of those 'acts of love' and endearment the husband would do for his wife." He scratched his head as he rolled up the leather envelope and stood. "I know it's not a total match, but me doing this for you made me think of it: I do this because I love you… and I want you to be safe."

For the first time in what felt like a lifetime, Destan saw a faint smile pull his wife's lips upward and strike a spark in her eyes.

It didn't last long, but it was a start.

"Ready?"

After picking up Trever's veil; clutching it to her chest, she nodded.

The belvedere whined as Destan opened the door, "So you want to come, huh? Oh alright. … Ya know? In fact, you'd be helpful to have along this time. But you've got to hide and be quiet, got it?"

Still unnerving to a certain degree to see, though getting less each time, the creature turned a midnight black and wagged his tail as he nudged Destan's hand to pet him. He knelled down and undid the orange collar, the belvedere shaking once really good and looking at him rather confused. Even Callimay was, "What are you doing? The collar isn't reflective."

"Real belvederes don't have collars." Destan reminded as he put the leather strip on the door handle. "It'd be a dead giveaway."

While on a normal basis that would've triggered her curiosity — and with what sign he just saw he was hoping it would — but she just said, "Oh," and continued on.

Though after a bit, seeing the precautions he was taking, she came to her senses and realized this had to do with Trever. The determination in his eyes grabbed her first… that and noting a hint of fear in them as well. And for some odd reason he wouldn't outright tell her where they were going. But the hints he "did" drop started clicking and so she did her best to claw and pull herself up using the rope Destan gave.

The belvedere stayed on the floor in the back, only the sound of his tail thumping being heard if either of them said something.

Heading west toward the border railway was her only clue right now. But they'd been driving for such a long time that she couldn't stand it, asking again, "Are we close? It's almost caller's warning."

"Pretty close," Destan nodded as he handed her a bracelet. "Do you remember this?"

It took her a few seconds, but her eyes got wide as she let out a small gasp, "It looks like what my mother had."

That's actually hers. Destan gripped the wheel and bit his lip before explaining as he put one on himself, "They're called reflectors. They make any clothing that's dark-colored on you look white… like a Falconer, basically. It activates when you put it on, then deactivates when you take it off."

"A… alright."

"Big Fella?" Destan asked as he glanced over his shoulder. "You can—what's his cue to turn white, Calli? I forgot."

"Relax, Buddy." She finished for him as she looked back.

So obvious. Duh. ~ It's a good thing she remembered, too. ~ Oh gosh, that's right. Destan rolled his eyes. "We're here. Ready?"

"What am I supposed to do?"

"Act like a Falconer." Destan smiled as he put the car in park.

"Excuse me?"

"Act like you own the world… like Gallia did. You remember her, right?" Destan shrugged his shoulders as he got out and opened the door for the belvedere. "Now it's nothing but strict business, Big Fella. Understand? Serious."

The belvedere changed in an instant; puffed up, looking more alert and stern as he rushed over to Callimay who just got out.

"We're at the Ferdinan, Faberton border, right?" Callimay shut the door, unable to keep from voicing her shock, "Why is the car—"

Everything has to look as inconspicuous as possible. Only another Falconer would even bother to look at the plates. And then it'd take them a while to track down that it's an old one. Come on.

It was the strangest thing for Callimay to see Destan with blonde hair: *I didn't even notice, did you? He restyled it to look~ Why did he do that? It doesn't look right at all!*

Him in all white would be — if things had happened differently — what he would have worn on their wedding day, but looking at it now she was half glad that never happened. He was tall enough as it was, wearing all white made him look like an absolute giant! Plus the color wasn't best suited for his rich skin tone… in her personal as well as professional opinions. At least not that shade.

Destan chuckled as he listened. He was glad there was something to help her take her mind off what was going on so she would act more natural. Though he did have his concerns she'd be "too" normal: *Maybe this would be a better illustration because I'm not telling you to lie: just act like you're protecting me from every Falconer in the world. Can you do that?*

Oh… her eyes lit up. *That makes much more sense.*

What we're looking for should be right over— ah! There it is. Destan looked around and then started walking.

There was a trashcan he walked toward, leaning over and picking up an orange ticket stub; throwing it in the trash. He then walked over to the nearest building and leaned against it, looking like a total jerk as he tossed his head and what could be said: turned his nose up.

For a split second Callimay had flashbacks to Toreon and Webb; having to fight herself for a few seconds.

This whole time the belvedere stood watch, scanning the people with the utmost scrutiny. Callimay wasn't sure what in the world was going on but trusted Destan would say if she needed to do something.

After a while he opened the paper he'd had hidden in his hand and read the almost invisible — it was that small — writing.

He pushed off the building and then glanced at his watch, checked his phone, looked around with an almost condescending look, then turned and bowed a bit to Callimay; gesturing for her to walk on.

As they came up to the booker's window, Destan said: *You ask him for two tickets to Berchshire. Alright?*

Berchshire!

Yes. One-way. He replied calm as he took her arm with a firm grip. *Calm down. Be… 'determined' when you tell him. Don't ask.*

O… okay. Determined. Determined. … Oh dear. She took a deep breath, squeaking out the first few words before clearing her throat and trying again, "Two tickets f— I mean two tickets for the noontime train to Berchshire."

That mess up gave her a bit of an irritated edge to her tone, even. Perfect. Destan chuckled to himself.

"Of course," the man at the window replied without hesitation. "Anything for a pair of such upstanding Falconers. … No need to pay. Thank you for your dedication to protecting us all."

As much as this man put up a "front", Callimay could hear the other side — what he "truly" thought and didn't dare utter out loud.

Hearing it made her want to do something: *Don't worry, Calli. He won't get in trouble for this. It's one of the Syndicate's perks, if you will. Since they have total power they get whatever they want no matter how inconvenient or expensive it is for those who 'have' to give it.*

But why are we using their own methods? I mean isn't that making us just like them?

Just as they came in view of the platform listed on their ticket, Destan took Callimay's arm and looked her square in the eye: *Now let me ask this: does driving a white vehicle make us Syndicate?*

N… no.

Does having white clothes, a dire wolf/eskimo mix, or a rather aloof character automatically make you or me a Falconer?

Well no.

It does give the impression to others that we are — I get that — but have we ever said a word to anyone we are Syndicate? The belvedere is ours, and yes he is a Syndicate tool, but do we use him as such? And the car, well that plate is a real plate for a vehicle that is registered… we bought the vehicle so we own the license plate number. — And before you say anything, it's a Crosswall thing with that all. — The color of the car? I'm not sure if you ever saw reruns of the 'old' show Knight Rider, but it's the exact same principle with any Shadow vehicle. We just transfer the color and license plate we own to this one for times like this for added protection; which by Crosswall law is totally legal.

But we didn't say anything when he said we were Falconers.

Would he have believed us if we said we weren't?

We still should've said it. She refused to budge.

He sighed in defeat as he glanced at the clock, and then smiled as he nodded her on: *You're right. Do what you can even though others may not acknowledge it because it's always the right thing to do.*

I guess I also don't want him to think he's alone; knowing what he believes. Or that it's wrong to think that way. And then the tickets—

The company will get reimbursed for our tickets, don't worry. … And as far as his fear to speak freely? That's why we're doing this all. Right? He smiled as he patted her arm and continued on. *I get why you're worried, Calli. I do. It's something I have to constantly be on guard for; and you're helping me do an even better job of it. Redje was really big on 'checking up on me' at first, and I quickly learned to appreciate it so much; just like I appreciate you questioning things. Okay? … And remember: if you feel like you shouldn't do something, don't do it. I don't want you mulling through this all in doubt, lack of conviction, no assurance, and questions.*

I'll admit this is a part of everything I didn't really consider at all. She sighed as they got in line. *Is Mr. Utree going to be coming to Bulwark anytime soon?*

Should be coming… week after next, I think? I'll ask when we get back. Destan ushered her on to the window.

℥

There wasn't much room on the train, but those who saw Destan and Callimay moved so there was a complete booth for them. Callimay felt infuriated even more than she already was: seeing how everyone caved

225

and basically begged for mercy when around who they thought were Falconers. What kind of freedom and safety were they enjoying from what all the Syndicate had done?

And the answer was: none. Absolutely none. It was nothing but the fear of tyranny.

The conversation with the booker went far worse than she expected: not only did he not believe her, but he was terrified. He started making a scene, begging her to have mercy on him and that he would get her better tickets. And everyone on the train she tried to tell to go back to their seats did about the same thing.

It was downright depressing for her to see this; and lit a fire in her soul that this fight had to be won. It wasn't just the freedom of left-handed people like herself on the line; it was the freedom of every person to have thoughts, ideas, and opinions that differed without the fear of being executed on-site. It would give those who didn't believe they had any power to do or change anything the courage to stand up and fight back; reminding them their voice mattered and evil wasn't going to win. And it also gave vindication and justice to those who had been tortured and left permanently scarred by the Syndicate.

As the train took off, her emotions were jerked away and replaced with memories. So many things changed in just over two years… even one, really. She never imagined herself in this position or situation.

She now saw so many hints of Doyen in Destan from their time together at the Society; what she could remember at that point, at least. What she'd brushed off as her just not knowing him or his extreme response due to shocking circumstances was — in fact — a different side of him reacting exactly as was necessary at the moment.

This all made her think about them now and what they talked about: her doubts and questions. He never lied to her about who he was when they first met. In fact the reason he never told her was because she never asked. Yes, she didn't know to ask; but his volunteering information wasn't in his character, anyway. And when she found out how wealthy he was, did that upset her in any way and make her angry? Why then was his occupation that much of a problem?

ॐ

226

Before she thought it had been long enough, the train began to slow as it entered Berchshire. Callimay tensed up, but not like she had in times prior. In a way she was tense because she was excited and nervous.

It was lunchtime, so as they stepped off, Destan suggested they grab a bite to eat, "That little place we went to last time was really good. They serve lunch, right?"

"Well, at least they 'did' last I knew." She smiled.

The same thing — pretty much — happened with the waitress at the small café bakery. They could "hear" her call them "deplorable people" and her begging a coworker to serve them so she didn't have to deal with them and what they made her think of.

Callimay was glad to know so many "normal" people weren't for what the Syndicate was doing, and gave her hope what they were working to accomplish would stick; that the political battle would be won and the International Law would be abolished.

⅁

When they got done, Destan came out and called the belvedere to them and started up toward the older part of Berchshire — the residential part. Callimay had a split-second concern someone would recognize her, but remembering what time it was gave her a bit of comfort.

Well that was until they passed by where she worked. She ducked her head to the side and took Destan's hand; speed walking past. He wanted to stop and look in, but knew what she was doing was for the best; so he fought the urge and kept on.

Before long they were out of town: *Where are we going?*

I'm just following what the note said, Calli. Come on.

When they got to where they were going she almost couldn't believe it. They were standing in front of the house Trever lived in.

Her heart skipped and fluttered with the thought of him being there, but the other side of her kept pulling on her; trying to get her back into the pit of despair she neglected to fill in.

There wasn't any uneasy feeling in the air; though. Her pessimistic thoughts couldn't cling to that. It was a cold day, but a beautiful one. And the fact the door was unlocked didn't bother her at all because Trever did that quite often when he would be at work.

Destan walked in first; his body language changing in an instant. Callimay could feel this release of tension and darted around, "Trever!"

"Hi Everlyn," he smiled as he opened his arms to her.

"Where have to been!" She burst into tears as she ran over and plowed into him. "Are you alright? What happened? Why wouldn't you talk to me? I've been sick with worry!"

"Well it wasn't because I wanted to. I didn't figure it out for a little while, but it seems I landed right in the lap of the Elites off the get go." Trever calmed as he held his sister close and let her cry. "Not only do they take their marching orders from Toreon, but they're an altogether different kind of ruthless."

"So they are…"

"Yeah," Trever sighed as he sat down.

"Well," Destan paused as he turned and stared out the window. "Well at least we know."

"Yeah…"

"What's wrong?" Callimay picked up on his tone.

"There's a problem." Trever paused as he tapped his stretched out fingers against each other, avoiding looking at his sister or brother-in-law. "There's… well from what I gathered there's over seven-hundred of them. Seven-hundred forty-six to be exact… not including Toreon."

What could be said in response to that? It was bad enough it was as bad as Destan feared. But to be far worse?

How in the world were they going to make even a dent in that amount? There were only three of them who were truly capable of taking them on. — Yes, Destan was the most powerful, but his "deadly flaw" was a major hindrance.

For the longest time nothing was said; the shock steeling everyone's voices. But Callimay started in a whisper, scrambling to find something to say because the stillness was too much for her to take, "So… since you found that out does this mean you're coming back? … Trever?"

"I'm gonna have to stay. I'd be exposing everything if I up and left right now." He shook his head as he stood and checked his watch. "And Kayla's not going to take it well if I dump her there. She has stable and strong ties where we are, but there's some kind of friction between her and those higher up. But, as usual, she's tight-lipped and won't tell me what it is. So, it may end up we won't be staying much longer anyway. I'll let you know when I can about how I'm doing. I'm sorry I scared you so bad. I can tell you haven't been eating or sleeping."

"I…" Callimay tried to defend as her brother's eyes narrowed.

"So I take it they have someone who can disrupt Calli's ability?" Destan started to piece things together. "Right?"

"I don't know what is what, but I'd guess so." Trever handed Destan a memory stick. "I have a feeling their code names are their abilities since they match what is written in a portion of their file describing said capabilities… but I'm no expert like you are in that department. This was all I could get right now. I hope it's enough to get at least a good start on things."

"I'm more than certain it is." Destan said relieved as Callimay came to his side.

"Take care. And like I said: I'll get with you when I can. … Guess it'll have to default the way we originally agreed to so there's no false alarms. I'm sure there was a bit of a tizzy about me not getting with you like I said I would. — I'm sorry, Everlyn." Trever shuffled toward the door, stopping as he looked over his shoulder. "If all goes well I'll see you in a few weeks. The Nest, right?"

Destan stopped his nod, tapping his lip a bit before answering, "Just plan on it, but it may just be us or the skeleton there."

"Understandable. I might even be late… or early; I guess it doesn't matter too much. It'll all depend on Kayla at this point. But I won't let it go any longer than… oh, say three months?"

Three months! That's quite a bit more than just a 'few weeks'!

"Sounds good." Destan nodded.

"Promise?" Callimay's voice broke.

"I promise. — Glad you could make it. I'll t—"

"Wait!"

"I have to go, Everlyn," he sighed as she ran over and clung to him.

"Come back. Please." She sobbed in a whisper. "I love you."

Trever closed his eyes, remembering what his baby sister said so long ago. It was much longer than he anticipated, but he did come back for her. And as much as he wanted to tell her he would be back, he knew better, "I love you too. Now be sure to eat and get some reset when you get back. Stay with Mr. Ruff and Destan. They'll keep you safe no matter what happens. Alright?"

Not satisfied with his answer, she refused to let go.

"I've really gotta go, Everlyn. If I don't, someone's gonna get a bit suspicious." He tried to pull her back to arm's length. "And know that whatever happens I'm alright with it. I know you're safe now. — Take good care of her."

"Now you're the one who's sounding a bit—"

"I know, I know." Trever rolled his eyes at Destan. "Now that the shoe's on the other foot I get it now."

"Take care." Destan nodded on.

℥

With nothing else to do and Destan wanting to ensure they wouldn't be seen anywhere near Trever, they spent what time was left for the day to talk about things concerning themselves… trying not to dwell on the bombshell Trever dropped.

Their conversations were rather sporadic and short-lived, but they kept in the "off topic" nature even though Destan could tell Trever being gone was still wearing on Callimay's heart. She was much better knowing he was safe, but the knowledge of what evil power was close to him that she couldn't fight? It was a good thing she hadn't processed it yet, or she would've most certainly been a nervous wreck.

Right at sunset Destan took his reflector off, checked the windows all around, and told the belvedere to hide.

"Where are we going?" She asked as he started toward the back of the house; her ripping off her reflector when he motioned to her, his eyes wide with annoyance for not listening to what he just told her.

"We can leave from the drop point in Downing. Where we were when we flew out here. Remember? … Do you think you can run that far? If you can't I— why don't I just jump us there?"

"It's not that far. Let me try. Okay?" Callimay petted the fluffy creature standing in her way.

"Until the slope starts to drop off. Okay?"

"Alright," she nodded as he opened the door. "Wait."

"What?" Destan asked concerned as he whipped his head around.

"What about the car?"

He took a deep sigh: *Way to scare me.* "It's been picked up already."

❦

It was hard for Callimay to not hear much — if anything — from her brother for almost a week at a time, but she knew letting go of this special way of communicating was best: the less she thought about who was stronger than her, the better. And it wasn't a complete loss. People communicated for centuries before in just as tense situations without the special aid she had.

When he got information out he always had a personal note in it for her; it usually telling her he was alright and not to worry which made her feel she had a responsibility to keep an even keel. And there was always the occasional one to Destan to keep watch over her.

All this time Destan was at a total loss as to how things should proceed with regards to the sheer number of these Elites. He had that gut feeling things were going to get delayed again, but he "was" hoping this would be a "little" detour which would only take a couple weeks.

But now? Now that light at the end of the tunnel started to look like the headlight of a train barreling down on him.

Going through the information Trever got both baffled and bothered him. He was expecting a bit more variety in the serums used. Yes, they were mixed following Baleck's known style, but they weren't really "that" different. It felt like a flaw which didn't fit Baleck's style; his achievements with these mixed serums were his pride and joy. Could it be these were the only combos that were stable enough to survive? Or was his talk about combining and mixing them more talk than reality?

Regardless, as it sat right then, if they could take one down, taking the rest with that same base "flavor" of ability wasn't going to take much effort. And so that narrowed things down to about a dozen bases.

And what put him more at ease was he didn't see the one Webb had anywhere listed.

Then it didn't.

When he got through the list he didn't have an answer about how Callimay couldn't get through to Trever: *Is this not the whole thing? ~ Trever would've said so. ~ Maybe he doesn't know it's not complete. ~*

231

Well let's just think of the worst case scenario again, shall we? ~ Well I was on the super conservative side last time, wasn't I?

Linton wasn't sure how to help when he found out. In fact the whole deal with abilities was something that took him a good bit to wrap his mind around. Yes, he knew about the Elites and spent time around them, but he didn't know just how dangerous they were because they never actually "did" anything around him. — Deep down he felt it part of his responsibility to help find a way to diffuse this rogue fuse Vashti found and was threatening to use; but didn't have a clue as to how to help.

Majesty Presley was a bit shaken by the news as well, but could tell by the hesitancy in Destan's voice he needed all the support he could get; offering a staging location of sorts for individuals to be based at which was as close to the Quimbergo border as possible once he was able to figure out how he wanted to handle that situation; if going after that location was his decision.

~ 15 ~

Between this news and trying to get things finalized with Linton — financial things they "needed" to get done — Destan was at a breaking point… and he knew it. But what could he do? He couldn't stop. Yes, he "did" have others around him who could help, but he still had to shoulder responsibility and keep abreast of everything.

So, stepping in like she'd always done and taking the brunt of the "backlash", Callimay took it upon herself to quickly find a way for him to decompress. Every idea she had was missing something, so she surrendered and used the only method she knew that would grab his attention: she demanded he take a day off.

Of course he wasn't having any of it, but she was prepared; saying because she was still learning how things were going to work with her "reading" his emotional state now, since her ability functioning as it was supposed to, "If you keep this up much longer something 'will' happen. And I'm just not ready for that yet, Destan. I'm not."

Even with that cold bucket of reality splashed in his face it wasn't an easy choice to make; but he agreed and she gave him two days to get things set so he could prepare and be confident in leaving for a day.

Ƌ

Come that morning Callimay was bustling about early, making sure everything was ready to go and they got out of there before something happened: *I mean if anything does 'happen' they can still get us. Doctor Gerould knows where we'll be. ~ Shouldn't you tell him that? ~ I… I'll wait to see if he is preoccupied with it or if he's able to let go on his own. ~ Well let's not take this experiment too far, now. ~ I won't.*

She jumped, gasped, and screeched when she turned around and ran into him; but was all smiles and laughs as he helped her pack their lunch at the same time as eating what she fixed for breakfast.

The belvedere was excited as well, but Callimay was firm: he had to stay behind. And not only that but she was going to be the one driving.

Destan got a bit stiff and formal, so she told him about his "safety net" which brought him down to the level of calmness she knew would be the most he could do.

❦

As he looked out over the familiar view of the waterfall, reminding him of the cliffside at the mansion, so many thoughts of a totally different nature began to run through his mind that pulled him away from all the mind-melting ones he'd been so preoccupied with.

It was lost to him for a while how so much in his life had changed in just a couple years… and all of the ways which were good. Callimay was, in ways he never envisioned, a blessing. She was first and foremost strengthening and encouraging him to walk for and with God; but it touched so many other areas to help him see the end of this heinous and crewel injustice was possible. In a way it was mind-blowing to think of how close they were; how far they came in such a short time.

Through it all she gave him such a wonderful example each day of what it was to love others more than self, and to do everything you could to protect those you loved. That reminder was what kept him going through some weighty times. And she always did her best to encourage him to keep doing the job he was; telling him he was doing the right thing and doing it well. And with the way things were going he needed that reminder… badly.

Callimay didn't want to interrupt, but at the same time she wanted him to remember she was there. So, she apologized for not having much ready; to which he smiled, "Just getting out of Deep Dark was enough. But then you said I couldn't wear my ensemble and had to spend the entire day with you? It's more than I thought possible right now… but you sure know how to convince a guy."

❦

As they came back up to the car, Destan noticed there was another one beside it. And it was one he instantly recognized, "What in the world? Why are they here?"

"I had to get you 'something' but I needed to keep it where you couldn't find it." Callimay giggled as she waved to the car. "And they said it'd be later before they could get here."

"Get me something? What in the name of…" Destan almost laughed as she grabbed his hand and started dragging him over.

Redje got out and then walked around, opening Tabitha's door.

Destan started to say something but stopped when he heard tapping on one of the back window as well as a muffled, high-pitched voice.

The father of this little voice winked as he plodded along, both the voice and tapping becoming more and more frequent. He laughed as he opened the door and helped unleash the fury of joy from her restraints; making sure she had her coat snapped as well as hat and mittens on before he released her into the wild.

"Desan!" Rose hit the ground running; the little pink fuzz ball on legs jumping for his leg when she got close. "Happy bewated— white, Papa? Bewated?"

"Close enough," Redje chuckled.

"Really?" Tabitha sighed. "We talked about this."

"You know she's not going to pay attention right now." Redje rolled his eyes.

"Happy bewated burfday, Desan!" Rose giggled as she looked up to him with wide eyes full of so much joy.

"I don't…" he sounded — and looked — baffled as he stumbled back from the impact.

"You don't think she'd miss her birthday 'and' yours in the same year… again. Do you?" Tabitha laughed as Redje handed her Benjamin. "Callimay was trying to ask me while she wasn't around, but Rose has a keen ear for the name of her 'Desan'."

"You all came?"

"We were due for 'family road trip'." Redje smiled as he came over and handed Callimay a box, then hugged Destan. "It's good to see you."

"Desan!" Rose jumped up and down as her hands that now looked like crab claws reached in the air for him.

"What?" Destan exaggerated as he, in one fluid motion, picked her up and tossed her in the air; her screaming with joy.

"Iza missed you wike 'dis' much!" She squirmed around in his arms, hugging his neck and then giving him a kiss on the cheek. "I wuv you, Desan. I wealwy do."

"I missed you too." He sighed as he freed one arm so he could give Tabitha a hug. "Thank you so much for coming."

"Doyen? Crying? Why I never…" Tabitha tried to make light. "It was the best Redje and I could think of on such short notice."

"It was perfect." Destan smiled, his glassy eyes sparkling with joy.

"He not cwying, Mama." Rose corrected as she puffed her cheeks and put her arms out. "Desan newver cwy! He wike Papa: stwong! … Wewl, Papa did cwy dat won time. … An I guess dat Desan did de won time, too. But dat it! — Wears de pwezent I got Desan?"

"Right here, Sweetheart." She handed her a small envelope.

"I made it mysewf, Desan." She said proud as she looked at it and then to him with her big eyes as she hugged it. "I dinnu wike de stuff dat was alweady made. Needer did Mama. I got it when I got Papa's for his burfday!"

"Well you've had this a little while, haven't you?"

"Forewver!" Rose exclaimed exhausted.

"Let's see what it is." Destan knelled down and let her sit on his knee as he took his gloves off and accepted the glitter spackled, pink envelope with his name jaggedly written on it… "and" misspelled.

Callimay chuckled to herself, seeing the glitter fall off the envelope onto his hands and Rose's lap. She was thrilled and started playing with it, rubbing it all over Destan's coat while he read the note Tabitha helped her write; her rambling on in her lisp-filled language, "Cwabby cwaws, cwabby cwaws. Dey awl spawkawee now! Wookie! Gwitter cwabby cwaws! Dey getted your nose. Ha! — I hurd dat people tink dis is fwom fairwees. But I know dat not twoo. Fairwees awn't weal. Gwitter is! Isn dat white, Desan? … Desan?"

He couldn't find words. In his hand was a heart-shaped key chain which had her and his names with a heart in between scribbled on one side, while the other said "I love you". It wasn't much, but it made Destan think about something: *Do you think? I mean~ Hold on there,*

Boon. ~ This isn't a bad thing. I've got to stop thinking that! Wanting a family with my wife if a good thing, it's a beautiful thing… it's what God intended for a husband and wife. Yes, the timing might not be best… but what if I don't make it? What does Calli have then?

She could hear as he processed the strong emotional reminder this tiny gift brought to the surface. At first she was willing to let it go, but then he started to spiral deeper and deeper: *Destan? I… I'm sorry. I was the one who said she could come.*

No, he sighed as he closed his eyes and hugged Rose tight; then let her go. *No, it's alright Calli. I needed this.*

"Doan cwy, Desan." Rose gasped as she put her little hands on either side of his face, leaving little patches of glitter on his cheeks. "Is awl white. I dinu huwt you, did I? Do you not wike it? I sowy."

"No. No you didn't, Rose. It's a beautiful present. Thank you."

"Oh goodie. I wouwd newver wan to make my Desan cwy." Rose hugged his neck again, her now convinced he wasn't "crying" crying.

"So. I finally get to meet the little man, huh?" Destan cleared his throat as he set Rose down and she ran to Callimay who was opening the box Redje gave her. "Is it alright if I hold him?"

"I'm fine with it… but are you sure?" Tabitha cautioned.

"I'm sure." Destan took a deep breath as he looked over at Callimay and Rose, them peering into a box at something dark. "How are you, Benjamin? Pretty hefty fella. They're feeding you well. That's good. — Looks like he's got the Manning chin. Skipped a generation, huh?"

"He does," Tabitha smiled as he tried to get his little arms out of their warm and safe home.

"A wiggle bug just like your sister. — Whose side is that from?"

"Destan," Callimay scolded.

"Hush, woman." He countered; her making a face at him.

"I bet Redje doesn't do that to Tabitha," she frowned as she put the lid on the box and stomped over. "Maybe Redje should take this back."

"Oh believe me," Tabitha laughed as she put her gloved hand on Callimay's arm. "Destan's nothing but a sad little babe who doesn't know the ways of the world… compared to my 'dear', 'loving', Redje."

"You're kidding me!"

"I wish I were." Tabitha looked at Redje out of the corner of her eye.

"But it's my way of showing you my undying love for you, Tabby Bae." Redje exaggerated; Rose giggling when she saw him kiss her.

"And your confidence that I won't leave you." Tabitha huffed as she ignored him; taking back Benjamin.

"So since I'm not so 'horrible', does that mean I get to keep the present?" Destan grinned as he winked, putting his hands on the box.

Callimay pursed her lips as she gripped it, "I don't know."

"'Can' Rej return it? Something tells me you wouldn't get a 'generic' gift." Destan raised his eyebrow as he played the box like a drum.

"No," Callimay sighed as she let it go.

"This is heavier than I thought! Geez! What did you get? An engraved lead stone?" Destan hoisted the box a couple times, laughing as Callimay made another face at him. "I'll stop. I'm sorry."

"You wong, Desan." Rose blurted out as she jumped up and down, clapping her hands. "Is a—"

"Shh!" Redje put his finger to his lips and shook his head. "It's a surprise, Sweetheart. Destan's supposed to find out himself."

Rose gasped as she clapped her hands across her mouth.

"It's not something— I don't know." Callimay sighed as she watched him open the box; him letting the lid fall to the ground. "I know it's a bit more 'practical' right now. And if you don't like it—"

"They actually figured it out?" Destan looked up shocked.

"Only took them fifteen years, but yep." Redje nodded as Destan pulled the tissue paper back to reveal the long Tantalum whip sword.

"D… do you like it?" Callimay asked worried as she crept over.

"You?"

"Well, Redje gave me the idea."

"Actually she jogged my memory." Redje gave a slight correction. "She talked about how you retired the dagger; so it came back."

"Is so heavy, Desan!" Rose leaned over and picked up the handle.

"Rose don't touch that!" Tabitha gasped as she reached out.

"Sweetheart, it's very sharp." Redje put his hand on Tabitha's and then kneeled down to take it from his daughter; sounding calm but stern. "And what have we said about sharp things?"

"But Cowimay said dat onwly de pointy end ez 'wealwy' shawp?" Rose asked confused. "It's not wike yours or Mama's."

"Roselyn!" Tabitha gasped again. "I told you—"

"It was onwly de won time you had dem out why you dwawling." Rose defended. "I dinnu get dem out. I pwamised I woodn't."

"Here. Let me hold it so you can look at it. — Is that alright Rej?" Destan asked as Redje looked at Tabitha.

"Tabby?"

"A… alright. Just don't touch it, Sweetheart. Okay?"

"Awl white, Mama." Rose nodded as she smiled; flinging her arms behind her and squirming in place.

"Your cheeks look like they're cold." Destan squeezed her one a bit.

She fussed as she shook her head, but laughed.

"Here. What do you think?"

"Is a wooks wike a bwack snake!" She ran and hid behind Redje's leg. "Snakes huwt ducks! I doan wike it, Desan. Put it back."

"Alright. Alright." He chuckled as he coiled it back in the box.

"She's right." Callimay's eyes widened.

"What? You're scared of them too?" Destan joked.

"More like terrified." Callimay shivered; then diverted, "Why don't you put it in the car and I'll grab the food."

"You brought enough for them, too?"

"You didn't realize how much you were packing?" She tried to keep from busting out laughing; then said to herself: *There's a hut not too far Tabitha was alright with. I didn't know how strict she was on Rose not being around Bulwark.*

She's always wanted Rose — and I know Benjamin — to have a normal and carefree life. Something she never had. She doesn't want them to even know it's an issue; she doesn't want them to have to comprehend what is going on and then try to explain no one can know. Destan sighed as he walked to the car. *It's hard because that means they can't go where they'd like to go or let her do certain things, but they're doing a great job with finding ways with our network of contacts. And let's face it: what she doesn't know about is pretty meaningless in the grand scheme of things. Plus — Lord-willing — they won't have to worry about any of that much longer.*

"Can wez wace dare?" Rose asked excited as she tugged on Destan's coat and looked at her father with glee.

"You sure you can you keep up?" Destan raised his eyebrow as Redje picked her up.

"No abilities." Redje frowned as Rose giggled and squealed.

"Agreed," Destan nodded as he looked back.

"We'll be there as soon as we can." Tabitha sighed as she waved on.

Destan and Redje smiled at each other, Rose clapping her hands and then wrapping her arms around her father's neck and snuggling close as she closed her eyes, "Go go go, Papa! Wealwee fast!"

Callimay stood there and again almost busted out laughing as the two grown men in front of her started sprinting; bickering and shouting at each other the entire way. Rose's squeals mixed in made it that much more amusing.

She knew this visit would help Destan, but the gleam in his eye at the mention of a race put more "life" in him than she thought possible. — Could she have been upset that it was Redje who did it? Of course. Was that a thought which crossed her mind? Certainly not.

🕉

As they came up to the door, Tabitha looked at the eave where a row of jagged icicles hung. She had a grin blossom on her face as she walked over, plucking one of the low-hanging ones off and breaking it into small pieces, "Oh I'm so glad you had second winter this year."

"What are you doing?"

She hushed as she looked in the window and then trotted over to Callimay, "Could you do me a favor? I know this is all for Destan's birthday, but I think he'll get a kick out of this."

"What?" Callimay asked rather cautious.

"Could you ask Destan in your superpower way to keep Redje occupied? Oh! And not facing the door. I don't want him to know we're here. If Rose says something don't worry about it. I just don't want him to see this."

"O… kay?"

A few moments passed, Tabitha prodding, "Umm… will you?"

"I already did."

"Oh! Sorry." Tabitha somewhat flinched. "I guess I was expecting some— oh never mind. What did he say?"

"He said it wasn't a problem." Callimay reached for the door handle. "What are you planning?"

"You'll just have to wait and see."

They came in so casual, Rose running over and going on and on about how Destan and Redje started having a snowball fight so "she" ended up winning the race. She sounded so proud as she talked a mile a minute.

Tabitha knelled down to Rose's level and put her finger to her lip before she showed her what was in her hand. Rose's eyes got as big as dinner plates as she had the biggest smile Callimay had seen from her. She tried not to giggle as she took the ice chunks out of her mother's hand, whispering, "Ooo Mama. Dey wealwy wet!"

"Shh, Sweetheart." Tabitha calmed as she looked at Callimay a bit confused. "Ca… Callimay? Would you hold her up?"

"Sure," she leaned over and took her in her arms, still confused.

"No, Cowimay." Rose shook her head, trying to wiggle and twist so she was facing away from her. "Iza gots to be facing Papa to do dis."

"Oh no," hers mouth fell open as she whipped her head over toward Tabitha.

"O… h yes." She replied determined.

"Wets go, Cowimay!" Rose nodded her head furiously, her lunging forward to get her to move. "But yooze must be quiet just wikes a ninja! You no how? Mama teached me!"

"I know."

"Oh goodie. We musts do dat, Papa must not knows we awe dare. And as I dwap dem in, you has to tug on his cowar. Dats de ownwy way dey wiwl go down."

She tried to suppress her laugher as she started over; staying in Redje's blind spot.

When they got right behind him, Rose nodded as she put her hands — which were dripping with water — over Redje's back and up to the collar of his shirt. Callimay pulled it back and Rose threw open her hands, the little frozen pieces of water free falling into their new home.

"Ah! What the— Tabby!" Redje stood straight up and started hopping and jumping around as he yelled; trying to reach the now numerous frozen pieces of water that were racing down his back.

The way Redje danced around looked more like he was being shocked by some electrical poker. Rose was giggling so much as she patted and rubbed his back, Tabitha trying so hard not to laugh too loud so Benjamin wouldn't cry — Callimay doing the same — while Destan let out the loudest laugh.

"Seriously?" Redje huffed as he tried to catch his breath, now untucking his shirt; sending some pieces flying. "What in the 'world' did you do? Crush them with a hammer? Gosh! Ah! Oh that's cold. — Tabitha Anime! What in heaven's name possessed you to do that?"

"There was ice outside. What was I supposed to do?" Tabitha stifled yet another laugh, Benjamin looking like he was just about ready to go full-blown angry mode. "It's a whole lot more fun than those big ice cubes. … Oh quit being a baby. They melt much faster since they're small. I could've just brought in a full-length icicle you know."

"Oh for love of…"

"You sneak up on him and…" Destan trailed off as he pointed at Redje while looking at Tabitha, him leaning on his knees as he tried to catch his breath; still laughing.

"I do too, Desan!" Rose piped in as Callimay put her down. "Mama wuvs to do it, but sometimes she howds me and wets 'me' do it! Duh won time I did it mysewlf! But I spiwled my gwass of wemonade which it. Oopsies! — Papa 'wealwee' yewl, dinu he, Mama?"

Redje grumbled as he shivered and shoved his shirt back in, "Too much like your mother."

"It's just my way of showing I love you," Tabitha batted her eyes.

"I… y… oh you just wait." Redje shivered again as his face pruned, him shaking his finger at her.

"I can go get some more if you'd like."

"No! I… I…"

"Yo-ou what?"

He wanted to keep going, but knew more ice could be awaiting him if he did, "I'm gonna stop. That's what I'm gonna do. Humph! No more victorious comebacks for you!"

Once the lingering snickers and banter died out, they sat down and had a wonderful meal; Destan looking relaxed and happy. Well that was until there were a couple comments made about a substance on his face. He all but scraped it trying to get off what was acting like it was permanently glued to his face; prompting Callimay to take over.

But even with her attempts it was quite apparent the glitter was happy where it was.

"I think I would have preferred the ice attack."

"Oh, hush," Callimay calmed his pouting fit as he rubbed and rubbed his face to get the shining little bits off.

"Geez! This is even worse than your makeup, Calli! What in the—where did you get this stuff, Tabitha?"

"Well it had glue on it, Destan. That's how it stuck to the envelope in the first place."

"Just great."

"Desan wooks so pwetty." Rose giggled as she crawled up onto his lap and stood on his legs to see his face. "Just wike my dawls."

"Ugh!" Destan threw his head back.

"It'll come off," Callimay assured as she tried to stop laughing.

"'Eventually', ole pal. Wear it as a badge of honor for now. Battle scars of one you… 'didn't' win." Redje winked. "Believe me, I know."

Destan shook his head as he sighed, wrapping Rose in a bear hug and swinging her back and forth as "punishment". Though with her squealing and laughing it didn't appear to be working as such.

After this was all done, Rose looked around the room confused, "Wear's de burfday cake? Desan must bwoa out his candles while he says his burfday bwessing! White? I mean I no it not wealwy wong to knot do, but how tan he which out it?"

"I don't need a cake for that." Destan smiled as he got up and walked behind Callimay's seat, leaning over and snuggling his head close to hers. "I'm thankful for the blessing of my wife and everything she's done for me. How she's shown me a beautiful side to life I'd have never known about without her."

She closed her eyes as he wrapped his arms around her even tighter.

Rose giggled as she put her fingers over her eyes and swung her legs back and forth; them slamming against the chair legs.

"And I'm also thankful for all of my friends, my Christian brothers and sisters, and the joy they bring into my life through their love and constant examples." Destan smiled as he looked across the table at

Redje and Tabitha. "They've helped me grow and reminded me I'm not alone. — Does that work, Rose?"

So lost in thought, she tilted her head as she looked at the ceiling for a while; and then nodded, "I guess since it not de weal day and you owld now ita wowk."

"Roselyn!" Tabitha hushed.

"She gets her one-uppin' from you, Rej." Destan made a face as he turned his attention back to Rose. "I am pretty old, aren't I?"

"Not wealwee 'dat' owld." She shook her head as she pointed. "You hear not gway."

"Oh…" Destan dragged out as he nodded in an exaggerated way; finally laughing. "Well thank goodness for that."

♉

"Thank you so much for coming," Callimay's voice sounded so content as she gave Tabitha one last hug once she finished getting Benjamin in his car seat.

"Like we said, we hadn't decided where our early spring trip would be, so this was perfect timing for us." She smiled as Redje popped his head up on the other side of the car, hinting to her Rose was fastened in and ready to go as well.

"It was a wonderful gift for Destan." Callimay smiled as she looked back and saw the now long and stoic look on his face: *What's wrong?*

Nothing.

Destan?

"You two take care. Alright?" Tabitha rubbed Callimay's arm as she waited for an answer.

"Oh! … Oh, we will. You have a safe trip back." She tried to pull herself away from the strange tension she felt building. "Are you going to get any chance to see your family on the way back? They don't live 'that' far away, right?"

"Benjamin isn't a big fan of car rides — Lord help me — but Rose is good about keeping him distracted and playing with him as much as possible. So the shorter the better for everyone." She sighed and shook her head as she started to look worried. "Callimay?"

"Yes?"

"I… please take care of each other. Come back to Rayleen, in one piece, happy, healthy, and real soon. We all miss you more than you realize and want you back home." She said teary-eyed as she gripped her hand. "I've loved getting to know you and I want to keep doing so. … I know it may seem out of the blue to say that, but your mention of me seeing my family? Callimay, I can't go back unless this all gets fixed. I know Destan said it was possible since you were able to get the Swinchpuck family on our side and things are stable, but for me to show up right now? I love them all so much and I know they love and miss me too… but I just wouldn't want to take any more risks than I already am. If Rose and Benjamin lost them because of th—"

"Lord willing, once we get one loose end tied up we're going to break this all wide open as quickly as possible. I promise you. Hang in there." Callimay wrapped her in a bear hug, trying her best not to cry. "You take care of each other. We're praying for you every day. Just please keep praying for us. This loose end isn't going to be an easy fix. In fact it's— just pray. Don't stop praying. We need it so bad for this loose end that we didn't expect to deal with. And right now it's going to take a true miracle to take care of it."

Both women spent a moment trying to get their emotions together, them both nodding as they squeezed hands.

"Tell Mrs. Manning we said hello. I know she had that scare a little while back with the stroke. I'm sorry I wasn't there to help."

"Redje's taking it the hardest. He doesn't show it but he is. It's hard for him to see her disoriented; thank God she remembers him. I don't think he'd be able to handle that. — She's basically his grandmother. — I'll see about mentioning you when I'm alone with her… but she 'may' not remember you." She sniffled as she died off to a whisper. "People she's met in the last couple years she's has issues remembering. I haven't said anything about it to Redje, yet. I just can't bear to."

"Whatever you think is best." Callimay encouraged as Redje walked over. "I didn't mean to make her cry, really I didn't. I'm sorry."

"This is all emotional for everyone." Redje sighed as he looked at Destan. "I should offer you the same apology."

Destan looked torn up and lost as his wife looked over to him. Her eyes got wide as he rushed over to the car and got in, turning it on.

"Go ahead, Callimay." Tabitha nodded. "We love you both."

"Let us know what's going on and what we can help with." Redje said as he waved to her.

She hated to run off, only getting out, "I… let me know when you guys get back. … I— I'm sorry. I need to go."

Callimay could hear the muffled voice of Rose as she ran to the car, scared Destan was going to take off without her. But the door opened for her and she saw Destan's arm withdraw. She slipped in and shut the door, him pealing out the second her door closed.

His thoughts were so scattered she didn't know what the root cause of this was; and even though terrified she dared to ask: *Destan?*

"I'm… I'm alright. I just wanted to leave before they did." He turned off the road and stopped the car, leaning his forehead on the wheel.

"Alri—"

"Calli?" He looked at her, eyes bloodshot and nose bright red… tear stains on his face. "Are you alright if I take a short trip?"

"Where to?" *Idiot! Why did—* "It doesn't ma—"

"Downing."

"A… alright." She nodded, hiding her shock as best she could.

"Okay." Destan put the car back into gear and kept going, sighing as he reached over with his trembling hand to take hers. "I love you."

ℬ

There wasn't anything — good or bad — said for the rest of the trip. Callimay wanted so bad for today to be relaxing; and while it was for so long… something happened and it all felt ruined.

He took a deep breath as he turned the car off and faced to her, "I'm sorry I… Rej asked me about something and it got me to thinking. He knows every year right around my birthday I go to my parents' graves; that it's… well it's a big deal to me. Last year I couldn't go and wasn't expecting to because I thought I'd still be at the Society, but he asked if things were at a spot where I went this year. … I think it is possible and I really want to, Calli. I just…"

The words he wanted to say he struggled to let find the air of life; yet the soft touch of his wife's hand on his reassured him, "I don't want to sound heartless because… I want to do it today, but I've always gone alone. It's always been my private memorial I give them each year. Rocher's only ever driven me from the station in Berchshire to Heirway and that was when I was younger. — But I don't… I don't want to push you out. Especially when you worked so hard to get me away from everything today. I just don't know how to make it so—"

"It's alright. I understand." She reached over and gave him as much of a hug as she could. "If you need to go by yourself t—"

"But I 'want' you with me."

She could feel the battle in him starting to escalate. He was fighting to keep her and function in these "strange" moments that still popped up every now and again. He wanted to win the battle as in keep her by his side, but there was obvious resistance to her being included.

"Destan? Destan listen to me." She soothed as she ran her fingers through his hair. "I'm not going to be mad if you go by yourself. I know what a… 'private' and personal thing it is to visit the grave of a parent. — I always went by myself. — Please calm down. I don't like you upset like this. I'm okay staying here. … And think of it this way: I'll be here so you don't need to worry about missing something. Sound good?"

"But I don't want to push you away." He grimaced as he buried his face in her hair. "I know how much it hurt y—"

"You're not, Destan. You're not." Callimay whispered as she fought back tears. "It's hard, I know. Believe me, I do. But you need this time alone. It's okay. I understand. And I 'want' you to have that time."

There was a little while that transpired before Destan calmed enough so she felt safe to let him be. And so he sat there and held her, waiting a few minutes before letting her go, "Let's go inside. Okay?"

"Alright."

As he got out, he saw her open the back door, "What are you getting? Oh just leave th—"

"Oh I'm not getting 'that'. It's the dishes and leftovers," she popped back out with the basket.

"Oh, Calli. I'm sorry everything—"

"This was all for 'your' birthday," she laid her hand on his cheek and then let it slide off and rest on his chest. "I just wanted today to be a break for you. To do what 'you' wanted. … I'd say I need to be sorry for that being uprooted, but I guess it— oh it doesn't matter. What's done is done. Redje and Tabitha have no ill-will about what happened. They told me so.”

“It’s the best birthday I’ve had in I can’t tell you how long. No matter if it was two months late.” He broke a sliver of a smile as he took his presents out of the back seat.

“It did get away from me, didn’t it?”

“Well let’s face it: we really didn’t have a chance before now with all that’s been going on.” Destan took the box with his sword from her.

“I’ve been dying to ask you this question: why did you want this kni— ‘sword’, I guess, specifically?”

“My hand-to-hand combat is where my strength lies, but I always prefer to have my opponent a healthy distance away so I can ‘see’ them and what they’re doing.” Destan started as they began walking back, him taking her hand in his. “Some Falconers love to have hidden blades and needles on them; and of course they’re laced in one way or another. Having their ‘prey’ close to them gives them a chance to use them with deadly accuracy. I don’t ever want to give them that chance. — I’m not answering your question, am I?”

“You’re fine,” she smiled as he stopped and looked down at the box.

“When you first talked about what you thought the Shadow symbol was you were kinda right… in a way. Remember you said the ‘S’ looked like a ribbon?”

“Yes.”

“Well, when I was originally shown the design I thought of the whips that ranchers use. — And as a side note: when I saw the veils I thought of duster coats too.” Destan winked as he bumped into her a bit and then started walking again. “When I really got to looking at the Shadow’s emblem I realized the ‘S’ wasn’t the guard of the handle of a sword or the curve of the crescent moon — even though they are — all I saw was this sword. Call me all geeky and nerdy; I don’t care. At the time that’s all I saw and thought about; and what teenage boy with my disposition toward that sort of stuff wouldn’t see that? But! I think there was something more than my eye for fantastic knives that brought that all about: my grandmother actually designed this sword specifically for me. She gave me the plans for it but I wasn’t allowed to open them until after she passed. … I’ve actually been able to see some of her collection that she designed herself and it's stunning. — Rocher told me he'd do what he could to make sure I got all of them; I've got a dozen or so right now. — But back to the plans for this one, the mechanics for it wasn't something that was mastered by the foragers and craftsmen the Shadows trusted. Finding the right material to make it was the other problem. It needed to be tough enough to take a beating while flexible enough to have the give needed in such a sword. Then it needed to be something that wouldn't weigh a ton. And — yeah, there's quite a bit that was wrong with this; which is why I was so shocked when I saw it — the whole issue of it being non reflective since it wouldn't be in a sheath? It took a while, but the last I heard, Tantalum was the material our smiths said would work best. It was still semi reflective, but they said it could be coated with a special, scratch-resistant ebonized finish to give it our standard matte black color. Sounds great, huh? … Yeah, there was still one problem left: Tantalum isn't a metal found on any other planet than the Homeworld. And even there it's super rare. There was a small amount known to have been purchased and brought to Quidoria, but I don't know who has it. And I have no doubt it is locked up tight and costs more than anything even 'I' could ever think of. — Speaking of which: what 'is' this made out of?"

"Umm. Well… it's supposed to be Tantalum." She said rather timid.

"What in the— how!" Destan stopped in his tracks and almost flashed his eyes at her. "I know this isn't something I usually say, but this is one of the very few things we can't afford."

"I don't know how it worked out. I just asked Redje." She bowed her head, her hands gripping the basket with an almost death-grip. "He took care of everything since I didn't know much about it."

"'He' paid for this?" Destan asked shocked, his voice sounding softer as he took a small step back.

"No," Callimay shook her bowed head.

He put the box down and kneeled in front of her so he could see her face, "I'm sorry if I sound mad. I'm just— who paid for it?"

"I did?" Callimay sniffled as her eyes darted back and forth.

"You!"

"I saved money over the years and still had what was left in my regular account," she began to explain as he rubbed her hands.

"Granted it still wasn't quite enough, so Trever gave me the last little—how in the world, if you say you couldn't afford it, could I?"

"Do you have the receipt for it?" Destan asked as he opened the box and moved the sword and then the paper in the bottom.

"There was this little note in the box when I checked it, but I didn't bother to read it." Callimay took the small envelope out of her pocket.

They read it together and figured everything out in the short few sentences, "Grandfather!"

"Brigon is the country that bought it. All of it?" Destan mumbled.

They sat there for a while and stared at each other.

Destan then picked the sword up to put it back in the box; his finger running across what felt like a scratch. He stopped and looked at it, "What's this?"

Callimay whipped her head around to see what was wrong, rushing over and seeing Destan feeling etchings in the flexible, yet connected sections of the midnight black metal, "Oh! — I thought something was wrong. — I was looking through your father's Bible one day and came across a note I knew was yours. It had those verses listed." Callimay bowed her head and wrung her hands. "I read through them and could see the theme of leadership and protection in them. Had I not done that I could've paid for it myself. But I guess grandfather just let me think I was the one who paid f—"

She stopped because Destan had thrown his arms around her and pulled her close. He was doing his best to hold back the influx of emotions he was feeling, but needed to let it out somehow. So he kept saying over and over again how thankful he was to her, grateful for what she did, and that he loved her so much.

✠

The rest of the walk was quiet; Destan ignoring the belvedere and getting ready to leave the moment he walked in. Of course it didn't seem like he would need to do much, but the fact was he spent quite a bit of time getting ready; coming out wearing a dress shirt and a pair of slacks… he even had his wool winter coat and fixed his hair so it looked a tad different than she was accustomed to.

He was lost as he looked around, asking, "Where are you?"

"I'm in the kitchen." She called out apologetic. "I'm coming. I went ahead and packed you something to—"

"C… Calli?" Destan asked rather unsure as his eyes darted back and forth as she jogged over to hand him a bag.

"What's wrong?"

"How fast can you get ready?"

"I… but I…"

"I changed my mind. I want you to come. … Please." Destan put his quivering hands on her shoulders and looked her dead in the eye. "Please, Calli. I 'need' you to come with me. I don't wanna be alone. Not when I don't have to be."

"I… I'll… just give me a couple minutes." Callimay fumbled as she took a hard swallow, trying to get her thoughts together.

"Alright." He sighed as he let her go.

She rushed in and scanned what she had, trying to find something black: *I… I don't want to wear this. Destan's not wearing his. He made sure not to wear it. This isn't just a run in the middle of the night. This is something important in such a different way. … Surely there's 'something' in this closet! Goodness gracious. I just don't understand why I don't have anything black. Oh! Wait! I could~ That's not a bad idea, Rose Petal. ~ But what if he doesn't have time to stop? ~ It's on the way. It'd be fine. ~ I know. But you know how he is about timelines. ~ Just ask him. It won't hurt anything. ~ Alright. …* "Destan!"

After calming her, he sat down beside her and took her hand in his; his voice so soft, "What's your question?"

There were a few moments of silence, but she gathered her courage — for whatever reason she thought she needed it — and said, "I don't have anything but my ensemble that's black. … At least not here."

"It's fine. I know your wardrobe doesn't have the bleak 'color'. You can wear your ensemble, it's okay."

"I know this means so much to you, though." Callimay fiddled with her shirt hem while looking in his sad, yet loving eyes. "I don't want this dragging along with us. I have a very nice black dress at the house in Berchshire I could throw on after we get into Downing. It wouldn't take me but a minute. I know exactly where I left it. I just don't know if… if you don't think we'd have time I understand. I j—"

"Y… you'd do that? Just for this?" Destan asked stunned as he almost flinched and pulled back.

"This isn't a 'just' type of thing. As much as I'm able to I want to help and support you. — For some reason I thought this would."

"The house isn't that far. I don't think it'd be a problem." Destan sounded a bit better; the sparkle starting to come back to his eyes. "You can wear that until we get there if you want. Though it'd be best if you wore your wool coat to help keep you hidden at first. Plus it's freezing cold out."

"Rocher is flying us there… right?"

"I forgot to ask bef—"

"Let me go."

"No. I'll go." Destan took her hand and stopped her. "Meet me by the ascent. Okay?"

"Alright," she nodded as she rubbed his hand before he let go.

℘

Callimay sat next to him in the jet and never said a word, knowing all too well what he was going through… and that there wasn't a word of comfort she could give. — Well, at least she couldn't think of one aside from the ones she'd been given by others that she appreciated.

When Rocher said they were landing, Destan snapped to somewhat. And it was at that point he "realized" she was there, "Why are you sitting there?"

"Oh, I'm fine." She replied a bit startled as she smiled.

"Remind me not to head straight there." He mumbled under his breath as he took her hand and looked out the window. "If I forgot you're with me right now then I'm most likely going to forget that."

"Alright," she encouraged as she leaned over and framed his face, giving him a kiss.

He let that small smile out, but it just had nothing to make it stick; and she couldn't blame it. It tried, it really did.

℘

Once on the ground and everything was settled, they started off in two opposite directions. He was "this" close to snapping at her, but the innocent tone of her voice reminded him she wasn't his enemy. She was doing what he told her to.

They stopped about a mile down the road and worked their way through the fields; getting in through the basement.

Callimay scurried upstairs and vanished into her bedroom; not waiting for him to come with her.

There was a certain hush in the air of that was comforting and calm as he wandered around the room after lighting an oil lamp he found. The ebbing flame was so soft as it fingered the furniture and other surfaces. Snow's blanket was tucked in outside; the clouds apparently not happy with the thickness since the new addition began to fall. The window panes were etched with beautiful and intricate frost "leaf" designs. — He closed his eyes and took a deep breath when he saw them, seeming to remember something happy and peaceful.

Not but a minute later Callimay walked out in a plain — but still beautiful — black, lace-covered dress with matching leggings, gloves, and short boots. She had her mouth opened to say something, but seeing how Destan looked made her stop. She folded her hands in front of her and bowed her head.

A couple minutes later, her glancing up a few times while waiting, she saw him stirring. His pain-ridden face, slouched shoulders, and quivering hands showed her just how close he was to losing it.

She ran over and took the glass jar filled with oil, quickly setting on the table behind her.

Now she understood more of why he was like that countless times at the mansion — now knowing what he went through — and she just couldn't stand seeing the man she loved like this. She knew he didn't like to be vulnerable when there were others around; and knew he still wasn't comfortable with her in certain circumstances, still, "Destan? I… I'll drive. Just let me know where to go when we get close to Heirway. … Destan?"

"I'm sorry," he mumbled under his breath as he closed his eyes.

"It's alright. Don't worry about it."

He leaned over and blew the light out, not looking any better but stabilizing, emotionally. He took her hand and pulled her close, saying a prayer before they left.

The drive was quiet though not nearly as tense as the flight; but it still wasn't the easiest. And it was for a totally different reason: Callimay knew the roads in Faberton were not the greatest, but add to that the fact they didn't put much into keeping them cleared during the winter?

Rose Petal, ask him. ~ No! He's just now relaxed. You know that. Everything's fine. ~ What about the pass? ~ I'm not even sure where the graveyard in Heirway is. I might not even need to drive through there. ~ Fine. But don't blame me if~ Oh, be quiet.

And as it turned out, Destan told her to turn off just before the pass. The road winded quite a bit as they went up, but it was in better shape… which struck her as odd because there was more snow: *Maybe they keep it clear because they get more up here? ~ That makes some sense. They would be accustomed to it and prepared. ~ How much farther? It 'is' winter, but the night only lasts so long, Rose Petal. ~ We've got plenty of time. Don't worry.*

Destan's voice sounded like he was frightened as he talked with her, him getting more and more anxious as they went along.

We're close. We've got to be. There's no other reason for him to be acting this way. — Oh, Destan. I… I don't know what to do to help. ~ Ask him, Rose Petal. ~ I can't. Look at him. If I… I just can't.

"This is it, Calli," he gestured to their left.

She pulled into the drive of an older cemetery that was "plain" and simple, almost as if it were a forgotten place. But then again, when Destan's parents died he didn't have "control" over the money his father had: *Maybe this was the best that could be done at the time.*

"Father's will stipulated he wanted to be buried here, Calli." Destan replied softly as he reached for the door and stared off into nothing. "This is where his father is."

"I… I didn't mean to—"

"It's alright." He took a deep breath as he looked around. "C… could you wait here? I… I don't—"

"Take all the time you need."

He got out and came around, reminding as he opened her door, "If anything seems off or you don't feel safe…"

"I'll come for you." She nodded as she got on her tip-toes and gave him a kiss on the cheek. "I'll be waiting here."

"I— thank you, Calli." He rubbed the side of her face.

"I love you."

It hurt to stand there and watch as Destan wandered away from her — although at first she had to fight the urge to help steady him since he staggered a bit. While she understood all too well how he felt; seeing just how much it physically affected him almost scared her. This wasn't her husband at all.

And then out of nowhere it hit her, looking at him at that moment. He was wearing gloves, a fedora, wool scarf, and a Crombie coat.

Okay, the coat wasn't that big of a deal because he had one just like it; but the scarf, hat, "and" gloves? Destan never wore such things! At least she'd never seen him wear any until now.

He soon disappeared so she leaned back against the hood of the car, keeping an ever watchful eye to make sure no one was around; but she became entranced by the snow while it drifted to-and-fro, as if it were swinging from limb to limb of invisible trees. Everything was peaceful and quiet. And while she couldn't see much, the view there had to be beautiful during the day no matter what time of year it was.

Then came a small skirmish within her. She knew she couldn't leave her "post" in watching over Destan's emotions, but she wanted so bad to let him have this time: *It doesn't hurt now so maybe I could. Just for a little while? ~ It's risky, Rose Petal. ~ I know it is. But he deserves his privacy. ~ But you kept on and on about how he wouldn't let you in? ~ This is different. Very different. I've always let him have his space about this. There's nothing I'm 'changing' if you think about it. He needs this time. He needs it so bad. Who knows what's waiting for us in the next weeks? Having this little time to let everything go? I know how it feels. You feel like you're with them again, their little child, free of cares, and blissfully unaware of so much. I know that's how he feels.*

Callimay knew he was at the grave sites, so she looked at her watch and decided to give him five minutes.

Everything was strange now that she didn't feel any pain, so turning off her ability almost felt bad and wrong; but she was trying to remind herself this was how it was supposed to be all along.

She checked her watch every couple seconds, gripping his wedding band that hung around her neck as she waited.

And waited.

And waited.

Just how long was five minutes, again?

But finally, it was over. Emotionally he wasn't "good" by any means, but he wasn't in a dangerous place. So she did her best to not "listen" and just keep an eye on his emotions.

It had been a half hour now and she knew with the time it took for them to get up there it was getting close to the max time before they had to leave. They needed to be airborne by the time the sun came up.

So as much as she hated to, she crept into the cemetery to find him and gently remind him they needed to leave soon.

As she tip-toed in, she heard a muffled wind chime. Against better judgement, she entertained this distraction and looked around, finding one next to a small headstone. Callimay didn't want to disrespect anyone, but she'd found Mrs. Berchoff's cleared before and appreciated whoever took the time while they were there visiting the site of their loved one to — in a very small way — pay their respects to her mother. She knelled in front of the stone and gently pushed the snow away, cleaning off the chime and stone itself. The chimes tinkled their high-pitch thank yous as they settled back into their accustomed positions.

You're welcome… Nathan. … You were only— not even a year? What does this part say? … You weren't even born! You died— I can't even begin to imagine the pain your parents w— Destan!

She felt a spike of some kind and took off.

While it wasn't a big graveyard, it was still big enough that she had to "look" for him… seeming to forget the fact he was the only one there so all she had to do was follow the footprints.

When she saw him she stopped dead in her tracks. He'd cleared away the snow from both plots and was sitting on a bench between them at the foot. He was hunched over with his head bowed and hands clasped in front of him, his voice so soft and sorrowful as he spoke out loud. — But something was different. What?

As she inched a bit closer, Callimay began to understand. Destan had taken the hat, scarf, and gloves off. The scarf was draped over his mother's stone while the hat and gloves rested on his father's. She clapped her hand over her mouth as she gasped, now understanding.

"I know. We need to go," he said a bit louder as he sat up, his deep breath filling the air around him with fog; him still facing away from her. "I know this is in some ways stupid and useless, but would you indulge me for a minute? — Father? Mother? I know you're not 'here', but this is where I left your physical bodies and where I come to talk to you when I can. … I have someone very special with me this year."

He slid to the one side of the bench and looked back at Callimay, reaching his hand out to her.

Upset she interrupted him, she stepped back and shook her head.

Unwilling to accept her well-meant, respectful distance, he let that small smile flash across his face as he motioned for her to come. And so how could she refuse?

She bowed her head and scurried over, taking his hand as she slid on the bench beside him as quiet as she could.

"This is Callimay. Maybe you remember her when we were visiting her family that one time. … Well, we've been married over a year now. I can say without a doubt she 'is' my Jewel, Father. I found her. And I promise you — as I've promised her — to do everything I can to keep her safe and show her every day that I love her." Destan finished as he looked over to her and then gave her a kiss. "Just like your example you gave me of how you loved mother. … And I know Calli would love to listen to you play, Mother. In fact, she knows how to play, herself. And how to play with me like you did. I know you two would get along so well. You're so much alike. You even both like your tea the same way."

There was this awkward silence as he stared into her eyes with his bloodshot, glassy ones; but as awkward as it was, there was a look of deep-seated love that captivated her and told her everything was going to be alright. That and his words showed her he was doing so much better; moving on as best he could from the past. He was choosing to remember the good there was and let what happened to him in the present interact with those memories.

"Stay here," Destan leaned over and whispered in her ear.

He went to his mother's stone first and kneeled in front, apparently saying something under his breath from the fog puffs of air she saw; he then took the scarf and put it on. He then did the same at his father's and came back to her and offered his hand, "Ready? I'll drive."

"I can. It's alright."

"You did an amazing job coming up here but I know that took a lot out of you." He took her hand as they continued along. "I'll be fine to go back. I promise."

He's not looking back? ~ He came here to see them and has peace again. … And I'd even be bold enough to guess it's even more so this year. Sure, it's not 'easy' but it's 'easier' if you don't look back. ~ It is.

♃

As they got to the western edge of Berchshire, Callimay could begin to see the change in the sky. She'd had the fleeting thought of stopping and seeing Mrs. Berchoff's gravesite, but she knew it was too late.

And really? She was alright with it. This trip was for Destan and she knew good and well if she went to that gravesite she's loose it and need time to get herself together so she could leave again.

"I know why you've been so quiet and kept everything to yourself this whole time… but I'm still your husband, Calli." Destan seemed to say out of the blue. "I'm not taking a break from it just because of this. If you have a request or a question, just talk to me. Okay? Nothing's changed. Yes, I thought I needed some space, but you reminded me in your beautiful and quiet way I need you more."

~ 16 ~

They were emotionally exhausted, but at the same time they were at peace and content. And when they came back to Deep Dark, there were a few encouraging messages from Trever which helped this transition even more.

He said he was going to stay longer; letting them know he was doing alright and Kayla wanted to stay since it was nice to have him around for so long. It seemed her relations with those higher up leveled off and was stable, so that helped his situation even more with those he was around. So this was going to give him time and access to find some kind of additional information they could use to take down the Elites — he wasn't just friendly with people there, he was getting in on meetings.

As good as this was, Destan and Callimay knew there were risks. Destan wanted so bad to have that fool-proof plan to get him out "and" take down every single one of those Elites — Toreon included —so they could have that assurance of security again so they could continue on. He didn't like everything being on hold… and he knew no one else did. But compared to the alternative, this was all they could do.

One of Trever's latest notes puzzled Destan and then made him overly suspicious. He refused to tell Callimay about it which was so far removed from what he usually did. In fact he would have "secret" meeting away from her and she couldn't help but think it was about that very topic.

It made her curiosity burn, but she kept telling herself it could do with something that she's forgotten… and Destan doesn't want her to remember. And in light of what happened last time, it helped douse the flame of her curiosity.

But still, what was it?

Aside from this all came some rather bizarre news from Linton, "I just got word the Artemisia was destroyed."

"Why?" Destan asked confused.

"It wasn't working like Baleck, and then their engineers, promised it would. Vashti was in one of her rage fits so she laid the first couple blows to it and then sent it off to be 'properly' destroyed."

"Well, even if it didn't have a thing to do with giving abilities to people, I'm glad they don't have it." Destan sighed as he flopped onto his chair, it rolling back a bit. "Why did she want it so bad, anyway?"

"Because she thought it would save her," Linton rolled his eyes as he crossed his arms across his chest, leaning against the wall.

"From what?"

"I'll give you one guess."

"Does she have some form of aggressive arthritis or something?"

"You're thinking too logically about this." Linton shook his head. "Think a bit more farfetched. Then you'll be closer."

He tapped his desk for a few seconds but surrendered, "While I usually don't mind doing this, I guess I just can't think 'that' illogically right now. What is it?"

Linton raised his left hand and nodded his head toward it.

"Seriously?" The baffled tone of his voice a perfect complement to the speed at which he turned his chair. "She thought that could 'cure' her of being left-handed?"

"Bingo."

"But it wouldn't do that even if it could cure diseases."

"Oh believe me, I even said that a couple times when she'd blather on about it. But she was bent on it being her answer to her problem because of some off-the-cuff comment Baleck said one time."

Still trying to wrap his mind around this idiocy, Destan rubbed his face, "But why is she wanting to do that? I mean it's not like she has to worry about anyone finding out."

"Believe me when I say she doesn't have any reasoning to what she does when it all boils down to brass tax. Especially when it comes to her personal life." Linton shook his head a bit as he recalled a couple instances; then switched the subject a bit, "In better news I did get some information on where they possibly trashed it. So it may be possible to get it working again if we can find it."

"But Aldred is the only one who knows about it and he's—"

"He's not dead. Severely wounded, yes, but not dead."

"How do know all this?" Destan asked his point blank.

"As far as Vashti goes, that is all my experiences with her over the years. Aldred is because I was there during the aftermath. And then what's happened since? ... I do still have a few connections that are safe since they're at odds somewhat with 'higher ups' due to various reasons; money, mainly. I give them a way to compensate the loss by giving me intel. Some offering much more than I originally ask for because of their growing distrust."

I'm inclined to trust him on this because of what details we have gotten about a growing number being dissatisfied with how the money is being handled... but I also know this trust can't be blind. Plus, he's had these contacts and has never said a word about them until now. Though I have to give it to him: he was upfront about it when asked. "Would you mind getting names and such to Traceur?"

"But I gave... was it Enforcer? He's about your build and height, peppered hair and mustache, about mid-fifties? At least I could've sworn I gave him all of that information." Linton tried to think back.

"Oh. Yeah, that would be Enforcer. He's been gone for a while, but I recall him saying something about having a list of something for me." Destan remembered. "That's probably it. I'll try to get with him later today and make sure he's got it."

ℬ

Destan called a special Ring Meeting of the Veil and any diplomatic persons to get input from others to help him come up with an effective strategy which would limit casualties he knew he needed to be prepared for, "I don't pretend to know everything and I do not want to give the false impression I don't need or want help and suggestions."

"Are there any weaknesses known for these 'abilities', as you call them?" One of the political figures asked.

"There are, yes."

"Is there any common thread to them?" The individual continued.

"There are a couple 'groups' — if you will — that each have that one, single, and even major thread." Destan replied as he looked over the table in front of him and then picked up a few pages. "But a single thread for 'all' of them? No."

"Is there any way to isolate those groups?"

"Yes and no. We don't have much in the way of information about where each 'type' resides within the location we know about, but I wouldn't be a bit surprised if the Syndicate took the precaution of having them 'mixed' to avoid such situations."

"I know this is a bit of a side trail to the main issue, but do you know the nature of the 'missions' they are being sent out on?" Another diplomat asked.

"That's unknown, as disturbing as it is. We have some suspicions and leads, but nothing confirmed. The names and profiles we've been able to get to our recluse ops haven't shown any sightings of them."

"Does you spy in their place know who delivers orders each week? Surely they're sent by a messenger. … Or is it electronically?"

Callimay was standing back a little, watching and listening to see if something might spark an idea in her mind, but couldn't help but notice Destan's subtle reaction to that last question which was followed by an entire team of veils bolting for one of the computer rooms.

Things continued as if nothing was out of the usual, but then everything happened. The chaos that was taking place from one of the video feed left Callimay shocked, but she was bewildered no one cared. All the other feeds were off; only the chaos visible.

That's not the president, Calli. Destan comforted, though his tone still hinted at him being frustrated. *I did this meeting on purpose. Trever warned me about this president; that his name was mentioned a couple times; though he never knew why.*

Abilities? She stood up, sounding scared.

Dakoe's to be exact. He sounded somber as he nodded. *I talked with this president a couple times prior to Trever telling me, and I thought I was just tired because I didn't see him, but someone else at times. Then when Trever said something my suspicions grew; and as you can tell, with what he said he gave himself away.*

He did?

I never said that where Trever was receives orders every week. I mean they do, but I never said it to him.

Callimay's skin crawled, thinking how far the Syndicate was willing to go to in order to take them out; but then she gasped when she realized, Destan calming her: *Trever's fine. I've been keeping in close contact with him. This guy didn't get any info.*

Some info was given to the others to assure why their feeds were cut for a short time; and then they continued along. Several promising ideas were given, but each couldn't fit the vital piece of preserving life into it: *Destan? Do you need to step back for a bit?*

No. I can't, Calli. I know I have to accept the fact someone most likely won't make it out, but I can't… He replied; an edge in his tone.

Well you need to take a deep breath and calm down at least.

I'm fine.

Look at your hands. She persisted as the frown on her face grew. *You're getting upset. I understand we need to get this figured out and finding a 'safe' solution isn't looking to be possible, but you need to calm down. Even Traceur can notice it. Look at her.*

Destan took her advice and looked as his hands, then Traceur who was standing opposite him with eyes screaming danger; then sighed as he leaned on the desk: *I'm sorry, Calli. … Maybe I should take a b—*

Fidus whispered something in Destan's ear, causing him to whip his head over and look at him almost frightened. He looked back to those around him, and continued on.

Of course Callimay wasn't sure what that was about, but trusted when he had time he'd tell her… though that came sooner than she expected: *Calli?*

Yes?

Go to my station and call the last number listed on the incoming call list. Fidus just told me Aldred called and wanted to talk for some reason but would only talk to me. I really don't want to wait and give him a chance to change his mind about talking, but I need to stay here. Could you see if you can get him to talk with you? Please?

O… okay. Did Fidus say anything about what I should ask about?

No. But Calli? Be careful, okay? He's — in a way — a kinda rough character. I know it's just a phone call and there's no guarantee he'll talk to you, but I just want you to know. He never sounds like he has any emotional ties to anything or anyone: doesn't really care who lives or dies kinda deal. He's about as neutral as possible, but beyond self-centered. If he starts asking or demanding money, don't say a word and hang up on him. I know it's rude, but you don't need to be put in the middle; and he 'knows' that. I'll take care of that if it comes up.

A… alright.

I didn't mean to scare you, Destan sighed, feeling a change in her emotions. *I just want you to be prepared and know he's the type who doesn't care about how his actions can affect others: good or bad.*

I understand. — You better pay attention. I'll go see what this is about. Callimay tried to smile as she picked up the phone.

One last thing. Don't use your name or title. Just say you're my wife; using my real name. … And he knows 'who' I am, so don't spaz out if he calls me Doyen. Just don't encourage him.

Got it.

The phone rang and rang. And then cut off. Callimay took the phone away from her ear and looked to see the phone still said it was connected, then put it back to her ear, "Hello?"

"Who is this?" A harsh male voice pestered.

"Is this Aldred?"

"I asked who is this." He repeated more stern.

"Destan's wife."

"I said 'he' was to call me." He huffed.

"Please don't hang up," Callimay said rather desperate as she sat down. "He's busy right now and asked me to. He knew to call you back as soon as possible but he couldn't get away from what he was doing. I'm sorry you're stuck talking with me. — What can I do to help? Is there a message I can give Destan?"

There was silence on the other end for a while.

Complete silence. No kind of any background sounds whatsoever.

How can he~ Focus, now! "Aldred? … Hello?"

"If it were anyone else I wouldn't trust asking this question, but for some reason I feel I can trust he told you the truth and you would give it to me." Aldred said rather upset; him hissing as he sighed before asking, "Did Doyen alter Chameleon at all?"

Well that sure is an odd question for him to ask and make this much fuss about. "While I know he never would have in the first place, he did — in fact — tell me he didn't change one thing about it. He said if he would have even tried he had no idea what he was doing; and if you found out he might as well have killed me himself. And so, in the end, if I didn't make it at least he did everything he could."

Silence again.

"A… Aldred?" She asked rather timid as she curled up in the chair.

"What?" He snapped back.

"I know you're not much for sentiments, but I do want to thank you for what you did. I know if you hadn't I wouldn't be here right now. Thank you doesn't seem like enough, but I'm not sure what else to say."

Yet again there was this ear-tingling silence on the other end, but it was louder; the type that felt rather daunting and frightening.

Why? Why was her honest thanks being accepted like this?

As she sat there, fiddling with an edge of her veil, she heard a comment from the meeting and thought of something, "Aldred, could I ask a question?"

"Depends on what you ask," he growled.

"I… I'm just curious about something. How much do you know about the serums? I mean, how long have you worked with them?"

"I've worked with them in different capacities for around twenty years, why do you ask?"

She sat there and thought for a little bit; her bighting her lip as her eyes widened. Was this something she should even say to Aldred? What if he told the Syndicate what they were trying to do? She'd be putting Trever in all kind of danger.

"Why did you ask me? Does it have to do with the Elites?"

"I—" she froze as she almost fell backward while shooting up from her chair. "How do you know about them?"

"I worked with Baleck, remember?" Aldred said rather arrogant. "Now why did you ask me? What are you wanting to know?"

Callimay didn't know what to do and missed the name mentioned, thank goodness. Destan was delving into something that sounded so very promising so she just couldn't interrupt him. But then again, if her idea could fix everything: *Destan?*

There was a couple seconds delay during which Aldred hung up the phone before she got an answer: *What is it, Calli?*

I… I may have an idea. Though Aldred hung up because I was taking too long. She sighed in defeat.

He motioned for Fidus and then whispered to him, after which he excused himself and rushed over, "What is it?"

"It's so obvious I don't know why it took me this long to think of it. Aldred knows about the serums to some degree or another from what he told me: he said it's been around twenty years that he's been working with them." Callimay began to explain; Destan's expression cluing her in that he knew where she was going. "Since we can't find anyone who worked at the Society as part of the team who did the initial processing — well, who is still alive, that is — he's the only one we know of who has any kind of working knowledge of them."

"Which means if anyone could figure out how to reverse the cementation and processing, 'he' would. — Did you ask him?"

"Well I— no. I didn't know if I should say anything. I was trying to ask you if it was okay but he hung up on me first."

"You're fine. And you did the right thing." Destan assured as he took the phone; stroking the side of her face. "If this works out like I think it's going to, I believe we found that 'way of escape' God's had for us all along, Calli. Pray it is. Pray hard. — Aldred?"

"Whatever it is it's going to cost you extra," he greeted.

Destan rolled his eyes and leaned against the desk, "I figured so."

"Oh, so you decided to grace me with your presence. I'm honored to be worthy of your time. — Why did your wife ask about the serums?"

"Are you where you can talk freely?"

"I'm always where I can talk." Aldred scoffed.

"I know you worked with my father toward the end of his stay in Faberton. Was there ever anything about reversing the processing and cementation that he worked on or spoke of? Any preliminary things? I admit I haven't looked through what I have, so I might very well have something, but I wanted to ask you first." *Pfft! Who am I kidding? I wouldn't even know I had it even if I read it.*

"I doubt you'd find anything even if you did look and had anything of any importance. When can you meet?"

"He knows," Destan whispered as he furiously motioned for a Veil who happened to glance over; and then said as calm as possible, "Name the time and place."

"Meet me in New Windsor at Chathum Cathedral. And please, don't let the brash child who came last time knock you out. I prefer there be no middle man. … I assume you would prefer after dark."

"Yes."

"Fine then. Second evening throng is at nine tomorrow. Arrive early so you can sit in the back balcony on the far right, front row. … And I expect payment up front 'plus' my extra fee."

"I'll have it," Destan started writing things down at rapid speed, almost slapping it to make sure Callimay was watching. "Now excuse me for asking a dumb question, but am I coming alone or am I allowed to bring someone?"

"I just assumed wherever you go your wife would as well. Though this seems like a rather dangerous thing to involve her in… all things considered. But who am I to voice such opinions?"

"We'll see you then." Destan agreed as he heard Aldred hang up. "Calli? How fast can you get an outfit designed for yourself?"

That was not at all what she was expecting his first question to be after that kind of discussion, so she sounded confused, "What kind?"

"Get everyone's thoughts and questions wrapped up last night. Calli got us our plan." Destan ordered the Veil who came over; and then turned and asked, "Calli, do you remember in ancient history class, the Renaissance period in… was it Europe? The dresses with the laced fronts and long, flowing sleeves; fancy braids and sheer veils?"

Well that was oddly specific. "Yeah?"

"Something like that. And don't worry about me. I've got something already." Destan answered before she got a chance to ask.

"It shouldn't take me but maybe a couple hours. 'Possibly' five."

"Good. Take it to Outfitter the second you get it done and tell him to drop everything else he's doing. Tell him to pull Noonflash if he needs to. It's 'got' to be done before tomorrow, dusk." Destan ordered as he rushed back to where the others were waiting.

ℬ

As she started to think, Callimay couldn't recall being under this type of time constraint; but part of her was thrilled to have this challenge to one, help jog her memory about her previous job and two, helped her feel like she was contributing to their efforts… all the while forgetting she was the one who came up with this plan in the first place.

But it was interesting to think how her chosen profession was something she would use so much in this line of work. And so as she put pencil to paper, she smiled.

The good thing was she was free to do whatever she liked, but still had a strong, basic design to reference. But then again: *I don't have a clue what Destan's outfit looks like. I know we don't have to be all 'matchy-matchy', but I don't want to look like I don't belong with him, either. … Maybe Outfitter can help.*

She slipped out and rushed over, catching him as he was just about to leave, "What can I help you with, Jewel?"

"Doyen told me he has a Renaissance-style outfit? He asked me to get one made but didn't tell me what his looks like."

"Headed to New Windsor soon?"

"Tomorrow?" Callimay said with a bit of hesitancy.

"Let me guess: drop everything and get to work. Am I right?"

"Yeah?" Callimay dragged out.

"Don't worry, Jewel. This isn't the first time Doyen's done this. In fact, when he asked for his outfit for New Windsor it was in much the same situation." Outfitter consoled as he patted her arm and turned to go back in. "This 'last second' notice stuff comes with this line of work, believe it or not. So don't be worried. I'm well accustomed to it."

He ushered her to follow him to the counter as he went on around, looking under at a row of books, "Now I should have his sketches— hum. Where did they— oh! I remember. Come in the back."

Callimay followed along, a bit of her giddy when she saw the rows and rows of fabric bolts. Granted they were all black, but something about this helped bring back memories of the couple times she got to go to the northwest seamstress division of the fashion distributor she worked for. Watching everything be picked, rolled out, pressed, cut, and then all the tedious work of making fabric into beautiful clothing she drew? It was such a thrill for her.

Outfitter went over to a drafting light desk with notebooks upon notebooks on shelves above it. He pulled a rather thick one out and started flipping through all the hand-drawn sketches of outfits Callimay did — and several she did not — recognize.

A tension of some type started to build in her as she waited to see what the outfit looked like: *Surely it's not like what I remember from the drawings of the men of those times in ancient history class. I mean… Destan wouldn't wear those balloon-like shorts would he? Would he? ~ He had a rattail for land's sake, Rose Petal. ~ I actually didn't mind it after that first week… but oh my 'word' I don't think I could stand him wearing something like that for even a minute!*

Now came the moment of truth — Outfitter tapped one of the pages and stepped aside so she could take a closer look.

She breathed a sigh of relief when she saw the pants; though made a comment, "A cape. Why am I not surprised?"

"That was actually my part. He wasn't too keen on it at first."

"Really?" Callimay asked rather shocked.

"I think he sees his veil as a part of him. This? This is clothing; and something that probably looks more feminine because of the styling and fabric used." Outfitter offered; trying to be logical. "Of course that is my opinion of how he reacted to seeing it. He never actually said."

"This really helps, thank you so much." Callimay nodded as she looked around. "Would you mind if I sketched mine here?"

"Not at all," he glanced at his watch." I'm gonna go grab something to eat and I'll be back before long."

"I'm sorry, Outfitter! I didn't know you were— I'm sorry! I know you've got to be so careful with your sugars."

"Oh you're fine. I was leaving a bit early anyway, so now I'm right where I usually am." He calmed as he reached for the doorknob. "Don't feel the need to answer if anyone comes in. I'll be back in a bit. Light switch is up on the right there."

"Alright," Callimay nodded as she picked up a pencil.

She got so caught up in comparing the two outfits while she worked that she started thinking she was at work; a few forgotten memories beginning to reform. Her body relaxed into its accustomed drawing posture; upset it had to adapt to how this light table was set up.

Callimay started recalling similar designs she did; one in particular she fell in love with in an overall way. There were obvious things she needed to change so it would work, but it was reassuring to her how things were falling into place so quickly.

The sketch was coming together and looking graceful and elegant. And then there was a stripping sound followed by a crack; a thick, hard streak now across the entire drawing.

This all happened because someone had snuck up behind her and wrapped their arms around her.

Panicking, she squirmed out of their loving embrace and jumped up, out of breath and wide-eyed.

"Easy! It's just me. … I guess you were really wrapped up in your work. Start to remember more things about then?"

"I'm… I'm sorry, Destan." Callimay tried to catch her breath.

"Are you sure you're alright?" He reached out, her flinching. "Calli what's wrong?"

"You just scared me." She took his hand with her shaking one and pushed it back. "So what did everyone say?"

Well, as long as you're alright now. ~ *What brought that all on?* "We decided we're all a bunch of idiots." He said rather confused as she nestled herself close to his chest.

"Huh?"

"You thought of the most obvious thing: just take their abilities away. In the grand scheme of things — if I'm being frank — seven-hundred and forty-six more regular Falconers is just a drop in the bucket. If they lose their special crutches — as I'll call them — then they may not be nearly as dangerous since they've slacked off on what would be their regular training. At least that's what I'm hoping for." Destan rested his head on hers as he held her close. "Is it done?"

"Yep!" She said chipper as she looked down at the paper, laughing as she picked it up, "Oh my. Looks like I was in mid stroke!"

Destan rubbed her arm as he looked at the page, "So is it white?"

"Oh heaven's no! We'd look like a chip from Reversi if I did that! It's going to be a burgundy color with gold accents. … At least that's what I'm hoping Outfitter can do. I was thinking of rose gold depending on what he has on-hand right now."

"Well there's no time like the present. And since we don't have much time let's go ahead and get what you need." Destan looked to see if anyone was out front, then started walking toward the bolts of fabric.

Instead of heading down any of the isles, he made a straight shot for the back. There was a door he opened and let Callimay in, turning the light on as he closed it.

There, to Callimay's amazement, was a massive room stocked from floor to ceiling with every color imaginable… and what looked like pretty much every type of fabric as well.

"What in the world!"

"Where do you think the fabric for our outfits when we went to Zervonith came from?" Destan replied as he almost laughed. "So what was the color were you thinking again? Burgundy? That's like the purple version of maroon, right?"

"I… I guess you could say that," she tried her best not to laugh as she turned and followed him.

"What type of fabric?"

"I was thinking a velvet, but if not—"

"Velvet…" Destan muttered as he scanned the area and shuffled over to a certain section of bolts. "Hum. I don't— ah! Here's some. No, that's not the right color. No, no, no— ah! What about this, Calli?"

"That's perfect!"

"Well I see you let yourself into my stash." Outfitter huffed as he slammed the door. "Again."

"You weren't back and this needs to get done." Destan made a face and continued, ignoring Outfitter. "Now. You said gold accents? What kind? Do you need fabric or just trim stuff? — Do you have anything rose gold back here, Outfitter?"

Oh how I hate it when he goes on these 'shopping sprees'. Outfitter grumbled as he followed along, him taking the bolts out of Destan's hand and making sure they weren't "mussed".

⅌

Destan refused to leave until Callimay got what she wanted, and then finished talking things over with Outfitter. He said it would be ready by the afternoon, but then remembered, "What about shoes and such?"

Callimay replied after she thought for a minute, "I have a pair that should work just fine. It's floor-length so it won't be a major issue."

"I'm assuming the coat…"

"Oh! Oh dear." Callimay clapped her hand over her mouth. "I totally forgot. And I'll need some kind of hair net at least if not an actual hat. Ah! I knew I was forgetting something! Give me a half hour and I'll have them, I promise."

~ 17 ~

Overseer was at Assembly the following morning and got to spend time with Destan and Callimay; their enjoyable and undisturbed lunch reminding them they needed to take these moments of calm and quiet to heart. They needed time to focus and regroup so all the effort they were pouring into what they were doing would have the best shot at lasting and fulfilling its purpose.

"I assume everything is going well?"

"Yes, Destan. Just fine." Mr. Utree nodded as he set his mug down. "There are quite a few who are missing you two. Though it sounds more like they miss Callimay. They know you come and go, Destan, but they want to get to know her better."

"I don't blame them. I feel the same way." He chuckled as he took her hand in his. "Is Rej still able to bring the boys or has someone else stepped in?"

"Oh that's right! You don't know." Mr. Utree snapped his fingers as his smile brightened. "Izon is actually bringing them. There's another person who's been brought on to work Sundays, so he said he was willing to take that responsibility off Redje's plate when Tabitha had that scare with her blood pressure and such during the pregnancy. And since then he's continued. … And the most encouraging part? He's been inquiring about things — mainly with Redje — but has reached out to others in the congregation over the past couple weeks."

"That's great to hear!" Destan smiled as he shifted in his seat. "How's Sonnie doing?"

"Hanging by a mere thread, I'm afraid. I fear she's slipping into a loneliness she doesn't want anyone to help her out of."

"He really did leave?" Destan sighed.

"Yes."

Destan was depressed but not too surprised, "Well…"

"We all know it was best for her, and I think part of her does too: a relationship that is abusive on a mental and emotional level is just as abusive as a physical one. But she's found herself without a companion and the type of 'attention' she has grown accustomed to having given to her. It's understandable — to a point — that she's going through a rough transition, but her desire to go back is concerning." Mr. Utree kept everything in perspective. "There are some younger wives who are doing what they can, but she's shying away because they have what she wanted and had to an extent, so she thought."

"You could give her Destan's number, if that's alright." Callimay offered. "I know I'm married, too, but rough transitions and me have become somewhat of good friends. I doubt I have everything she needs as far as encouragement, but I would like to try. And maybe just talking on the phone would be better for her so there's a bit of 'disconnection' if you will since she wouldn't 'see' me."

Mr. Utree looked at Destan who nodded.

"When I see her next time I will be sure to give it to her." He smiled as he looked at his watch. "Well, I have a couple things to tend to, and I know you two have a trip to finish getting ready for."

"It was wonderful to spend lunch with you," Callimay shook his hand as she stood.

"I think Patricia's getting a bit jealous of me getting to see you so much." He chuckled as he offered her a hug. "But that'll be changing soon — right, Destan?"

"Lord willing." He nodded as he put his arm around Callimay.

"Safe travels tonight."

ℬ

Sometimes I have to wonder. Callimay smiled to herself as she fixed Destan's collar.

"About what?"

I feel like a child playing dress-up when we go to places like this. She started to blush. *Somehow the seriousness of everything fades. …

274

Not that I completely forget! I know this is very serious. I just— I never thought I'd get to wear the types of clothes I designed for so long and knew I'd never be able to afford.*

You 'are' a jewel on every level. Destan gave her a kiss and then took her in his arms: *I'll admit that knowing you enjoy this in that way makes my job in this that much more enjoyable as well.*

"Why are we talking like that? It's not like anyone is around or what we're saying is… 'sensitive'."

He stared at her, then chuckled as he shrugged his shoulders, "Well I was just going with the flow of things. You started it."

ᚦ

When they arrived, Destan pulled in the parking lot and found a spot as close to the exit as possible. A minor detail with where they were and whom they were meeting; but nonetheless, a detail that couldn't be overlooked because of the inherent risk.

The way his cape flared and snapped in the breeze added to the drama of everything; as if he were making the statement he had arrived and everyone needed to pay attention. A somewhat similar feel to how he was in Zervonith. And as Callimay pulled her veil over her face and took Destan's arm, she felt like he was parading her around. The flare of that long-lost memory made her shiver, but she knew this was nothing like what Toreon did. She knew Destan wasn't putting on a "show"; the wind was the one causing all the dramatic "look at me" issues. — And the fact was, it would continue to do so until they got inside; no matter how he tried to wrangle it. So, why fight it? Enjoy it.

And as far as "showing her off"? Of course he was. But he wasn't treating her like some "thing" that had no will of its own. He wanted others to see her because he wanted them to see just how special she was to him. — Which meant there were those here he knew; Doyen being able to relax enough so husband Destan could sneak in for a bit.

As they came in, there was an instant and abrupt change Callimay was not expecting: all those there spoke in an extremely eloquent and older fashion manner which was right on par with Rocher. Some even a tad more! But what took the cake was the fact every individual there was of an extremely high financial standing: hearing their comments about Destan and Callimay being mere "commoners" — let alone foreigners — didn't hit her as hard as it might have before, but it was still bizarre: *I mean… Destan has money, and quite a bit of it. ~ These people must be the 'mega-rich'. ~ They'd have to be!*

But, that all aside, since they were invited guests there was a higher level of respect and tolerance given that was frustrating to her: they were being nice to them because of who they knew, not who they were.

As they came up to where they would sit, there was one minor detail Destan forgot: *I can't believe I forgot that.*

It's alright. She laughed to herself. *Just don't leave without me.*

I couldn't. You've got my heart.

She whipped her head up, startled he said such a thing.

Being with Mr. Utree showed me that I've neglected to remember — on a consistent basis — the little things; how important they are. Nothing about what we're doing should ever make me forget that.

I love you.

Love you too. Destan helped her put her veil back and then escorted her to her seat.

When he sat down, he was quite thankful for the fact he could at least talk to her: *Either someone else is wearing your perfume or it's much stronger today.*

It's me. I was rushing to get it on — I forgot it — so one thing led to another— well… no. Come to think of it, since you didn't notice it in the car then someone else must also have it.

A little time passed with nothing happening, so Callimay sighed: *I have a question; completely unrelated to why we're here.*

Ask away. He replied as he casually looked around.

I thought these kinds of places had separate entrances for women and men?

Destan pondered for a bit, part of him glad to have a distraction of sorts: *That is a logical thought and historical fact, isn't it?*

I was just wondering. It doesn't truly matter.

No, I remember asking why, once. And somehow I figured it out — or in an off-handed way was told — but can't recall.

There were comments made by some of the men near Destan that reminded him: *Ah! Duh. How could I forget that? It's money.*

Oh-kay? Callimay dragged out as she raised her eyebrow at him.

Unlike some places, daughters are given priority when it comes to an inheritance. Similar to the idea of a dowry, but the daughter retains control of the inheritance when she's married. Her husband is only an heir — if you will — in that he gets control of it only if he outlives her. But if they have a daughter it's automatically given to her.

So is that a societal thing here or a religious earmark?

Religious, which has become societal.

Gotya. — He's here. Where, I'm not sure. Callimay sounded very serious as she greeted the woman who sat next to her. *He doesn't seem 'tense' or 'flustered' as far as I can tell.*

That's even better. If he's calm, we're safe.

Several minutes passed and no sign of him anywhere; it becoming quite apparent he was in no rush to complete the transaction. But, she relaxed when she was reminded he had money in this; he wasn't going anywhere without it and wouldn't risk letting anyone swoop in to capture them prior to him getting it. So, they sat and waited.

And waited.

And waited.

It wasn't until everything was done and people were leaving that he sat right next to Destan, "Emotionally stirring performance, wouldn't you agree? Quite the enlightening spiritual experience."

"Well, as a concert it was very entertaining; some of the best musicians and vocalists I've heard. But 'enlightening'? Emotions will only get you so far, especially if you're not careful to keep them under control; wouldn't you agree?" Destan replied in a professional tone as he turned to look at Aldred, catching a glance of Callimay getting up from her seat. *Head on down. This shouldn't take long. Stay with the ladies who sat next to you for as long as you can. Alright?*

Okay. B… be careful.

I promise. I'll see you in a bit. He nodded her on.

"She's doing well," Aldred looked back at Callimay and waved to her in a respectful and flamboyant way.

"Yes she is," Destan sighed as he reached in his pocket, gaining a glare from Aldred who reached for his side. "I'm only getting what you requested for payment. … There."

"I apologize for neglecting to remember who I was dealing with." Aldred let out a shaky breath as he cleared his throat; his shoulders relaxing as he smoothed out his coat jacket.

"What's wrong?"

"What would ever make you think something was 'wrong'?" He asked perturbed as he snatched the two cubes away from Destan.

Really, Aldred? That's the best you could do? ~ Let's not press it.
"What do you know?"

Aldred eyed the money in his hand for a few seconds, flipping it through his fingers; then asked, "Did you look through the paperwork you have?"

"Yes, and like you said: there wasn't anything there."

He nodded as he took a deep breath and sat back, "As far as mere calculations and computer projections can show, I was able to use the preliminary data your father compiled about removing serums from individuals. But, it's never been tested since I didn't complete it until years after the work in Faberton was ended and thus did not know of anyone still alive who could even be considered as a test subject. — To put it plainly: I need at least one individual of each type to see if my calculations are correct. Preferably a couple to be sure it is universal and effective. … I assume you know what I mean by 'type', or am I going too far?"

"You mean the three fundamental bases, right?"

"Oh good. You understand." He nodded in the most condescending approval possible.

"I could—"

"Don't be all high and mighty saying you'll be the Guinea pig along with your brother-in-law. You're a full-blown Cliffhanger and he's a Salvage which would give me absolutely no concrete data for Primes. Let alone the fact you may not even survive such a procedure."

"Salvage? Primes?"

"Your brother-in-law's emotional trigger is a border type." Aldred explained in a surprisingly helpful tone. "And have no fear, I don't have contacts within your circle. I was the one who put him through processing in Gastonia. — And technically speaking, your wife could've been considered a Salvage because of the spindles."

"Oh." Destan said quiet; feeling somewhat blindsided. "But you said she's alright now?"

"She is. And so now she could be labeled a Prime: those who fall into the desired parameters with complete and full cementation results. The Prince — and to my knowledge every Elite — are as well. And so if you are in any way concerned about risking their lives unnecessarily, as bizarre as that sounds, it won't be an issue to my knowledge."

"How much time do you need to test your theory?"

"Since you know about them I'm sure you can figure out where some will be," Aldred stood as he handed Destan a piece of paper. "Bring them to this location. Within a week, preferably. It'll take me a week after that to get results."

"How do I know the information you'll give me is correct?" Destan narrowed his eyes as he stopped reaching for the paper.

"I'll let whoever you want, stay and watch what happens. They can read what the computers tell me and then observe whether or not the individuals retain their abilities. … The rest is left up to trust. Like what was spoken of tonight."

"Why are you being so accommodating? This isn't your style?"

"Your wife told me you didn't alter Challenger. For some reason I believe her." Aldred folded his arms across his chest. "Is there a reason I shouldn't believe her? 'Did' you alter it?"

"If I did and something happened to her it would've been my fault. How could I live with myself knowing I lied and cheated only to be the one fooled and left with nothing? How would that be showing the love I have for my wife?"

Aldred stared him down for a minute, then finished, "So for as much as I'll ever know you weren't the one who killed Baleck. Which leaves me with the only answer I feared all along. … And so I believe a clean conscious allows a person to act rationally and for the good of humanity. I trust you will give me the same level of trust."

"I don't get you, Aldred." Destan stood and called out as Aldred started to walk away. "You're so cold and calculated yet you care about how someone met their demise. … Why?"

"I don't have the time and I doubt you have the money on-hand to pay for that information, Doyen. Plus it's something that's just personal in nature. — One week. That location. No need to call or knock when you arrive. I'll be waiting."

One question was bugging Destan to no end; so he asked, "Were you ever at the Society other than with Trever?"

"Like I said," Aldred snickered as he glanced over his shoulder. "I don't have the time and you don't have the money."

"Alright," Destan sighed in a grumble and then left himself.

ॐ

"Oh, there's my husband," Callimay smiled to the ladies with her.

"Will you be joining us later for the spectacle?" One lady asked as she took her by the wrist, her voice sounding like she was pleading.

"I… I'm afraid not tonight. Thank you for inviting us, though."

"Well, I understand how things can be sometimes, but be sure in the future to reserve enough time when you grace us with your presence. It would be simply smashing to have the both of you in our viewing box. — It is a daring thing you did."

"Excuse me?" Destan asked confused as Callimay took his hand.

"Going outside to find a mate."

"Oh!" Destan dragged out in almost a chuckle, but quickly caught himself. "Well when a man is smitten, he's smitten."

"I won't deny that." The lady nodded; her nose a bit turned up. "But I do give my hearty approval."

"I'm glad you see in her what I did and still do. And thank you for keeping her company." Destan caught a glimpse of Aldred and waved to him as he walked by. "Good evening to you all. Enjoy the spectacle."

"She is of a noble blood in character so I have no doubt she will rise to her rightful status in good time. — And we shall. It is always an exhilarating culmination to an already emotionally captivating day." The lady nodded as Destan bowed to her. "Good evening."

~ 18 ~

The second after they got back, there was furious work done to get a working plan together under the extremely tight time constraint Aldred gave. Trever, of course, was the original — and best —plan, but he couldn't be reached.

Thursday rolled around and still no answer.

"I really don't want to do this but we've run out of time."

"His last message talked quite a bit about Kayla. Maybe she's around him too much for him to get away." Callimay tried to calm. "And with that blocker — or whoever — around, I just can't get through to him."

"Maybe," he groaned as he ran his hands through his hair.

"Destan? I know you don't want me to go, but we're the biggest and most obvious target they'd jump on."

"I'm a big enough target by myself."

"But I'd be able to keep you safe," she raised her barrier after she hugged him; explaining when she saw the shocked expression in his eyes, "I finally figured out how to do it. Took me forever but I finally remembered each time it happened and what I did: if I think you're in danger and I hug you or try to shield you it activates. Gotta admit it took me a while to do it on my own without you; but I've been able to get my imagination going pretty good so I can envision you with me. … Knives, bullets, and spikes can't penetrate it. Traceur tried it with me the other day. I can't even feel it anymore; not even like I could when Baleck touched it the one time. I can only feel the inside when I touch it and that's not painful at all. … 'Please' Destan. Please let me come. I'm feeling better. I am. … It's why I did this, isn't it? Train so I could stay with you?"

He sighed as he pulled her close and buried his face in her hair, knowing good and well she was right, "I wish this were all over, Calli."

"We're both tired. I know. But this is the last push. We've got a wonderful reward waiting for us on the other side of this 'final exam' if you will. ... Right?"

Destan broke a sliver of a smile as he rubbed her cheek, "It's a wonderful reward to look forward to."

They stood there and stared at each other for a while, the belvedere seeming irritated with the silence.

"Alright," he rolled his eyes as he shoved the creature to the side. "Wear something warm and easy to move in. What about that purple sweater and slacks?"

"Since when did you notice my wardrobe?" Callimay laughed as she raised an eyebrow.

"I always have," he turned his nose up and huffed. "I just didn't have the need to say anything about it before."

❦

The trip to their drop-off was stressful for Destan; regret flooding his mind every second for letting Callimay come. And yet the second they left their detail of security, he flipped... as if accepting reality. They were just north of the Passes at the Quimbergo/Crosswall border — and a Shadow-controlled one at that — so there were no issues with them not making it through border security.

Once through, Destan jumped them to the outskirts of the closest station; having to take a few minutes to catch his breath, "I guess I should've been using it every now and again since everyone knows... but you needed this time without worrying about me. — I'm fine, Calli. Just give me a minute."

Now she understood the "other reason" he mentioned — aka didn't explain — when telling her they were going to go through the border checkpoint. She looked at him kneeling in the snow out of breath and recalled even more memories she'd forgotten; and some she wished would've stayed forgotten.

"It seems like that was forever ago, huh?" He took a deep breath as he looked up and smiled as much as he could.

"Somehow it does," she nodded as he stood and took her hand. "And yet it doesn't seem like we've been married but a couple months."

He could hear the hidden pain in her voice, "I'm sorry things—"

"It's just that good times fly by while the 'less than favorable' times linger… and then I still have some patches that are empty which make things feel awkward."

"We've been through quite a bit."

"And yet we're still going."

She could see him smiling and his eyes sparkling as he nodded, then his expression turned serious when they heard the hissing sounds of the train, "It's just pulling in, good. Don't let go of my hand, alright?"

An initial squeeze of his hand was her answer, but with each step they took toward the station she tightened her grip.

Do you see him? I hear so many voices but nothing that helps.

No, Destan looked around as he fed a meter with a few cleats and then let her through. *But he might be at the other end. I just hope we find him before we get there. He obviously uses his ability while he's there, so we won't be able to talk like this. And I don't want that.*

ᛞ

The sight that welcomed them in the foremost car was a bit of a shock: there wasn't a seat to be had which made the spacious car feel like a sardine can, the rumble and buzz of the constant conversations enough to make anyone's ears throb.

Oblivious to one annoyance and taking advantage of the other, Destan started looking for what Trever described as the briefcase the contact would have; this all masked as him looking for empty seats.

No one in that car had it, so they continued on… the next car being the same.

What in the—

They wouldn't have stopped if there wasn't room. And he'll be on this train. Don't— oh! Destan's dragged out realization interrupted when he heard a comment made. *It's liberty pay period.*

Excuse me what does— "Excuse me." She repeated when a man pushed past her.

"What?" The man growled as he turned. "Do y—"

"It's just a bit crowded, it's fine." Destan's eyes flashed and fists clinched; but diffused the situation as fast as possible, nodding her on.

Why did you—

It was best this way. Believe me. Just keep moving.

By the time they got to the next car, Callimay stopped him from opening the door, "I'm not moving until you tell me what this liberty pay period thing is." *I need a break from the noise, anyway.*

This isn't the time, Calli. We can't chat about~ You're supposed to be blending in while looking, right? … Well? Blend! "Every year," he sighed a bit as he worked to unclench his fist. "Two weeks are set aside where the government collects no taxes on anything."

"Anything?"

He nodded and took her hand, starting off again: *'Any' thing.*

So all these men are out buying things? In the middle of the night? She sounded so confused as she looked at the likes of those who were crowding that car.

No, Destan strained a chuckled out as he worked to get past a few men without gaining unwanted attention and keeping his wife safe. *They look like they're headed to work. At least this group does.*

But why are they going 'to' work? Why w— oh wait. You said no taxes on 'any'thing.

Destan exaggerated a nod as he opened the door to the next car.

Two weeks! But how can companies afford that!

Since they don't pay taxes either, of course they max production, imports, and exports. — Most guys make enough during these two weeks of brutal work so they can take the rest of the year off. AKA: it's all they need to live off of for the whole year. Of course not all can take this workload: if you sign up for it, you have to see it through or get fired. Which is probably why most of them are this cranky.

That's crazy! The amount of— what? She asked startled; Destan stopping out of nowhere, her slamming into the back of him.

There was the chance he overlooked him — or Toreon was making a surprise visit this week — but Destan couldn't see that being the case: *It just doesn't make sense we haven't seen him yet.*

This determination in Destan was showing signs of weakening, but didn't truly waver until they got to the last car and still nothing.

Let's sit down. Callimay calmed, knowing he was getting upset. *Regroup and then try again. … Okay?*

But there's no two seats next to each other.

It'll be alright. We've gotta sit down at 'some' point.

Destan grumbled but ushered her to what looked like the only booth with seats left.

But, a couple moments later he shot to his feet.

Well that didn't take long. Where is he?

I didn't like what I was hearing. Destan looked around for another place to sit. *And don't listen to what they're saying.*

Callimay death-gripped his wrist as she bowed her head.

Across the hall was the only other empty seat in the car. And seeing a new group of commuters coming, Destan sat down and gestured for her to sit on his lap.

While any other time she would've objected to this purely out of embarrassment, the feeling of her skin crawling from being watched made her welcome this closeness to him.

And then they heard the door behind them open.

The android conductor stopped where they were and didn't have any concern for the situation; saying in its automaton male voice, "I'm afraid the misses will have to find a seat of her own."

"There aren't any together," Destan objected as they both looked up.

"I'm afraid that goes against all safety codes."

Like you can really care about someone's safety you hunk of junk. And that person operating you 'knows' good and well her safety is better where she is right now. … Who knows. That person running you could be a sicko themselves and so they 'want' that.

Destan looked back at the place where the two seats were, furious and unwilling to move; his jaw tightening as his fists clinched.

The men there smiled and cat-called, "Oh she'll be fine." "Come sit with us, chickie baby." "We don't bite."

Hearing what the men were now saying out loud made him even more furious. And then the android not changing its command threw him over the edge. Callimay almost fell down, Destan shooting to his feet like he did before. He glared at the camera on the android who was a good three feet shorter than him: *Sure I could level the stupid thing, but it's not the 'source' of the problem. It's those jerks and the person running this stupid thing.*

In those few moment Callimay got to her feet and wrapped her arms around his.

Feeling her trembling helped him back off a bit; him now pushing past the android to start toward the front of the car.

A man offered as he stood, "I'm happy to take that seat so they can sit here."

The android turned and looked up and down, shaking its head, "It's only one seat."

"Oh don't think anything of it." The man brushed off. "I only had my coat on the seat next to me. … There. Two seats for two people. And right beside each other. Everyone's happy, right?"

"Thank you," Destan bowed his head in respect as he all but pushed Callimay to the seats before anyone could do something; sheltering her the best he could from the lingering snickers and whistles.

The android rolled over and looked up and down a couple more times, then nodded before it left; the men across the hall still carrying on though not as loud.

"I appreciate your willingness to give me that security; thinking of my wife's safety." Destan thanked as he offered his hand to the man sitting across from him. "It's good to know there are still those around who notice and do something."

"I know how precious things need to be protected from those who don't appreciate what they even have." The man nodded, a faint smile on his face as he set his coat in his lap.

Half out of curiosity and half desperate for a distraction, Callimay listened to see what the man was saying.

Oddly enough, she couldn't get in. She tried again but met the same resistance: *You don't think he has an ability do you?*

You mean the blocker?

Yeah.

He glanced at him again, then brushed it off: *I highly doubt it.*

It's just odd that there's nothing there.

The stress of everything could be causing you some issues. Don't think too much about it.

Callimay sat back and closed her eyes, trying again: *True. … That was the one type we couldn't find in the list and Aldred really wanted. It'd be amazing if he was one of them; this situation actually giving us what we've been needing.*

That would be really nice, though that kind of stuff usually just happens in movies. Destan chucked to himself as he looked at the man in a casual manner, his eyes subtlety changing. *Wait a second! The briefcase! It's under his coat! … It's him! We found him!*

While thrilled, something didn't feel right to Callimay: *More like he found us. You don't think—*

"Are you two from around this area?" The man asked seemingly out of the blue as he looked to Destan after looking outside.

"No," he shook his head; scratching his head to try to keep his surprise and shock unnoticeable. "Thank you again about earlier. My name's Quinton and this is my wife Everlyn."

"Nice to meet you, Quinton… Everlyn. I'm Stall." The man smiled; reaching out and accepting Destan's hand this time. "Quite the original names you two have. Where are you from?"

"You could say that," Destan smiled as he glanced at Callimay. "We're originally both from Faberton, though we met in Gastonia."

"It's strange how you find out you lived right next door to the person you marry and yet you had to travel halfway around the world to meet them." Stall chuckled as he sat back. "If you don't mind all the questions, why are you two here?"

"I had some last-minute business come up that couldn't wait."

"You can tell me to back off and I won't take offense. I'm just a curious person by nature."

"I'm sorry if my answer is coming off that way. Guess I'm still a bit worked up because of them." Destan glared across the hall out of the corner of his eye.

"Completely understandable," Stall glanced over to the others; them quieting down immediately before he looked back. "So! What part of the ring you heading to?"

"Northwestern."

"Ah," Stall nodded as he relaxed, revealing momentarily a security cuff on his left wrist. "We might be getting off at the same stop."

What are they having the Elites do, anyway? I get they're hiding them, but we've never gotten information about one being encountered anywhere except for that one. Callimay questioned when she saw the extreme measures taken in order to keep this information guarded.

That one was just the tip of a small iceberg we found of replaced individuals. Lots of recluses are getting vetted right now to see if any of them have been found. But that's just one form of them. The rest? Still trying to figure that out. Though I do have to admit: the cuff doesn't mean much. It's standard issue for any Syndicate correspondence. Destan was quick to cut off the tense conversation. "Oh, you're getting off at Northwestern, too? That's a coincidence."

Stall nodded and smiled as he checked his watch and then shifted how he sat to relax more.

Destan looked at the train's tracking system and saw they had a couple hours: *Just relax, Calli. We've got time.*

She took his arm and snuggled close to his side, but even though she closed her eyes she couldn't sleep. And some of those nagging reasons were the same ones which kept Destan a bit on edge. It was enough to have a rather high-ranking Syndicate member sitting right across from him, but then the other men who were threatening his wife in the most disturbing of ways? With no one in "authority" caring? A moment's doubt crept in: was the right they were doing worth it with this type of danger so close? And then in the grand scheme of things, would their sacrifice and effort change anything with what seems to be such a large majority of people acting as these do? They didn't care as long as they got their money. It didn't matter where it came from.

A refreshing feeling of relief washed over him when the, shall we say "unsavory characters", got off at the next stop; as did pretty much everyone in that car. Of course they made sure to get one last "word" in before they left, laughing to each other, but there were a few who said what little they could to voice their displeasure and apologize; even though they were not the ones at fault. — There were people out there, but as usual they were the minority and usually quiet because of that fact. But they did what they could when they could.

$$\mathfrak{SD}$$

The world outside flashed by as they sped along with the moon towering above; almost full as it broke forth with all its glorious light over the frozen, jagged terrain. It sparked the snow, it glittering and gleaming; piled almost to the height of the windows near the tracks and sprawling out as far as the eye could see.

This frosty view drew Destan in; him finding himself not able to look away for a few minutes. His mind took him back on that train during the winter, protecting the woman he loved while they ran from those who were looking feverishly for them to end their lives. The feeling of her right next to him helping erase the dull, throbbing pain he was constantly in; the occasional jars of the train making sure to keep him awake. It was still burned in his memory, seeing the terror in her eyes at certain moments; him recalling how for the first time that look terrified him as well. She'd made him see so many things through a different lens… the lens of reality and humanity.

His peripheral catching movement across from him brought back the harsh reality: they were on this train "trying" to get caught. They were, in fact, running "toward" those who wanted them dead: *Remind me how is this— what am I doing! ~ Boon, calm down. You two have got this. She knows what's going on; and she knows you're not going to let them take her. Things are different. She's much more capable of protecting herself and you're not injured. Just take a chill pill and think things through. This dude isn't Elder.*

Doyen? Are you listening? … We're in position. Steer clear of Timber Avenue. Syndicate webs in each of the allies there. Chicane said out of nowhere it felt like.

In allies? What in the world do they have them in allies for?

If I knew that I wouldn't have found them in the first place.

Where are you set up, then?

Not too far off. Katgoo Street; just two more clicks to the west. Third ally to the right. Small curiosity shop there. Chicane relayed.

Got it. Any word from Liberator?

None yet.

Destan sighed, now worried Trever was being lulled into staying on purpose because they knew who he was. And if they did, could they be expecting something like this? Was this a frame up?

I mean with those webs where they are it could very well be one. ~ Boon, you need to stop. This is not who you are: jumping to conclusions left and right. ~ Are you accusing me of overthinking things? ~ Yes. Yes I am. So quit it. We're almost there. No time to second guess things. Stick to the plan.

Doyen? Can you hear me?

What is it, Enforcer?

You've got a half-dozen Falconers waiting at the first station. And by their looks? They match what Liberator said to be Elites. He commented as he looked through his scope.

Good. Any matches?

Still running them through the database.

*Speed it up. We've got no time left. *

Will do.

Calli?

I know. We're here. She opened her eyes and stretched a bit.

"It's a late evening," Stall commented as he smiled, checking his watch. "But I guess business will do that at times."

"Yeah. Not fun to get that call, but I'm getting used to them." She smiled as Destan put his arm around her.

"I know we haven't talked too much, but I've enjoyed our little conversation." He smiled as the train hissed; those outside starting to make their way for the doors.

They all waited for the initial group of people to rush out and then on, but there was some level of a commotion toward the front of the car that stopped everyone at one point. Destan and Callimay turned to see what was going on and saw the group of Elites coming down the aisle, comparing people to a manifest each of them held.

Destan grabbed Callimay's hand and jumped up, stopped by Stall, "Where are you off to in such a hurry?"

He punched Stall, knocking him to the floor, then rushed Callimay out; making sure to make as much of a scene as possible so the Elites would see them.

Did they bite? Chicane asked.

Like sharks that just smelled blood. Destan smiled as he looked back. *Any matches, Enforcer?*

Just came up. You've only got two types though. Not three like Aldred's asking for.

Well, hopefully we'll add a couple more to our merry band. What are we looking at?

Elemental and physical manipulation. Four are forms of Sinew, one is Machinate, and the other is Epicenter.

Mental is the most dangerous and the one we 'need' to know can be reversed. Destan grumbled as he looked back to his wife before checking to see how close those behind them were. *We need— wait. The contact! Stall! Where is he?*

Just getting off the train. He has a couple escorting him. Enforcer said as he switched his focus.

He's our third category.

Huh? Chicane asked stunned. *How'd you figure that out?*

Jewel can't get through to him… she told me she can't even feel him to try and get in. The blocker could be someone else and projecting their block on him; but… we can't take the chance of losing him if he is. — Fidus?

I'm on it.

Be careful. We don't know exactly what he has — if anything — or what he can do if he is indeed the blocker. Keep a sharp eye on your emotions and what's going on around you. Destan slowed a bit, "Calli? What's wrong? Are you alright?"

"The cold is just wearing on me faster." She almost moaned as she fought to keep up with him, grabbing her side. "I'll make it. It's okay."

"No," he stopped and picked her up.

They both looked back, seeing the small group of men and a single woman turn the corner: *It's twilight, Veils.*

Locked and loaded. Enforcer hunkered down and took aim.

Net is concealed and ready. Chicane peeked out from his hiding spot to scan the area again.

"Just hold on and be my second pair of eyes," Destan whispered as he took off; being mindful to not trip his ability. "I'll get us home, safe and sound. I promise."

Them not having to go so far made things better. The group stayed together and didn't have time to split up. But even so, the woman "vanished" prompting Destan to tap his ability and run; though not having the outcome he was expecting.

She appeared right in front of them and he didn't have time to react. He plowed into her like a bowling ball into that one rebellious pin that refused to be knocked down so a you had to be satisfied with a spare.

Callimay was jarred from the impact; her ribs beyond angry — the temporary pain relief Baleck and Aldred giving her choosing the worst time ever to wear off. And even though she tried to keep quiet so those chasing didn't have reason to believe they had an advantage, her cry of pain wouldn't be silenced.

Hearing this, Destan jerked back and rolled to the side so he was the one on the ground; his eyes becoming wild with fear for a few seconds as he tried to catch his breath and make sure his wife was okay.

They looked up and first saw the lady knocked out cold; then down the street to see the small group closing in on them. One on those in the group fired a shot, Callimay throwing up her barrier as fast as possible.

"Will it move if you do?" Destan grunted; getting to his feet.

"Sadly, no," she breathed heavily as she swayed a bit; trying to catch herself but needing Destan's help.

"Let it down, it's alright. You've gotta save as much of your strength as you can. We're not alone. Enforcer and a couple others are keeping an eye out." Destan calmed as he picked her up and then put his hand against the dome that looked like the casing of a snow globe.

It vanished and he ran as fast as he could; again, being extra careful to not trigger his ability. He knew the less he used it the better things would be for Callimay; and the better the Elites could keep up.

Doyen? Chicane asked as he took hold of the door frame.

I feel it. Destan turned and jumped behind the group. *I've gotta get him off the ground… Calli? Do you feel better?*

Yes, she nodded as he set her down and framed her face.

Run as fast as you can to the drop point. Don't stop or look back.

"No!" She argued as she grabbed his arm; her nails digging into one of the still tender spots from his surgery. "I'll get caught in the web if I do that. Let me take care of Epicenter."

"Calli!" Destan began to get angry as the group finally realized where they were.

"Then let me go back and help Fidus. Please! I don't want to get caught with them." She pleaded; her eyes now soaked with terror.

Knowing he had to stop this bickering about who had the best idea, he caved and pushed her on, "Alright. Go!"

Fidus? I'm heading your way. Callimay took a deep breath.

Alright, Jewel. He replied, sounding a bit winded.

"Let her go. She won't get far." The one man said as he grabbed the other's arm.

Enforcer?

Scanning now, he replied, feeding off of Destan's worry.

"So here you are, the 'great Doyen'." The one who appeared to be the leader taunted as he sauntered back and forth while eyeing Destan. "And might I add even more so that you're one of us. This is indeed a great honor."

You've got at least two dozen more closing in on your six, Doyen. There's no way to make it to the drop point. Enforcer was quick to inform as he repositioned himself.

What about Jewel? Destan asked worried.

There was a brief pause as Enforcer searched through his scope; finally finding her in a small group of shoppers; gripping her side as she fought to act natural: *I don't know how on earth she did it, but she's in the clear.*

Chicane? Did you leave one of the nets at the original drop point?

No.

Can he get there, Enforcer?

He's got a small window but he'd have to run like never before to make it.

Get it where we originally planned: on my side of the web, though.

What!

Just do it! You've got just enough time to get there before we're surrounded. Let me know when it's ready.

Moving now.

I've got company up top. Enforcer hissed as he saw movement on one of the other buildings.

Anyone we know? Destan asked as he started looking around, using Toreon's ability to see how many there were.

In fact, yes. Enforcer said with a bit of satisfaction. *I've still got a score to settle with her. The one from Faberton that night you were shot. She was there.*

Ingrid! Destan whipped around and looked up. *That's... that's not her. But Toreon even said—*

Doyen!

He rolled out to the side of the street, barely missing being hit by the rubble flying through the air from the shockwave Epicenter dished out.

Chicane?

Just one more minute.

You've got fifteen seconds.

Destan heard a few shots ring out from above him and then shouts from others who were still a bit off. He darted toward the ally that had the Syndicate web, hoping with everything they'd follow him: *Come on. Come on! Be selfish. Get all the glory for yourself. You don't need backup for just 'one' me. Right? ... Right. That's it. Follow the leader.*

Chicane whipped his head around when he heard thundering steps, seeing his superior barreling down on him with a group in tow.

Here we go. Good, bad, or indifferent... this is it.

The two stood there facing the five men who knew this was a dead end... in more ways than one. They laughed as they inched closer, "What are you gonna do now, Doyen? And I see you've found yourself a friend, too. Well this just keeps getting better. Did you find the nice little welcoming gift we have for you?"

"Not today," Destan mumbled under his breath; grabbing Chicane's arm and bolting toward the web.

"What the—" Chicane gasped.

"Stop them!" The leader gasped as they all started running. "The Monarch wants him alive."

But quite on the contrary, he only "looked" like he was going to run head-on into the web like an absolute idiot. He jumped out of the ally at the last moment; leaving the small group with no time to react. They were caught in the Shadow net which was between Destan and them the entire time.

Chicane and Destan ran back to get them, hearing voices very close by, "How are we going to do this?"

"Hold on," Destan put one hand on the web that encased the five men and then looked out toward the extraction point.

While he was able to make the jump to the exact point he wanted to — much to his surprise when he saw where they ended up — the first step he took was the only one he remembered.

☎

He felt like a prisoner in his own body; him unable to move, his eyelids unwilling to open and his mouth refusing to let any words out. The only sense still functioning was his hearing: several voices — though words undistinguishable — close by.

Unsure of why he was in this predicament, Destan tried to force himself to move. It was then he started to feel he was surrounded by something wet and ice-cold: *I'd say I'm in a morgue, but the days of ice slabs has long-since ended. ~ Form of new torture by the Syndicate? ~ I highly doubt it. They wouldn't do this. … But what 'is' causing me this much of an issue? ~ I mean I know I jumped pretty far, but I didn't use my ability hardly at all before it.*

A few more minutes passed before he could move freely and open his eyes; Chicane still in a panic from what happened and then his superior passing out.

Once he got his bearings, Destan assured Chicane everything was okay as he helped him to his feet.

But it was quite clear: his body still wasn't ready. So, he rolled over and laid there in the snow for a bit, trying to focus on gaining back what energy he could.

The second he felt he had enough, he asked: *Enforcer?"

The little— she got away again. He growled. *Are you alright?*

Did someone get the other two?

They're secured.

And Jewel?

No word from her or Fidus.

Alright. Get to the alternate point. I doubt you'll be able to make it through to us right now.

On my way, Enforcer got ready to take off.

Fidus?

Where's Jewel? He asked in anger, almost.

What! Destan sat up far too fast; almost passing out because of how dizzy he was.

She never showed up. I got him, though; so no need to concern yourself in that area. I'll need to be picked up at the alternate p—

Calli! Destan stumbled to his feet and started running. "Calli!"

Nothing.

Calli!

Still nothing.

"Please, God! Don't— Calli!"

Destan, what's wrong? She asked worried.

*Why didn't you answer me?*He asked out of breath as he dropped to his hands and knees.

I couldn't hear you. What's wrong?

Why didn't you meet up with Fidus?

I got caught— oh but don't worry! It was by Trever. It's okay. Callimay gasped when she realized what she said; trying to explain. *I'm not hurt. I'm fine. We both are. W—*

Where are you?

Just outside of town. Due north of where we were. There's a small tree grove here. She explained as she looked around her. *Why do you sound so tired? What's wrong?*

I just jumped six people 'and' myself about ten miles. Destan breathed heavy; him finally admitting to himself just how much he did. *I'm just worn out and then on top of that was scared about you when Fidus said you weren't with him.*

Callimay sighed as she motioned to Trever: *Just stay there. We're coming to you. It'll take us a few, but we're on our way.*

I think I can see where you're at. Meet me on the northwest side. Destan kept going, feeling some better since he could hear her voice.

But as he kept on, he was struggling to keep conscious: *Been a long time since we've felt like this. ~ And it's one thing I never missed. Geez! I didn't think it'd take 'that' much out of me so fast.*

Right as he got to the tree line he felt something sharp graze his leg and then heard the release of a pin. It was a faint sound but something that made his eyes widen as he lost his balance and fell backward.

Callimay had just come around one tree and caught sight of him when this happened; her screaming as she started running. Trever held her back; his voice as stern as it was when she was at the hospital in Faberton, "You don't know where the web is, Everlyn!"

"Well hurry!" She cried as she pushed him ahead.

As they got closer, she could hear her husband grimacing and hissing through his teeth; his emotions spiraling out of control: *Destan please listen to me. I know it hurts. And I know this may sound like I'm heartless, but try to calm down. You're going to hurt yourself more if you keep getting angrier. … Destan? Destan can you hear me? Destan!*

"Calli?" He gritted his teeth as he tried to look back for her. "Where ar— ah, geez!"

"Don't move!" She started to run.

"Calli don't!"

"Everlyn!" Trever grabbed her and pulled her back to him.

"He needs help, Trever! Let me go!"

"That web's hot!" Trever hushed. "If the weight on it releases it's going to blow this whole section sky-high."

This did nothing but send her over the edge, Callimay screaming and flailing as she fought her brother to let her go; her actually biting him… but to no avail.

Get her out of here. Do it now and do it quick. I don't know how much longer it'll hold. Destan breathed heavy, eyeing Trever. *And before you offer any cruel rebuke: yes, I wasn't paying attention since I couldn't keep conscious or steady. The jump I made took everything out of me. I set myself up for this. It 'is' my fault.*

I… I don't… Trever started, stunned by the sight he was seeing and what he knew was going to happen. *I can't—*

"There's got to be a way!" Callimay wailed as she continually tried to free herself; her side acting up again, but her refusing to stop. "We can't leave him! They'll kill him! … Trever!"

She was going to keep on with her tirade, but the pained yet clam voice of her husband captured her attention enough so she'd listen, "I'd jump, Calli, but I don't have enough energy left in me and I don't know if I'd clear the blast radius. I'd say I wasted it getting those others out… but if it saves lives, it's worth it."

"But there's got to be a way to disarm it!"

"Callimay Rose Nevrille!" Destan bellowed. "Get a grip or so help me— ah, gosh!"

Now she was frozen with fear, looking at the man she loved straight in the eye. He had a couple cuts on his face and several on his arms and legs… she knew the wires were digging into his back this entire time.

"I just don't want to give up when I'm right here," she cried as she became limp in Trever's arms. "I can't not at least try."

"You're not giving up on me. You never have the whole time we've known each other. In fact I don't think you could ever give up on someone. — Be strong for me. I love you." Destan sighed as tears began to stream down his face.

Trever couldn't find anything to say. He'd condemned Destan so often for being the one to make the sacrifice and leave his wife alone — even though it was to protect her — but now he couldn't bring himself to even think it. He saw the pain and fear in Destan and saw the love and torture in Callimay. What he saw he finally understood: Destan loved his baby sister… "truly" loved her.

Get to the extraction point. Tell Fidus what happened and then take her to Brigon as soon as you can.

It was hard to hear that order a second time, but was there hope this would have the same ending as last time?

I'm going to try and jump, but I have got no energy right now; and you two need to get a safe distance away, regardless. Destan reminded as he tried to keep his breathing calm and slow. *I'm hoping this ends like last time, okay? — Ah, geez! — And so… let Quandary know.*

Trever nodded as he picked his sister up and started walking away.

Callimay beat her fists on him and screamed, "Destan! No!"

❧

Once they were about a mile off, Callimay heard Destan's calming and loving voice: *Dear Heavenly Father? Sometimes the path we put ourselves on isn't what would have been best, but we know that every turn affords us an opportunity to be Your lights to those we are around. If it be in Your will… let me be able to get out of this and back to Calli. But no matter what happens, give her all of Your strength, peace, and comfort. Help her see the good in this and remember her first love has always been You. Help what I've done that put me here be of benefit to countless people; that what we're dealing with from governing bodies can be stopped so we can do more of Your work with less frustration. In Your Son's Name I pray, amen.*

Amen, she quivered in response.

I love you, Calli. I always have. I even think I did when we were young. I just didn't want to admit it.

I l— she stopped when she saw the explosion. "Destan!"

Trever was in so much shock he let her go. She ran as fast as her legs could carry her; her ribs killing her a bit more with each step so she couldn't breathe. But she wasn't about to stop; she had to know if he made it or not.

But how in the world could she? Where would he jump? Could he jump far enough to get out of the blast radius? And if not there would be no way for her to know. That entire section of the forest was splintered, still raining debris, and in flames.

Destan? She cried as she ran around the area, not focusing on any one location too long. *Destan can you hear me? Destan please!* "Oh God please!"

A few minutes later Trever showed up. She looked back at him, her hair a complete mess and her eyes wild with fear, "Did you…"

"I'm so sorry, Everlyn." He shook his head.

She crumbled to the ground and screamed, sending ice cold chills down Trever's spine. He tried to comfort her but she pushed him away and rocked back and forth; grunting and wheezing as she tried to catch her breath that had no intention of doing anything but running as fast as possible away from her.

He looked around; his flushed face now looking more worried than anything. Trever knew it was dangerous to stay, but something inside couldn't bring himself to pry her away. How was he supposed to take care of her? How could he comfort her? And while he worshiped his baby sister, it hit him in that moment he didn't know the first thing about serving her, being there for her… knowing what she needed.

The cold, hard fact that smacked him in the face was: he really didn't know how to love her.

"Everlyn?"

"Leave me alone." She sobbed.

"No, Everlyn, we need to go."

"I don't care anymore. Let them find me."

"Yes you do. You do because he's always done everything to keep you safe." He knelled next to her and put his hand on her shoulder. "Now come on. We can't stay here."

"I can't just leave. I have to find him."

"There's nothing here, Everlyn. Destan's not here."

"I know that!" She yelled as she shoved him away. "I… I know that. But… but I… I've got to find—"

"Everlyn listen to me. Destan's alive. I heard him just a second ago."

"W… what?"

"He's out there," he gestured to the blackened night. "Somewhere. We need to find him and get him back. He's in bad shape. Come on."

"Y… you're sure?"

"Positive. Now come on." Trever helped her to her feet.

Callimay started looking every which way, trying to find the man she loved while preparing herself for what she may see. She tried to reach out to him but couldn't find him. But that didn't detour her; she knew he'd have to be in so much pain and beyond exhausted. He probably didn't even have the strength to reply: *Destan probably used his last little bit of energy to tell Trever what he did.*

After a while she was confused, "Did he say where he was? I don't know that he could've jumped this far."

"I— let's just keep going. It's probably more this direction."

She grabbed his arm and yanked on it so he turned around to face her, "Did you actually hear Destan? What did he say, exactly?"

Unable to look at the truth contained in the fire burning through her eyes, Trever looked away.

"You lied t— why! Why would you do that!" She screamed as she slapped his face.

"It was the only thing I could think of to get you to leave."

"Give me false hope so that I have to go through everything twice? What's wrong with you! Do you hate me or something?"

"No, Everlyn! No I don't!"

"Then why would you do this? Why would you lie to me! You know it's one thing I absolutely hate!"

"I… I needed to get you out of there before someone came to investigate. I did it to keep you safe. I swear. I meant well—"

"You didn't have to lie. No one ever has to lie! Nothing good has 'ever' come from a lie. Ever!"

"But I meant well," he tried to defend; his shoulder dropping as he watched her storm back and forth.

"I'd hate to see you mean the worst for someone. — Why are you doing this to me! Why!"

A faint voice brushed through the following moments of raw and angered silence, "Calli?"

"Destan?" She whipped her head around.

"Everlyn, I'm sorry."

"Shh!" She waved her hands. "Did you hear that?"

They stood as still as statues to listen in the frozen countryside that was now pitch black because of the storms moving in.

And listened.

Trever sighed, "Everlyn we can't stay here. We've got to get going or we'll be stuck out in this storm."

She sighed as she slumped her shoulders and collapsed; unable to hold back the flood building in her eyes.

"Calli?"

"Everlyn? I heard it."

"You're just lying to me again. Please stop." She pushed him away and got to her feet; starting to plod back. "I just thought I heard him, I know that."

He heard the voice a second time, "Everlyn, I'm telling the truth. I can hear him."

Knowing he'd lost her trust so he was alone to find Destan, he took off toward the direction he heard the voice; confident she'd follow at some point.

Sure enough, Callimay came lagging behind — not wanting to exert any more effort or emotion since she didn't have anything left but fury for her brother's antics. With each step, the sub-zero temperature gave the snow you stepped on that unmistakable, shredding sound which perfectly mimicked nails on a chalkboard; her trust in her brother being shredded more and more. Each foggy breath held the unspoken words of her hatred for her brother. Every tear burned with the anger she could barely keep contained.

But it washed away when she saw blood spattered snow around a body, their shredded clothes littering the ground around them. For a moment she stood there speechless from the regret of her anger, the fear of what she saw, and the horror of what her mind was concluding.

She ran over and flopped to her knees beside him, her hands quivering as she dared to reach out to him.

His eyes flickered open for a second when he could hear and feel her beside him.

"You're alive? Destan? Destan can you hear me?"

While not able to say anything or move much, he leaned his head into her hand.

Shivering and almost convulsing from the emotional rollercoaster coming back to the station, she started bawling as she swept his hair out of his face, gasping as she whipped her head up, "He's freezing cold, Trever."

"Do you think you can stand me picking—"

"What's going on?" Chicane asked furious as he ran over.

"I'll explain later." Trever shushed. "Help me get him up."

~ 19 ~

"For the 'final' time: get back in bed!" Doctor Gerould ran over and caught him before he fell; almost glad Destan was in so much pain this time. *Maybe it'll help him remember. ~ Oh who are we kidding? He's too stubborn to remember regardless of what pain he's in.*

"I'll be fine. I need to get to Deep Dark so I—" Destan winced, the belvedere rushing over and ducking under him to help keep him on his feet. "So I can see how Calli's doing."

"Your body's taken a beating: inside 'and' out. If you want to kill yourself, do it on your own time… and do it so it actually works." Doctor Gerould scolded as he helped him back into bed. "She told me she'd be back in a few minutes. You can wait that long."

The belvedere flattened his ears and looked so pathetic and confused as he rested his head by Destan's hand. He let out a puff of a breath, catching his attention, "It's all backward and wrong, I know Big Fella."

A few minutes later the belvedere rushed to the door and whined as he sniffed and pawed at it.

Callimay opened it a few moments later and rushed over to Destan, ignoring the creature begging for attention, "I'm sorry I took so long."

"It's alright."

She said something muffled as she gave him a kiss and snuggled her head close to his; him smiling and relaxing as he closed his eyes.

"So… what happened?"

"Fidus and Chicane said things are going well. And Aldred gave you a round of applause for giving him multiple of two kinds to see if it will truly stick." Callimay summarized. "He gave me a—"

"Chicane? But Enforcer was supposed to go?"

"That's what I thought you said, but when I asked him, Enforcer told me it was Chicane who had that detail."

"Eh, it doesn't really matter." Destan shrugged off. "As long as someone was there."

"Anywho." Callimay reached into her one pocket. "Aldred gave me a list of names and said while he wasn't there personally, he helped find them for the team they ended up using. He said this was your reward for your 'extra work'. He said you'd understand what this was an answer to."

"Give this to Chic— well I guess Enforcer. Tell him we need to find every last one of them and bring them in." Destan's eyes got wide as he scanned through the rather long list of names.

"Wouldn't that be more of something in line with what Gumshoe would do? Or at least what he should head up?"

"He's back?"

"Just got back."

"Then give this to him."

"Who are they, anyway?"

"The faculty at the Society. — Yes, I know most didn't survive that holocaust, but they're the ones who had direct access to the serums and knowledge of how processing worked. They have to be interrogated. And as much as I hate to do it, we've got to destroy every last piece of scrap paper and file my father wrote about them; even the stuff about us. It's the only way to keep this from happening again. … But…"

"But what?"

"We're going to have to wait until Aldred's part is completed. He may ask for something."

"Who's to say he will keep his word?"

"He always has, Calli. It may seem like he doesn't but he's quite literal and contractual — if you will — about his help. If you ask one question more than what he agreed to he knows he's not obligated to answer; even though to us it's a natural extension of logic that deserves answering, or an action which is deemed necessary. — I know he's not a 'kind' person, but for as much as I trust others… I do trust him in this area." Destan calmed as he stroked her hair. "He's a brilliant scientist; the only teenager to get clearance to work with my father in Faberton.

But he didn't want to work for anyone once he 'tasted' wealth, he told me one time. … More like once he tasted the addiction of gambling."

"But it's illegal."

"In most countries, yes it is. But Caudree as well as Agroos Union allow it for 'entertainment'."

"Oh. I seem to remember something about that. Isn't it some huge 'festival' type thing they do?"

"Uh-huh. — What about what happened in Quimbergo? Any word from Trever as far as what they're doing? I know he said he was going to go back, but was he able to? I know I fowled things up really bad." Destan scolded himself as he looked at his bandaged arms and hands.

"Trever was able to get back in by the skin of his teeth, he said. The man on the train must've projected his block in general when he was around; it doesn't sound like Trever was 'targeted' according to what he told me. — But anyway, we were able to talk and he told me Toreon came and locked everything down. … It sounds like they're moving everyone to different locations within the next couple days so we won't be able to find them." She tried to break the news as softly as possible. "Aldred said he'd know first thing tomorrow if what he came up with would work. He's also working on the mechanism right now so it's the right amount to reach everyone in the facility and would be ready to go immediately after he found out. And if he needs to adjust something it wouldn't take long… as long as this works in the first place."

Destan sighed as he kept fiddling with her hair that was done up like it was on a regular basis now, "Did he say what type it is?"

"Air; which was why I couldn't go. He didn't want to risk me being exposed because of the danger that would be for you."

I can't figure that guy out anymore. "How's it being armed?"

"That's… well that's the bad thing." Callimay stuttered as she bit her lip. "To ensure the Syndicate can't disable it, it can't be on a remote or even timed release. Someone will physically have to set it up and turn it on."

"So that means whoever does it will have to physically be in the building." Destan finished as he shifted, wincing a bit. "Not the best thing right now, but…"

"Trever said he'd do it but Aldred's against it."

"And for good reason," Destan nodded as he sighed. "But he's the only one who could do it on such short notice. … It's his call, Calli."

"I know," she sighed as she bowed her head.

"Hey, look at me," he put his hand under her chin. "I was stupid and reckless back there and this is causing things to cascade into borderline madness. … I… I know you're tired of this all."

Callimay mumbled as she closed her eyes, "If this works then that means Total Eclipse can start."

"No. This 'will' work. I have faith in Aldred and Trever both. And that all means we're one step closer to going home and leaving this all behind us."

Her eyes became glassy, part of her becoming borderline indignant: *Why am I like this! I… it's not—*

"My ray of sunshine's just tired. She's tired of all these ups and downs. And it's okay to feel that way. I mean weren't you the one to say that about emotions in the first place? … Calli? I mean they do change. And my goodness what you've been through is going to make it more of a challenge."

"I just—"

"You don't want Trever in danger just like you don't want anyone else in danger. I get it. But I also know you understand that's impossible with what we're doing. Just take a moment and step back." Destan put a hand to her lips as he worked to sit up. "Elder's gone. And once this first big push is done I'm stepping down. Fidus and I've already talked about it and he understands and agrees. Our job is to offer protection for those who want to make this nightmare end. To make sure the Syndicate isn't capable of pulling the insane power-grab their founders did with the Eradication. We're going to be the first line of defense in what I'm sure will be be the Syndicate's show of force; but in the long run, it's up to individual governments to step up and do their part to protect the people they were set in place to. … I'm serious about this being over and us going 'home' home, Calli. Not just wherever we sleep at night, but back to what you and I have built and fashioned into a home. I want that home to grow… maybe even move somewhere to the country and build a bigger place if we have enough little ones needing their space."

His last comments tugged at her rather raw heart.

"I… I know we don't talk about a family directly because it's hard, but we both need some encouragement to keep going this last little bit." Destan reached out and framed her face. "It's so close. I can see it. And with these Elites gone it's going to make our lives so much easier. … Am I helping you any with this? Calli?"

She smiled as she tried not to start crying, "Yes."

"Is there anything else I can do to help?"

Callimay shook her head, "You've taken the first step, I need to take the next one since you're injured. And don't fight with me about it. What do you need from me right now?"

"I just need you." Destan sighed as he opened his arms and let her curl close to his chest. "Right here for the rest of our lives."

╯

Destan was all but fuming when Doctor Gerould came in later that day, but he had every right to eye the rebellious young man as he gave strict orders: if he wanted to heal he couldn't get out of bed for any more than a minute or two when absolutely necessary.

Of course Callimay did nothing but sit and let them bicker about it. She knew Destan understood; but she also understood Doctor Gerould knew it was hard for him to be "chained" like this at a time when he couldn't afford to be. This "bickering" was Destan coming to terms with what Doctor Gerould knew was a challenging reality.

But neither of them were willing to make that admission; and so the bickering continued for a few minutes more.

Once everything settled — the two refusing to talk to each other so Doctor Gerould left — Traceur walked in.

The second the gnawing tension greeted her she started to back up; Callimay smiling as she started to follow, "Heading to Deep Dark?"

"Yeah," Traceur's voice was fused with confusion and fear.

"Oh good! I'll go with you."

The belvedere wanted to come, but Callimay shook her head, "You just stay with Destan, okay? I'll be fine."

Huffing as he bopped his nose against her leg a few times, the fluffy creature giving up and plodding over to sit beside Destan.

After they left, Doctor Gerould slipped back in the room.

"Seriously! I only did it for the exact reason you said."

Destan threw the covers over himself while he flopped on the bed; hissing from aggravating everything, but with only himself to blame.

"I… I just wanted to talk with you while Callimay wasn't here."

"What's wrong?"

"It… well, it's your heart. I can't say what did it for sure, but if I had to guess, it was the jump you made with so much extra 'baggage'."

"H… my heart? Like… it's damaged? … How bad?"

"Enough that I 'strongly' suggest you ask Aldred if he can find something capable of at least suppressing your abilities. And in a form that wouldn't be transmittable to Callimay for obvious reasons." Doctor Gerould didn't bother to beat around any bush; his tone reflecting the serious nature of this all.

But he softened as he continued, "Now you're heart's functioning fine, no abnormal rhythms or tissue damage, but it appears as if your heart was 'stunned'. It looks like a perfect case of what we call stress cardiomyopathy. In and of itself it isn't something uncommon as far as being found in people without abilities when they're overwhelmed with stress or powerful emotional episodes, but you present a different set of variables that I want to make sure don't cause any permanent damage."

"I don—"

"Now give me a second to explain." Doctor Gerould pulled a chair up; his tone much more like a concerned father. "Basically your body is flooded with a high level of adrenaline and other hormones that are normally released when you would be under stress: fight or flight. They interact with your heart to help it function at a faster rate so your body can respond to the situation the brain says it's in; but in this case there's just too much for it to handle at one time and your heart doesn't know what to do with all the excess it has to process and doesn't have the stamina to do it any longer. — Under normal circumstances the patient is kept on a strict cardiac diet and bedrest for a few weeks; recovering as if nothing ever happened and the heart showing no signs of damage. But as with Callimay's brain: if it's not allowed time to heal, the next episode causes more weakness which 'lingers' and can start to effect the tissue permanently."

He paused for a moment, letting this sink in as much as possible; giving Destan the chance to ask any questions.

A blank stare was all he was given.

"I know I don't know much because I am speaking as a doctor without true knowledge of the serums and their effects, but relaying what I see in 'normal' people and then offering logical conclusions based on what subtle differences I'm seeing because of your 'unique' situation… I'm confident this isn't something that is of catastrophic importance today. Urgent? Most certainly. But if you stop, step away, and listen to your body; I don't see why you can't bounce back from this: completely."

The belvedere had his nose snuggled under Destan's hand and whimpered as he petted him rather sporadic. What he was thinking about now wasn't what he was potentially facing, but the fact this was something he needed to find a "tactful" time to tell Callimay… and in a way he could get all the details out before she started calling every doctor on the planet to figure out how to find a cure.

Of course, Doctor Gerould sat there and didn't say a word either way. It wasn't in any way easy for him to tell Destan this. He knew him too well. The changes he was going to have to make were going to mess with his duties that were becoming more and more pressing; and his usual segmenting thought process couldn't juggle two things — of this caliber — at once, even if his life depended on it.

"There's… well there's no 'permanent' damage right now… right?"

"Correct."

A sigh of relief helped calm the churning fear in the air, the belvedere rooting his nose further under Destan's hand.

"I'm sorry, Destan. I truly am." Doctor Gerould clasped his hands and shook them; his head hung in shame. "I wish I could be more help than I am about this all."

"It's not your fault. I'm the one shooting myself in the foot; albeit unknowingly. Thank you for telling me… and when Calli wasn't here."

"I thought it best to let you tell her, or at least let you decide how and when to tell her."

"I'll… I'll figure something out. — Lance?"

"Yes, Destan?" He shut the door and turned back.

"How long do I have to rest and such so everything's copasetic? In your opinion."

"At least two weeks. And rest assured, it's not 'strict' bedrest, but a heavy restriction on weight lifting, emotional situations, and stress."

And right now of all times. Destan closed his eyes as he clinched his fist. *So, basically strict bedrest.*

"What happens with the Elites is all between Aldred and Liberator. We're just curriers and backup at this point; and we've got everything set for what we're able to anticipate and handle." He did his best to keep things in perspective. "Remember: the first part of what happens after this is purely political in nature. And the next phase after that is really up to the Syndicate. If the financial fiasco can hold their attention long enough, it can buy you the time you need while not dragging this out any longer. I'll get with Linton—"

"But I'm assigned to Majesty Presley. Well… I assigned myself."

Doctor Gerould eyed Destan again; that being his "fatherly" cue of: Destan better calm down and listen, "As long as things go as planned, your brother-in-law will take your place. And if not, Callimay c— don't even 'think' about arguing with me. You know when she finds out she'll step in anyway. She's not the type to sit on the sidelines and let everyone else take the brunt of work. You know that."

Coming to the realization talking about it was only going to get him more worked up, let alone the fact that "is" what his wife would do, he took a deep breath and laid back, rubbing his face.

"Let this mission with the Elites play out first, 'then' we'll address all that. Alright, Destan? … Destan?"

"Alright."

"Just get rest. Coadjutor should be in after dinnertime to check your wounds. In the meantime, if you need anything, Coadjutor said he'd be around while Torpid and myself are observing what Aldred's doing."

ℬ

Callimay ran down the hall, stopping short at the door and cracking it open just enough so she could poke her head in.

"Shh," she calmed the belvedere as he whined and nudged her hand, him tapping out a dance of foot-fire as he stood there: *Destan's asleep. ~ Looks like Fidus is going to be the one making this call. ~ I hope he doesn't get upset. ~ Thing is, you tried, Rose Petal. You know how important him getting his rest is right now. This is why Fidus is here. ~ I know. ~ Well then 'do'.*

When she got back an hour later, Destan was still asleep. She sat there with her head leaning on the bed, closing her eyes to rest. The belvedere was quiet as he crept to her and sat in front of her, resting his head on her lap as he sighed.

Next thing she knew, she could feel Destan undoing her hair and brushing it out with his hand.

"It's starting to get longer, finally." He smiled as she shot up. "Sorry. Didn't mean to startle you."

"I… I'm fine. — Yeah, it is." She brushed off and curled up next to him; finishing rather quiet, "Everything went just like Aldred hoped it would, so Fidus is on his way to get things to Trever."

"But I thought y—"

"I… I was going to wake you but you need your rest. I'm—"

"It's alright." Destan rubbed her arm. "It's not like I lose some achievement or something for being left out. Fidus is the most senior active Veil right now and the one who is supposed to be making those decisions in circumstances like this."

"Aldred still wasn't thrilled Trever would be the one doing it, but Trever wouldn't budge because he was the only one who could do it in the time constraint we are under." Callimay said rather nervous. "I asked about him wearing a mask, but Aldred said the particles were far too small for any mask to do any good with as close as he would be. He had to make it that way so they couldn't 'escape'."

"It's harmless to 'normal' people, correct?" Destan asked concerned.

"He said once it got into fresh air its 'contamination zone' would be less than a mile and would dissipate in less than an hour; but he said it in and of itself isn't a 'bioweapon' which would affect 'normal' people at all. And by the info Trever got us, no civilian is within a five-mile radius of the place, anyway."

"Good. … What's the ETA?"

"Caller's warning."

"Is there a recovery team on standby?"

"Yes. They're leaving in a couple hours. And the weather looks a bit calmer. … Destan?"

"Stay here, Calli." He shook his head.

"Alright," she sighed as she hung her head. "Chicane said he would stay around the area until those Elites were ready to bring back."

"Is anyone with him?"

"Coalesce left with Dozer and a few others."

"Good," Destan sighed as he lay back, wincing a bit.

"How can I help?"

"I'm alright," he smiled as the door opened. "Mender said you'd be by about now. Figures it'd be right as I get settled."

"Did he say why?" Coadjutor asked as he shut the door.

"Yeah," Destan grunted as Callimay helped him sit up.

♭

The next several hours were some of the most nerve-wracking ones Callimay could remember. Destan had been through these types of situations with other deep recluses, so it was easier for him to relax; though he couldn't as well this time because the belvedere was whining and pacing the floor.

"Be quite!" She hissed as she stomped her foot; the belvedere cowering from her.

"Calli you've got to—"

"Shh! I think I heard someone." She flew to the door and opened it; leaning out into the hall.

Her shoulders dropped as she leaned back in and closed the door at a snail's pace; her leaning her head against it.

"Calli just come sit down. Trever knows what he's doing."

"Maybe I should g—"

"You'll just be doing the same thing there and you know it. Just stay here. No matter the outcome, I want to be with you when it comes in. Two minutes difference won't make—"

"Do you think something's going to go wrong!"

Trying not to groan too much as he rubbed his face, he sighed, "Calli, look. The fact he got back in and nothing happened after all this. His cover is still in-tact. He's as safe as he has been this entire time."

♇

The light on his phone came on, Trever's attention trying to slowly shift from Kayla to it so she wouldn't be curious. She kept talking as she got glasses down from a cabinet; him sending a quick reply before deleting it all while her back was turned.

"We're all out, I think," he shook his head as he got up, answering her question.

Kayla groaned as she opened another cabinet, "Oh yeah, that's right. I forgot."

"I'll go to the store real quick. Want me to get something?"

"You know we're not supposed to leave and don't forget you're on really thin ice right now… for whatever reason." She finished as she twisted her lips and glared at him.

"They're just jealous. — I've got a hankering for something other than what they fix, anyway. I won't be gone but what… ten minutes tops if I order it before I leave?" He shrugged his shoulders as he grabbed his coat. "So what do you want?"

She grumbled, but eventually caved, "Well, what are you getting?"

"Hopefully some Crab and Sodd if the Whistle-Stop is still open. Want some Krumkake?"

"How could I say no to that?" She smiled as she sighed wistfully. "It does sound really good. And it has been a long time since we've had a 'good' meal. … Do you need some extra for a tip?"

"You know I don't tip," Trever rolled his eyes. "It's their job. I don't get tips for doing a good job, do I? So why should certain people get special perks with my hard-earned money when I don't?"

"Excuses, excuses," she made a face at him as she opened her purse. "Now give this to them and quit bickering with me."

"Fine," he took the money and gave her a kiss. "I'll be back in a bit."

"I'll cover for you while you're gone. But it's up to 'you' to figure out how you're going to get the front guard to let you go."

"Every man's heart and brain are tied directly to his stomach, Babe. You know that." Trever winked as he opened the door. "I'll be fine."

♇

"What do I owe you?" The man guarding the gate whispered as Trever slipped him a small bag; them both scanning the area.

"Just get inside and get some rest tonight before too late, huh?" He slapped his shoulder. "That's thanks enough for me. — And really? 'I' should be the one thanking you."

"It was worth it, believe me. And I will for sure."

℔

From what looked like a dead sleep, Trever jumped to his feet. He got in his closet to grab his coat; checking the hall before sneaking out. And then as if pacing himself against cameras and security, he would check his watch and then pause — it almost looking like he was counting — before rushing to certain spots and hiding.

He reached his target room and slipped in just as a couple security guards rounded the corner.

Once they left he wedged a chair under the door handle and started looking around. He took out a package that was no larger than a light novel and set it on the floor, reading the note with it as he moved certain levers to certain positions.

The directions were pretty straight-forward and simple which made up for the fact getting into the air vent was ridiculous: *It's not like this thing is big enough for a person to fit into! Why did they make it so… hard! Come on!*

Once it was in place, he sat and waited.

And waited.

I got here too early.

Time dragged on as Trever watched the second hand on his watch tick by the last couple minutes. There was a five-minute window where are the guards would be inside. He needed all of those five minutes to ensure the aerosol got to them.

Aldred told him they needed to be exposed for at least thirty seconds for it to work. They figured out it was going to take at least three minutes for the aerosol to make its way to the farthest parts of the building complex, so he had to time this just right.

While Trever didn't see anything when he set it off, he felt a breeze and then an overwhelming sensation of dizziness. He decided it wasn't enough and smacked his head as he got it out the vent; him staggering over to the furthest corner of the room. In a rather futile effort to limit his exposure, he sat there and kept his hand over his mouth and nose.

He heard voices outside and saw the handle giggle, him panicking a bit since they shouldn't be there at that time, but nothing else happened and they continued chatting and laughing as they walked away.

Oh! I forgot. … Where's the scanner? … Forty-five, three, and twenty-seven. Two minutes. Alright. Trever sighed as he took a small phone-like device out of his pocked fiddled with it before setting it down so he could start putting the vent back in place. *Now let's hope this goes up easier. Please don't strip on me. … Come on.*

Out of nowhere the door burst open; people shouting, "Down on the ground! … Now!"

Stunned, Trever whipped his head around. The blinding light which met him only made his dizziness worse; him stumbling off the boxes he was standing on. A few more demands were shouted, him unable to get his thoughts clear enough to figure out what to do, and then he felt a heavy and painful sensation on the back of his head and his left side.

ЗD

The clock's second hand started another minute, Callimay fidgeting in every way possible as she tried to keep from pacing. Destan was passed out and she made sure to put the damper on the belvedere so he wouldn't whine all the time: *One nervous Nellie is enough for right now. At least I can do it and be quiet. ~ He's sleeping an awful lot. ~ H… he is. Hopefully it's— no, it's fine. It is. He needs this.*

She glanced up at the ceiling, sighing as she closed her eyes; finally letting everything go and in a manner of speaking, "giving up" what she knew she couldn't control. That release of worry helped so much because the next thing she knew, she was being shaken awake. She stopped screaming when she realized who it was; their motioning reminding her Destan was still asleep.

Terrified, she scurried out into the hall with them, asking winded, "What's wrong?"

"All I wan— why is it that you automatically think that? Does something always have to be wrong when I look for you?" Fidus raised

315

his eyebrow as he folded his arms across his chest. "And are you okay? I didn't think I—"

"Because I can't remember— oh never mind." She rolled her eyes; part of her so relieved to hear what he said. "So what's the 'good' news you have for me! How's Tre— Emissary? I mean Liberator."

Fidus paused for a moment, mouth wide open, and then sighed, "The news I have is just that: news. Aldred got a reading that the aerosol was released."

"And?" She dragged out; her eyes and voice washing over with fear.

"It was only active for a half minute or so and wasn't fully activated. He said it's most likely Liberator fell unconscious from the high levels of the aerosol he inhaled; him hitting something on the device as he blacked out. And the way he talked he wasn't too surprised."

"But you said—"

"We don't know if it's bad or not." Fidus' voice became stern. "We can't jump to unnecessary conclusions without any other intel."

"But if he can't—"

"If he's not at the drop point by caller's warning and Aldred says it was activated again, we'll know why." He refused to cave.

Doing everything possible to keep that positive outlook Fidus had, Callimay nodded as she took a deep breath, "Okay. … Sounds good. But… but shouldn't we have something ready to go if he doesn't?"

"I agree," he stepped aside and let her pass; him continuing as they walked at a rather brisk pace, "We need to get a secondary team on their way and in place so not a moment is lost. Our primary team may need to shift their detail if something has gone wrong."

While her mind was full of terror from the what-ifs, another side of her kicked in. She thought it was just due to her training — neglecting to remember what Destan told her during her first run.

"Get with Aldred and see if he can have another machine ready to go within the hour. It could be he wasn't able to get it off at all if things did go south."

There was a Veil who joined them at the main door to the medical wing, Fidus nodding to them.

"You do know that means he'll be expecting—"

"Y… yes." She fought to keep her composure. "I know that, Fidus."

$\mathcal{SB}$

"Go ahead, I could use the sleep anyway." Trever said with a bit of a lisp because of his busted lip. "Just don't throw water on me after I'm out, okay? Not like I can go anywhere when I'm asleep anyway and it'd just waste good water."

The guy gripped his hair a bit more and then tossed his head back as he let go.

"Well it was worth a try," Trever mumbled as the man stormed over and spoke with a couple others.

A door at the far end opened, him not able to make out who it was: they were slender and tall but that fit about half the people there. And yet it only took a couple seconds of them bickering for him to realize who it was; him shaking his head as he chuckled to himself.

"And what if what I just said is true? Do you think the Prince will let this slide? As if you matter much being a standard deviation." The person threatened; everyone allowing them to walk by.

They sauntered up, tilting their head and leaning in to affectionately brush the side of his face… stabbing him under the chin with their spiked fingernail, "Why do you do this to me time and time again?"

"Well this sure wasn't intentional, I assure you, Kayla." He grimaced as he looked up.

She leaned in and whispered, "Please tell me this is something Elder wanted… for whatever reason."

"And if it wasn't?" He looked at her out of the corner of his eye.

"Okay," she sighed as she took a step back and wiped her finger off in an overly dramatic way. "Fine. We'll do it your way. Enjoy it."

Without another word she left; all the others in the room shocked and left scrambling to figure out what to do. But one of them who had been sitting at a table the whole time got up and picked up the phone-like machine Trever had; swinging it back and forth like a fad fidget spinner from centuries past.

Kayla will get me out, but if she tries to get in contact with Elder I'm dead meat. ~ So do we stall or break out? ~ How about option three?

$\mathcal{SB}$

Meanwhile, Callimay was being tested to what she believed to be her max. Deep in her heart she knew she couldn't go because of the risk she would be in of losing her ability and what affect that would have on Destan; but superficially she didn't feel she could trust anyone to save her brother except herself and felt enough time would've passed before she got there for the aerosol to do any damage.

Yes, this was a major conflict she was having —understandable to a point — but it was causing issues beyond herself. Major issues, in fact.

"You have to stop, Jewel." Traceur finally spoke out; her slamming her hands on the table and glaring at her. "Elder is dead. We are not a threat to you anymore. I know it's hard to grasp sometimes and you still have moments where you can't remember things, but it's the truth. Trust us! We know what we're doing! The longer we wait like this the more likely something 'will' happen to Liberator if it already hasn't. Those going to help him have families waiting for them, too! Please, Jewel! Think! Think and then act on it… now!"

And that was all it took; Traceur's bolstering confidence — albeit extremely direct — to remind Callimay she wasn't alone, her concern wasn't well placed, it wasn't just Trever who was in danger, and she had to make a decision right then.

Tears welling in her eyes, Callimay hung her head and then nodded, that signaling to the group there they were cleared to go.

Doctor Gerould put his hand on her shoulder as he stopped next to her, "I know you understand Traceur, but don't take things too hard. Just keep trying to reach him, okay? Don't give up. I… I'll make sure you get contacted the second we get him clear."

ℬ

While there wasn't much known about the entire layout of the place they were going to, Trever got them quite a bit of information they were able to use so they understood what they were getting into. And then something unexpected happened, someone running up to Tracer with a phone, "It's for you."

"Hello?" She stood up and trotted away. "Are you sure? … Is that all you've gotten? Any word— alright. … Oh? … Well that helps quite a bit. … Uh-huh. … Okay. Yeah, keep me updated."

All eyes were on her as she came back, sighing, "Well we have one thing that won't be any concern: the recorder/transmitter for the exposure verification was turned back on. All readings show every individual was exposed. So as far as any extra 'firepower' goes, there is none. And as it would turn out, the information that was transmitted for that all showed the location of every individual. The signal was still being transmitted while I was on the phone, and Coalesce said he'd be sure to give us any further info about locations or if we lose it."

"I'm assuming we're getting those images as well?" Someone tapped their hand on the table.

"It should be coming through any moment, yes." Traceur sat down and started working. "The only thing is they said the image is 2D. We'll have to guestimate which floor each individual is on."

This all took a load off of Traceur and her team, but also Callimay. It gave her a new hope that Trever was okay. She still couldn't reach him — and it concerned her as to why: if everyone was exposed, she should be able to get through — but she clung to the hope she now had. And she kept staring at one hotspot on the image for some reason. It was brighter than all the others. Surely that meant it was him. Right?

He'll be okay. He'll be okay. … God? Please let him be okay.

℥

The stress of everything, lack of sleep, and lack of knowledge as far as what would happen and how fast… Callimay's mind was starting to slip; there being moments she wouldn't know where she was or who she was talking to. Seeing the fear in her eyes at one point, someone called for Auditor, and she did her best to keep her calm and keep everyone else from badgering her.

"Why don't you go see Destan?" She smiled as she put her arm around her and walked away from the group. "I know seeing him would help you right now."

"I…" Callimay stuttered as she fought to think.

"How about this?" Auditor kept every word positive as she led her on; waiting for them to be out of Deep Dark when she finished. "Why don't you go see Destan and I'll go get some food. Sound good? … Callimay? … Is there something you'd like me to get, special? I know it's been a while since you've eaten anything. And Destan wouldn't want to see you like that."

Her lack of response started to worry Auditor more and more.

But not wanting to trigger something, she just kept walking and saying the same thing in different ways; her breathing a sigh of relief when they were right outside Destan's room.

"Here we are! You go on in and I'll—"

"What is this place?" Callimay gripped Auditor's wrist, starting to cry. "W… where am I? Who… who are you?"

Not fully prepared, but knowing she had to be a source of trust and calm during this storm, Auditor took Callimay's hands in hers and looked her in the eye, "Do you know your name?"

That answer came in the form of seeing this young woman's eyes widen with terror as she yelped a bit, then screamed and jumped when the belvedere barked and pawed at the door.

"Easy."

"Why can't I remember anything?"

"Just come in here, I'm sure you'll start to remember." Auditor coaxed as she reached for the door handle.

"What is that in there!"

"It's your belv— dog. And your husband is in there, too."

"Husband! I…"

"Just try. I'll leave the door open and do whatever I can to help you feel comfortable and safe. Okay?"

Some part of Callimay knew she could trust her, but she didn't know why and it bugged her so much. She nodded and took her hand, flinching when the oversized white fluff ball of a dog bounded out… and then stopped. He knew she was scared. So he whined and sat down, stretching his neck out to sniff her hand that she jerked away.

"He is big, isn't he?" Auditor calmed as she put her arm around her, chuckling. "Let's go inside real quick, huh?"

"O… okay," she shied away from the belvedere as she followed.

The second she laid eyes on Destan her mind was desperately trying to find his name. She recognized him and knew he was her husband, but why couldn't she remember his name? Why didn't it make sense that he was in a hospital bed? What was under all the bandages he had on? What happened? Did she know what happened? By what Auditor told her she should!

"Why don't you sit here?" Auditor offered as she guided her to the closest chair to Destan's bed. "There we go."

"What happened to me?" Callimay shivered as she reached out and gripped Auditor's hand; begging her to stay. "Don't leave. Please. I… I don't— how come I can't remember anything?"

Auditor was trying to remember what music ended up working for Callimay, but knew the fastest way would be to contact Mender; which made her cringe a bit. But she pulled herself together because she knew this young woman needed help she couldn't give; and the one who had it would be civil with her about this request, "Sweetie? Would you mind if I stepped out to make a phone call? I'll leave the door open, I promise. I won't be but a couple steps away if you need me."

"Who are you calling?"

"Your doctor. He knows of something that can help you remember."

"This has happened before?" Callimay mumbled under her breath as she looked around her.

"Is it okay?" Auditor barely tapped her shoulder; trying to smile and be encouraging.

"Y… yeah. Yeah, it's fine."

"I'll be right outside." She repeated as she gestured to the door.

Once outside, the belvedere whined at her and flopped down on all fours; his ears flat.

"I'm worried, too. But hopefully he'll remember what she needs." *Oh why does it have to be him who knows.*

"We just land—"

"What music was it you prescribed for Callimay? Do you have an extra disc of it somewhere?"

"What happened?" He jumped from his seat; catching the attention of all who were nearby.

"Everything's just been too much for her to process, and with the exhaustion from the stress I think she took a nap and didn't have it with her… and it's snowballed into a breakdown of sorts."

Doctor Gerould dragged his hand down his face, "I knew something wasn't right when I— how bad is she?"

"Well I have her trust, so I'm able to talk with her and be around her. But she can't remember anything. I 'think' she recognizes Destan, but the poor thing's terrified." Auditor smiled when she saw Callimay.

"Umm— just a second," Doctor Gerould paused to answer a question first. "Is there a speaker in the room?"

"I… I don't see one."

That's odd, I thought for sure it was there. "Have you looked in the suite? The original disk should be there if nothing else."

"I was trying to not leave her if at all possible and not have others around." Auditor sounded a bit testy.

"Eavesdrop should have a copy of it. I'll call her right now and have her bring it to you. — By the way, where are you?"

"We're with Destan in his room." She poked her head in and waved to Callimay as she nodded.

"I'll make sure she knows."

"Thank you." Auditor took what appeared to be her first breath as she hung up; smiling as she came in and sat down. "He said he'll have your aid for your memory here as fast as he can. Another lady will come here, but I trust her, okay?"

"What is it that helps me? How long have I been like this? Does he know?" Callimay gestured to Destan.

"He knows and he's been by your side the whole time to help you."

Callimay began to tear up as she bit her lip; so much guilt building inside of her for some reason, "Did my memory loss cause this?"

"Oh heavens no, Sweetie." Auditor's heart broke just a bit. "This has nothing to do with your memory lapse. He had a… a work accident, that's all. The bandages make it seem a lot worse than it is. It's just cuts and scrapes. And as far as what helps you? It's music, believe it or not."

"M… music?" Callimay raised her eyebrow.

"Think of it this way: when you're asleep, your brain usually uses that time to relax and sort out your memories from that day. Well, your brain's been hurt a couple times and starts losing track of memories when you're asleep. The music helps stop that."

"I was hurt?"

"But the best part is that the music works. You just forgot to have it playing when you took a nap earlier today because you were really worried and stressed out." Auditor tried her best to explain on a very basic level. "It'll be okay. You just need to rest while listening to some peaceful music. Sounds nice, doesn't it?"

"You're sure it works?"

"I am, Sweetie. I am." She patted her hand as she heard quick footsteps. "Oh! That must be the lady I talked about. Let me go check."

Everything done and now behind her, she closed her eyes and took a deep breath as she stretched; calling the belvedere to her as she got ready to leave. Part of her felt better since everything was done, but the other part was broken beyond repair.

Callimay wandered around for a while and eventually found herself on the beach. She sat there as the tide began to creep in, trying to sort out everything.

The belvedere would bound up and down, barking and nudging her arm; but even he couldn't get her to let go of her despair. And before long, the tide was up enough she wasn't on dry sand. The belvedere whined as he sat beside her and he put his chin on her shoulder; her turning to hug him as she cried.

"The tide's just about to get to the point you won't make it through the pass, Rose Petal." Someone said rather quiet and calm as they came out from the cave. "You never liked your hair being wet and in your face. I doubt that's changed."

"It doesn't matter."

"Oh don't say that. Things aren't that hopeless."

"What happened to him? Am I ever going to know?" She sobbed as she stared out at the waves. "What if…"

"Maybe you won't, and maybe you will, but you can't give up like this." The person sighed as they sat beside her and petted the belvedere. "You fought so hard to help him remember who he is and who you are to him. Keep that fight in your heart right now. Don't stop trying. Even if he is gone, you've got to keep going."

"Don't I get some time to grieve and process this all, though?"

"Now it's not been settled that you were too late to get him help. Don't hasten grief when you don't have to. Enough of it comes on its own. — But even if it is that way, you have to learn to grieve 'and' live at the same time. I had to for twenty years, Rose Petal." They sighed and rubbed Callimay's shoulder.

"Mama?" Callimay screamed as she sat up.

There wasn't anyone around. In fact she wasn't down on the beach even. She was on a sofa next to Destan's bed.

Her eyes were wide with terror as she rubbed her temples: *What just happened? H… how did I? … What happened?*

She sat there, working to calm her breathing, and then laid back down and sighed: *Trever? I… I love you. I wish—*

Everlyn? Well it's about t—

Trever! Callimay shrieked as she opened her eyes and jumped to her feet. *W… where are you?*

Oh, you know, just trudging through the 'wonderful' winter wonderland of Quimbergo like any 'sane' person would be at this time of year. He almost laughed. *How about you? … Everlyn?*

I… I'm just so glad to hear your voice. Callimay finally got out as she collapsed to the floor; crying. *You're alright?*

Just cold. — Look I'm sorry I missed the pickup. I hit a snag with the centuries and Kayla… but it's all fixed for now. No worries.

You're alright, right?

I'm fine, Everlyn. His voice sounded like he was smiling; a possible eye roll also involved. *So did it work?*

Did what work?

Did that thing not send the info?

Oh! I… I'm…

Are you okay? Trever stopped, picking up on her confusion.

Callimay rubbed her face as she sighed: *I'm a bit foggy. I'm sorry.*

What happened?

I… I don't really know. I… I can't remember. I can't remember even coming back to see Destan. She looked around her.

Just relax, his worried tone quickened his steps. *I'm on my way back. Is Destan awake?*

No.

Is your music on?

She listened for a couple seconds, then nodded: *Yeah.*

He relaxed a bit as he sighed: *Okay good. Just stay put and I'll come there when I get back. Okay?*

Alright.

℘

Trever and the group who came for him had to stay at Aldred's lab for "decontamination" so they wouldn't carry any of the aerosol back and risk stripping Callimay of her abilities and do who knows what to Destan. So it ended up that Trever had to call and find out how his baby sister was and apologize for not remembering he'd have to wait to come back.

During this time Aldred was able to confirm Trever did not have any abilities any longer and there were no adverse effects from him being so close to the source, "There's no reason to think otherwise. The scanner shows the exact same levels, most being higher, than what the test subjects readings were. None were lower, so in my opinion there is nothing to be concerned about."

Destan looked around him and then asked rather quiet since Callimay wasn't around, "Is there any way for you to take the chemical you used and… I guess 'dilute' it?"

"Whatever for?"

"Let's just say since I'm the first cliffhanger to make it this long I'm discovering major health issues that need to be managed."

"And you're wanting to address the source, not the symptoms."

"Exactly."

"How bad is it?" Aldred asked as intrigue coated his voice; it sounding like he was taking notes.

"Nothing permanent, but the way the doctor talked it's not that far from that."

"What specifically is it affecting?"

"My heart."

Aldred took a bit of a step back, as if hit with a strong breeze, then replied in a tone that sounded taken aback, "I'll look into it. Do you need an answer by any certain time?"

"Just as soon as you can. And don't let my wife know. I haven't said anything to her yet." Destan wrapped up as he saw her walking over.

~ 20 ~

Now knowing the Elites were not in any way a "danger", Linton wasted no time putting the plan of crippling the Syndicate's finances into full-on frontal attack mode. Some family members had to be present with their lawyers to close their accounts since the amount of money being moved was far more than any estimates the Shadows made — a terrifying reality-check for Destan, seeing just how much "power" they had — so arrangements for transportation and guard details were set, checked, rechecked, and adjusted a few times.

It was orchestrated so all the money would be ripped from Vashti's hands in one fell swoop; causing the most chaos and panic possible. The political battle could begin without being noticed nearly as much because they wouldn't have any substantial amount of resources to dedicate to it. — After all, they were all about money. That was where their power came from. And with the amount being stripped from them? There was no way this wouldn't affect them… instantly.

Practically the second Trever walked into Bulwark everyone started packing their things and helping get whatever else was needed to be taken to the Nest ready for transport. He said he would take Destan's place in Brigon since he was one, a blood relative and two, in much better shape physically speaking; assuring Callimay before he left he'd make sure things were all squared away at the Nest.

Destan still wasn't where he needed — or wanted — to be, but he'd have time during the first couple weeks at the Nest to let his wounds rest before he would most likely be called upon to do his final part.

Callimay was working on packing, the belvedere trotting back and forth from the closet to the bed as she got things.

"Calli, why aren't you packing in there? You wouldn't have to walk so far. And really, we've already got things there. It's not like you need to do all this right now. I'll make sure it's sent back to Rayleen."

"I'm fine," she smiled as she looked over the edge of the suitcase. "I get to see you this way. And I do have to do 'some' packing anyway, so might as well just do it all right now!"

She came back a few more times, stopping this last time to catch her breath and rest for a moment.

"I'm well enough to sit in a chair," Destan grumbled as he started to get up.

I can't even take a breath without you spazzing out. Oh how I fear being pregnant on that front alone. You'll kill yourself with worry! ~ And suffocate us with his well-meaning worry. "Don't you dare get up!" She ran around and put her hands on his shoulders — just about the only place on his torso that wasn't cut. "It's fine. I need to walk around and get used to these shoes again. Okay?"

Destan sighed as she helped him back into bed and went back to the closet, "Are you sure you feel well enough, Calli? I mean you can get new shoes if it'd—"

"I don't think I could make a long run, but it's not like I can't walk at all." She said as she took an awkward step and fell onto the bed.

"Calli!"

"I just stumbled over the step," she huffed as she got up.

"Sure." He dragged out.

"I did! I just tripped."

"Only takes one time," he laid back and shook his head.

Unwilling to let him win this silly fight, but realizing the wisdom in his words, she conceded, "I'll see what Outfitter's got left in my size that's flat. Surely he's got something."

"I'm sure he does. — Oh! Don't forget my whip sword. It's in its box on that far top shelf."

Of course you put it up there. Why would you put things where I could possibly reach them? "You never took it out this whole time? Well then why in the world did I get it for you?"

"I did several times, I just put it back because… well I didn't want to leave it in the combat room. And thankfully I don't need it while we're here." *At least not anymore.* "Though it'd be best if I put it on from now on so I can get used to it."

℔

Before too much longer, Callimay was done and had Rocher take the suitcases to the jet. Destan was up, working on the computer, oblivious to the two of them talking. Rocher took advantage of this and requested she follow him into the hall; saying in a still hushed tone, "Milady? Are you quite sure Sir is able-bodied to embarking on this trip; as well as what is surely to follow? The projected timeline for the Arena is not set in any form. It could take place in mere days."

She sighed as she bowed her head and rubbed her arms, "Destan refuses to wait any longer. He… he's not bad, but I know those stripes on his back still aren't healed enough for him to move like he wants to… and I even know he will need to. He won't even let me look at them. — I tried to get him to wait, but he's dead set on this. He's got some kind of compression shirt he's wearing to help keep them from reopening… but it's a painful process to get it on in the first place."

"Pray tell, did Mender give you any kind of concrete timeline as to when he anticipated said stripes to be properly healed?"

"Last I heard, another three weeks providing he doesn't do anything to irritate them: and that shirt could even do it."

"Well then, I suppose all that can be done at this point is wish for the Syndicate to linger and wallow in their money woes for as long as possible." Rocher took a deep breath and nodded; now finishing what he intended to say all along, "Everyone is assembled and prepared for Sir to address them. As I understood it, we were only awaiting a few scattered recluses to join."

"Oh, I forgot! Thank you for reminding me. — I don't even think Destan remembered. — Once he's get dressed we'll be there last night."

When Callimay got back in, the belvedere whimpered and whined as he nudged her and then ran to the closet, "Destan?"

"I'm… fine." He replied a bit pained.

She ran over, finding him leaning on the back of a chair, "Destan what happened? I— you should've asked me to help. You can't be doing this. You'll cause— you know what Doctor Gerould said."

328

"I thought putting a shirt on wouldn't be such a— ah! … A painful thing." Destan heaved as he bent over even more.

Callimay didn't know what to do, but felt she needed to.

But what!

Reaching out to him, she hesitated. Part of her felt if she touched him she'd make his pain worse — which seemed so stupid to her, but when she looked in his eyes she couldn't help herself.

Not sure what to do himself, the belvedere sat next to him and stared at him, his ears twitching and head bobbing back and forth.

As she smoothed out the wrinkles of the shirt, Destan looked up and took her hand, smiling as much as he could as he pulled her close, "I know you don't know what to do. It's alright."

"I'm sorry," she cried.

"Now you know how I felt when you were in so much pain," Destan tried to be light-hearted as the belvedere rushed to their side and he started walking for the door. "Are you sure you have everything?"

"Yes." She nodded as both her and the belvedere supported him while he hobbled toward the door.

"Oh! I forgot. My veil. It's on—"

"Just sit down here and I'll get it." Callimay gestured toward the computer desk.

"Are you sure you should be wearing this? It 'is' heavy."

She walked as Destan put his hands over hers, prompting her to look to him, "I'll just wear it for the meeting. I promise. And I'll only wear it during meetings until the Arena. … Deal?"

"I… alright." She sighed as her shoulders dropped.

"Would it help if I asked you to help me put it on?" Destan groaned as he stood up, using the desk to help support his weight.

ℬ

They took their time walking to Deep Dark; Callimay becoming more and more tired as they went along: *What's wrong, Rose Petal? ~ I don't know. I'm just worn out. … I know Destan's in pain, but~ Tell him. ~ No. It's not that bad. He's got enough on his plate right now. ~ What about the whole big blowup of you being against him not telling you things when~ Alright! I'll tell him after the meeting. Satisfied?*

Rocher helped Destan down the stairs as Callimay followed, but had her attention diverted by whining, "Oh Buddy. You can't come with us, alright? Just stay here by the door and keep watch, okay? … And you need to hide for a while, okay? … Good boy. I'll make sure you get some moonlight soon."

The fluffy creature sat and whined as he sniffed toward Destan, but did as was told and sat still, turning midnight black. She hurried down and stood beside Destan as he talked with Nexus, "The last one is connecting right now, Doyen. Shouldn't be more than a minute."

He sighed in relief as he took Callimay's hand and hobbled to the middle of the circular portion of the room, nodding to Fidus who then addressed everyone, "It is time for the Veil to conceal all Shadows and eclipse the moon."

To that comment everyone stopped talking and gave their full attention to Destan. Callimay started to leave, but he took her hand: *Just stay here. For one it'll help me keep my balance better. And two? … Well I'll just let you guess that one.*

A few shallow and labored breaths helped him prepare himself to say in a loud and clear voice, "Thirty years and nine months ago to almost the exact day, Commander formed a team of trusted individuals who knew the despicable injustice being dealt to those who were left-handed, and sought to overturn what heinous law gave the Syndicate its birth and authority. Innumerable hours, tears, sleepless nights, altercations, battles, victories, and losses were endured to bring us to this point. We have lost many of our number who made breakthroughs so Total Eclipse and the Arena would even be a reality. And yet each and every individual here has offered their own expertise and talents, as well as their share of blood, sweat, and even tears to continue finding breakthroughs to make such efforts as swift as possible while at the same time putting just as much effort into eliminating as much loss of life as possible. You all are an amazing group. You've endured several scares with Narks — our latest one shaking us to our core — and yet you have all risen to the challenge. I'm proud to say I am a part of this group. You all have my deepest thanks and gratitude for what you have given up so others such as us in the generations to come won't have to endure such hostility. … Total Eclipse is beginning tomorrow. Everyone is well aware how their details and duties are to proceed and the risks involved. I know the reality of death has always been on each and everyone's minds since they began their regimen to become a Shadow. And I also know this final step will — in many ways — feel like blind-navigating a live Syndicate web. With this in mind, it is well known my beliefs in regards to my obedience and service to The Living God. I know many of my comrades share this belief and also share in the peace of knowing whatever the outcome is for us individually, we have a reward awaiting us far greater than the physical freedom we are striving for right now. For those comrades I want to encourage and remind you not to back down. Fight the good fight. Finish the race. Remember your reward and don't lose sight of it. To those who may not know of what I'm speaking, I know a Holy Bible is within your reach wherever you are. The words written on those pages are powerful and eternal. They are what guides a person to a lasting relationship with their Creator and Lord. I know I have spoken with several of you, and others have made this known to yet others, but I want to take this last opportunity before we begin this last surge: this may be uncomfortable for you, but I cannot stress enough that only by obeying the commands given within God's Word can peace be ensured, victory be possible, and the day of judgement be looked to with joy and longing. If you have not obeyed the commands written within God's Holy Word: to believe Who God is and His Son Who walked on the earth so long ago. Have faith in what The Scriptures say concerning Him Recognize your need for such redemption by confessing Who Christ is, to turn away from your life in sin. And to be washed clean in the waters of immersion in The Name of Jesus Christ for the forgiveness of your sins and the precious and powerful gift of The Holy Spirit Who gives you the power to live a Godly and holy life bringing glory and honor to God at every turn; I beg you as your friend and comrade to open your eyes to how serious this is. To know there is hope beyond this life we now live. To see that there are spiritual battles being waged every day that we must win. And to understand I am not doing this as a commanding officer, but pleading as a comrade — a fellow member of mankind — to those I love, trust, and honor to look at themselves and value themselves of what God already has seen them worthy of."

There was a few moments of the most awkward kind of silence — it felt peaceful and happy yet on-edge and uncomfortable — before Destan began again; taking Callimay's hand and bowing his head as he spoke with a kind, yet firm tone, "Dear Lord? I pray You would be with each and every one of us. Nothing is done that escapes Your notice. We are all accountable to You. I pray we would all conduct ourselves in the way worthy of You and Your Son. If anyone hearing these words needs You, may they seek truth and not delay in making this decision. — We do not know how much longer we have to live; I only ask those who need to turn to You will have every opportunity to make this decision. For those who are Your children, help us to have clarity of mind and a heart to do Your will. Help us to have strength in this fight. Give us Your peace, Your strength, and the victory that only You can give. Be with us all. Guard us and lead us. Keep us unified and let our focus never waver. May You be glorified in what is done, for we know that victory is granted only by You, and You alone. And I pray others will see Your light in us in how we conduct ourselves and what we say. I pray this all in Your Son's Name, amen."

A wave of "Amen," rolled through the room as people lifted their heads. Destan took another deep breath and finished, "May the new moon continue to rise on you all. If there is ever an instance where one of us is lost and no one is there to thank you for what you have done, may I be allowed to say this now without causing anyone any distress: 'may the stars accept you as guide and guardian'. … Thanks for what you all have done for others can never be fully expressed, but I know this blessing and gesture is held in high regard by all here. It has been a true honor to be your commanding officer these six years. I pray for your safeties and those whom we are protecting. Godspeed to everyone in their runs. … And let the Veil be lifted so the Shadows can be seen."

Destan took Rocher aside and spoke with him, then came and gathered a few things from his desk; Callimay helping him by holding the duffle bag he had ready. What he was packing didn't make much sense, but then it hit her: this only served as a distraction.

He wanted to be the last to leave.

The belvedere was still sitting up by the door, his tail thumping echoing through the now empty and bare room.

They stopped where veils and knives were kept as a memorial of sorts for those who came before; the long row that ran the full length encircling the main room. Destan opened the one case and gripped his father's veil, its familiar feel saying goodbye for the last time, then brushing his hand over Callimay's mother's.

He looked at her and smiled as much as he could, resting his forehead against hers while rubbing the side of her neck as he closed his eyes and whispered, "Ready?"

"They didn't die in vain, Destan." Her voice tried not to crack, but failed miserably. "They did so much to keep us safe and give us the life they always wanted for us."

One last time he looked back as they started up the stairs, seeing the map that shone on the floor, "This is really it. I'm ashamed to say this, but I never thought this would really happen."

"And Elder wanted you to keep thinking that, but you didn't."

"Not when I met you. Not when we were at the station in Brigon. I can't help but think that was the moment I started to break free from Elder's grasp. It was the oddest thing: I remembered 'why' I was doing this all. I felt fear for what felt like the first time in that moment because I imagined you being the one screaming for me to protect you. And at that moment I felt ashamed. I knew I hadn't done what I needed in some instances in the past. — That's why I believe that's when I started to break free: I started to remember. — I had someone so close to me, so innocent and precious, it forced me to remember I 'had' to fight for this day to happen. I couldn't let things continue to ebb and flow: just like Linton. I had to push ahead, make progress happen, and break through barriers."

"It's been a long road." Callimay encouraged as she rubbed his arms. "Much longer for you than me."

"I've been in this room for eight years now… and today's the day I leave it forever. And I'm not saying it to be dark or depressing. … No matter what happens we're never coming back. Had your grandfather not given us the invitation he did, we would've needed to find a way to get back here if things didn't work; but I'm so glad that's not what our backup plan is; that you don't have to stay here. This ends today. What follows this? We pray and step out in faith."

She started to look sad as she listened to Destan. Something in her knew this place was so much of who he was and knew in a way he was trying to process how to handle everything being different regardless of what happened.

And it seemed a tiny bit of him was scared to make this transition.

"I remember when the map went completely black." He smiled as he started up the steps. "Elder was furious and trying everything to rip the credit due you away with the most stupid of comments. Everyone was as joyful as I'd ever seen them when Brigon's light was turned black. … I know I said it then: that I wished you could see what you'd helped accomplish in that moment. But I know this is all God's doing in the end. But you let him use you for this."

"I love you, Destan."

"I love you so much more, Calli." He opened the door and ushered her out; her refusing to move. "What's wr— why are— what in the world are you doing here!"

"I was worried I missed you. — I would've been here sooner but a little 'stole away' was trying to tag along." The person apologized as they backed up so Destan and Callimay could walk into the hall. "And I hope you're alright if I wear this. I know I'm not supposed to, but I feel kinda exposed without it."

"I'm glad I found out before we left." Destan's tone showed more of a perturbed side than that of shock. "You don't need to be here or go with us. You need to go home… now."

"I'm doing my job as the protector of my family. I'm not about to shrink from my responsibilities. Especially not now. Right now's the most critical time"

"But you're doing your job already, Redje." Callimay stepped in, trying to help keep Destan calm. "You're a guard of our second largest Safe Haven. That in-and-of-itself is being the protector to your family and fulfilling your responsibilities to the Shadows. Someone has to keep those places safe. If things go wrong you're the last line of defense to make sure everyone gets out. You know that."

"I left them in good hands." Redje shook his head. "And thankfully I was able to get Tabby to see she needed to stay: it's not her job to do this, and she shouldn't with her health or the children."

"We all have our roles; and yours is to stay in Safe Haven." She continued to rebut in a reserved and polite, yet firm manner. "Health? Has something else popped up? Are her and the baby okay?"

"Look," Destan said loud and stern. "As much as I admire your willingness to sacrifice everything to keep those you love safe, you're being stupid and illogical. As your best friend and brother in Christ I'm begging you to go home and be with your family. You made a promise to Tabitha and you have Rose to take care of plus your newborn. And if Tabitha is having medical issues?"

"I und—"

"'A-nd', as your senior commanding officer I'm 'ordering' you to go back to Safe Haven. What Calli said was right: if this all goes south you 'have' to be there in order to get everyone evacuated. … Plus, as much as this personally hurts me to say it — part of me yelling not to — you can't wear that veil ever again in an official manner. You know that, Rej. Once you step down you're done." Destan kept his cool, almost cringing as he finished. "If I have to send a detention escort with you I will, so help me. You've abandoned your detail without authorization. … Please Rej, don't make me do this."

He stood there and was stunned to hear what he did, though part of him was fully expecting it. It was as if he just needed to be reminded; be comforted and encouraged that his role was serving its purpose and he was doing his part to protect the lives of those he cared about.

And so he accepted defeat, "You… you two are and have something very special. Don't 'ever' forget that. I've heard Tabby tell you on a couple occasions, Callimay, but I'm going to say it again: you two make sure to come home… to Rayleen, here, in this life, on Quidoria. We love you both and want to stay a part of your lives."

"Lord willing, we will."

"May the new moon continue to rise on you." Redje smiled as he accepted Destan's hand, then gave Callimay a hug. "Godspeed in your runs. If you ever need someone to talk to, don't hesitate to reach out… in whatever form you need. Just, don't cut out like you did last time."

"I'll make sure that doesn't ever happen again." Destan smiled. "Tell everyone in Rayleen we miss them and are grateful for their continued prayers. They mean more to us than they realize."

"I will, but before I go I want to be sure and say one right now. That is if you'll let me stay that long before sending me off in cuffs."

🕉

The flight there was crowded, Callimay excusing herself to the lounge not but a second after they were at cruising altitude. But after a minute or two the door opened, Destan poking his head in, "Feeling alright?"

"Better," she took a deep breath as she sat down.

"What's wrong?"

"I'm not usually one to be claustrophobic, but I guess being so high in the air and moving so fast just makes me feel like I need more space than I have with this many people." She rubbed her arm as he sat down next to her.

"Raven was spacious, wasn't she? — You're 'sure' you're alright?"

Callimay nodded as she leaned against his arm, "How are you?"

"Glad my veil is off, that's for sure." He smiled as the belvedere pawed at the door. "Of for the love of— come in, Big Fella."

"You're going to make sure and get your rest, right?" Callimay asked worried as he sat back and winced a bit.

"I promise you I will." Destan nodded as he kissed her on the cheek. "You look tired. Are you sure you're alright?"

"I've been a bit tired lately, but I'll be fine."

"Tired? When?"

"Well, I guess it was mainly when you were trying to get your shirt on back in the suite."

Destan let a sigh of frustration out as he brushed her cheek.

"It's nothing like that. I don't feel the pain anymore."

"You don't feel the pain but you still have the other side effects. Aldred warned me you would. You're still going through what you did before, just without any pain now." *I guess that pain was a 'help' in that area, as much as I hate to say it.*

"Oh. … Well now that I know at least it makes sense. I'm alright, Destan. Really."

"Did you remember your speaker?" Destan jerked a bit.

"I packed it, it's fine."

"But you—"

She waved her wrist in front of his face; showing the thin black band she had on. "Remember?"

He twisted his lips as he grumbled to himself.

"You're just focused on everything else. It's fine." She put her finger against his lips. "You can't remember everything all the time."

"I'd been meaning to ask, but now finally remembered: what made you think to get that in the first place?" Destan questioned as he took her hand and tapped the band.

Without any hesitation, Callimay stated in a quiet but deliberate tone, "Because I'm terrified of forgetting again; especially now that things are ramping up. I don't want to be stuck somewhere and not have it with me. — I'm just glad that it can tell when I'm asleep so it'll automatically turn on."

❦

It was strange to be at the Nest and know there were so many others there as well. Sure, they stayed in the cabin portion like usual — fixing meals, sitting around to chat, and watching the belvedere have fun in the snow — but knowing just on the other side of the wall and under their feet were about two thousand people at any given moment? It made Callimay a bit, well… uncomfortable.

"It won't be for very long, I promise you. And not anyone can just come up here."

"I know I shouldn't feel like this." She smiled as she kept washing the dishes. "For goodness sake, I mean there were just as many if not more people at Bulwark. I guess since I knew that's the way it was there it didn't occur to me. Here was, well… a special place for just us. … But you're right."

"My ray of sunshine," he started to think as he stroked her hair. "Are you doing alright? I mean, aside the awkwardness of everything? Are you really tired, still?"

"I'm okay now. What about you?"

"I'm not gonna sugarcoat it, I'm bushed." He took a deep breath as he rubbed his face. "I think I'm gonna head upstairs and rest for a bit."

"Destan? … W… what's wrong? I mean… you don't give up like this. I'm the one practically forcing you to relax." She bit her lip as her hands began to quiver at her side. "Is it your back? Is it that bad? Is that why you won't let me see it?"

"Let me get upstairs and then I'll tell you, hum?" He asked as he fiddled with her hair again, still smiling as he fought off another yawn.

🕭

As much as he could have brushed it off or pushed everything aside, Destan faced this issue head-on and didn't hold back; telling Callimay exactly what he remembered Doctor Gerould telling him.

It was a crushing reality she had to deal with. And in a way it didn't feel real. Destan had always been so strong, so healthy; in a way she felt she was losing her safety net she'd let him become. Fear began to claw at the web of protection encircling her; it beginning to fray and strain. But then she looked at his eyes. She saw he had hope. He wasn't gone.

"Calli? It's still hard for me to think about, even. It is so odd, but God's giving me this chance to find out now and stop things before they get worse. ... Calli?"

While she knew he was trying to help, all she felt was the shame crushing down on her: *How is it I'm giving up so fast now? Why can't I... why can't I cling to hope anymore? Am I losing myself in that sense? Is this all bending and twisting me to where I don't even know who I am?*

"No, it's not Calli." Destan took her hands; leaning over so he could see her eyes. "You reacting like you are is just natural shock. What sets you apart is how you move ahead — the fact that you 'do' push on."

Her shoulders dropped as he pulled her to himself, her trying not to cry, "So wh… what can I do? Is there anything I 'can' do? I mean it's something medical. How— are you in pain? Are you just tired?"

"Just tired. My chest might feel… 'heavy' at times, but usually I just get tired out of nowhere. And all those things are getting looking into right now. Lance said I just need to keep my cool as much as possible. So I need you to remind me. Remind me like I've asked before: our goal, our home, our family. Be the woman who is brave and courageous to stand up to the monster in me; who knows how to defeat him."

This tugged at her heart, her nodding as she sniffled and wiped her face. It was one thing for him to have deep cuts from razor wires, but to have a problem with his heart? Your heart is what kept you alive. If something went wrong, that could— it terrified her in an altogether different way. And then something he said struck her odd, "Th… that's why you've been talking with Aldred so much, isn't it?"

He nodded as he continued to rub her arm.

"B… but Doctor Gerould said there was no permanent damage, right? I mean, this is something you can… I guess 'manage' so nothing is permanently damaged? Right?"

Destan nodded as he yawned, leaning his head back against the pillows Callimay helped him prop up.

"And rest is the best medicine right now? Well, that and you not tapping into your abilities."

"Yes on both fronts. And if all goes well and we both can keep up on things, there won't be any worries at all." He closed his eyes as he pulled her hand over and laid it over his heart. "I probably should have waited to say something once I finished resting. I—"

"No! You're fine," she whipped her head around and put her free hand on his face. "You rest. I'll be okay. I… just get some sleep."

"I love you, Calli." He said rather groggy as he squeezed her hand.

"I love you more, Destan." She replied teary-eyed.

~ 21 ~

Destan was down for most of the following week, but once Sunday rolled around he would hit the ground running each day. This stark transition concerned Callimay to no end, but he sat her down and explained Doctor Gerould gave him full clearance and that what he was doing could be labeled as, "therapy and rehab".

Of course she objected because that was "his" definition and not what Doctor Gerould instructed, "You can't just do something and call it 'therapy and rehab' because it has the appearance of being healthy and beneficial. And doing too much at once isn't helpful at all. It's just as bad as if you were to injure yourself again."

In a way, Destan missed these little "discussions" they would have with each other. Not that he enjoyed talking about bad or sad things, but it was the fact they were getting to spend time growing together and learning how to best communicate their feelings, and feeling free to open up about these kinds of things. He understood, and enjoyed the benefits of letting his emotions be laid bare in front of his wife.

⁐

With them all settled in and things as stable as they could ever be, Trever and a group of other Shadows and Veils got ready to take off for their details. Destan tried to talk with him but there seemed to be this reluctance since he saw Destan's "advice" as being judgmental of his actions and lifestyle. So right before he got in the car Callimay ran out.

"Everlyn, I've gotta go. You told me everything was alright."

"I know, I just… I just wanted to give you this." She handed him a book. "I remember you saying last week how much you liked to read."

He looked at the printing on the spine and then handed it back as he shook his head, "I don't need that God stuff, Everlyn. I've got you."

"But I—"

"I'll get with you as soon as we get there." He reached out and gave her a hug. "Now get back inside before you freeze to death. I love you."

She stood there unsure what to do. She'd never been shut down like this by anyone; let alone someone she loved so much. The part of her that knew the danger her brother was headed toward — what might happen to him — was screaming and crying in despair. They just found each other and yet she might lose him… and this time it would be for eternity.

As the car rolled back out of the drive, the wind smacked her in the face, waking her up to the fact she was standing out in a frozen tundra. But even then she plodded back inside, trying so hard to hide her bitter grief with being physically chilled; hearing a tender voice, "He didn't take it?"

"No," she sniffled as her shoulders dropped.

"You've done all you can. If he won't read it or listen, what can you do?" Destan comforted as he wrapped her in his arms. "It's not like you can 'make' him do the right thing."

"It just scares me."

"I know it does," Destan sighed as he saw Rocher walk up.

"The last of the stationary details have departed. I— are you quite alright, Milady?"

"No," she shook her head as Destan let her go.

"Sir?"

Here came another opportunity. He had so many and yet each one ended the same: *Here goes nothing… most likely.* "She tried to speak with Liberator one last time before he left… trying to give him a Bible to read."

"Religion is not for the heart of everyone, if I might be so bold to remind you." Rocher seemed to nod in approval. "And as I've heard you say on several occasions, it 'is' the person's choice."

Destan groaned internally as he worked to choose his words wisely, "I have, I won't deny that. — Why? Because it's true. But wouldn't you agree that not all choices are the right ones?"

"Without doubt."

"Is that any different with this?"

"I see nothing wrong with a person finding the need of having something to ground oneself in for good, but I also see no evil in keeping things fluid so various situations can be tended to as desired for the greater good to come from it."

"Good isn't subjective. That's the thinking the Syndicate uses."

"Oh I mean nothing of such wild and hideous situations. But for the sake of this discussion I remind you of this: when Milady was on death's door. It was a situation where deception and lies would be quite useful and allowed."

"But I didn't do any of that and look at the outcome." Destan tried to stay calm as he continued to discuss and debate with his great uncle. "And it's only from your perspective that what the Syndicate is doing is wild and hideous. They — for the vast majority — believe what they're doing is right. Why else would they turn on their own families and murder their siblings and children? They believe the lies; their own lies. They have fallen for the delusion of this being right and one's duty to society. Doing what you think is right based on a standard 'you' or some other man sets is one-hundred percent of the time a skewed standard that is going to be detrimental to someone innocent. There is a level playing field and standard that isn't bias, but there is only one. And this Book contains it."

"The hearts within all mankind know what is inherently right and wrong in this life, Sir. Those in the Syndicate know in their soul that what they are doing is wrong, but choose to live the lie with which they tell others to also convince themselves; thus justifying their every evil action. Commander even acknowledged this."

"Grandmother was not the know-all say-all be-all in this area, either." Destan sighed as his hold on the Bible tightened.

"But you do not deny and cannot that the truth of men knowing inherently what is acceptable exists. Even that book of yours says so." Rocher pointed at the black leather-bound book with a bit of anger.

"It does say that, yes, but it goes on to say in that very passage that leaving any man or woman to their own devices with no dependence on God leads to corrupt thinking, a darkened heart, and a debased mind which defies even the laws of nature written on their hearts. Without the standard being followed, there is no way to adhere to what their heart knows instinctively to be truth." Destan opened it and flipped to where those words were. "You can't cherry-pick things out, Rocher. If you're going to use these words against me you've got to make sure you know what you're talking about. You've got to take everything in context. You've even said so various times concerning other things. … Just look at it."

Rocher reached over and closed the book in Destan's hand, sighing, "You worry far too much about others' choices for their personal lives and use only one deity's book to base your beliefs and judgements, Sir. I agree this religion has opened your eyes and heart that were so scarred and vengeful, but do not think some revelation can make you become so high and mighty to believe this is the only way and only deity which will offer salvation for any individual. — Now I believe I have other duties to attend to."

Destan rubbed his face half in frustration, feeling as defeated as Callimay was. He set the Bible on the desk closest to him and leaned against it, shaking his head as he mumbled to himself.

"Destan?"

He took a deep breath and looked up, trying to sound better, "What is it, Lance?"

"I… I overheard what you and Sentinel were discussing. I wasn't meaning to pry, but something struck me." He paused; his voice so curious. "You said some people think they're doing good but they don't base it on what even the laws of nature which were put in their hearts say. Saying those in the Syndicate are doing that exact thing?"

There was pause, confusing Destan.

While it appeared Doctor Gerould was trying to process something, or attempting to justify something to himself; there was something else he latched onto.

"Is there something I can help with, Lance?"

"Would you mind showing me where the passage you were talking about is?"

Not wasting any time, he snatched the Bible up and flipped as fast as he could to it; a shot of relief running through him, "Here. … Take all the time you need. Keep it if you want to. I have another. And if you have any questions, I don't ever pretend to know everything but I know that book contains them and I'm more than willing to sit down and find them with you."

Destan couldn't deny the joy he now felt; knowing this would help to some extent, comfort Callimay. Yes it wasn't the individual she initially intended to reach, but sometimes what you plan for isn't the outcome which is given in that moment. As he cracked the bedroom door open he could tell from all the tissues everywhere and how sad the belvedere looked that she needed to hear this, "Calli?"

"He says he loves me yet he doesn't even care to appease me and 'take' the book?"

"Would you want him to just take it to keep you happy and not actually do anything with it?" Destan tried to calm as he sat down and stroked her hair. "That wouldn't help any, right?"

She sighed as a sob jumped out, "I just don't… I don't understand. From what mother wrote, both her and father were Christians and raised us all that way. At least we were taught there was a God and we needed to obey Him. I just don't— how can someone walk away like that? How can someone be so indifferent about a thing like eternity? Isn't he afraid of what comes after dying?"

"I know it's hard, Calli. But didn't Dakoe do the same thing? Yes, it was a bit different in circumstances, but at the core wasn't it the same thing? He walked away, was indifferent about his eternity, and only feared Toreon's power over him. Trever's doing the same thing; though I don't know what he fears more than eternity."

A shaky breath accompanied with sniffles was all she got out.

"We can't give up hope. Remember how I said that when Trever didn't even know who he was? There's still life in him, Calli. Yes we can only do so much, but we can't doubt the power of the seed we're sowing. He might be resisting it right now, but who's to say that he might not come across someone at a later time and they put it in a way that knocks him off his feet and wakes him up?" Destan tried to encourage as he rubbed her neck. "I know I've got to remember that myself right now."

"Why?"

"Rocher," he sighed. "For all intents and purposes we had what he would call an all-out fight and disrespectful argument. I really thought I had him where he couldn't explain his twisted justified self out of it, but his took what Scripture said and bent it all around 'his' viewpoint in order to justify everything he's doing and believing — or in this case 'not' believing. … I know how hard it is to see those who are your family and so close to you be unwilling to listen. It tears at your heart and wrings your stomach."

"How long have you been trying?" She asked as she looked up.

"Ever since I was immersed… what, almost nine years ago, now? … But even with what happened today — how I almost didn't want to say anything because I knew how it would end up — I'm hoping that debate woke Lance up a bit. He asked to read the passage I was trying to explain to Rocher." Destan tried to sound as optimistic as possible. "So nothing was wasted in me saying what I did just like nothing was wasted in what you tried to do for Trever. It just didn't reach the one either of us was aiming at."

~ 22 ~

Come the next morning, Destan was all keyed up for some reason. — They'd switched their schedule to coincide with what times those who were working on the political front would be working, so this really was morning as most would know it. — He'd been up for almost an hour pacing the floor, waiting for Callimay to wake up: *Just wake her up, Boon. She'll be fine. ~ No, she needs to wake up on her own. It's best that way for her mind. It's just best this way. I can wait. ~ Well then cool off and calm down!*

He whipped his head around when the belvedere perked his ears and looked over toward her and saw her yawning as she sat up, "It's nice to wake up and feel rested for a change."

Seeing how calm and content she was, it drained all the nervousness he had. He sat and took her hands as he smiled, "The switch helped some, then?"

"For sure," she yawned as she nodded; and then froze when she realized, "Oh goodness! I'll get breakfast fixed really fast."

"It's okay. Yes, it's getting 'late' but I've just remembered I've got to keep an even keel. And part of that means keeping a steady schedule with you and not rushing around."

"Well, I can at least fix something easy." She petted the belvedere.

"How about some eggs and sausage? Maybe some fruit?"

"Perfect. I'll be down in just a minute."

ॐ

When they got done and headed to the bunker, there were quite a few Veils already hard at work; either on the phone or having a video call with contacts in various countries; this hum of voices almost deafening. But for as much as it sounded like chaos, no one looked frazzled or unsure of what to do; some even laughing from time to time.

Callimay went to her station and brought up her computer, finding a few missed calls from Trever and some messages. She put her headset on and listened, glad to hear things were going well and he was safe.

There was even a message from her grandfather telling her he loved her and reminded her Destan was her leader but also her helper. And she needed to remember she wasn't alone and be there for Destan so he knew the same.

Destan didn't have an assignment — now, that is — but he had to concede his role as leader was to keep the overall goal flowing. And so being separated like that made Callimay feel like she was — in a way — living out one of the wartime movies she loved watching. She was one of the supporting characters who were responsible for piloting a battle ship while Destan stood on the bridge of the main cruiser and called the overall strategy. It was so strange to be in this position, and yet she wasn't scared like she thought she'd be. She had a level of protection being where she was, even just physically. She wasn't like Trever, her grandfather, and the rest of her family were: "exposed".

Everything was set up so there would be support for posts at all times, rotating three Veils who would only cover one individual the entire time; being mediators to get information from other countries when there were questions or requests.

∛

For a little while, this political "coup" against the Syndicate was going exactly how it was originally planned all those years ago: their money was the biggest factor in keeping everything running — including their political hold — so they had to focus on that. But as expected, before long they started taking notice. And yet they couldn't abandon their financial situation due to the fact they'd done so much in the way of "fancy" transactions and routing of payments — or payoffs — that this friction and uproar wasn't going to subside overnight. And to those with the most invested? Their slush-funds mattered more than the International Law itself.

"You both look exhausted," Tabitha groaned as she slouched.

"A bit," Destan nodded as he rubbed Callimay's arm.

"How are you holding up?" Redje asked as he leaned forward.

"As well as can be expected. I haven't heard a word from Aldred since we got here, so he's either taken off to gamble his wad or too absorbed in his work." Destan replied, trying to smile. "You?"

"Hunkered down and doing what we can to help each other." Tabitha replied, Redje frowning and refusing to answer.

"I know it's hard, Rej." Destan tried to encourage. "But you've got a beautiful wife and two adorable children who need you there."

"I'm doing my job, I know." He sighed as Tabitha gave him a hug. "And I know there are many others who would in one way or another love to trade places with me. ... Any word from the Monarch?"

"Not so much as a degrading remark in one of their public addresses... well, any different than the usual." Destan almost laughed.

"I heard rumblings that some Falconers filed a class action lawsuit against them for unpaid bounties in Arable." Redje prodded.

"It's more than rumblings. And it's more than just a group in Arable. They're crumbling apart from the inside." Destan nodded, sounding much more positive. "That one they can't keep under wraps because it's the biggest one with the best 'backing'."

"You think they'll tear themselves apart completely?" Tabitha sounded hopeful.

"There's that chance, though I see the Law being taken down as enough for them to call a truce with enough of them so they don't lose their livelihoods altogether." Destan cautioned.

"How's Mrs. Manning doing?" Callimay asked out of the blue.

"Much better," Redje smiled. "Thank you so much for the prayers. We both know they're what helped her turn that corner."

"That's great to hear." She said cheerful.

"Mama?" They heard a faint voice call out.

"Sounds like Benjamin's hungry." Tabitha said in passing as she got up. "I'm coming, Sweetheart. — It was great to talk with you. We're still praying for you."

"We need to go, too." Destan checked his watch. "You guys stay safe and keep alert."

~ 23 ~

"Calli? Calli wake up," Destan bit his lip as he shook her gently, the belvedere hopping up and down beside him. *I shouldn't be doing this. I really shouldn't, but—*

"Huh?" She asked groggy as she slowly pried her eyelids open.

"You okay?"

She covered her eyes as she sat up, "Yeah. What is it?"

He took a breath before reaching over and brushing her hair out a bit, "Just get ready and come down to the bunker as fast as you can. Sound good?"

"O… okay," she yawned as she worked to get herself awake.

🜉

When she opened the door, the belvedere greeted her and started down the staircase in a fury, bounding over and sitting by Destan; looking back and barking at her as if to tell her she needed to hurry up.

No one was working. All eyes were on her. Callimay lowered her head and made a beeline for Destan, scared by all the attention.

After he gave her a kiss he sent the belvedere to the stairs and sighed as he squeezed her hand, "It's okay. Everyone's just kinda on-edge because the Monarch's going to call in just a couple minutes. They're doing a public call so everyone in the world is going to see this."

"Do you know what for?"

"I want so bad for this to be a surrender, but from everything we've gotten and from just plain common sense, I know they're not going down without a fight." He grumbled a bit as he reached over. "Here, let me put your hood up. … Feel okay?"

349

She fumbled to fix the part that was tugging on her hair and then finish securing it; caught off guard when Destan took her wrist, "Easy there. You don't have to cinch it down 'that' far. We're not going out in a howler. Just keep it on so it covers your face."

"Okay," she took a deep breath as she unclasped it.

The regular lights went out, red border ones glowing enough so you could see vague outlines of all those standing beside and behind them.

Fidus walked up beside Destan, opposite Callimay and took a deep breath; Enforcer and Traceur beside her. They all stood there in silence; the air with each passing second becoming more and more electrified with tension.

Destan had his head slightly bowed so his face was concealed. He could feel the uncertainty in Callimay's emotions, so he took her hand and leaned over to give her another kiss: *You don't have to say a word. I'll do it all.*

Not wanting the fear to defeat her, she nodded furiously as if trying to shake it out.

Nexus called out, "They're here. Everyone standby."

Seeing how the young man she'd loved for so long fade into the battle-hardened leader just from hearing those words hurt her heart a bit; its pang she felt so often and wasn't sad to not feel anymore. But here it was again, coming back strong as he let go of her hand and looked away.

It wasn't at all the time for this to rear its ugly head, but all Callimay could do was bear under it like she had for so long; the welling tears refusing to be contained this time, though. She wanted to run off, but it was too late. The screen came on, though was darkened so the light wouldn't reveal much at all.

Looking up and seeing her blood relatives standing there; their aura of superiority and hypocrisy diverted her emotions to frustration and anger. She clinched her fists and bit her lip. What she wanted to get off her chest would have to hold on a bit longer.

"The war between us has, for the most part, been kept from the eye of the public so as to keep the innocent shielded from knowing of your despicable presence. And so, over the years you passed from the thoughts of all; nothing more than a fanciful myth or urban legend.

You didn't exist but in the minds of conspirators and the hearts of the wicked." A man in all-white reminiscent of the flamboyant nature of what Toreon would wear — hiding his face behind a masquerade-type mask — called out in a condemning way. "But enough is enough! It's time the people of Quidoria know who the demons are we've protected them from; who is single-handedly responsible for the issues so many of our hard-working Falconers and Informants — those now struggling to support their families — are dealing with. These people are no cartel, pirates — not even the Fringe — they are an evil this world has never known or ever will."

You described yourself so well. Destan chuckled to himself.

Toreon stepped up and continued this bashing of an introductory monologue, "These individuals drenched in darkness call themselves the Shadows. And as their name and appearance suggest, they operate under the cover of darkness like only those who are in the wrong do. Their leader is nothing but a Derelict 'boy' whose judgment is clouded continually by the distraction of his childish wife… who also professes to be a Derelict. His closest circle — known as the Veil — work to threaten the livelihoods of those who are lawful and peace-loving; the results of which we are dealing with this very day. Without mercy they cut down the spies we had in their midst; the latest being a brave man who selflessly took the mantle of resorting to this life of crime in order to bring about justice and peace to the world he loved."

You—

Let them finish, Calli. Every word that comes out of their mouth is really just more ammo for us. Destan grabbed her wrist.

A moment of what felt like powerful, mocking silence was followed by the clacking of a woman's high heels. She was dressed in the same style of clothing, her stepping down from her thrown-like seat as she spoke up in her shrill, alto tone that was all too familiar to Destan and Callimay, "Yes, we know all about the heinous debauchery you have pulled my beloved Swinchpuck family into and how you've worked to upend the law and order Quidoria has enjoyed since the Void era brought on by you 'Derelicts'; pushing the Homeworld away from us through your thoughtless trade practices. But let it be known this will not prevail! You leather-laden slime that call yourselves Shadows and

Veils have been a thorn in humanity's side from the beginning of your existence. It is time you face us and let us see the power you supposedly claim to have. … Well? What do you have to say? … Speak up!"

Destan snickered a bit. He'd been given control of this conversation. — They, for all intents and purposes, were fighting with themselves and he had to admit it was amusing to a certain extent to just stand there and let them continue.

And so he took his time to respond; taking a deep breath before his booming voice asked, "Where do I start? You didn't give me much guidance as to what charge I had to defend first, 'Queen'."

"Y—" Vashti reached for her sword as Olderon stepped in and grabbed her wrist; whispering something to her.

"Well, I guess I could begin with the Nark you spoke of, 'dear' Prince," Destan said as a sarcastic act of being arbiter of the situation. "His selfish act of 'sacrifice' through suicide was made when he was attempting to murder an innocent woman who was at death's door already; his last effort failing so his only closure — apparently — was to escape the punishment of his actions. He was in no way an advocate for the life of those who were innocent."

He paused to give them a chance to say something, and then continued, "As for the personal attack on me and my mental maturity, you know very well I have broader shoulders that bear more weight than you ever could. Our time together in a more 'informal' situation proved that beyond the shadow of a doubt. Furthermore, let it be known my wife has never been anything but the strongest source of encouragement and steadfast love. Having her around me this entire time? She has saved my life on multiple occasions."

The silence after each of his responses was making the Monarch appear almost laughable.

Seriously? Still nothing to say? Destan did his best to rein in his bantering side. "The debauchery you speak of, 'Queen', can find its roots in your betrayal of those you were given by God to love. And yet the Swinchpuck family who took you in was willing to finally stand up to you because of their knowledge of this type of treatment you showed; admitting just how deadly it is and that their ties to you needed to be severed not only for their good, but yours. — And do not assume those who work under the cover of dark 'are' the darkness in regards to doing what is wrong. We only do so to protect ourselves while we expose the true darkness is in you; the darkness you are afraid people will see if you were to turn off the blinding, burning, branding light you shine on everyone. The tide is turning. It is not us whom you are fighting anymore. The world is seeing the dangerous laws and evil acts you condone for what they truly are. They are standing up and refusing to go along and be slaves to the Syndicate and accept the 'protection' you offer them. You're nothing but an over-sized mafia with a waning grip on your territory. — Why are the tens of thousands of us standing up at once? Because that allows millions to openly question what they've wanted to for so long. Terror is not comfort, nor tyranny protection. We've fought you out of the spotlight because we are not the focus. We are not the ones who are to be glorified. We only seek to protect those who are being labeled a disease, who are manipulated and treated in the most heinous of ways by your Falconers and the Informants who support you. People have known we exist because in their hearts they couldn't imagine an evil like you existing without any stopgap also existing. It wasn't myth, legend, conspiracy theory, or a wicked dream. It was common sense. And now that you've confirmed their hopes, realize that now you are fighting humanity, not just us. We may be standing on the frontlines, but those standing behind us are growing in number by the second. They know the International Law should have never been proposed, let alone run through and ratified like it was. They regret how the Syndicate was so easily given the power it was. — Let it be known here and now that the Shadows do not assume to seek such power. We only seek to protect those who would stand up to you and ensure your voices are heard. It will be the choice of those who call Quidoria their home whether or not you are judged in this lifetime as being wrong; but make no mistake, your judgement 'will' come and the punishment will never end."

"How could anyone believe that a group of obscure and shadowed individuals who won't even show their faces and use voice changers wish to protect anyone?" Vashti scoffed as she rolled her eyes.

"You yourself hide behind a mask, Queen." Destan prodded, not giving an inch. "We veil ourselves to protect not only our identities but those whom we love and fight to protect. We value the bond love brings into our lives. Something I doubt is still alive in you. Why do you hide your face, Queen?"

"How can you claim to love others when you cannot save your own from us?" Olderon stepped in, Vashti visibly shaken.

"We've saved more than you would care to admit in comparison to those we regrettably lost. And those of our number who have been lost made the sacrifice to protect the people they love… unlike the menace you spoke of earlier. I personally know your latest execution victim did just that mere moments before she was taken down." Destan's heart felt a bit of relief; knowing he was doing all he could to vindicate Canary to the world. "Do not think her loss is forgotten by any of us… nor any of the others in this world who saw that public murder."

There was a moment of silence that felt like a total victory for Destan and everyone in the room with him, and then he spoke again, "You spoke of us facing you and showing you our power we've claimed to have. I know nothing of this claim. The only thing we want to accomplish is give the people their power back to choose. In fact, that power is being handed back to them as we speak."

"Silence!" Vashti screamed as she pushed her husband to the side, and then calmed before she continued; almost snarling through her teeth. "Now you listen to me, 'Doy-yen'. We will snuff out each and every last one of you Derelicts and make you regret everything you've done and said. We will wipe you off the face of Quidoria for good. I'll die before one of you slip through my hands."

"Then you should make the ultimate sacrifice for the Purge and start with yourself." Destan came back without hesitation or mercy. "You, your husband, 'and' your son… Vashti. There was no reason for your sister to die by your hand when, by your standard, you were more guilty because you yourself are left-handed."

She stood there, mouth open, and then started to rail when her husband silenced her. He then took a moment to compose himself and puffed up his chest; showing confidence as he attempted to do major damage control, "Only someone who was desperate to find justification would spout off such ridiculous claims. What would make you think anyone would believe what you say?"

"I don't have to make people believe me. Reactions speak volumes. Your Queen has betrayed you." Destan shook his head ever so slightly. "People know she was adopted by the Swinchpuck family; why the massive distancing they've done recently isn't the ground-shaking 'woe is me' surprise you're wanting to maintain so people take your side. And there are those who know she had a sister. If people were paying attention and knew the language she was speaking — the woman who was the last of our number you executed — they know she called you 'sister', Vashti."

"As the commander of the Elites — the Syndicate's most advanced group of Falconers — I give our formal declaration of war and set the decisive battle for the night of the blood moon. Tomorrow. Abaddon Plain. Dusk. … I take it you are familiar with the area?" Toreon blurted out; trying to divert attention away from the bombshell truths Destan dropped; secrets held by dozens upon dozens of those in proper as well as shallow graves across Quidoria.

Callimay was crying now; her heart could rest. It was out in the open. People now knew. They now knew just how sick and demented Vashti was. What they did with this knowledge was up to them, but Callimay's heart wasn't burdened with that grief. In a manner of speaking, she felt this was her "vengeance" against Vashti. Making sure she knew that what she did to her own sister wasn't hidden or secret… the truth being spoken was pure vindication.

Destan, meanwhile, chuckled to himself; Toreon's statement was insignificant in every way imaginable. But, he humored him and replied in a stern tone, "As leader of the Shadows and head of the Veil, I know the cruel reasoning behind such a choice of time and place. But even with these 'Elites' you have mentioned, we do not shrink from our responsibilities to protect and defend freedom. And though we regret you have chosen this path of destruction and violence, we will not shrink back. And so I accept. Dusk at Abaddon Plain. Tomorrow."

There was a moment of bewildered silence from Toreon and his parents to Destan's quick and affirmative answer. They looked utterly laughable as they stood there and didn't say a word in reply.

"What is wrong? Has the strength of truth, the power of freedom, and the rawness of vindication utterly crushed your false sense of authority and security? … May truth continue to be found in the hearts of everyone and shine brightest from this day forward; shining the true beacon of light to the world. A hope that will—"

The screen went black and so without any lighting anywhere, it felt like they were in a pit; Destan's voice echoing endlessly that there was hope and truth to be found.

With that done, hushed voices started to rise, sounding secure and encouraged; cheering erupting from some sections that quickly spread because… why not? This in-and-of-itself was a victory. Destan took the hidden, painful truth so many had borne and told the world in a clear, precise, and bold way that left them with no excuse. Whatever people said or did from this point on would prove exactly where they stood: and would undoubtedly give those who hid their true feelings the assurance they weren't alone. And when you know you're not alone when fighting for what is right, it gives you that much more courage.

Destan comforted as he reached and took his wife's hand, "I know that was bitter-sweet and I'm sure you want to talk — I felt a bit torn myself when things started, like I abandoned you — but for right now we've got some work to do. … Okay?"

Hearing that brought her to her knees… literally.

Not wanting to draw attention to her and doing his best to help, Destan called the belvedere down to help her up since he couldn't bend over much. As the belvedere thundered down the stairs; a few others turned back and came over when they saw her.

"I'm… I'm fine." She put her hand out to them. "I just— I'm fine."

Destan nodded them on; helping support his shivering wife as he asked, "Is something else wrong?"

"Everything and yet nothing," she answered without hesitation.

"Calli, I—"

"I can make it." She smiled as she threw her arms around him; the feel of his arms around her so comforting. "Just let me have this one hug. Please."

A few moments passed as she gathered herself; seeing everyone bustling around bringing something to the forefront: the task that was thrown at their faces looked near impossible. Why did Destan agree? How in the world were they going to prepare everything in such a short amount of time, let alone get there safely? The Syndicate having an "honor code" about rules of engagement was laughable at best.

Don't let this trip you up, Calli. I knew they'd do it this way. In fact I think most of us did.

Huh?

Now before I say this don't get all bent out of joint or be a downer about what you think. Okay? — They want us to react just like you are: think it's impossible. Give up and walk away. Run and hide.

Her shoulders dropped as she bowed her head; her sighing.

I thought I just said not to—

"Doyen?" Someone called out.

He acknowledged the person, but didn't leave, "Calli?"

"That's why I have you. To help remind me." She looked up at him with a soft smile on her face. "Right?"

"Right." His small smile jumped out as he nodded. "What's up?"

"Traceur's on the line."

"Good. — What's it look like?"

"I wouldn't have the foggiest idea." Traceur's whispering voice sounded irate.

"They've got it blocked off?"

"Just like you thought." She growled. "There's not even a gap big enough for me to slip through."

"Don't waste time and take any more risks. Get back last night."

Callimay came up and took his arm, trying to be supportive.

"Well, it's a good thing we 'horde' physical maps, isn't it?" He tried to be light-hearted. "Curator?"

"Here!" a young man popped up from one of the tables where a group was discussing things; him moving so fast his chair shot back, slammed into the wall, and fell over.

"Get me every map we've got for that area. Get Bailiwick and Sketcher and build us a holo as fast as you know how."

He grinned as he nodded, "You got it!"

Within the hour, the three individuals came back and uploaded the map to the main floor.

Much to Destan's chagrin, what he thought was going to happen did: between hot-beds of webs at the western edge where it was wooded and the fact the rest of the area was flat and wide open, this wasn't going to play to their inherent strengths. Long-range weapons were going to be a game changer. — For everyone to be given orders to use firearms? It went against everything he'd been taught and everything he'd done up to this point.

And yet he knew stealth didn't matter. He knew this order was one he was going to give at some point, "The standing codes and expected conduct of any Shadow of Veil are very clear about this, but I want you all to know that we've come this far holding fast to this conduct because we 'are' different than the Syndicate. I'm sure it won't take long for there to be justification for firing at will, though. Don't let them take someone down before you engage. Understood? … From the weather reports, it looks like the chances of us working under less than favorable conditions is as high as it could be." *Lightning at night. A 'lovely' little gift just for me, I'm sure.* "Since we won't be there until dusk there's a chance the squalls will die down, but the terrain's going to be ruined: slick, messy, and treacherous."

He stopped to give a moment for everyone to take it in, ask any questions, and then kept on after the last comment was made, "I'm going to do my best to isolate the Prince as fast as possible and keep him occupied. I know some of you are aware, but I'll remind everyone: he has capabilities beyond the realm of nature as we know it. Due to the efforts of Liberator he's the last of these Elites we know of from the records we have from the Syndicate. If they somehow got any out or are holding a secret stash of them somewhere, we'll know right away. … And if that comes, Jewel and myself will do all we can to assist."

That all left a horrible taste in his mouth, even though it was a risk he had to acknowledge. But he couldn't leave it like that, "But the likelihood of that being the case is pretty much zero from comparing what intel we have from the Society, what Liberator got us, and what Aldred has told me, personally. So thinking of it that way and recalling what the Prince said, it sounds as if they still believe they have all those we dealt with, in-tact."

This helped ease the tension in the air and his own emotions, "Let me remind everyone so when it happens the knee-jerk reaction those who see it will have is limited. The Prince is capable of teleporting from one place to another, rendering himself practically invisible at times and free to attack at any second from any side. It's my hope that his love for spectacle and his personal hatred for me will allow me to engage him fully before everything breaks loose. I'm capable of everything he is, and more… though it's best for me to limit what I do."

An awkward pause came, Callimay looking over at her husband who was staring at his hand. So she tried her best to explain, "Because of a situation forced on him by Elder and those working with and for him, Doyen's circumstances with his extra abilities are… well they're a challenge because these abilities are fueled by emotions. And Doyen's are strong negative ones. So he requires my assistance to guide him so those emotions don't take him over and send him into a blind rage."

Not knowing if what she said was helpful or just compiled the confusion of everything, Callimay stopped talking; wanting to run over and hug her husband but also knowing that wasn't the help he needed at the moment.

"What is our best course of action if he does break off you?" Someone asked from the far back.

This broke him free of his thoughts; Destan looking at Callimay for a moment, her nodding.

"If that becomes an issue, you're going to have to rely on Jewel's cues like I did when I first engaged him in this state. — Which means there will need to be at least four Veils who take on the duty of protecting Jewel if things come to that. She'll need to focus on him and then contact those in his path which will leave her vulnerable. — Some of you have already experienced her ability to talk to your minds, but I know there are many of you who have not. It may be a bit unnerving at first, but trust that voice you hear. You'll recognize it as hers and she'll only use it if you specifically need help."

Traceur stepped up and said, "I'll be glad to be one who falls back to defend her if necessary."

Auditor, Curator, and Coalesce quickly followed suit; a few others bickering with them that they wanted to do it and got up before them.

"I appreciate your willingness," Destan put a hand out; part of him chuckling and the other gladded at this response. "But we just need four. Auditor, Neurosan, Curator, and Enforcer will be the four."

While the others wanted to object, they knew better.

But Destan knew Traceur was the one who was going to say something regardless, so he remaindered her, "I've set aside four details headed by Gumshoe and Traceur to hang back until the blood moon arises so we have support that can detect suspicious movements on their side; acting as a second wave. They'll come at this area from the opposite side so we have the Syndicate surrounded, and hopefully by then we will have some visual on the moon so we know when Total Eclipse has come."

This discussion continued for another ten minutes, so many details brought to light and cemented; but finally it came to a close, "I can't think of anything else. And us adapting in the moment is where we shine. Godspeed, shot straight, stay aware, trust your instincts, focus on what's in front of you no matter what; and may we all convene at this table once this is over."

☫

When they took a short break as the sun came up on the day of the Arena, Destan's phone rang, "How are things on your end?"

"I think the more pressing question is how are you doing?"

"As ready as we can be given the circumstances. Just keep praying. Please. We need them."

"We're spending the whole day in various homes until we hear from you."

"That's all we can ask for. Thank you Overseer." Callimay smiled as she squeezed Destan's hand.

"The Monarch made the announcement, as I heard, that they are going to allow this to be covered and shown to the world."

"Well, I guess I should've seen that coming. Though it does mean the possibility of them allowing civilians to broadcast it instead of their own people is something we've got to consider. And then if they do use their new night vision cameras our snipers will be in a world of hurt."

"Not just a possibility," Overseer corrected. "Tate and Fredric got called to leave immediately for Crosswall."

Destan slammed his fist on the table, clipping the edge of his plate which sent it flying across the room.

Callimay gasped as she looked at him with his head in his hands: *Destan don't give up. Not now. It's alright. We'll figure this out. Please don't give up.*

It's going to be enough for us to keep each other safe, Calli. With them doing this? How... I...

She scrambled to think of something, "I... do you... is there a way of getting in touch with them, safely?"

"Yes," Mr. Utree replied without hesitation.

"Maybe this wouldn't work, but give them the contact info for Nexus." Callimay continued, Destan looking over at her confused. "I say this because I remember when there was a controversial, high-profile live feed about ten years ago. There was a big to-do about the fact 'live' feeds were delayed, if even for just a few seconds, and that none of the stations were doing their job of monitoring and filtering like they were supposed to. If that still holds true, Nexus could have control of the delay and maybe remove any of our movements so the Syndicate wouldn't see them? Maybe? I don't know."

"It's worth a try." Overseer encouraged. "I'll contact them right now and then let you speak with Nexus and them about it."

The conversation ended and Destan stared at his wife: *Why didn't I think of that? It's so simple yet— what's wrong with me? Smallest thing happens and I fly off the handle.*

"You're nervous just like everyone else is but able to channel it much better. It's just this hit a bad spot for you. Keeping everyone safe is your weak spot. They know that. They know it because of me. And they're got to try every underhanded thing they can to get under your skin. — But now, if this works, we'll know where 'they' are! Nexus can get us intel which our second wave may not be able to notice. ... Come to think of it, by the Monarch flaunting this like they are they're actually helping us!"

"We'll only have the cameras from Kerogen though. I'm sure they'll have others there as well. And then Nexus is only one person."

"Let's not get into all the details yet. ... It may not even work." Callimay faded out at she finished.

"But it's a shot we have at turning something horrible into a great opportunity." Destan took a deep breath and smiled.

Nexus said she'd need quite a bit of help, but told them it was possible to use the delay to manipulate any footage that would be funneled through. The issue of that help was resolved when guards from various Safe Havens started calling in to report the worldwide broadcast; asking how they could help. Nexus said it'd be easier and faster to spread the feed over several servers in locations throughout the world that would be closer to the end locations so if the Syndicate were monitoring it they couldn't pin-point one, exact source. And with Abacus and the tech team scrambling their VPN points, them finding the source would be that much more difficult if they caught on.

This encouragement was also a level of comfort and security for Destan. And he had to fight to keep that when he looked over and saw his wife getting her knives ready: *This is stupid! I can't let her—*

"This is my choice." She looked up at him, dead serious. "And I have to be within a certain range to watch over you at the level I need to. I know the risks I'm taking. But for as scared as I am of what may happen to me, I'm more scared of losing you by not doing anything. I'm ready for whatever may come. Everything we've been through, every moment of my training… it was all for this moment. I know it was."

He rushed over and took her in his arms, letting his whirlwind emotions let loose.

She was crying as well, but got out, "I know earlier you were only steeling yourself because of the unknown of what was going to happen during that conversation. You had to do it, but I know you felt that pang too. And you listened to it, you didn't forget it. I know you love me and that the past, as hurtful as it was, is there to remind us both how far we have come and that giving up or even just slacking off isn't an option… even if I have troubles remembering it at times."

Every word she said brought more and more clarity to their minds, every tear shed and moment they held onto each other brought their hearts and souls that much closer.

All this time the belvedere sat and watched; Destan realizing his block was still on; him almost laughing as he sniffled, "His not barging in even annoys me, now."

The creature was thrilled to have that connection back, running over and snuggling close to Callimay's side to comfort her. She smiled as she rubbed his ear.

"Just in case," Destan reminded as he took her right hand. "Okay good. You've got it on."

His mentioning her music band made a thought jump into her mind; her not thinking it through before she blurted it out, "Where would we go if something did go wrong? I mean I know we'd get to Grandfather, but how would we get there?"

He sighed as he rubbed her shoulders, not answering for a while.

"I'm sorry I said anything." She bit her lip; furious with herself.

"It… it's okay, Calli. It's something I've got to have set in my mind, regardless; so if it does happen there's no wasted time trying to figure out what to do. — Everyone knows to get you to Brigon if things go south. But if things…" he paused as he tried to keep himself calm. "If things are the point of utter chaos and you're alone? You run in the direction that gets you going in the direction of Brigon and 'never' look back. Go it?"

She fought back the thought of her left alone; that fear crippling her emotionally for a while. Would it even be possible for her to leave and get to safety if things came to that?

϶

Unlike so many times when they went on a trip, the belvedere wasn't bounding with joy as they got ready to go. He knew this was serious and would jump at the tiniest of things he felt was out of place as they got ready to go; but wouldn't go overboard.

They passed by Canary's home, Callimay having to look away the entire time so she wouldn't get emotional. She sighed when she heard the belvedere whimper and whine, "It's okay, Buddy. I'll be alright."

Destan reached over and took her hand in his, comforting her as much as he could as they continued on; doing his best to not say much to himself so she wouldn't hear.

They were the first ones to arrive at the meeting location just as he wanted it to be. The storms were still rolling through but he knew it wouldn't be too much longer before they'd clear out. And after he took a quick look around, he found they were alone as could be: *They only stayed long enough so we couldn't get any early intel. … Figures.*

In his attempt to keep both himself and the woman he loved calm, Destan blurted out when he got back and locked the door, "We're having waffles for breakfast."

This sudden random info dump was so far off base from what she was expecting that she actually laughed, "With what?"

"Didn't think that far yet…"

Unable to keep it in, this randomness so far-fetched and ridiculous, they both busted out laughing.

Trever and others who were at active and guard posts left messages of encouragement and thanks, making Destan feel like he was giving this his best.

"I know we can't run right back to Rayleen, but how soon do you think we'll be able to go home once this is done?"

Destan didn't want to answer at first, but knew having something to cling to in that area in particular was what they both needed, "It will depend on what happens with the authorities here in Crosswall: if we're detained or not. Maybe a half a year? They won't let us just leave, and I wouldn't want or expect them to."

She took a hard swallow, but tried to stay positive, "Well that's not that bad. Though we'd miss Rose's birthday."

"She's not going to be happy about that, is she?"

"Oh I think she'll understand. … What should we send her?"

"Hum. What would a pint-sized girl with me for a boyfriend want?"

"Oh hush." Callimay shoved his arm.

"You're right. She wouldn't want — let alone 'need' — anything. 'I'm' her present."

"I'm trying to be serious." Callimay made a face.

"I 'am' being serious." Destan cut to a normal tone and looked her in the eye.

"I… I know you are."

Knowing he sucked all the light-hearted life from the air, he sighed and nodded, "You 'are' right, she'd still like a little something extra since I wouldn't physically be there. … Huh. Well… I 'don't' know what to get her. Last year I left seeds with Rej she wanted—"

"Seeds?"

"She's starting her own flower garden like Mrs. Manning has. Some things she could take parts of — I can't remember the big ole technical term for that — but there are some, and of course they're her favorites, that just don't work that way. And some aren't 'cheap' if you know what I mean."

"Oh."

"Thinking a bit more about it, there was this one thing she asked me about. … But I don't know if Rej and Tabitha would want her to have it with Benjamin…"

"What is it?"

"A pond."

"A… pond?" Her dumbfounded look and voice paused. "Seeds and now a pond?"

"For her duck."

"Her, duck?" Callimay stuttered, sounding more than just confused. "What? A duck? But she doesn't have one."

"You have a wonderful memory." Destan tried to be sarcastically in shock; then confessed when she slapped his arm. "She 'wants' one. Tabitha said she couldn't have one until she had somewhere to keep it. — Hence a pond. — She's not a fan of the wallpaper in her bathroom being splashed. And don't ask how I know."

"Okay."

"I thought about having it run from their yard to ours; and seeing about putting some of the Koi fish that I rightfully own in it."

"I think she'd love seeing them."

"Then that's settled. Even if they say no, we'll put one on our side so I can get some Koi shipped from Zervonith."

A tap came on the window, Destan and Callimay both jumping.

He rolled the window down and asked almost flippant, "Why are you here so early? And standing in the rain?"

"It may not let up, so best get used to it now." Fidus replied stern as he leaned on the door frame. "The first wave is starting to arrive."

Oh! Guess it is about time, isn't it? Destan cringed as he nodded and turned to Callimay, "Let's do some more recon, shall we?"

"Okay." She let out a shaky breath as she put her hood up.

"Calli." Destan stopped as he grabbed her hand. "Calli look at me."

"What?"

"Say my name."

"Destan?"

"No, 'say' my name." He shook his head as he framed her face with his steady hands.

Callimay worked for a few seconds to calm herself, then smiled and opened her eyes, "Destan."

"I love you." He sighed after he kissed her.

"I love you too." She closed her eyes as he rested his forehead on hers; the grip they had on each other's hands almost hurting, but neither of them daring to loosen their grip.

"We're so close to going home. Just one last push." He whispered as he rubbed the side of her face. "And then we won't ever have to look back at this, you won't have to wear black all the time, and I won't be constantly pulled away to make decisions which could be life or death ones. We'll be able to enjoy our marriage and live the life I've dreamed about and wanted for us from the moment I saw you."

Callimay tried her best but couldn't keep from crying, "Promise me you'll listen to me. With it being more difficult for me to notice changes in your emotions and not being used to this type of situation, I—"

"I promise you: I'm going to fight this monster in me so you don't have to work so hard." Destan pulled her closer. "And remember: you still feel the other side effects. Warn me when you're getting tired."

"I will."

Another tap on the window perturbed Destan, "Let's go."

🕮

The belvedere stuck to Callimay's side like a huge, ultra-protective briar. Destan didn't see anyone so he kept going, them now cresting the hill to look at where they'd be that evening. Something "felt" strange but he couldn't put his finger on it. And it didn't have to do with the fact the belvedere started crawling in front of them and growling.

"Why's he doing that?"

Destan had Callimay move behind him, but the belvedere finally got to the point he jumped on Destan and barked at him. He cycled through his vision modes and eventually found there were low-lying webs everywhere, "They must've found out their Elites are 'broken' and know they can't win by themselves, anymore. Though I guess I oughta feel relived at the same time: that means that was all they had."

"What are we gonna do?"

"Stay here. Keep your barrier up until I get back." He turned to her, finger pointing straight at her. "I'm going to check something."

"Destan! Don't g—"

"Calli, you need to stop. We're in a war. What I say goes… unless I'm losing my marbles. I'll watch myself and take the Belvedere. He seems to know where they are."

"Okay," she nodded as she sent him to Destan.

The creature didn't want to leave her, but once her barrier went up he followed Destan without looking back.

Lightning flickered and flashed at more frequent intervals; the thunder booms making the soaked ground tremble. And not wanting that "annoyance" to cause him issues, Destan waited a bit before he worked his way to the closest anchor point: *Hum, no weight trips. … Looks like they put these in rather fast — for them, anyway. Much better job that whoever Elder had do that one trap, but still. ~ Done today when Traceur was here? ~ Totally possible. … Not as bad as it could be, but still enough to catch someone off guard in a bad way.*

He double-checked to see which wire was the top-most, and then both ends to make sure it wasn't armed before getting to his feet. His back complained; him wincing as he took hold of the anchor, but he didn't dare show any kind of reaction that his worrying wife could see. They were going to be in much worse situations than this before long. Keeping her calm until then was the best thing.

After thinking it through for a bit, he took a few seconds to tap Trever's ability and rip the anchor out of the ground. And while the amount of effort he put into it was what he needed to for a standard anchor, this one went flying out of his hand.

Just as he was programmed to, the belvedere pushed Destan down and to the side, standing over him.

"Look, I appreciate the thought — I really do — but get off of me, Big Fella. It can't come back at me."

While glad the belvedere was so protective, his back made it crystal-clear: he physically wasn't ready for this battle.

But what could he do?

Hiding this pain wasn't too challenging, though. He got up and shook his hands out as he looked out over the area: *At this rate this is gonna take forever even with them easily removed.*

Even with every Veil and Shadow working nonstop there was no way they could clear this in time: *'Not' by accident! … I should've known they'd pull something like this.*

As he stood there and thought, the belvedere whipped his head around and looked at the tree line, growling and snarling.

Calli? Someone's here.

She reached out and wasn't surprised: *Toreon.*

"Are you against fighting a fair fight?" Destan stood up and called out, making sure to check the surroundings as he started back toward Callimay. *Fidus? The Prince is here. Keep everyone hunkered down for now. This area's covered in webs. Do 'not' engage.*

On it.

"I just came to tell you you're in the wrong place." Toreon appeared right in front of Destan, smirking. "You always had a knack for being in the wrong place so I thought I would be of some help to you this time around. Umbrella?"

"Don't even start," Destan took a deep breath as he tapped his side, feeling the lead goggles. "We both know you said this place. In fact the whole world does."

"I'm not much for wearing glasses. My nose just is so delicate because of my allergies. I hope you understand. — And as far as the location… well, I forgot about the webs. My apologies for my oversight in that area." Toreon said so innocent as he backed up a couple steps. "I don't have a thing against a fair fight which is why I came to tell you."

"I have a solution," Destan inched his way between Toreon and Callimay. "How about you surrender? Then we can avoid any loss of life and no one has to know you flubbed the location. I mean it'd keep your image as untarnished as possible, considering the circumstances."

Toreon laughed for a while, then cut off to a serious tone, "You don't get it, do you? The second Eradication — the Purge that you've been working yourself to death to curb? This war is its birth: the fall of the Shadows will cement it happening. All your Derelict brothers and sisters won't have anyone to run to once you're gone."

"What about your parents… and even yourself? Will you still be alive in this 'pure' world you talk about?"

Toreon's eyes narrowed as they began to burn with anger, "Linton's betrayal on that front alone will cost the entire Swinchpuck family their lives."

"You underestimate the power of truth and freedom." Destan warned. "Anyone with a half-functioning brain knows your mother admitted to being left-handed during that broadcast… and 'she' knows it. Nothing can keep her, your father, 'or' you safe from that, now."

"Well, you won't be here to see how it's handled, so telling you is pointless." Toreon shrugged off.

Destan smirked a bit as he rolled his eyes, "Sure, whatever. — Now where is this war taking place since you said this wasn't it?"

"Oh, that's right." Toreon snapped his fingers. "Now what did mother say again? … It's right on the tip of— oh yeah. The Citadel's Field. I'm sure you're aware of this place. I can take you there; it's not too far from here."

"Is that place even big enough for your Elites 'and' us?" Destan almost laughed as Toreon started walking away. "And what's this about you doing the exact thing you accused me of back at the Society? Setting another double standard for yourself?"

"Excuse me?" He stopped and looked over his shoulder.

"I didn't say you could leave."

"Shut up, punk," in one fluid motion Toreon whipped around and drew his gun. "Your dirty trick to get the Elites was far too low."

Callimay screamed as the belvedere jumped in front of him, bearing his teeth; but Destan didn't move an inch. In fact he grinned and almost belly-laughed as he pointed, "You can't do that and you know it."

A quick look down showed a crisp, tiny red dot rock-solid steady on Toreon's chest. He twisted his lips for a moment as he gestured to one side, "Well neither can you."

While not as visible, Destan could see red dot on his chest, "You've gotta admit I wasn't the one to lose their cool that brought this all on."

"Would one shot be nearly enough for me?"

"Oh I know you won't go down 'that' easy. But just because there's only one sniper on you doesn't mean they can't get more than one shot off in time. … Dusk, Prince?" Destan over exaggerated.

"Don't keep me waiting." Toreon whipped around and threw his nose in the air before he vanished.

Callimay lowered and then raised her barrier when Destan got close enough, a nervous wreck as she checked him over for injuries, "What happened? Are you alright? What did he say?"

"He's changed the place," he tried to stay calm as he kept scanning the area.

"Okay," she froze for a moment; then looked for the answers on the ground, only able to manage some rambling thoughts. "Why didn't you get him? What made him draw his gun on you like that? What kept him from shooting you? H—"

"I need you to calm down, okay?" He took her by the shoulders and looked her square in the eye.

She took a hard swallow and then nodded.

"You know he loves to toy with people. — Sure he wants me dead, but this was 'way' too easy for him. And I couldn't do anything because he had a Deadeye close by… a sniper." Destan clarified as he looked back. "But it wasn't Ingrid."

"How do you know?"

"I'm not sure. I could just tell it wasn't her."

"So… now what do we do? Can we get the area cleared in time?"

I wanna just send her back. This is too much for her to handle and we haven't even started fighting yet.

"No! No please don't! I'll stop. I promise." She pleaded as she threw her arms to her sides and stood tall.

Fidus?

Yes?

Give the all clear.

The profound moment that occurred before Fidus responded was a dead giveaway: *The Prince just told me they've moved the location.*

Where to?

Citadel.

"You're joking," Fidus jogged up to the two of them.

"Oh how I wish I were." Destan grumbled as he ushered Callimay on. "Pass the word along and get Traceur rerouted."

▘

While everyone was infuriated to hear the change, once they let the initial edge wear off they weren't that surprised. And really? In light of the conditions the original location was in, this change was a double benefit for them: they wouldn't have webs to deal with, plus they now had confirmation the Syndicate's Elites were wiped out.

A mystery to Callimay as to why this new location still wasn't ideal, Destan explained they were now going to be fighting in an enclosed area that was almost like a stadium. And then the distance they had to travel wouldn't give them much time — if any — to do surveillance.

They sped along through vast open areas; Destan doing all he could to avoid towns and cities for two very obvious reasons.

When he pulled up, the gates were opened and there wasn't a soul in sight — visible to the naked "or" ability-aided. They got out and he had her hunker down with the belvedere while he went back to the car; releasing the break and letting it roll through the gate to see if there were any traps.

Nothing happened.

Destan jumped to the car and stopped it, taking a moment to check things before he took a quick run around the area.

"You didn't see anyone?" Callimay asked as he helped her up.

"Yep."

"But that doesn't make any sense! There's got to be someone somewhere. Why would they just leave this wide-open?"

"This place is miles bigger than you think. Leaving the front door open isn't compromising any security for them. This place was built to be its own defense. Those gates are never closed."

"Then why—"

"Just because, okay?" He hushed as he looked around. "Once Fidus and the first detail get here we'll start in."

"But there's still an hour or so before it gets dark."

"It's going to take us all of a half hour to get to the Field."

The second Fidus showed up with Rocher and Chicane, Destan asked, "Where's Enforcer?"

"Already on the move with his detail," Fidus nodded. "Should be stationed within the next ten, or fifteen minutes."

"Good. Let's get our markers set as fast as possible."

"The Field?" Chicane asked as he checked his leg satchel.

"That's what I was told." Destan sighed as he nodded. "Did Curator get us anything?"

"Not much, but it's a start," Chicane held up a computer.

There was a narrow, long draw bridge past the first open area which spanned a torrential river a good two-hundred feet below them. Even though he checked it he was still leery as they crossed; the deafening sounds of crashing water still able to reach up the stone cliffs and make the bridge quiver.

The storms were gone, but the lingering lightning added to the dim lamps stationed here and there as they jogged along; the puddles almost piercing in their splat-sound when they'd hit one.

While it went against everything she'd been trained to do up until then, she had to remember: stealth wasn't what they needed. They were being watched every second, now. And while Callimay couldn't sense anyone nearby but she felt that sensation of being watched more than anyone else in the group.

Destan wasn't willing to rule out Toreon appearing at any moment; him not letting go of her hand while his other hand was at the ready on his pistol.

At one point the belvedere took the lead and trotted along at a steady pace, not stopping unless Destan or Callimay did. He looked confused when they got to where the path split into several different ones with staircases going every which way.

"I stopped being of help with knowing where we were about five minutes ago," Chicane sighed as he kneeled down and found a good spot for one of the sensors he took from his satchel.

"Fidus?" Destan asked; working to keep the fear in his gut from sparking anything that would send Callimay overboard.

"I... I can't remember." He scanned the area a third time. "I know this is the right direction, but I don't remember these stairs."

Doyen? Can you hear me? Enforcer chimed in out of nowhere.

What is it?

Turn around and get back to that first light post. Take the path that splits off from what would then be your left.

Chicane picked up the sensors and ran with the group to take the new path; the sense of time slipping away from them becoming more and more prevalent with the blackened sky above them. Destan told Enforcer to be sure to leave one of his tags just in case so everyone else knew that was where they needed to turn.

Before long they came up to an ornate doorway carved out of pure white marble; Fidus nodding as he told them they were very close. It was the head of a sea snake, its eyes red prisms that looked like they would burn a hole through your soul if you looked at them too long.

This was the only time Callimay paused… more like stepped back. The door through that section was the opened mouth of the snake; its fangs dripping rain water and pooling on the walkway under them.

It's not real. Destan calmed as he rubbed her hand.

It doesn't matter one way or the other to me.

Close your eyes and let me lead you. … Like when we were in Rayleen that first time for the ball. … Calli? Remember?

She took a deep breath as she nodded her head furiously, shifting her grip on Destan's hand as she closed her eyes and bowed her head.

They continued on though, her fighting the urge to scream and run off when she felt the water she knew came off the fang splash off her shoulder and hit her neck.

But it was over. Now it was time to run again.

So when they stopped, Callimay opened her eyes to figure out what was wrong. And yet she didn't say anything when she saw they were in a hall which — to her — looked like it would easily seat the entire population of Quidoria: *What in the world is this place, anyway? None of the architecture matches, it's a maze within a maze, no one lives here… why! What is the purpose of this place? Who has this much money to build this for no 'usable' purpose? I mean is there any purpose to this all?*

The walls of this hall had to be just as tall as the river they crossed was below them. Columns lined their path with the same snakes winding around them. And then at the other end of this hall was a massive staircase illuminated by light coming through the window which was the Syndicate emblem.

It took them all of five minutes to cross the hall and get halfway up the steps; the sound of their footsteps echoing like thunder.

As they got to the top of the stairs, the belvedere began to glow. But that's not what made Destan tense. It was the fact his snarls and growls were being replied to with the same sounds, though fainter.

Sure enough, once they made it to the top they saw the Monarch and Toreon with their hoard of belvederes… all thirteen alphas.

Callimay glanced at Mr. Ruff and noticed he was still bigger.

But why? How would Vashti allow that?

"Stay here, Buddy." Callimay calmed as she put her hand on him. "And hide."

He looked back as his eyes got so soft, and then sat and yapped at her as he turned midnight black.

Not a word was said by anyone as they waited. And much to Callimay's surprise, everyone was content to stand where they were: *I mean I know the movies depict it like this, but I didn't think it actually happened like this. It just doesn't seem right.*

From behind the Monarch the lot of Falconers and Elites showed up, making the way things stood right then impossible for the Shadows to win. — And had there been no kind of "honor" about this war it would've been just that.

Before long the others showed and took their places behind Destan; even them just the tip of the iceberg which was about to descend upon the Syndicate.

Once she scanned over who was there, Vashti nodded to Toreon and he vanished. Destan flinched, but Toreon only jumped to the middle of a central, domed, grassy plain. He held his hands up and bowed his head, telling Destan he wanted him to come talk.

"God be with us," Destan muttered as he let go of Callimay.

He marched out and took the goggles off his belt, "Glad the games are over with, Toreon."

"You know I'm gonna miss our little chats. I really am." Toreon laughed as he shook his head.

"Much as saying this to you seems wrong, I have to thank you for what you did for Calli in Zervonith." Destan almost choked.

"You might want to take that back later on." Toreon looked up at Destan out of the corner of his eye, that Cheshire-cat look in his eye.

"You won't ever be able to touch her again."

"We'll see about that." Toreon almost whispered as he winked, then vanished and reappeared in front of the group of Syndicate Falconers that had moved up.

Destan instead turned and walked back, Fidus and Callimay taking a step forward as he called out with a voice that had the strength of presence he'd always shown, but held a hint of pleading from his deep desire for no one to die, "Alright. You've had your fun, Vashti. Now hear me: this needless bloodshed does 'not' have to happen. There's been more than enough of that over the years. You can stop this, right here, right now. Let the people decide whether or not they want you. Quit abandoning the very group of people you are a part of. If you don't see yourself as evil while being left-handed, then why would you claim we are? Stop this madness! … You'll accuse me of being weak and backing down by offering this olive branch, but I want my stance to be crystal clear: I don't want one person to die tonight."

"I won't rest until every one of you are gasping for air and begging for us to end your miserable lives." Vashti yelled as she drew her sword and pointed it at Destan. "Kill them! Kill them all! And don't think for one second that anyone who thinks of leaving will find any consolation from me. I'll kill you where you stand if you even toy with the thought of retreating!"

A war cry rose from the Syndicate's side, followed by Toreon yelling, "Leave Doyen for me! Leave no one alive!"

As he vanished, every Falconer ran toward the Shadows.

Destan vanished as well and landed just where Toreon was.

It seemed like a replay of just over a year ago between them, but Destan was more in control of his emotions and he had more of an arsenal to pull from in regards to abilities. Toreon knew this and had prepared; knowing if there was any hope he'd be able to best Destan he had to drag things out… much like his plan last time. — Albeit maybe a stupid idea knowing what happened last time, but still, it was really the only chance he had: the cliffhanger monster inside Destan had to be awakened and prodded in every way, and time was the only true way to bring him out.

Meanwhile, Callimay, Rocher, Fidus, Chicane, and everyone else dispersed. And much to the advantage of the Shadows, there were culverts, shrub areas, and lower terrain places to hunker down in and use for cover… though that initial thought was soon shown to be nothing but a deadly lure. An entire squad was picked off before Fidus called out, "Deadeyes on our six!"

Callimay looked around and could tell the high rises all around were perfect spots for Syndicate snipers: *Enforcer? … Enforcer? Enforcer are you there?*

Sorry, Jewel. He said pained and slowly. *There's… thirty, or so, up high.*

"Enforcer!" Callimay screamed as she looked up. "Auditor? We've got to get those snipers taken down. — Chicane!"

"What?" He called out.

"Get a group and start up that side. Now!" She screamed as another Shadow beside her fell into her. "Go!"

The sight of death and chaos around her started overwhelming her as she worked to scale the side of the terrace and work her way up. But then something snapped when she heard Destan: *Do what you can, Calli, and know that's all anyone can expect. It's all God expects from you. But you've 'got' to do everything you can. So go!*

She reached out and started finding one after another, letting the team that followed her know where the snipers were: *They seem to be concentrated on this side, but I doubt they're all over here.*

At one point her grip slipped and she started panicking, but Auditor reached out and caught her, "Come on, Jewel. We're almost there."

They both looked up and saw the barrel of a rifle.

Once Callimay got her footing Auditor reached up and yanked the gun out of the person's hand, Callimay getting up as fast as possible and getting them down to the ground.

"Go on," Auditor called out as she took the rifle and started looking toward the other side, a shot ricocheting right next to them. "I got this. Go Jewel!"

Each second she spent standing still only let the fear grab hold, so Callimay got over to Chicane and started up again to the next level, "You've been hit!"

"It's nothing I haven't dealt with before." He hissed as he kept on.

It seemed like a lifetime for Callimay to this point. She glanced back down to where everyone else was and saw the belvedere fending off at least four of his counterparts. She knew which one was which, but the Veils close by couldn't since they were all black and snarling at each other. She screamed, "Buddy! Calm down!"

He whipped his head around to look for her as he reverted to his white color; the Veils around picking the others off in a matter of seconds. The creature then took off toward another group, keeping them occupied so those who were there there could take them down.

Callimay finally made it to the top tier and looked to both sides, seeing they'd finally secured that side and had pretty much taken down all the snipers across the way.

"Get back down there, we'll keep things controlled—"

"Look out!" Callimay gasped when she saw what was above her and shoved Chicane to the side.

"Find Traceur. She should've been here by now." Chicane winced as he got up.

Come to find, both the sensor Chicane and the tag Enforcer left were removed… Traceur and the others didn't know which way to go.

But, by this time Traceur said it didn't matter because they were in a better position and would be able to take down the reinforcements scaling ladders on the outside like fleas: *We're well within striking range, Jewel. I know we're supposed to hang back, but we just can't.*

She checked one more time before starting down; having to now shove her fear of heights away.

When she got to where Auditor was, Callimay asked her if she was doing alright, "I'm fine. I can't say how long this ammo will hold out but I'll do what I can. … Here, take these."

"Antidote?" Callimay questioned when she opened the bag. "But—"

"I know there's been a few bitten. We've all got it on us, but having an extra boost never hurt. And with all the chaos going on someone could've lost theirs. … Just do it if you have a safe second to do so."

"Alright."

"Stay safe, Callimay. I mean that." Auditor grabbed her arm. "And thank you. Thank you for everything."

"Stay safe, Sophia." Callimay fought back tears.

The second she hit solid ground, Callimay put her plan she forged into action and took off running; helping anyone she could as she worked to get to the belvedere. She couldn't see Destan but could feel he wasn't doing the greatest.

She got to Rocher, telling him Destan needed help but she couldn't find him, "Give me that bag so you can move easier, Milady. It's best you get to him."

Not wasting time, she handed it over and got ready to take off… then froze, "Buddy? Buddy come here!"

They heard what sounded like a rumble of thunder and then the belvedere jumped over the brush and barked at Callimay, him looking worse than she was expecting, "I— Buddy where's Destan? Find him."

He sniffed the air for a few seconds and then took off, "I'll cover you Milady. Go!"

Callimay vaulted over the brush and took off as fast as she could, having to stop and put her barrier up when a Falconer jumped out at her. She took her Seaxes out and then waited for her opportunity when they'd be vulnerable.

The belvedere came back for her, running circles around her and then taking off again.

"Destan!" She screamed out when she felt what she knew was a spike in his emotions.

Unable to neglect those who were calling to her, Callimay stopped to help how she could; gasping each time she tripped and stumbled over those she knew and were now lifeless: *Destan where are you! Please! Des—*

"Calli get down!" She heard him yell.

When she looked up she saw Toreon's father standing there.

Even though her heart felt lighter from the public broadcast, seeing him face-to-face brought back every ounce of anger she had, "You! You murdered my mother! She was your sister-in-law! How could you do such a thing!"

"So you 'are' her daughter?" Olderon paused as he shook his head. "She needed to be rid of. I let her stay too long. — There are always 'trivial' sacrifices which must be made for the greater good."

"Trivial? You sick, demented—" She hissed as she pulled her gun.

"That is one way to word it." Olderon replied as he noticed her shaking hand. "Though I would much prefer sick and demented to weak and spineless."

"Valuing life isn't being weak!" She fought back tears.

"Then why do you have that thing pointed at me in the first place?"

She knew he was trying his best to mess with her mind, but the thought of being hypocritical paralyzed her.

"Just kill her!"

That shrill voice woke Callimay up; her throwing her barrier up.

Seeing she was pinned down but safe for the time being, Rocher jumped to Destan's aid.

Toreon found his weak spot and was doing everything he could to make sure Destan felt as much pain as possible; adding to it by doing everything mentally he could with his comments.

"You can't stay in there forever… niece." Olderon scoffed as his towering figure loomed over her; her backing away and tripping so she felt to the ground. "If for no other reason your weak heart can't take what is happening to everyone else."

"What are you waiting for!" That same voice scolded as they ran over and slammed into the barrier. "Wha… what is this? — You! You evil little witch! How 'dare' you turn on your own blood."

"How dare I? … How dare 'I'!" Callimay jumped to her feet and screamed. "'You're' the one who turned your back on me. 'You're' the one who had my family murdered! 'You're' the one who murdered your own sister! 'You're' the one who dared! Not me."

"Vashti don't," Olderon grabbed her wrist.

"She deserves to know what pain she's caused!" She lashed out at her own husband; her coughing up a handful of blood as she crumbled to the ground.

Even though she was baffled by Vashti's last statement and shocked by what happened; Callimay used this moment to get away.

Or at least she tried.

Olderon grabbed her by the hair and threw her to the ground, his voice not wavering, "I'll let this be quick."

He put the barrel that felt like a branding iron against her forehead, Callimay unable to do anything.

The next second a gun fired, blood spraying across her frozen face.

Time ceased to exist in that six-foot square of space and time while everyone around kept on. Her eyes stared into the eyes of someone who should've loved her, who should've fought to protect her. A tear was at the ready to slide out of her eye, but there wasn't enough time for it to.

Someone ran up, dropping to their knees beside her as they started to speak to Olderon, "Was that quick enough for y—" *Too high, again? But I swear I fixed the sight.* "Everlyn! Come on. W—"

"You! You little… just die already!" Vashti clamored to her feet as she started firing at Callimay and Trever.

He let out what sounded like a war cry as he picked her up and leaped over the nearest bolder, and then peeked over for a moment before looking at her with wild fear as he failed to catch his breath, "You okay?"

"W… why are you—"

"When the location was changed grandfather sent me. Well… he let me go after I kept pestering him." Trever explained as he reloaded, and then repeated, "Are, you, okay?"

"Y… yeah?"

"Then what in the world were you thinking, taking the two of them on by yourself! Do you 'want' to die!" He took her by the shoulders and shook her a bit.

It struck Callimay then that what she did was indeed extremely naïve and foolish. Even though Olderon was willing to talk with her, he showed that he wasn't going to let her live in the end, "I just—"

"You can't just go wandering off, Everlyn!"

"But I didn't— watch out!" She shoved Trever to the side.

He rolled over, yelling as he drew his gun, "Where!"

"Right there!" She threw a few spikes at…

Nothing?

"What do you mean!" He yelled back as he whipped his head around to figure out where the person might've gone.

"Who are you!" She screamed as she stood and grabbed her knives.

"Everlyn—" Trever quickly fired a few rounds to cover her. "There's no one there!" *Don't tell me they've released some bio weapon.* "Get down! You're in the open!"

Out of nowhere she flew back and hit the ground hard; Trever now realizing: *We missed someone!* "Everlyn where is he!"

He was going to be taking an enormous risk of killing one of their own if he missed, but Trever knew they couldn't let someone with that kind of ability escape.

Callimay looked like she was slashing at nothing with her Seaxes, not answering Trever for the longest time as she yelled at the person only she could see, "Tell me who you are!"

For all he could tell, whoever she was up against was quite a bit stronger than she was; she was on defense far too much. But he couldn't step in like he wanted to. He couldn't see them to help her in close-range combat. So he kept calling out to her.

And then what he feared happened. He saw her drop one of her Seaxes as she grabbed her arm; him mumbling something before he aimed and fired several rounds while running to her.

Trever threw himself across his sister, cradling her head and repeating over and over, "It's okay. I'm here. I love you, Everlyn."

What felt like a minute passed and nothing happened.

"Everlyn? Everlyn is he still there? Can you tell?" He refused to move; him still breathing heavy.

"I… I don't know." She winced as she pushed against him.

"I'm not moving until I know he's gone."

She refused to stop, screaming as she pounded on his chest, "Trever please! Get off me!"

Reluctant, and for good reason, but unable to see his baby sister like she was, Trever rolled to the side. Callimay scurried a little bit away and worked to catch her breath; scanning the area for a few seconds.

"Do you see him?"

"N… no." She heaved as she put her hand out to brace herself so she could get up. "Ah!"

He was just about to say something when he felt a bullet graze the size of his face.

Ducking to the side a bit, Trever turned, gun already drawn as he yelled, "Put your barrier up, Everlyn!"

Over the next couple seconds Vashti and Trever exchanged fire, it only being interrupted when Canary's belvedere thundered in and knocked Vashti to the ground; not hesitating to latch on to her arm.

Nearby Falconers and Elites rushed over, Trever yelling, "Let her go! Get away from there!"

Not wanting to let her go, the belvedere had to be ordered a second time; him then running over to Trever.

♄

Of course Destan wanted to get Toreon at least "immobilized" within a few minutes, and he really thought he could, but apparently Toreon brushed up on his technique since the last time they fought. And so this fight was playing into the hand of Toreon… and both of them knew it.

But that didn't mean Destan was worried. Oh no. In fact this was his way of showing he'd brush up as well during the past year. Yes, the remarks chafed him, but they didn't rile him like they did in the past. Whether or not Toreon meant what he said, when it all came down to it, he was only spewing out anything and everything he could think of that would poke and prod at Destan's only "weakness": Callimay. He's matured and moved past those inflated insults getting to him.

Add to that the other abilities Destan was able to utilize and things slowly began to swing in his favor. — A faster swing would always be beneficial, but at least it was heading in the right direction.

They did an almost never-ending dance around their two guns that were kicked, flung, and generally yeeted around the twenty-five-foot area they were battling in; both of them somewhat distracted by the "ease" of those weapons compared to what they had on them which did just as much damage when used correctly. And in close-quarters, those other weapons were actually more beneficial.

Toreon was able to land a hit that sent Destan flat to his back. And of course there just had to be a rock that was jutting up and hit where several of the stripes on his back intersected.

He fought through the pain, doing everything he possibly could to hide it… but he knew Toreon noticed.

Now it was a race against time. Destan knew his stamina was going to drain quicker with each passing second; regardless of whether or not his back took another hit.

And so the whip sword came out to keep him at bay. Since Bander — the only other person in the Shadows who knew how to wield such a weapon — was in deep recluse, Destan's training was extremely limited. Now that's not to say the weapon was by any means useless in his hands, but it wasn't at the caliber it could be and he wanted it to be.

All things aside, this abrupt change in fight-style was just what he needed. Toreon had no idea about this weapon. In fact that was another reason Destan wanted it: he had an automatic upper hand because the fighting style for it wasn't something "standard" training covered. And it showed in Toreon; he was having to stay on defense constantly until he could find some way to counter it.

Destan got into a rhythm and knew if he timed his next attack correctly, things would be over enough for him to take a rest.

And they were looking to go just like that as he spun around that last time.

Except…

Toreon jumped behind Destan at just the right second; ready do deal the blow that would end this war in the most devastating of ways.

But it didn't happen that way due to the one person who'd always been there for Destan; stepping in at crucial moments to ensure he was able to fulfill the task his grandmother knew he was destined to.

The Katana now buried in Toreon's chest was thrust in just that much more by its wielder; the point the person made being cemented as he hissed, "You've taken your last life, 'Prince'."

They let go as he stumbled back in shock; crumbling to a knee.

Then something unexpected, yet predictable, happened. He yanked the Katana out of his chest and grimaced as he raised his gun, "You're going with me, old man. See you in—"

"No!" Destan yelled as he reached to shove Rocher to the side.

"D… Destan!" Callimay cried out as she watched in horror.

Time felt like it stopped again as Rocher fell into Destan's arms.

He rocked Rocher back and forth, moaning and heaving, "No no no. Wake up! Come on. You're too stubbor— you can't die! I didn't… I—"

"Do not give up on this war merely for my sake, Destan. ... You," Rocher began coughing up blood as he wheezed. "You have made me, your mother, father, and even your grandmother so proud. You've redeemed your mother and brought honor—"

"Rocher!"

Callimay could feel something building in Destan and had a bad feeling: *What's this? I can't get a— oh no.*

Unable to pick and choose, she just screamed for anyone to hear within her limited range: *Everyone get down! ... Now!*

She threw up her barrier and got on the ground, hoping it would help protect her from the shockwave she realized Destan was about to release. He lifted his head and screamed in anger and frustration, the ground shaking and then a ripple of impact shockwaves spreading out.

Ѧ

It worked, but Callimay was exhausted. She let the barrier down and laid there for a solid minute, trying to get her breath back. She then stumbled to her feet, looking around half-dazed and bewildered. The moon was eclipsed, causing the area to have eerie shadows hanging off every darkened area, but something else bothered her more. In fact it was the lack of something: no gunfire numbing her ears and no one else left standing. — The belvedere was a little ways off, cowering and whimpering; as were the last two of his counter parts.

The area around her was littered with countless bodies; part of her wondering if anyone survived that shockwave. This stillness made Callimay's skin crawl and her spine shiver... it didn't seem real. In fact it made her feel like something was wrong and they were about to be dealt some major blow out of nowhere. How could the chaos and mayhem they were in moments ago be gone like "that"?

Not wanting to be alone, she started stumbling and staggering in the direction of Destan, dizzy and in a fog she hadn't been in for quite some time. But even so she knew something wasn't right. Something felt very wrong.

Where is he? I... I know he was— "Destan!"

Still disoriented, she fought through it and finally got to his side, dejavú of Ginger's nightmare she was trapped in flooding through her.

She screamed and pounded on his chest; a wild fury of uncontained emotions which couldn't comprehend how to handle the situation doing the only thing they knew to.

But her pounding turned out to be the best thing she could've done. While not the "suggested" method of CPR, in this severe case it was exactly what was needed. Of course she didn't know that it worked until he reached up and grabbed her arm.

"Destan?" She jerked back; eyes still wild with fear.

It took him a good five minutes to fully come to; but he got his bearings and rolled over to get up… seeing Rocher.

Tears began to pour out of his eyes as he took the lifeless body of his great uncle in his arms, clutching it as he rocked back and forth, "No. No. No this can't be real. You can't be gone…"

Her heart now feeling the same yet different pang of sorrow and loss made her wince as she crawled over and wrapped her husband in her arms; trying not to cry, "I'm so sorry. So very sorry."

"This isn't real, right Calli? … Right?" Destan tried to justify as he threw an arm around her and gripped her tight.

"I…" She started crying as she leaned over so her cheek was against his. "I…"

"Why! I… I don't… I don't understand. He wasn't…"

"Destan I…" she started looking around, worried everyone would start waking up soon. "I don't mean to sound heartless, but—"

"He's 'dead', Calli! He's dead and he wasn't saved!"

"I know!" She said a bit louder as she jumped when she heard movement behind her. "Traceur?"

"What happened?" She asked scared.

"I'll explain later." Callimay shook her head as she glanced over Traceur's shoulder. "Is anyone else awake?"

"Those of us who were highest up are perfectly fine. We're trying to get as many of them subdued while they're out; and tend to our own. … Is Sentinel really…"

Callimay hung her head.

"I'm so sorry." She bowed her head. "I… I don't mean to—"

"Go on. I'll be there in a minute. — Buddy? … Go after the last two, don't let them get away. Go on."

The belvedere took off, Callimay trying to figure out how to say something to her grieving husband without making him upset again, "Destan? … Destan, Rocher 'chose' what he wanted. I… I know it might not help that much, but it's not your fault."

"I wasn't paying attention!" He pounded the ground beside him. "I got too lax about things and— I thought if I—"

"Destan please," she collapsed beside him; drained because of what she went through and now his emotional self-condemnation.

He sat there and brewed for a minute, unwilling to listen to her pleas — not doing what he promised her he would. But thankfully his emotions were beginning to level, though this was only half the battle and Callimay knew it.

One by one, others began to rise from the littered landscape; Veils and Shadows frantically trying to take advantage of the situation they found themselves in. The belvedere kept the last two of his counterparts cornered; them being taken down first thing so there wasn't that concern left. Some Falconers were doing their best to act dead so they would be passed over, but one-by-one they were discovered; scuffles breaking out to get them under control with an occasional shot piercing the chilling silence.

Callimay tried to leave a few times, but Destan wouldn't let her go.

"Just… one more minute," he repeated for the fifth time.

"Destan?" She tried to soothe as she rubbed the side of his face. "Destan we'll come back. We're not going to leave him here. I pro—"

A shrill scream caused them to whip their heads around and look to see who it was; them scrambling to their feet and running as fast as they could in the direction of it.

When they found who screamed and realized why they did it, the two of them were hit with another round of gut-wrenching grief.

Chicane was in his sister's arms as she rocked him back and forth, much like how Destan acted with Rocher. She was hyperventilating as she kept repeating the same phrase over and over again, oblivious to the world around her. — What she was saying wasn't in a language Callimay knew.

From how he looked, one could easily guess he fell from where he was when Callimay left him.

What caused his fall?

It wasn't Destan's~ it couldn't be. Traceur said those up that high were still conscious.

In this whirlwind, Callimay felt a strong hand on her shoulder. She flinched and jumped back.

"I didn't mean to scare you, Jewel. I'm sorry."

"Oh," she tried to catch her breath. "It's you, Fidus."

"We have reports coming in that a group of higher standing Syndicate members with some of their Elites are taking refuge near where Canary was stationed. Liberator and I are getting as many together as possible to head down that way right now. ... I'm not expecting you or Doyen to accompany us — nor Traceur. I just wanted you to know we're not MIA." Fidus said with compassion. "I'm sorry for both his and her personal losses."

Having that reassurance and reminder helped Callimay so much; her shaking his hand as she nodded, "Let me know how things are going and if you need any backup. I'll make sure to leave a channel open for you."

"Very well," Fidus nodded as he waved his hand and then took off back toward the entrance, several Veils and Shadows following him.

Callimay kneeled next to Traceur and tried to comfort her, but she refused to let her brother go or listen to anything said; fighting back at the outstretched hands that wanted to help comfort her.

"Alright, Traceur. I... I'll leave you be."

Feeling useless and her exhaustion catching back up, she got up and looked back to Destan. But he was gone; he'd started back to Rocher.

What was she supposed to do? Yes, she didn't have anything left in her, but she knew she had to try to help those hurting.

And yet no one wanted her help which made her feel even worse.

As she started back, the belvedere limped up to her, whining and whimpering all while his tail wagged, "We need to get you looked at, poor thing. You did a wonderful job, Buddy. Thank you so much for being there for me... for everyone."

He barked and then twitched his ears when he heard Destan's voice, limping over to him and lying down beside him as he began to howl while waiting for Callimay to get to them.

He'd laid Rocher on the ground and was staring at him, tears streaming down his face. Then looking over to his wife, he winced as he accepted her opened arms, "This wasn't supposed to happen this way. It… I just…"

She looked at all of the bodies everywhere and sighed. They both knew there were going to be casualties, but it was more than they ever thought: in a way she didn't feel the price for their freedom was worth it, now.

"I should've seen those deadeyes. I even looked up but didn't bo—"

"Please don't blame yourself. Please, Destan." Callimay immediately calmed as she clambered to hold him tight. "Even if you would've seen them who knows what you might have not noticed instead. Maybe it would've helped, but that's something we'll never know for sure. Just… just rest. I can tell you're in so much pain. Please."

"I should be happy you're alright." Destan began to cry as he growled. "What is wrong with me!"

"You're in shock. … We all are. I know we are. And it's okay." She hushed as she rocked him back and forth, the belvedere beginning to whine and yap. "I love you… so much."

℔

With all that happened so quickly and with all the emotions and adrenaline pumping through her, her body felt like it had been up for two weeks. But closing her eyes did no good. When she did, she could still see the blood and carnage, hear the yells and bullets, feel the fear and terror… part of her wondered if she'd ever be able to sleep again.

This grueling night came to an end as the sky began to lighten. It gave hope things would change; and change for the better.

Fidus got in contact to say they broke in the compound and the military arrived to take them into custody: *You?*

No, Jewel. They were sent by the president to aid us.

Oh thank goodness. She put her hand over her heart as she sighed.

Though they did put trackers on us and required us all to remain under house custody in either Crosswall or Gastonia. They won't allow Brigon because of your family ties nor Kerogen for Doyen's.

What about—

They've yet to say anything about Ferdinan, so there might be a possibility to remain at or close to Original Safe Haven. At least it might until the initial decision is made, one way or another.

Destan told me about that, and I don't blame them.

Neither do I. In fact, I would have done it myself. — They said once they secured these here they would be heading up your way to finish cleaning up everything there. So be prepared when they pull you aside and clasp that cuff on your ankle. Not that it hurts or anything, but it's awkward to say the least. … Aside from this, how are you all doing? Are things quiet now?

It's quiet and everyone's accounted for.

How many?

Tell me you didn't lose anyone. Callimay begged.

A few injured, but we're all okay.

Oh thank you, God. — There's… I couldn't stand to keep counting after the first hundred. Callimay broke down. *Destan's writing them all down. It's in the thousands and he's not done. I just can't— I can't bear to accept how many died.*

By your actions, Jewel, you saved countless more. I hope you realize that. I know I was one of those who were saved and I'm eternally indebted to you. Fidus tried to encourage as his voice hinted to him working through his own grief. *I understand how upset you are and this wasn't the outcome we were wanting… but you did what any Shadow and Veil has sworn to do: preserve life to promote freedom. We all knew this was a reality: some of us 'were' going to not survive this war. I know Doyen was hoping it wouldn't turn into a bloodbath, but he wasn't ignorant of it either. You always prepare for the worst while hoping for the best. — I believe he's tried to look more for the best since you came along. And that's okay. There is no shame in wanting that. … But I guess he didn't consider Sentinel dying as part of that worst case scenario.*

The hard thing is he did, Fidus. He thought about it far too often. Callimay bit her lip as she watched Destan continue to walk down the rows of bodies and take down their names. *That's what made it a million times worse.*

Their differences in religious views?

Yes.

Up until about an hour ago I held an even stancher view on things than Sentinel against Doyen; albeit very silent. … But seeing how so many things culminated so perfectly with you two at the helm tonight and how we indeed only had to fight this one battle for this war of ours between the Syndicate and Shadows to be finished like Doyen predicted was possible against what we all assumed to be the case? It has led me to believe I may be wrong. … I may not agree with Doyen and yourself on certain things, but your God seems to be One Who can sway the outcome of situations that just don't seem possible; and turn bad situations into great victories. — This all has made me a bit more open-minded about things. And I'll even admit a bit curious.

The warm embrace of comfort that enveloped Callimay because of what Fidus was saying helped her devastated heart so much, but knew for Destan it still wouldn't erase the pain of losing Rocher for eternity: *I'm so glad to hear that, Fidus. Thank you so much for telling me. It means the world to me to hear what you have reflected on from what happened. Seeing God's deliverance among so much grief, pain, and sorrow. — Make sure the injured get the medical attention they need. We're trying to get some of ours out right now.*

I'll see you back at th— well I guess not.

Let me know what they say about Ferdinan.

Will do. If it's alright I'll make sure I'm there. Let me know where you'll be going, regardless.

Alright.

🕉

It was half-past three in the afternoon before anyone showed up to help transport the Falconers who survived and get the rest of the injured to area hospitals. But being realistic about it all, they got there extremely fast: they had to get through the maze of this place, too.

Destan was sitting on a stone wall, lost in his own world as he read through the list of casualties and didn't see Callimay walk up to him, the belvedere still by her side; or hear her ask, "Destan?"

She took a breath as she closed her eyes and then reached out and took his hand, "Destan? They're ready to start moving the bodies."

"Huh?" He looked up at her, still laboring to breathe and almost straining his eyes to focus.

"Extraction teams are here."

"Oh. … Alright." He nodded as he hopped down, grimacing as he stood up straight. "I'll need to get their personal files so their families are contacted." *And I thought the Right of Respect was horrible.*

"Don't think about that right now. There'll be time t—"

"I need to Calli," Destan shook his head; his somber tone not condemning but still serious as he looked across and saw two Falconers still being guarded. "Is that the Monarch?"

"It's apparently two of their personal guards. Trever took down Olderon just before I got to you; and apparently Vashti took off before you flattened everyone." *So much for no mercy for retreating. Such a hypocrite.* "Fidus along with some others followed after her and pinned them down."

"This may sound cruel in a way, but—"

"She only cared about herself… just like she always had." Callimay bowed her head to hide her rolling her eyes. "I hate that she is blood kin to me on that front, alone."

"No regard for life and no love for anyone… makes me grieve for the brother Toreon slaughtered." Destan sighed in frustration as a few military officers came up, switching his focus as he put his hand up. "No need to go in to all the explanation and such. We were told about the trackers."

The men stood there a bit shocked, yet relieved at the same time.

Callimay had to take her boot off so they could get hers on, perturbing Destan just slightly.

But what was the start of things going overboard was when one of the men said, "We'll have to detain the belvedere. We were informed it is yours and supposedly not a threat?"

"As long as no one hurts her or her brother… who apparently isn't here right now," Destan nodded; looking around for a bit to see where Trever was.

He went with Fidus. He's fine.

"They're the designated keepers, then?"

"Yes." Callimay replied. "My brother was with the other group."

"Alright. — Radio down to the team there and have them find—what is his name, ma'am?"

"Trever. Trever Presley."

He got back on his com and relayed instructions, finishing as he addressed Callimay while taking her arm, "We'll need to keep at least you, ma'am, until this is all settled so the creature will go with us."

"Absolutely not," Destan pushed him back and pulled her to him.

"I'm afraid you don't have a say in this, sir. Please don't add insult to injury. We're only doing this as a temporary precaution until the courts decide what's to be done about this all and we're able to confirm everything about the belvedere." The man stated calm but firm. "We just want to ensure everyone is safe through this process."

"I can sever the tie that would cause the belvedere to even realize he was separated from her. Wouldn't that be good enough?" Destan tried to back off but not be separated from Callimay.

There was a hushed discussion between the two men as well as those on the other end of the com; and then the one who spoke before answered, "We'll have to have of our technicians witness the process and do some preliminary tests, but if that's the case then no one would need to stay."

"Where is he? I mean the technician." Destan clarified.

"'She' is actually in bed, but we can get her to come in."

"Then we'll all go." Destan all but ordered. "I'm not leaving my wife and that's final."

They heard one of them say "wife?" under his breath in a shocked voice as he side-eyed them; the main one speaking nodding on, "That's perfectly fine."

ℬ

The walk back through the Citadel brought an ugly truth about this place to light that Callimay had wondered: it was empty of humanity on any and every level because it wasn't a place built to protect, house, or support life… but an elaborate death trap.

She had to choke back tears at certain moments, remembering when Enforcer talked with them or when Chicane would place a marker… or even Rocher would make a comment. Yes, she knew she was in shock;

but what she wasn't prepared for was what was going to come: the nightmares, the memories, the pangs.

Of course she knew Destan was familiar with this and would power through at first, but she also knew this wasn't something someone needed to be comfortable with. It wasn't a lifestyle that was healthy in any way. And it wasn't the right way to honor those who died.

While sitting in the back of a police vehicle wasn't something that was on any bucket list she had, it was at least comfortable and those who were with them were kind and helpful.

At one point it hit her, though: *Will they let us go and stay under house arrest? I mean with the broadcast they've got to know we both have abilities, right? ~ Then this would all be a lie about the belvedere, wouldn't it? ~ There's no way for us to get out. Destan's in no shape—*

I forgot to tell you; Nexus contacted me about an hour ago. They didn't end up doing anything except go to the Monarch's one main conference room to listen to Vashti blather on in one of her rages before this all started.

So they don't know?

I highly doubt it, Calli. He winced as he tried to sit back and relax.

Well, I guess if he's not worried about it then I shouldn't. ~ Why don't you listen for a bit just to be sure? ~ It wouldn't hurt any. … Oh how I'd feel so stupid for falling for such a 'beautiful' lie after all the hard work we've put into all this and—

Don't get yourself all worked up. Destan reached over and took her hand in his, patting it a few times. *If it'll make you feel better, go ahead. But don't read into what they're saying. Okay?*

Sure enough she never heard anything that suggested they lied, and when they arrived they were still as nice as they were before; helping Callimay support Destan as they got to their holding cell. They even made sure they had plenty to eat and drink and did what they could to give first aid to the two of them as well as the belvedere — though his help was more as a protection for them than anything, and that was more than understandable.

Now alone to wait for the technician to arrive, Callimay could feel just how cold and damp the room was; but the latter was most likely just the fact they were soaked to the bone.

Destan was in a daze, but the moment he felt her beginning to shiver he pulled her close and moved so he would be shielding her if anything happened.

The belvedere was upset the entire time; hobbling back and forth, glaring at every individual who walked by… though never barking or growling. — Apparently being in a small cell with iron bars for a door didn't sit well with him.

With the door just down the hall opening and closing so many times and the amount of constant talk there was, the two of them drifted off several times; only to be woken and drift back off again and again.

Callimay could feel the belvedere nudging her hand and heard him yapping at her; but pushed him away, saying groggy, "We're tired, Buddy. And Destan needs all the rest he can get. Go l— oh!"

"Our technician can see you now." The man opened the door.

As Callimay moved, Destan jerked awake.

She began to panic, hoping he would listen to her before reacting, "It's okay. I'm fine."

"Who d— w… what's going on? … Oh. — Are they here?"

"Yes." The man nodded as he smiled. "This way please."

🕉

As the door opened, the belvedere shoved his way in, his happy bark and foot fire hinting someone was in there he already knew. And sure enough, when Callimay looked around the edge of the door Trever was sitting there, smiling, "Hey, sis."

Emotions bubbled out of her eyes as she ran up to and paused when she had to figure out how to hug him with her hands cuffed; Trever even having trouble holding back his relief.

The three of them would've been content to just stand there and give each other silent comfort and relief, but Callimay could feel someone staring at her. And sure enough, sitting across from them in this small interrogation room was a middle-aged lady. While not cruel looking, her gaze over her large-framed trifocals was one of impatience… though completely nonverbal.

Now with their attention she nodded toward the chairs across from her without much of an emotional response, "Please have a seat. … I was informed you have a map of the creature's computer makeup, is this correct?"

"Yes," Destan nodded slowly as he handed her his computer; his cuffs catching on the edge of the table so the computer went flying across the desk at her.

She raised her eyebrow, a look of suspicion and distrust on her face; it plain she was fighting to keep from yawning.

Destan was just about to explain where she could get to everything, but she cracked the entire security system on it within a few clicks and had everything she needed… and more. He was more than a bit upset it was that easy for her, but he took it in stride and realized it wasn't a big deal at all. There wasn't anything he had to hide. If they wanted all the information he had on that machine they were welcome to it. He only carried what he needed and made sure everything else was never traceable or remnants readable. — It was just the thought of their servers being "that" vulnerable that annoyed him. But then again, it's just as likely she was on-par with Abacus' programming skills.

After working for a while, she looked up again, "So he operates by way of emotional interface with his keeper? Does that sound familiar to you at all?"

"Yes," Destan replied as he reached over for Callimay's hand, wincing a bit.

The lady let out what sounded like a condescending sigh, "I take it you first accessed him though a Bluetooth connection?"

"Yes."

"Let me see him while I run some diagnostics." She peered over her glasses yet again and then gestured beside her.

Destan nodded, so Callimay got him up, "Buddy? Hey. Go say hi to the nice lady. … Go on."

He raised his head so he could see over the table to Trever, as if asking for sure before he hobbled over; ears flat and tail almost tucked between his legs.

A total surprise to the three young adults in the room, the second the lady touched his fur and he sniffed at her hand, she was nothing but a softy; her tone completely changing, "Well hello there. Aren't you such a big boy. … Oh, aren't your eyes just the most beautiful— I see you got hurt. Those others are nasties, aren't they? But you're nothing like them, are you? … Well, we're about to find out."

This sudden shift hit them as bizarre to say the least. She noticed and snickered almost as she explained, "I apologize for such a kind attitude toward the creature in contract to my formality with you. … It's not that I view you as criminals or anything of the sort; I'm just not what you would call a 'people person'. — And being called in during the middle of the night does also give me this edge."

She did various things first to test what she had: making the belvedere lie down, bark, wag his tail, run around the table, and even growl. Her eyes lit up with each successful try, it being hard for her to stop herself.

"Do you have what you need?" Destan finally asked.

"Oh." She sat up and pushed her glasses up. "I'm sorry. Yes. I know exactly how to set the block on that coding so we can run the rest of our tests."

"Could I ask a favor?" Destan stopped her as she stood.

"What?"

"I admit I don't know everything as far as how he was 'made'. And I don't even know if you would have any knowledge if it's possible."

Her shoulders slumped as she sighed, "Go on."

"Is there any way to eliminate the poison in him so he's 'safe' to be around anyone if he got upset for some reason that didn't warrant his, um, 'lethal' protection?"

Her eyes had a gleaming spark rush through them as she glanced at the creature and then back to them, "I can't make any promises, but you raise a good question that's worth investigating. All the Syndicate's assets are under quarantine, but I can ask for information regarding the belvederes since he's my personal case. — Granted, it will most likely be denied, but it's worth a try."

"Thank you." Destan nodded as he sat back.

"Come along now, my little man. Let's go get you fixed up." She ushered the belvedere out, him following her command, not even looking back at Callimay to say goodbye. "Oh! By the way, my name is Lieutenant Sinclair. Molly, Sinclair. I'll make sure they give you my number before you go. I'll keep you informed and hopefully will have him returned to you before autumn. ... Rest assured I know his function is to protect his keeper. Yes I did alter that so he would obey me, but I will reset everything to the way it was when he's given back."

Callimay relaxed, knowing she wasn't going to lose the very thing her mother left her to protect her.

"And as a person note," Molly whispered as she poked her head back in; her winking as she rolled her fingers on the door. "I'm glad you were able to get done what you did. Here's to it sticking, finally. ... I'm a Southpaw as well."

"Wait!" Callimay jumped up.

"What?"

"Maybe I'm prying, but I just have one question." Callimay bowed her head and clasped her hands in front of her. "Is that why you're not a people person like you said earlier?"

"I think you answered that yourself." She had a small smile start to grow on her face as she started to shut the door again. "Someone will be in shortly to take you where you need to go."

~ 24 ~

The next few weeks entailed Destan and Callimay traveling to each, individual fallen Shadow and Veil's family to give them the news that their loved one had passed; their house arrest being given that one "exemption" because of Destan's status. There were several who had no family, making their burden somewhat lighter in a way — and yet knowing that individual was completely alone and fighting so hard… it almost made it unbearable at their funeral.

A couple families refused to let them attend the funeral — Destan saying at one point he was getting a chance to see the type of person Tabitha's mother was and how futile his idea was.

"Why would you say that?" Callimay asked as the person driving them pulled out of the parking lot.

"When I picked her up I wanted to meet her mother and give her an earful about what she was doing to her daughter who was still alive. … Now I'm not excusing her actions at all, but seeing what I am now I can understand it a little bit more; and realize it wouldn't have made any difference to say anything."

Every other family they went to, on the other hand, was beyond grateful for what they did and the strength they had to come and bring the news themselves.

One in particular was hardest on Callimay and Destan… and it just so happened to be the last one: *I had absolutely no— not even an inkling he was married.*

How did you find out?

Traceur broke down and told me yesterday. Destan sighed as the car stopped in front of a very simple three-story house.

As they got out they heard the sound of chickens clucking and children laughing. It wouldn't have been much of a shock to hear, but they were out in the middle of the countryside of Crullar. Callimay whipped her head around and saw Destan cringe. Traceur got out and went on ahead of them; little children running around the back of the house and bolting for her when they saw her, "Auntie! Auntie Tiffany!"

She dropped to her knees and braced herself for their hugs, somehow able to keep from crying.

An older girl poked her head out a window on the second floor; waving and calling out, "Eh! Who be it?"

"It's Auntie Tiffany, Mummy!" The one little girl yelled as she jumped up and down.

"I woondered when ya'd be back. I'll be doon in five shakes."

Callimay's heart was racing like every time before, but this time it was trying to race while breaking at the same time. She let out a tiny yelp, Destan putting his arm around her to encourage her to keep walking, "I'll tell her."

"No, Doyen. I will." Traceur shook her head as she walked up to him and put her hand over his. "I changed my mind. It's best if Daisy hear it from me. … I just couldn't come alone."

Destan nodded and looked up, seeing this girl who couldn't be any older than seventeen "feel" her way out to the porch. All her children crowded around her, every one of them unaware of the gut-wrenching news coming.

"Someone which ya, Sissy?" Daisy tilted her head a bit.

"It's some of Christian's friends from work. They're—"

"Oh I wish he would've warned me so— Rainy?"

"Yes, Mummy?" The same little girl hopped up the steps and took her mother's hand, swinging it.

"Na that be fer later." She shook her off her hand. "Ya go take ever-one in and rustle up some snacks. Ya hear?"

"Okay!" The little sweet girl giggled as her siblings chased after her.

Each moment they saw this beautiful family was only making their pain that much worse. No wonder Traceur said she needed help.

When they came in the living room her smile vanished; her flailing to grab Traceur's arm as she pleaded, "Why didn Christian cum?"

"Daisy just calm down."

Callimay could feel the life drain out of this young woman as she clung to her sister-in-law, "He's nuttin' but injured like 'n last time… right? … Sissy? I no he be sayin' this last time was gonna be rough, but he said he'd be back fer the birth. He promised mae!"

Traceur broke down, "I'm sorry, Daisy."

She clasped her shaking hands around Traceur's arms, letting her guide her to a chair.

Her eldest son poked his head around the corner, his green eyes as large as dinner plates. He looked about seven, maybe eight.

"Mum?" He asked scared as he crept into the room and tugged on her sleeve. "Mum wha did they due? Why isn't Pop comin' home?"

Without saying a word she pulled him to her and wailed, a crash being heard in the hall followed by slapping of bare feet and a rush of little pigtails crowding around her, "Mum? Mum don't cry!" "Mum where it hurt?" "It thu babbie?"

The little boy looked back at Destan and Callimay with judgement and contempt on his small, but expressive face, "You get yerselves oot oh here, ya murderers! Don't ya dare tooch Mum! … Leave! I'll get ya fer this, I swear!"

Not wanting this to get any more out of control, Traceur looked at them with sympathy while trying to calm him, "Izack? Izack listen to me. They didn't do it. They tried to save—"

"Be gone which y'all!" Daisy screamed, all her children now glaring at Destan and Callimay.

"I… you better go." Traceur said under her breath as she nodded toward the door, rushing them over.

"I'm sorry, Traceur." Destan sighed as his shoulders slumped.

"I knew she would take it hard, but I swear I didn't think she'd lash out like that." Traceur's sobs began to become hiccups. "I'm sorry. … Thank you for coming… and helping."

"Leave!" Izack whacked the bat he had on the floor a few times. "Leave afore I 'really' hurt ya!"

"I don't know what you want to do with these, but they're yours… 'theirs'." Destan handed Traceur Chicane's knives and veil. "I… I'm so sorry. I… I just…"

"I'll get them calmed down and she'll want these. I know she will. She just needs some time." She cringed as she turned to leave, then whipped around and grabbed Destan's arm. "Please come to the funeral. I'm begging you."

"But I—"

"I know they won't want you there, but 'I' do. Please." She begged.

But that's not what happened at all.

Daisy was a completely different person at the graveside service. She apologized for how she treated Destan and Callimay… even for how Izack did, "If yer ever 'round these parts, stop in and stay a while. We'd love ta have visitors who knew my Christian; and I'm sure Sissy would love ta see ya. She's talked 'bout ya quite often these past few days."

Izack was still mad at them, refusing to say he was sorry: *So much of his father in him.*

Hopefully he can learn to focus that passion and use it to help others and not wrap himself in it. Destan replied somber. *Though I wouldn't know if that trait comes from his father or not.*

Amen to th— what?

I'll explain later.

✠

Things with the political battle hit stark resistance with the outcome of the faceoff between the Syndicate and Shadows; but for as much of a defeat as it was at first, the voice of the people of the world drowned them out in election after election; progress began being made.

Governments were looking to collaborate with others; but even that met staunch resistance from the general public — they were not going to repeat what happened last time. The "good cause" they did it for last time ended up like this; they weren't going to do it again. And so started independent efforts by each country to set up realistic and sustainable efforts to detain Falconers and Informants; most starting off with some form of a plea bargain: turn themselves in to receive a lighter sentence with the opportunity of parole.

Many lower-level people took advantage of this the second it was put out; and some even moving to different countries in order to take advantage of leniency. But that was quickly quelled; again, the people not wanting to interfere with what other countries had put in place. The goal of giving the people back their power was gaining ground.

♗

Being confined to the Minka — and the blessing of them being allowed to return to Ferdinan was beyond shocking to Destan — was the most pleasant "imprisonment" they could've asked for. The change of the seasons was going to be breath-taking; and it was giving Callimay a chance to see yet another side of Destan: he truly tried so hard to please his grandmother and conform all he could to her cultural traditions. And yet being there reminded her of one funeral they hadn't been to.

"He wanted to be cremated and his ashes put in what you'd probably know as a mausoleum. … And they've already done it."

"What!"

"Regardless of what his dying declaration would've meant to the family, I'm still viewed as the black sheep of the family because of my mother." Destan calmed as he sat down on the bed. "And you already know they're the type of people to visit the iniquities of the father on the son. As much as I would've liked to have be there, it wouldn't have done any good. He's gone. It's done. And me just continuing to 'blacken the family honor' wouldn't help my cause with the rest of them."

"I'm so sorry," she kneeled in front of him and took his hands.

"I know this isn't easy on you either, Calli." He let that small smile flash across his face. "Regardless of how much it hurt emotionally, you powered through and have been such a trooper though this aftermath."

"Nightmares will fade with time. … They always have."

"But memories will still be there. And their triggers." Destan softly reminded, but not in a condescending way.

"Time will help. It always does." She smiled as a tear ran down her face. "We made it. Just a little bit longer and we get to go home."

"Maybe even go on a true honeymoon." Destan started crying as he tried to laugh. "And build our home into our own little nest."

"This is all over." Callimay kept repeating as she threw her arms around Destan and snuggled herself against his chest. "Now we get to rest and build our life together."

Why can't I believe this is happening? I've wanted it for so long.

The End

We made it!
Now to relax.